Witchlight

Jessi Zabarsky

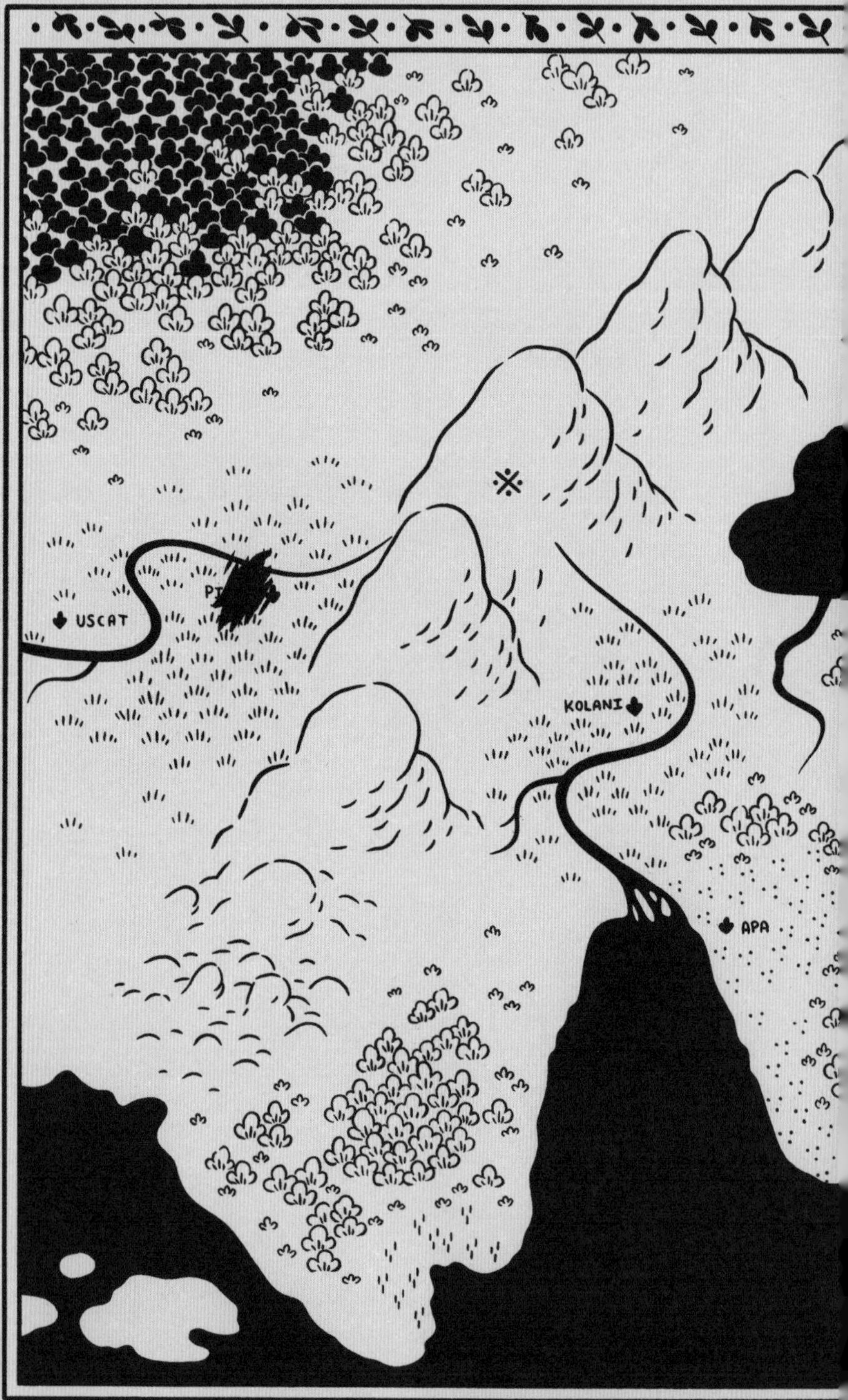
USCAT
KOLANI
APA

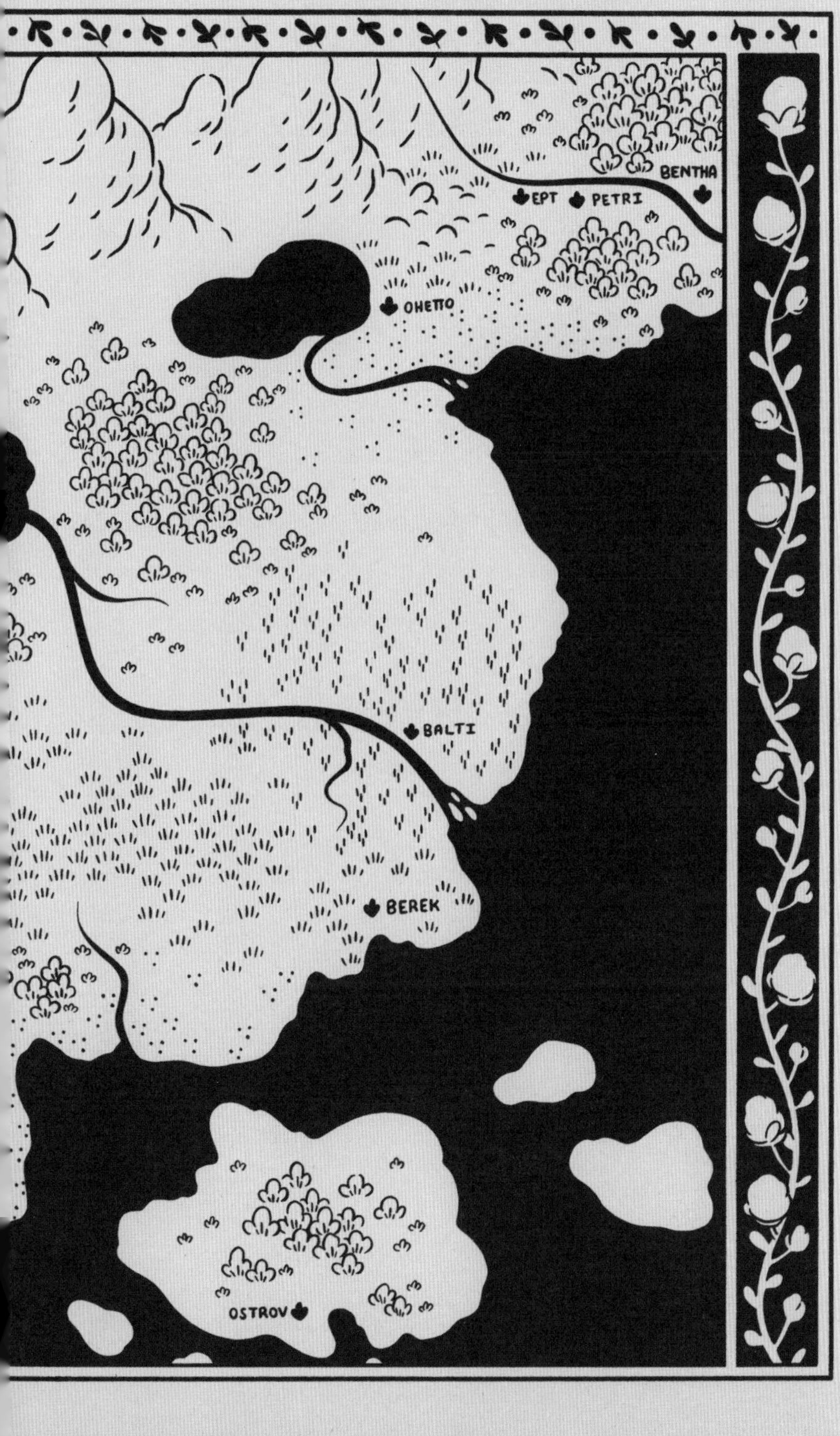
BENTHA
EPT
PETRI
OHETTO
BALTI
BEREK
OSTROV

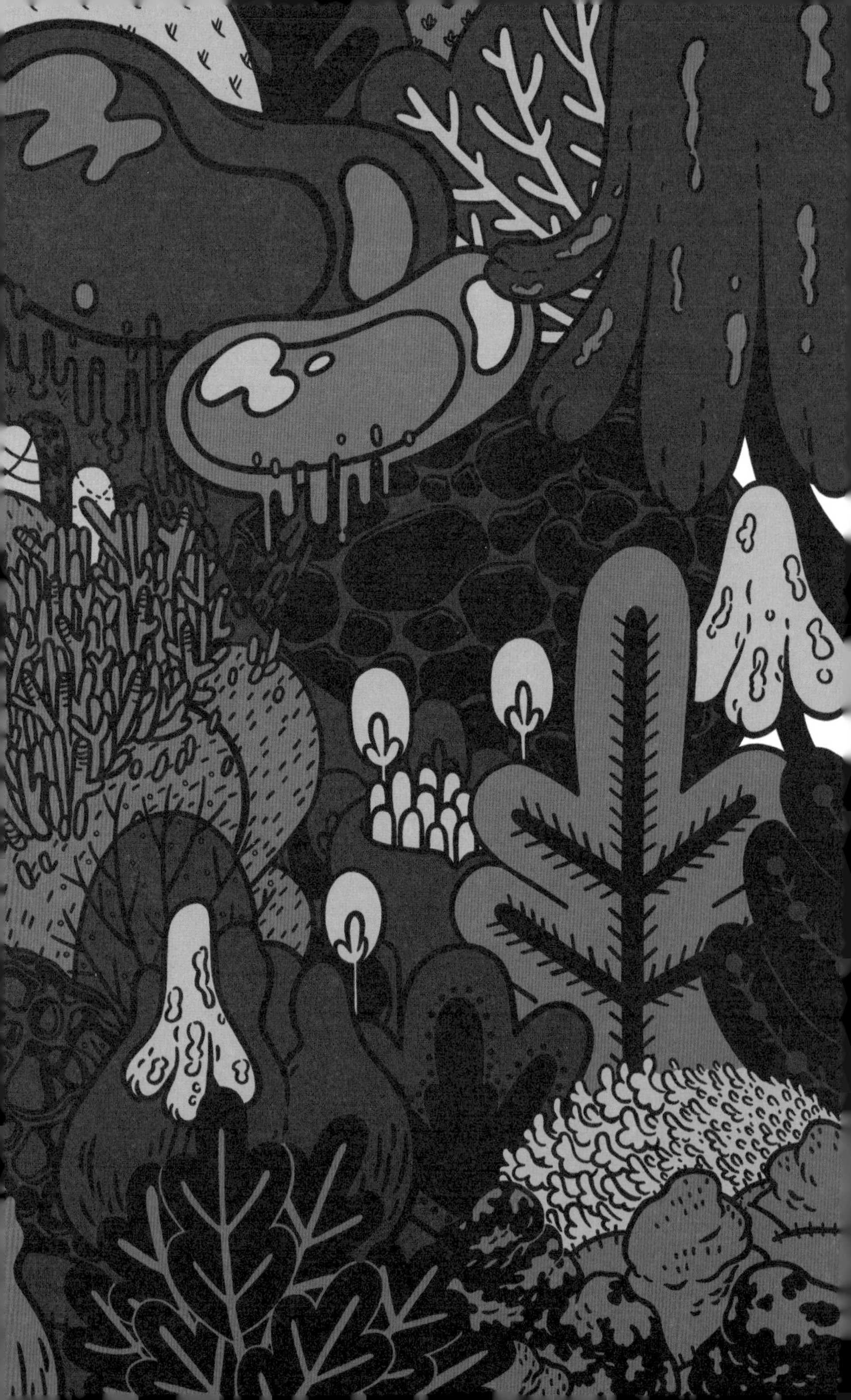

Witchlight

Jessi Zabarsky

with coloring by Geov Chouteau

RH GRAPHIC

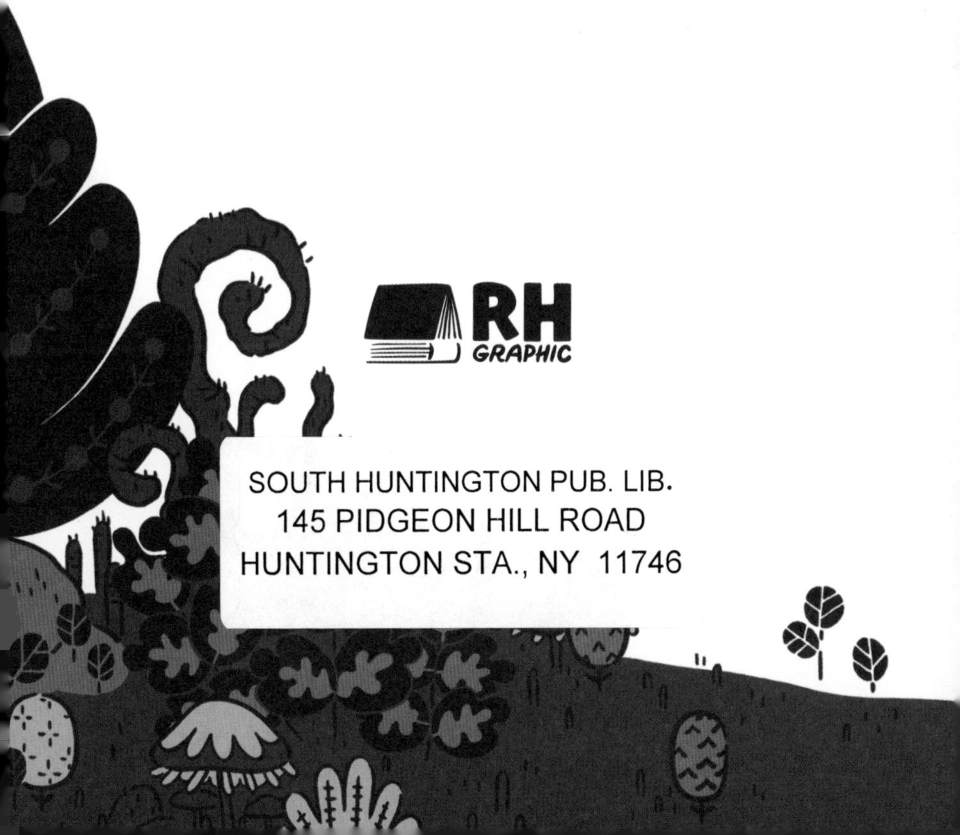

Witchlight was drawn with ink on paper, then lettered and colored digitally.

Text and art copyright © 2016, 2020 by Jessi Zabarsky
Cover art copyright © 2020 by Jessi Zabarsky

All rights reserved. Published in the United States by RH Graphic, an imprint of Random House Children's Books, a division of Penguin Random House LLC, New York. Originally published in the United States in different form by Czap Books in Providence, Rhode Island, in 2016.

RH Graphic with the book design is a trademark of Penguin Random House LLC.

Visit us on the Web! RHKidsGraphic.com • @RHKidsGraphic

Educators and librarians, for a variety of teaching tools, visit us at RHTeachersLibrarians.com

Library of Congress Cataloging-in-Publication Data
Names: Zabarsky, Jessi, author, artist.
Title: Witchlight / Jessi Zabarsky.
Description: First RH Graphic edition. | New York : RH Graphic, [2020] | Audience: Ages 14–18 |
Audience: Grades 10–12 | Summary: "Sanja gets taken by Lelek, a witch, and they find themselves on an adventure to discover the truth about Lelek's powers and each other"—Provided by publisher.
Identifiers: LCCN 2019025813 | ISBN 978-0-593-11999-0 (paperback) | ISBN 978-0-593-12418-5 (hardcover)
| ISBN 978-0-593-12001-9 (ebook) | ISBN 978-0-593-12000-2 (library binding)
Subjects: LCSH: Graphic novels. | CYAC: Graphic novels. | Witches—Fiction. | Ability—Fiction.
Classification: LCC PZ7.7.Z33 W58 2020 | DDC 741.5/973—dc23

Designed by Patrick Crotty
Colored by Geov Chouteau

MANUFACTURED IN CHINA
10 9 8 7 6 5 4 3 2 1
First RH Graphic Edition

A comic on every bookshelf.

To the best park in
the Cuyahoga River Valley

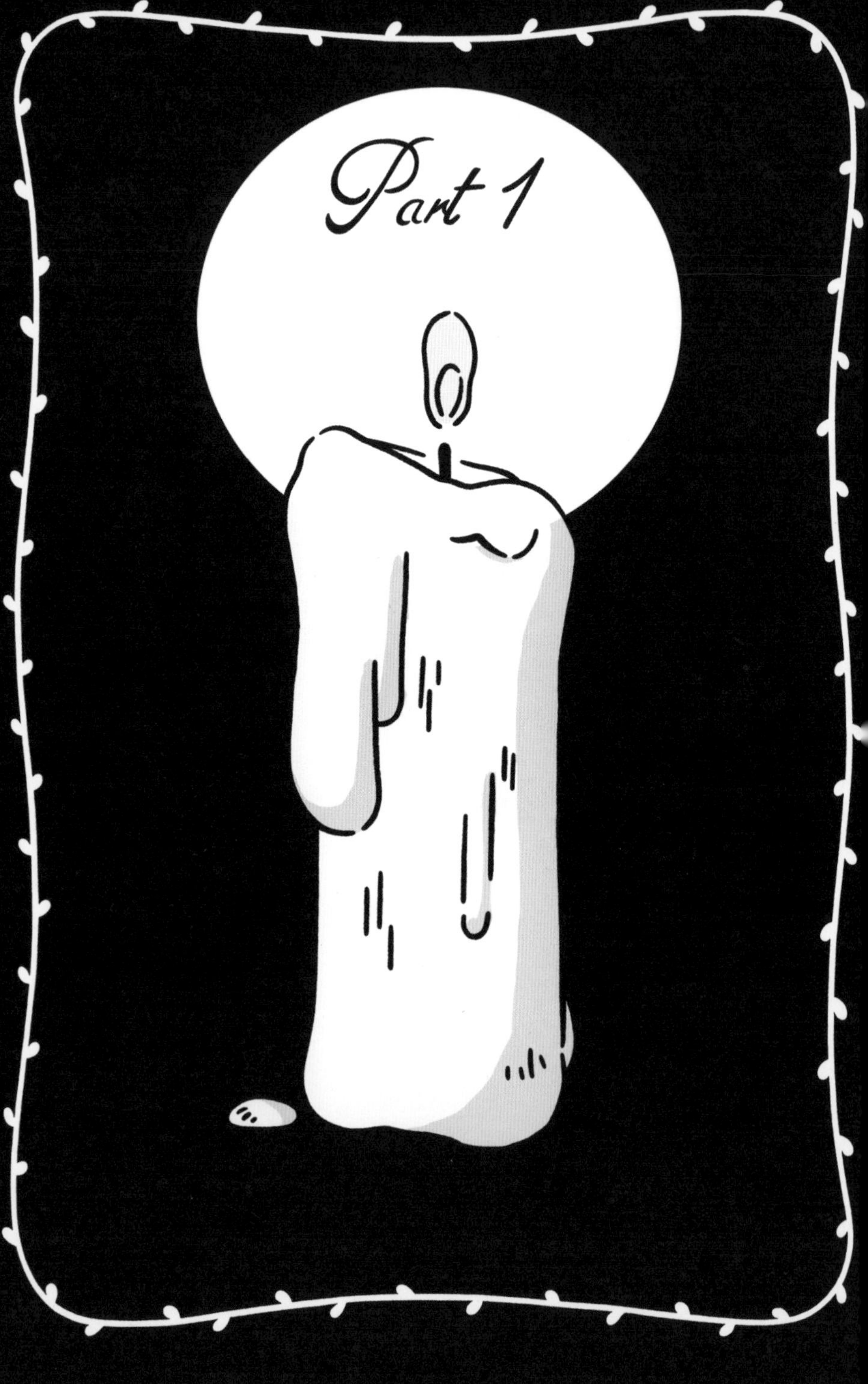
Part 1

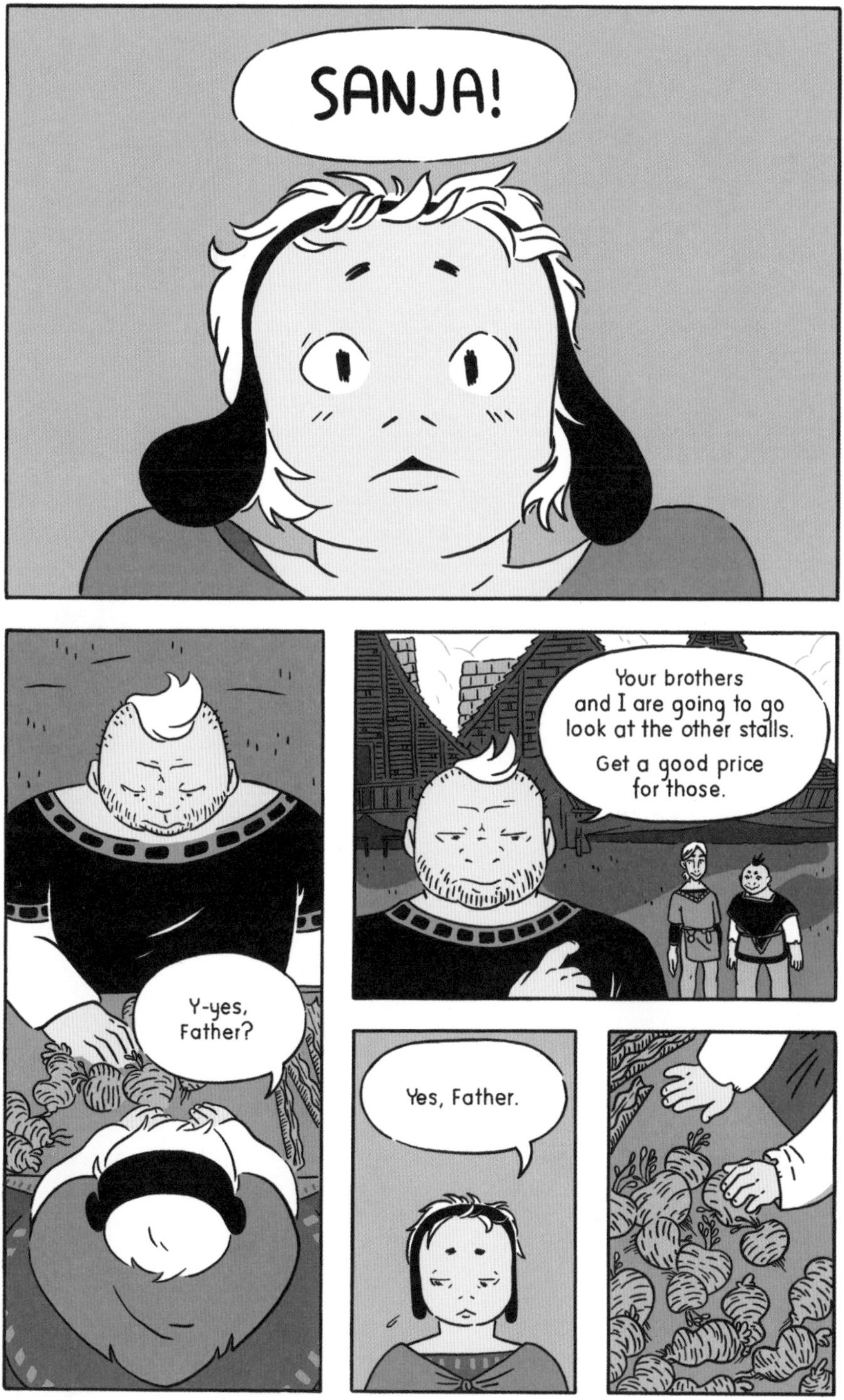
SANJA!
Y-yes, Father?
Your brothers and I are going to go look at the other stalls.
Get a good price for those.
Yes, Father.

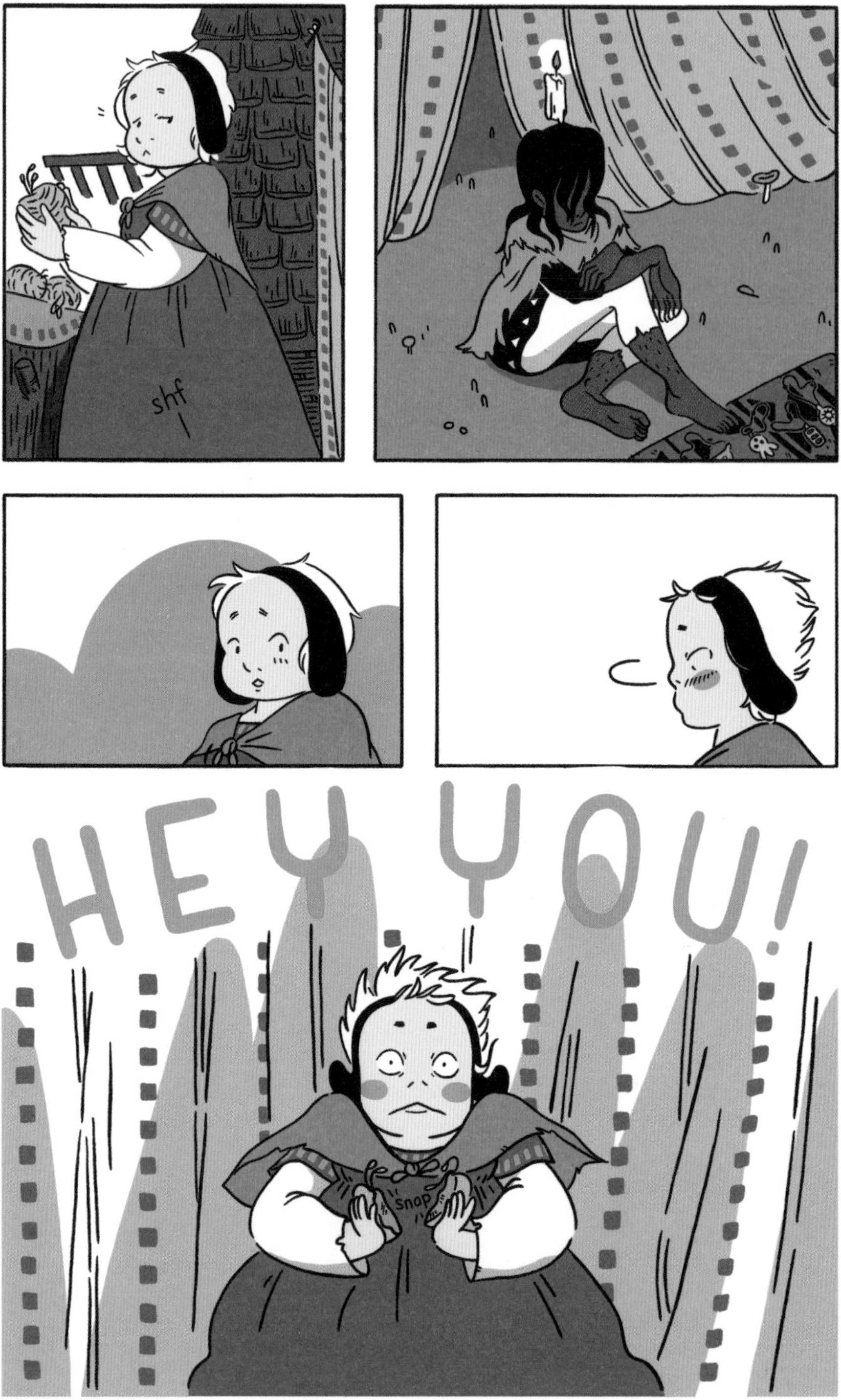
shf
HEY YOU!
snap

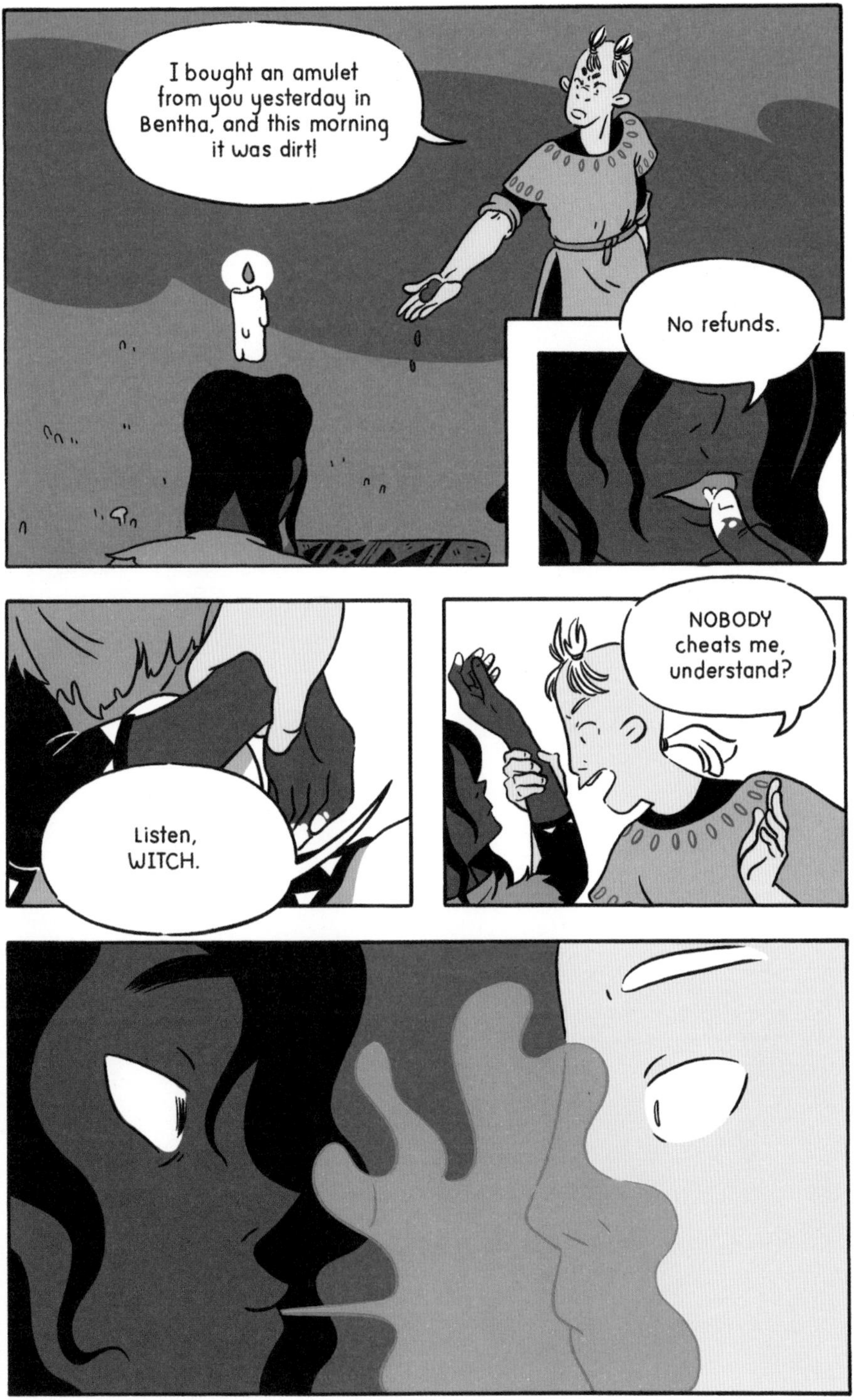
I bought an amulet from you yesterday in Bentha, and this morning it was dirt!
No refunds.
Listen, WITCH.
NOBODY cheats me, understand?

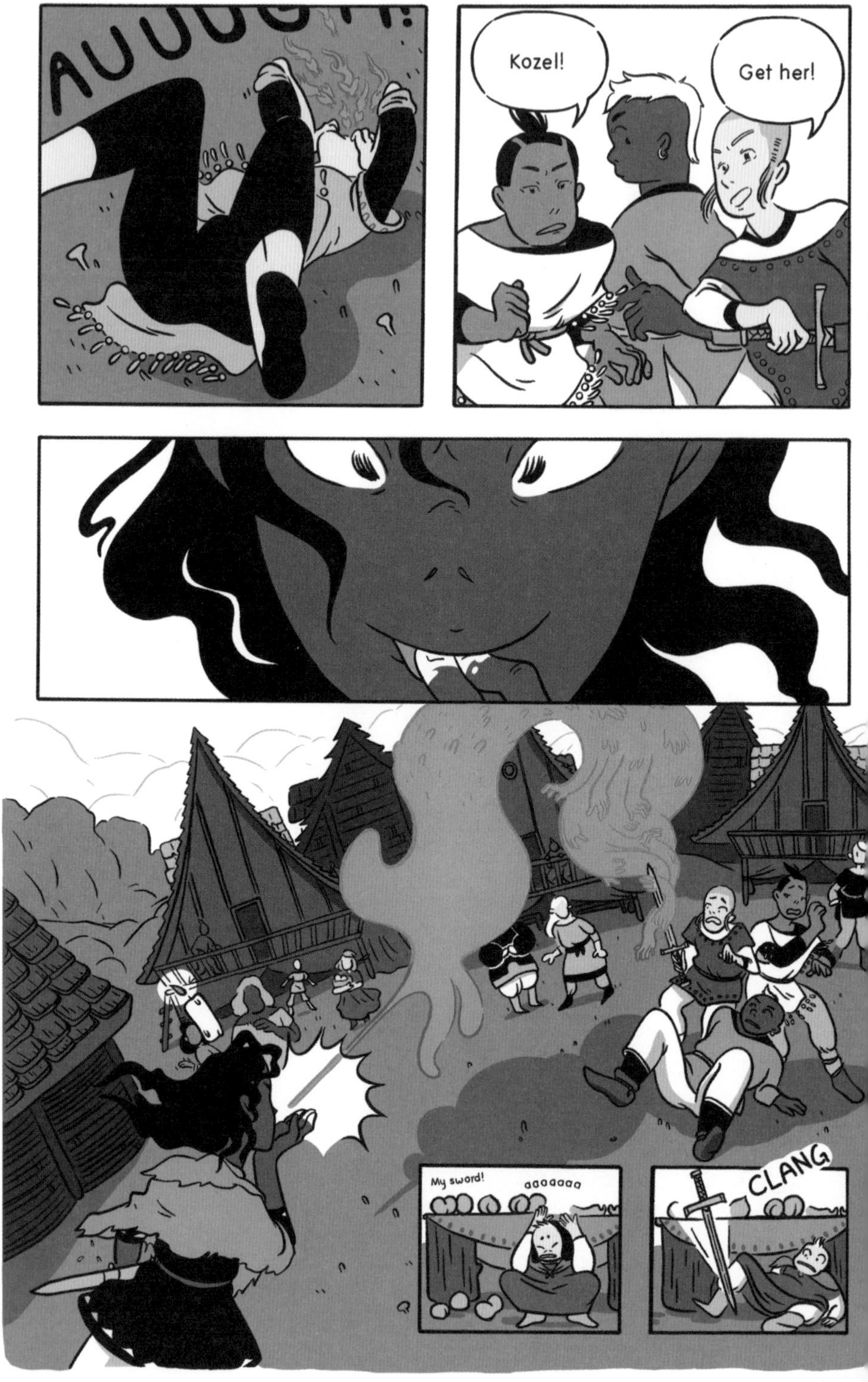
AUUUGH!
Kozel!
Get her!
My sword!
aaaaaa
CLANG

tmp
tmp
tmp
Blast!
ugh
Kaff
Kaff

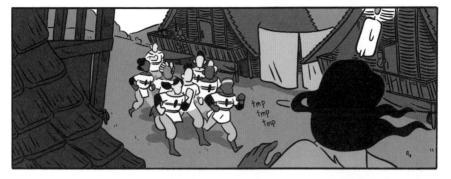

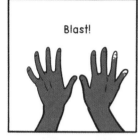

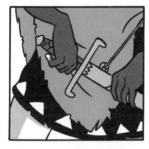

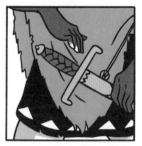

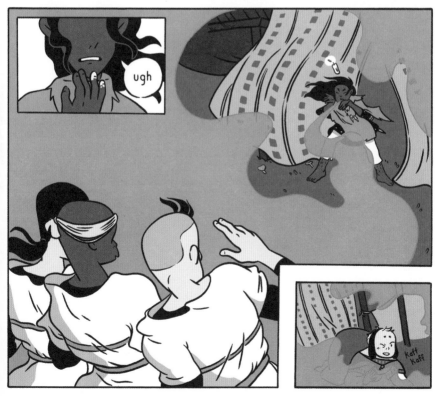

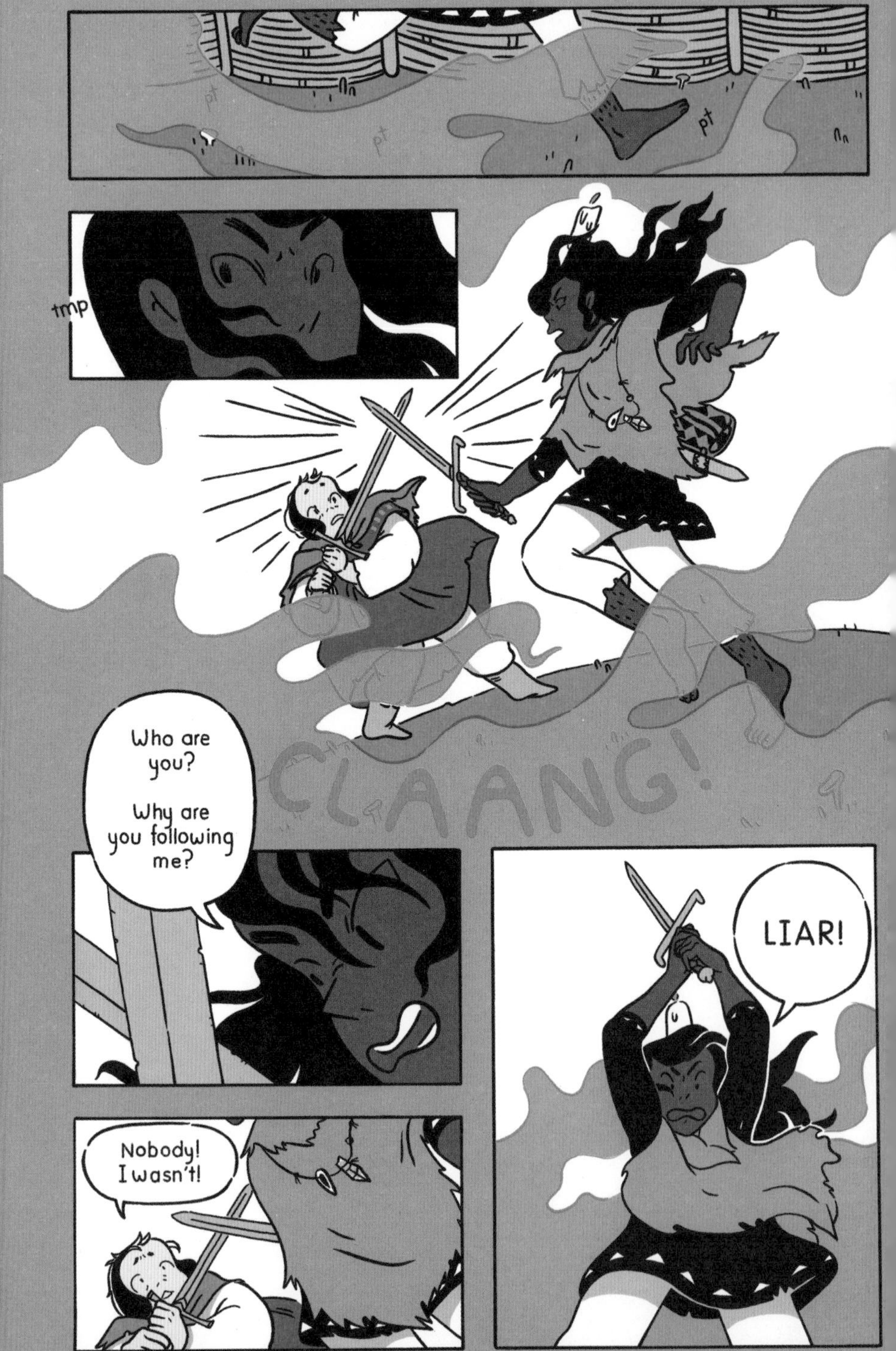
pt
pt
pt
tmp
CLAANG!
Who are you?
Why are you following me?
LIAR!
Nobody! I wasn't!

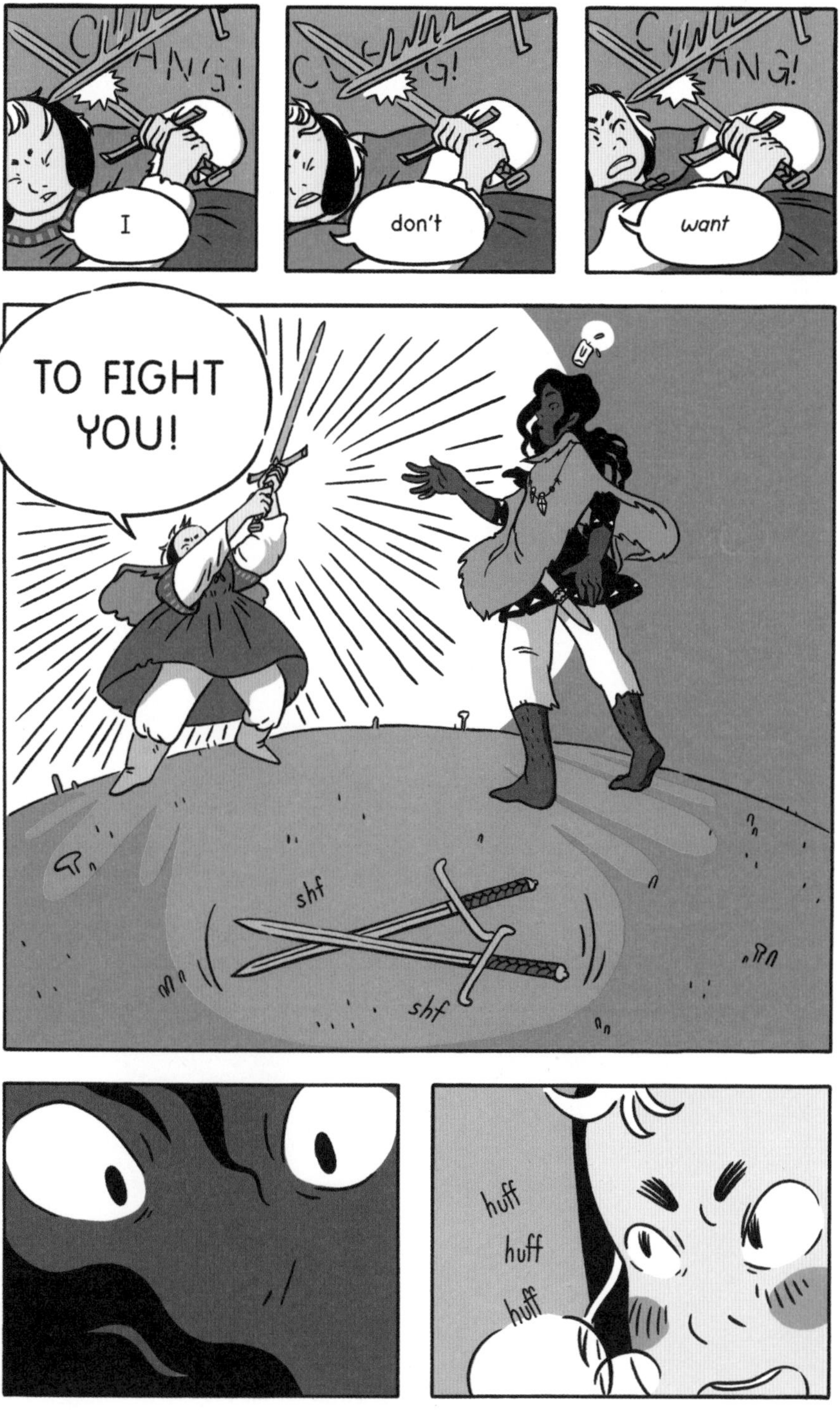
I
don't
want
TO FIGHT YOU!
shf
shf
huff
huff
huff

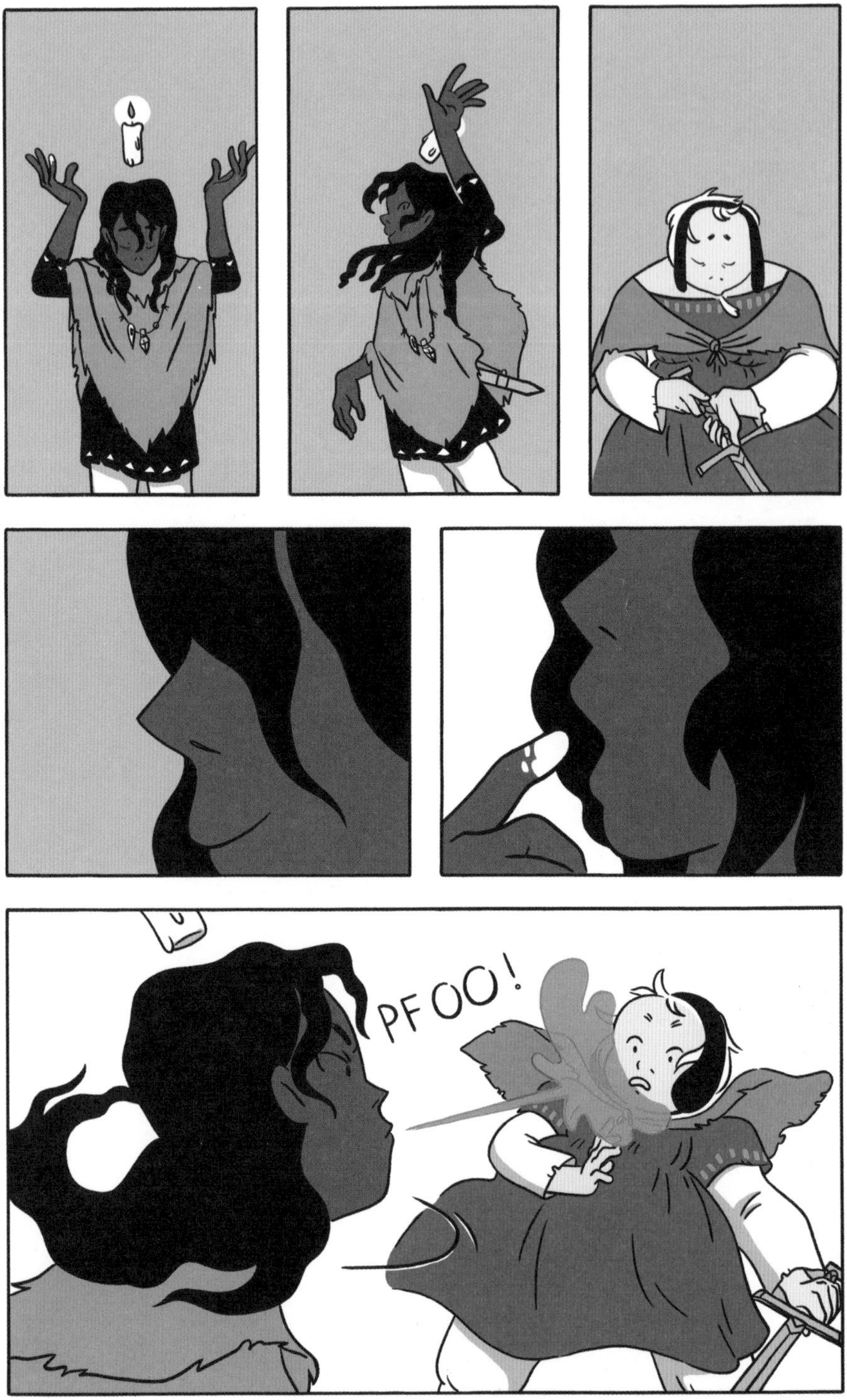
PFOO!

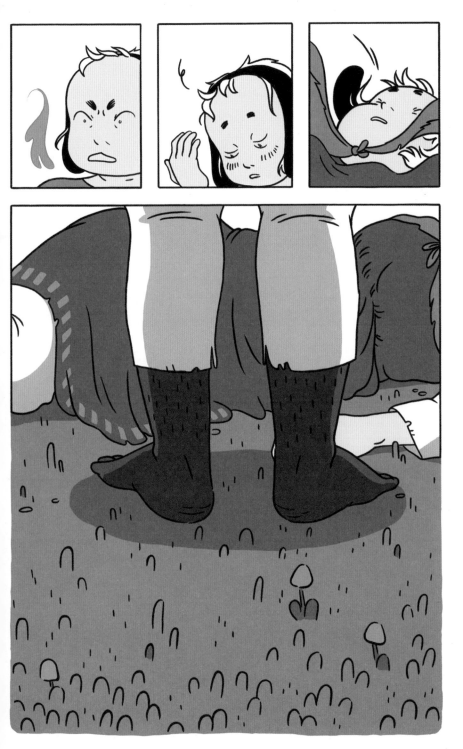

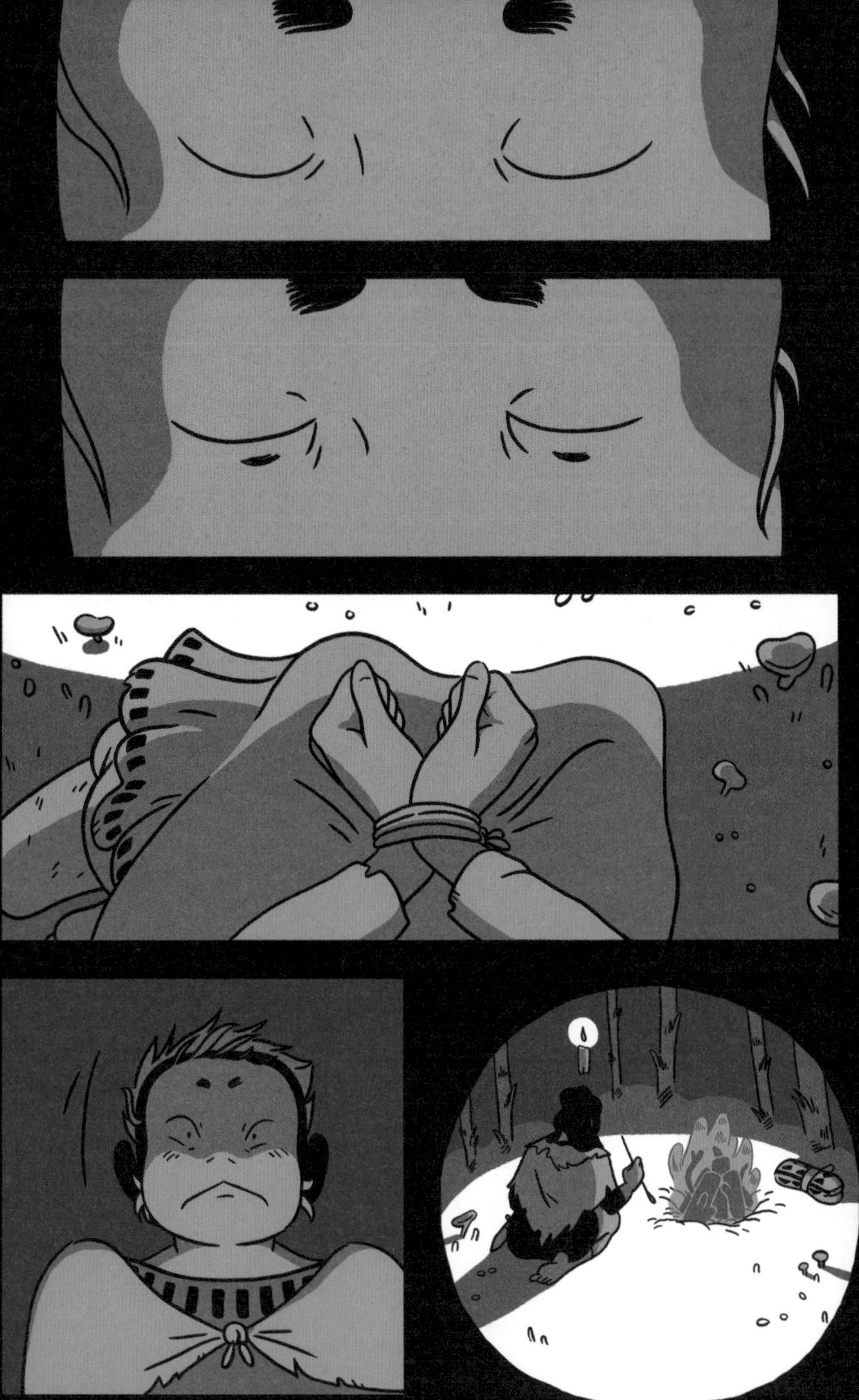

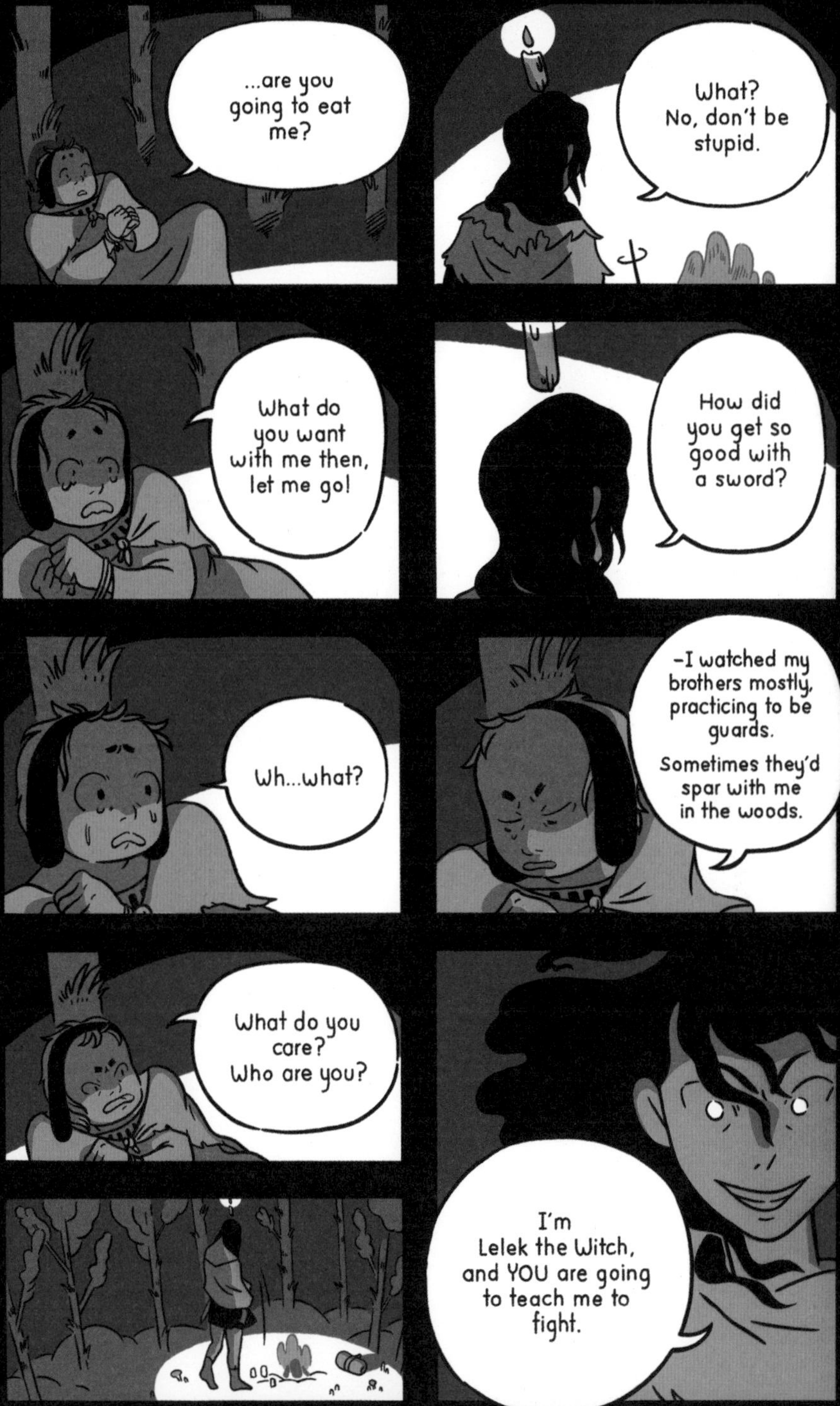
...are you going to eat me?
What? No, don't be stupid.
What do you want with me then, let me go!
How did you get so good with a sword?
Wh...what?
-I watched my brothers mostly, practicing to be guards.
Sometimes they'd spar with me in the woods.
What do you care? Who are you?
I'm Lelek the Witch, and YOU are going to teach me to fight.

What are you doing?

Making more potion, I used my last on you.

So... potions are your specialty?

Ha. Not by choice.

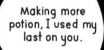

So—

Oh.

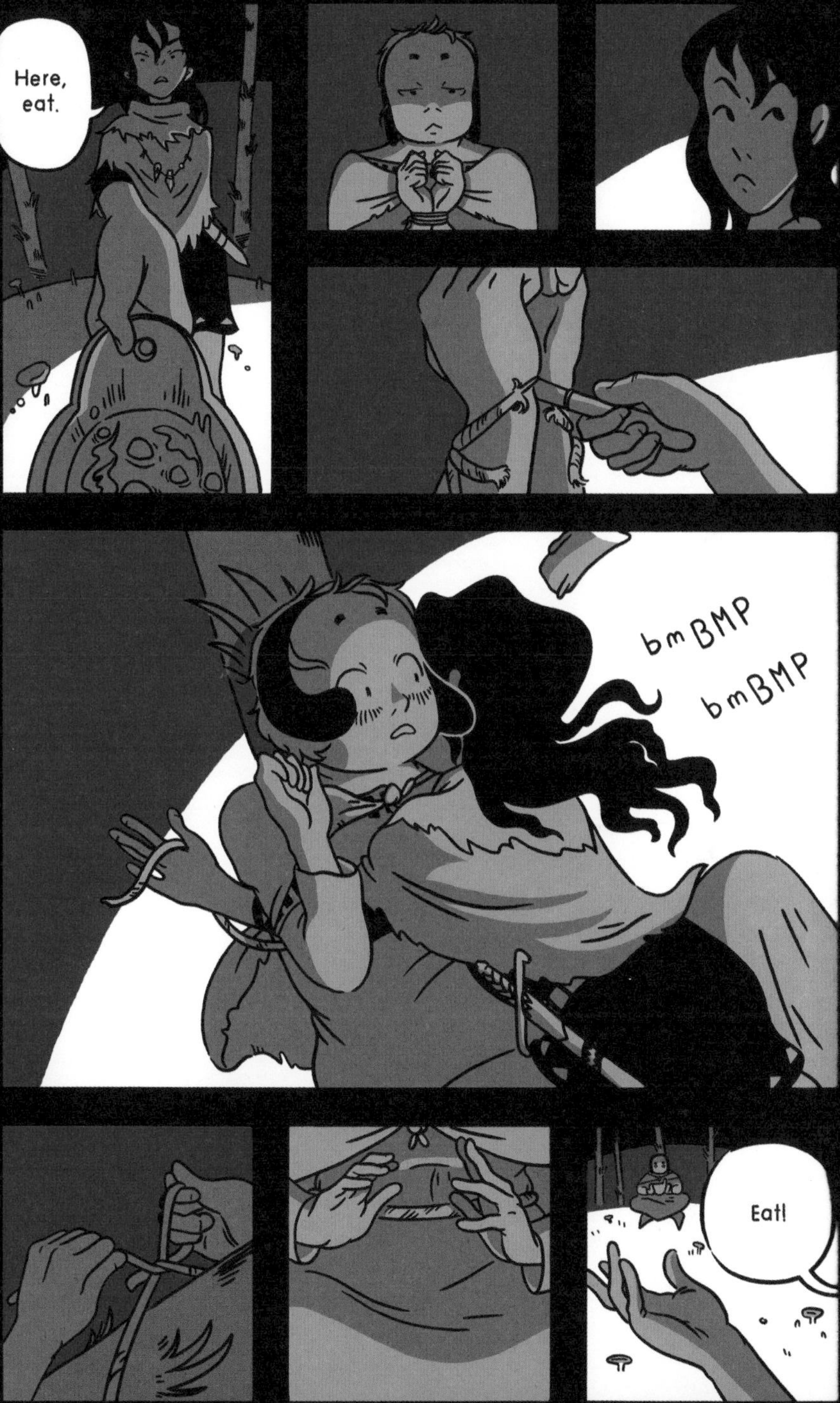
Here, eat.
bmBMP
bmBMP
Eat!

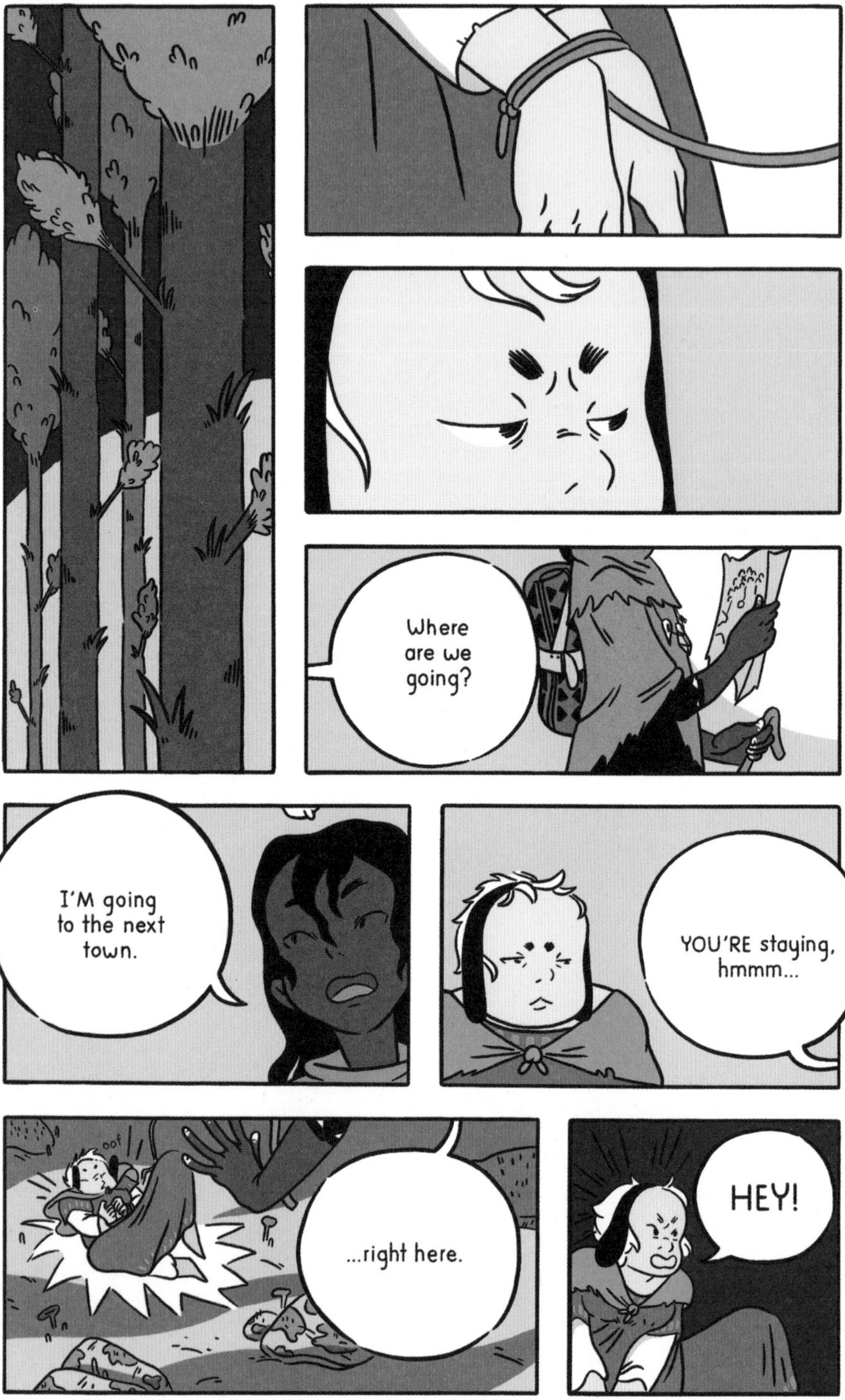
Where are we going?
I'M going to the next town.
YOU'RE staying, hmmm...
oof
...right here.
HEY!

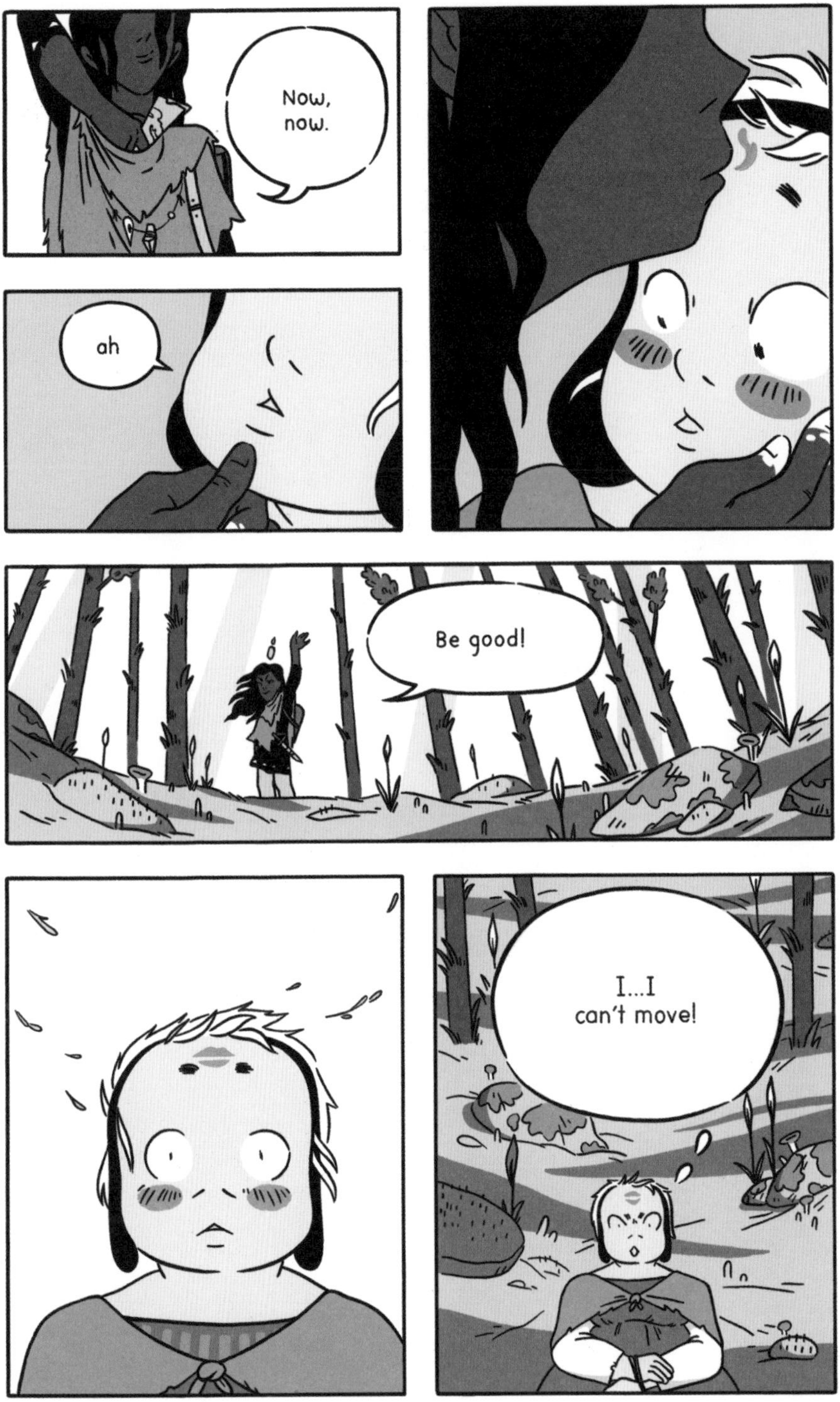
Now, now.
ah
Be good!
I...I can't move!

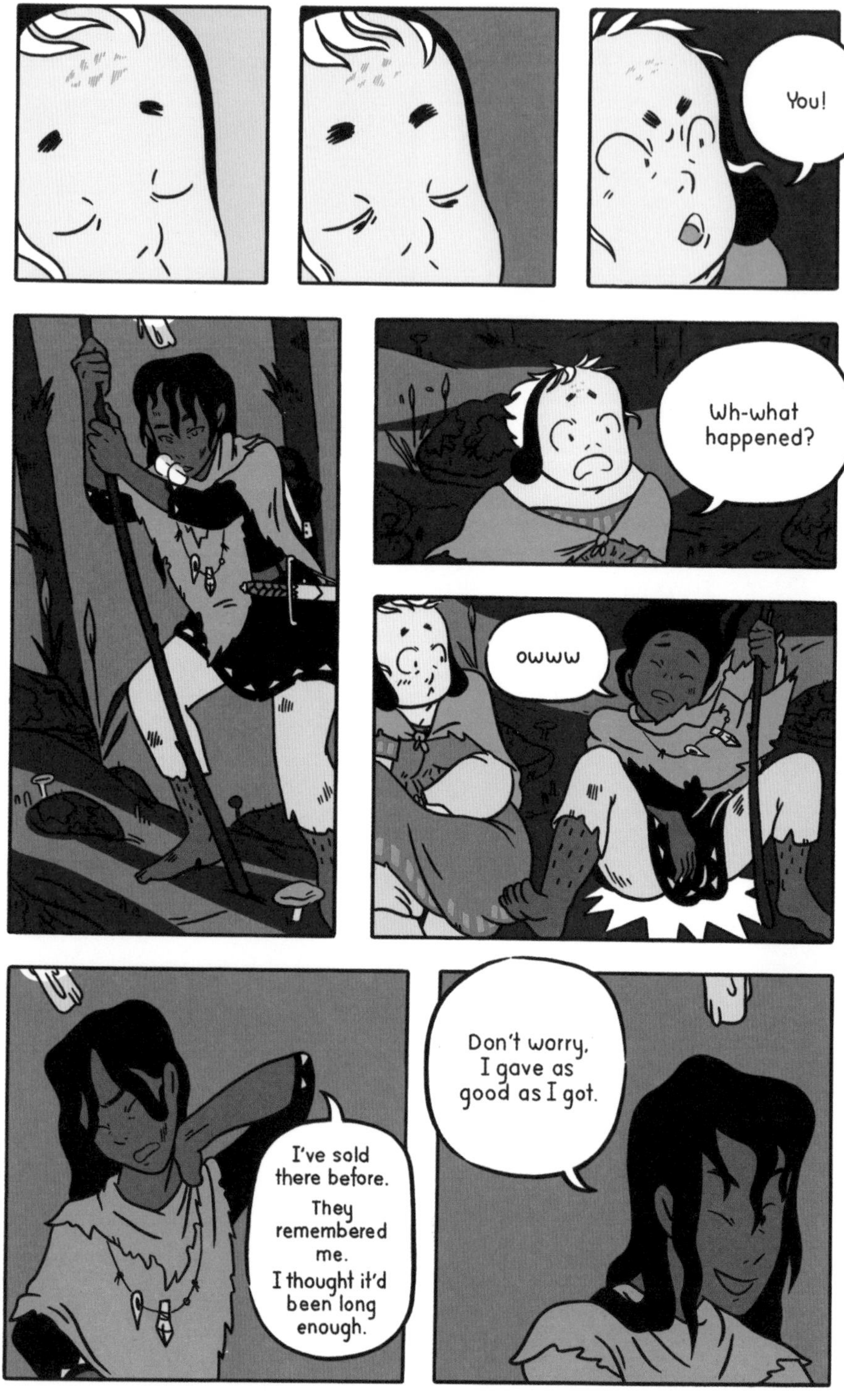
You!
Wh-what happened?
owww
I've sold there before.
They remembered me.
I thought it'd been long enough.
Don't worry, I gave as good as I got.

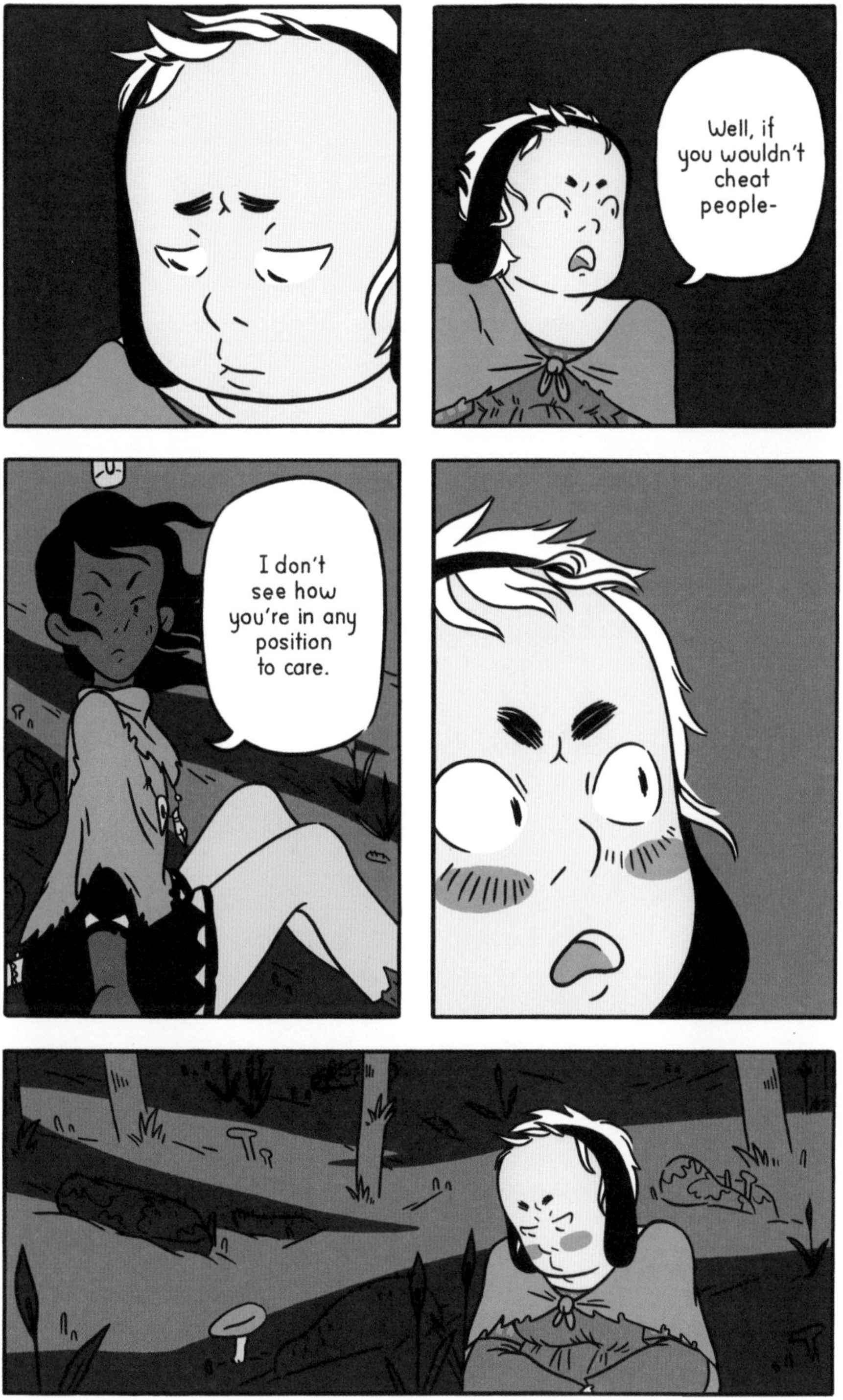
Well, if you wouldn't cheat people-
I don't see how you're in any position to care.

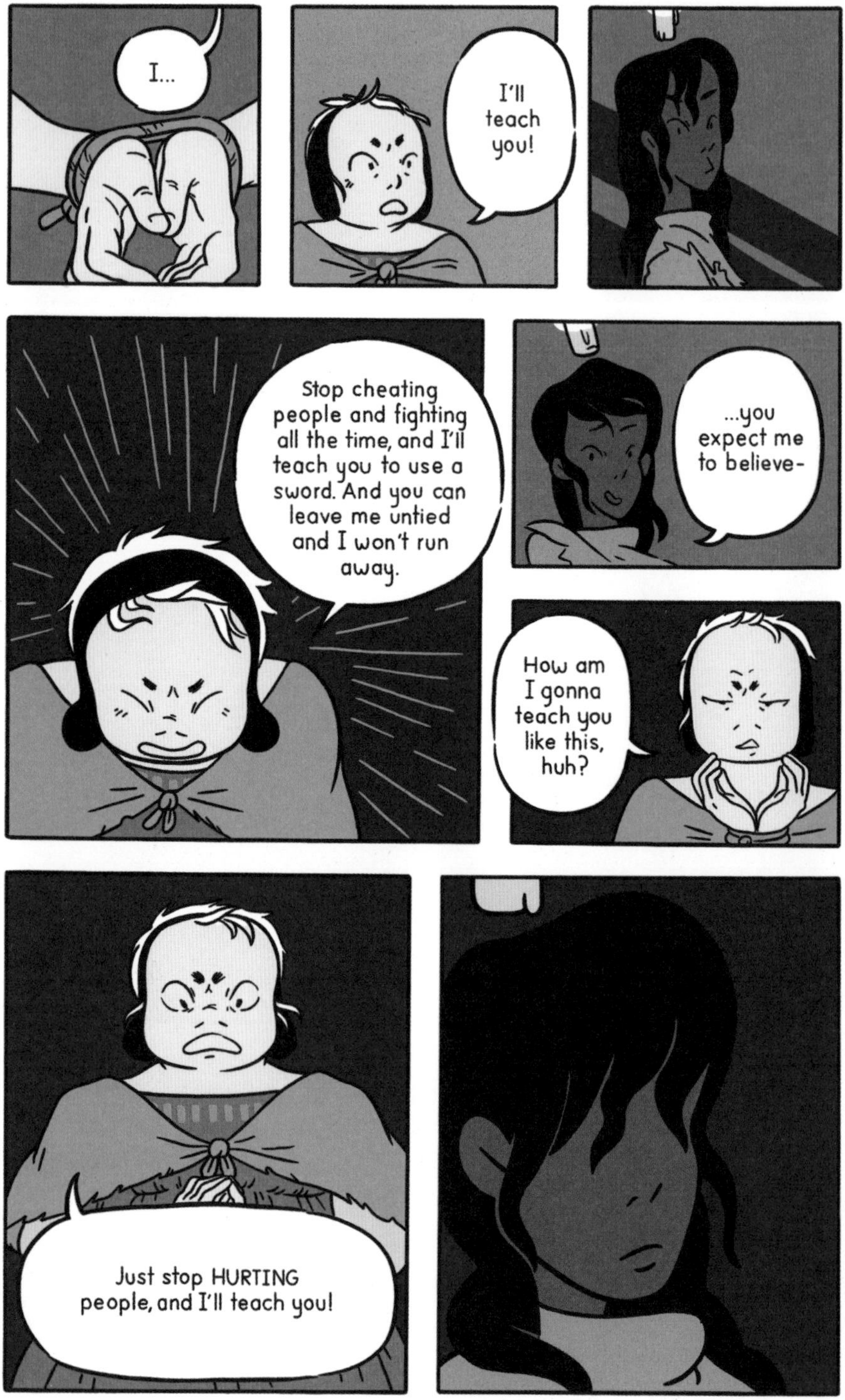
I...
I'll teach you!
Stop cheating people and fighting all the time, and I'll teach you to use a sword. And you can leave me untied and I won't run away.
...you expect me to believe-
How am I gonna teach you like this, huh?
Just stop HURTING people, and I'll teach you!

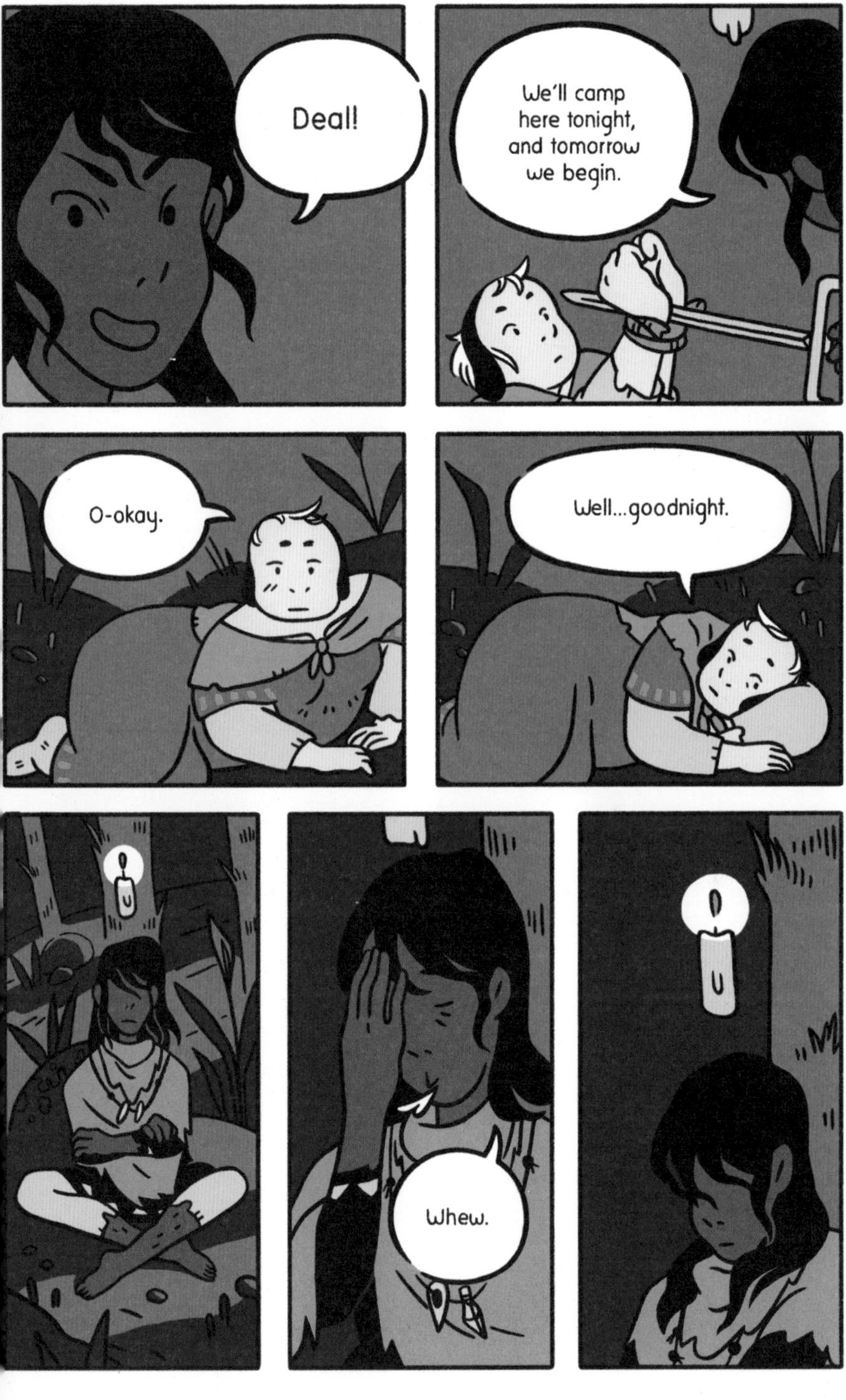
Deal!
We'll camp here tonight, and tomorrow we begin.
O-okay.
Well...goodnight.
Whew.

Part 2

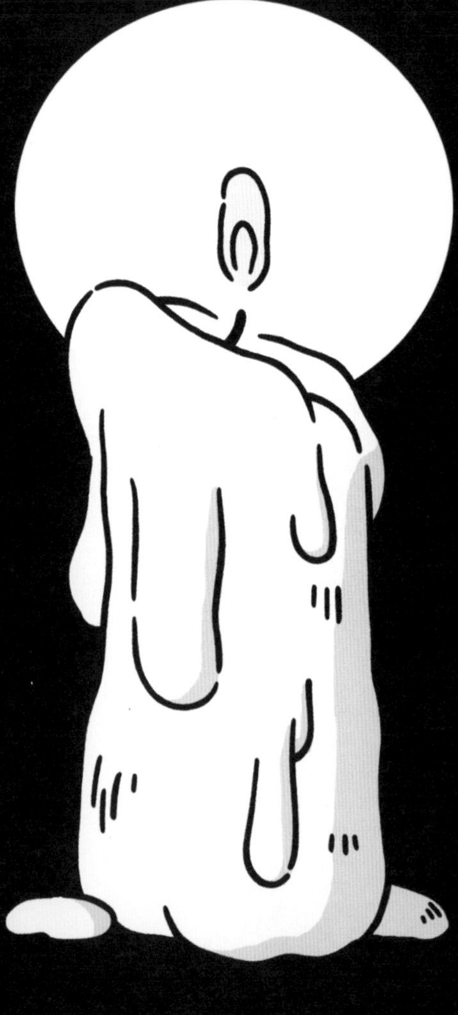

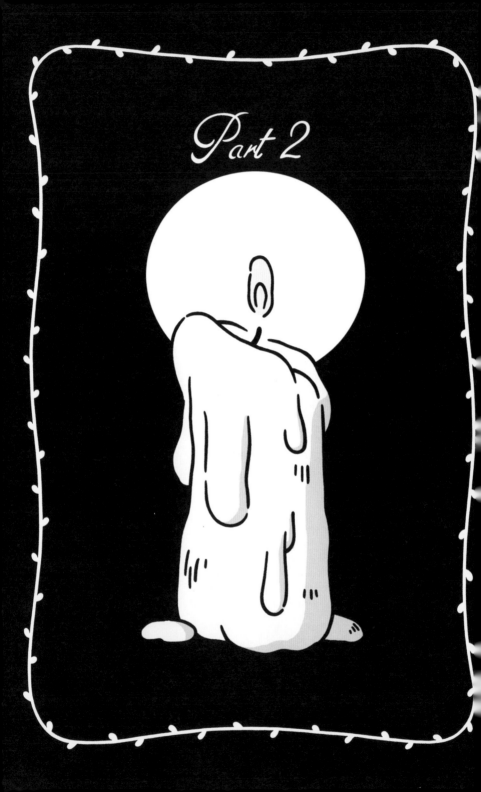

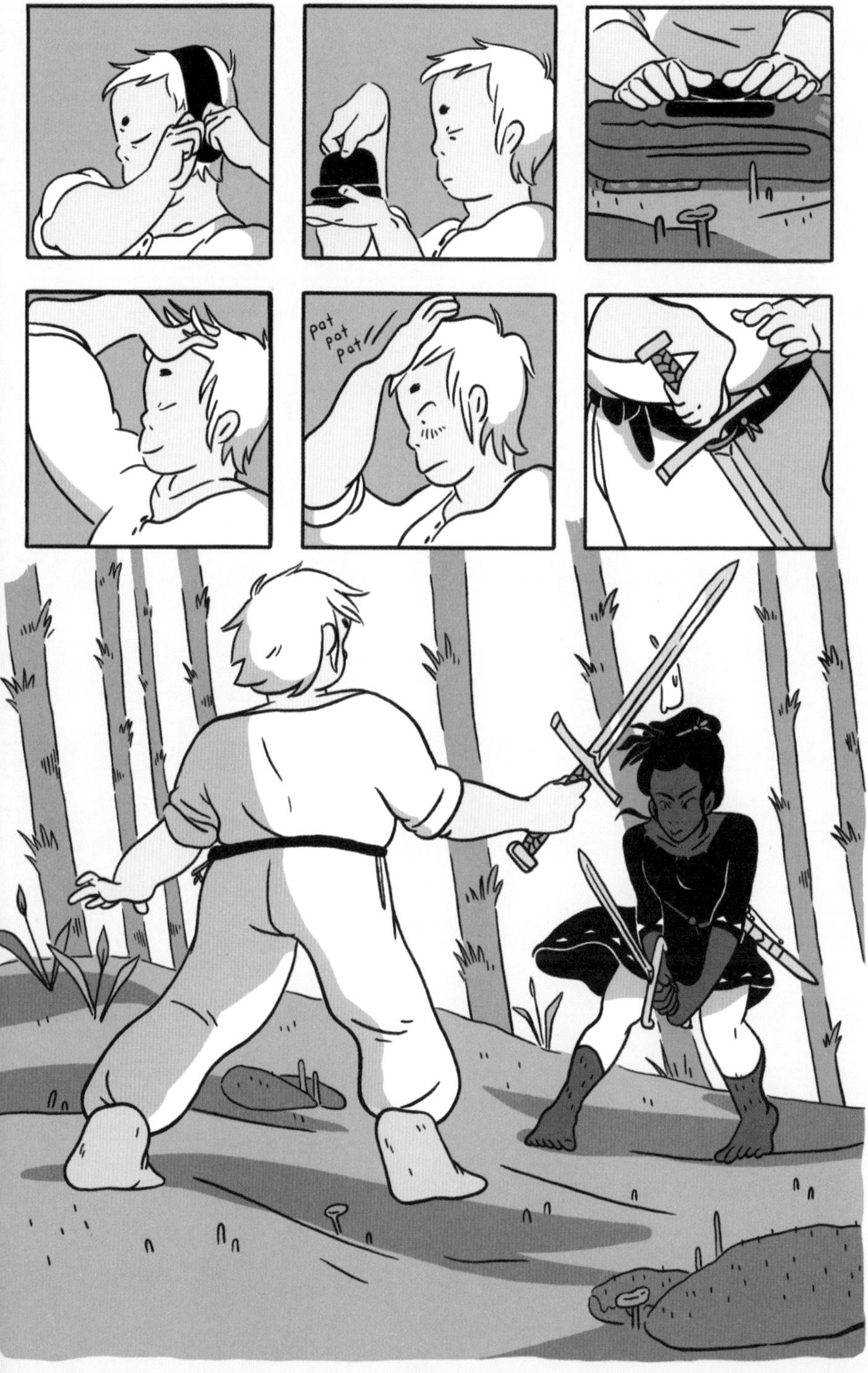
pat pat pat

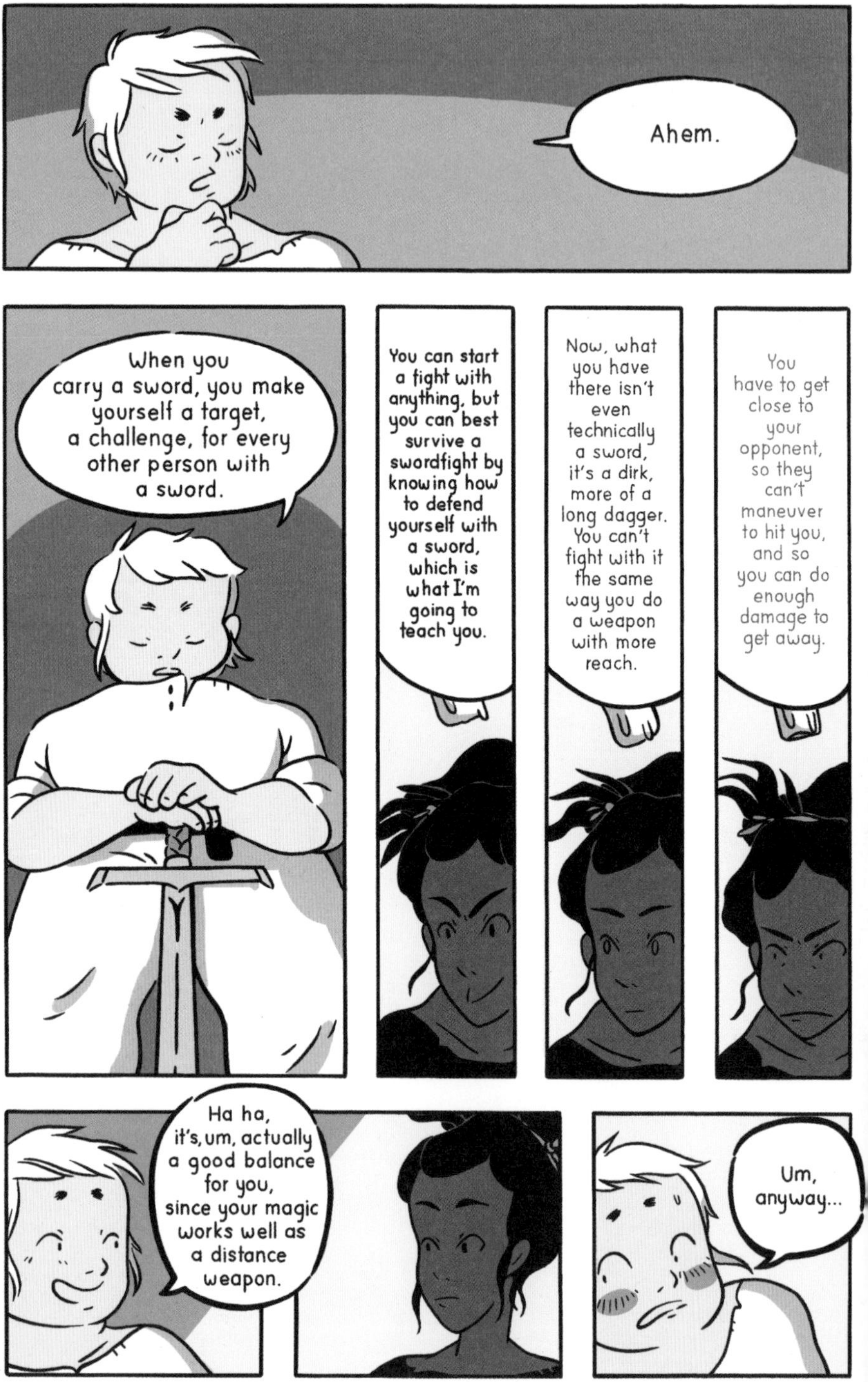
Ahem.
When you carry a sword, you make yourself a target, a challenge, for every other person with a sword.
You can start a fight with anything, but you can best survive a swordfight by knowing how to defend yourself with a sword, which is what I'm going to teach you.
Now, what you have there isn't even technically a sword, it's a dirk, more of a long dagger. You can't fight with it the same way you do a weapon with more reach.
You have to get close to your opponent, so they can't maneuver to hit you, and so you can do enough damage to get away.
Ha ha, it's, um, actually a good balance for you, since your magic works well as a distance weapon.
Um, anyway...

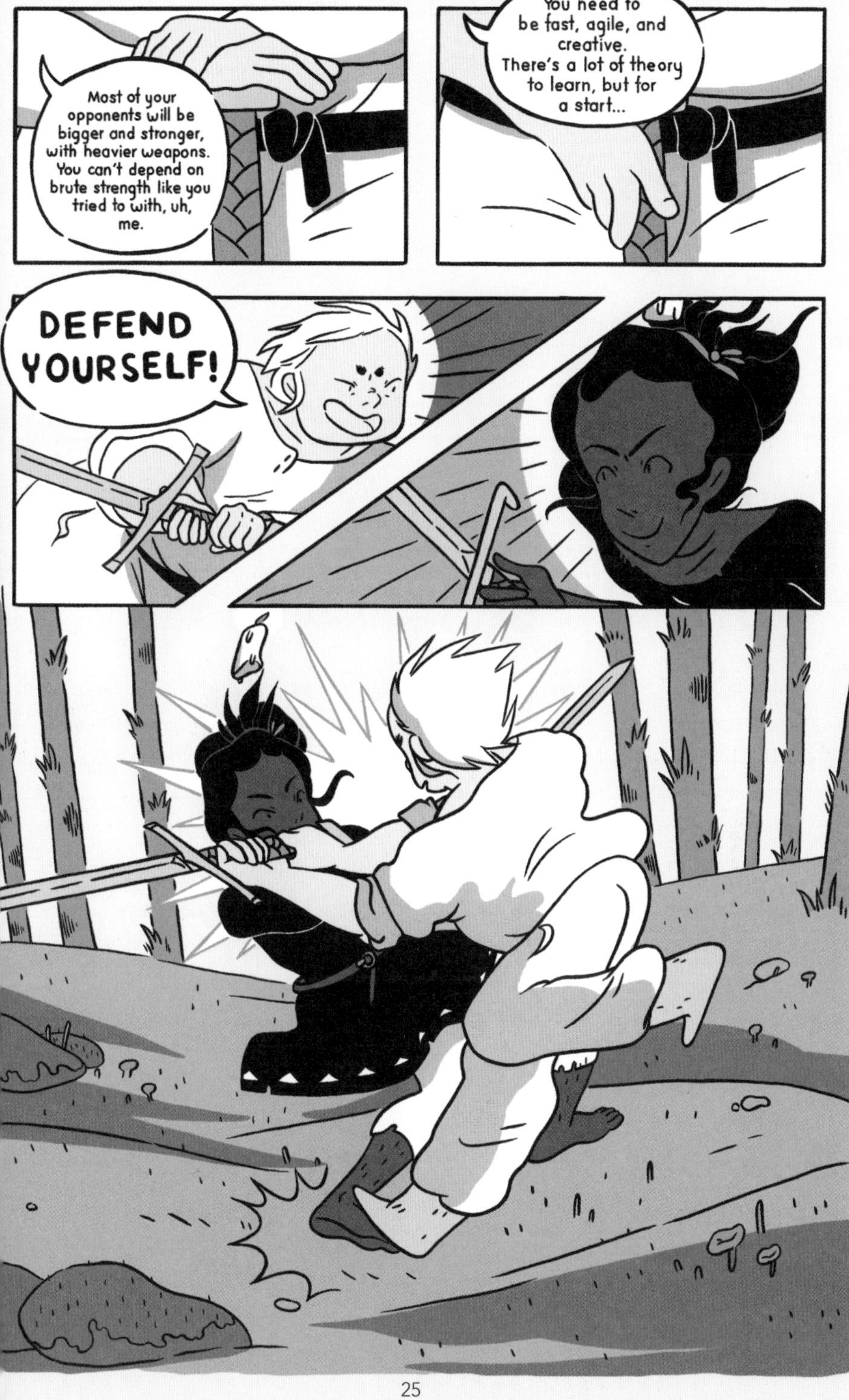

Most of your opponents will be bigger and stronger, with heavier weapons. You can't depend on brute strength like you tried to with, uh, me.
You need to be fast, agile, and creative. There's a lot of theory to learn, but for a start...
DEFEND YOURSELF!

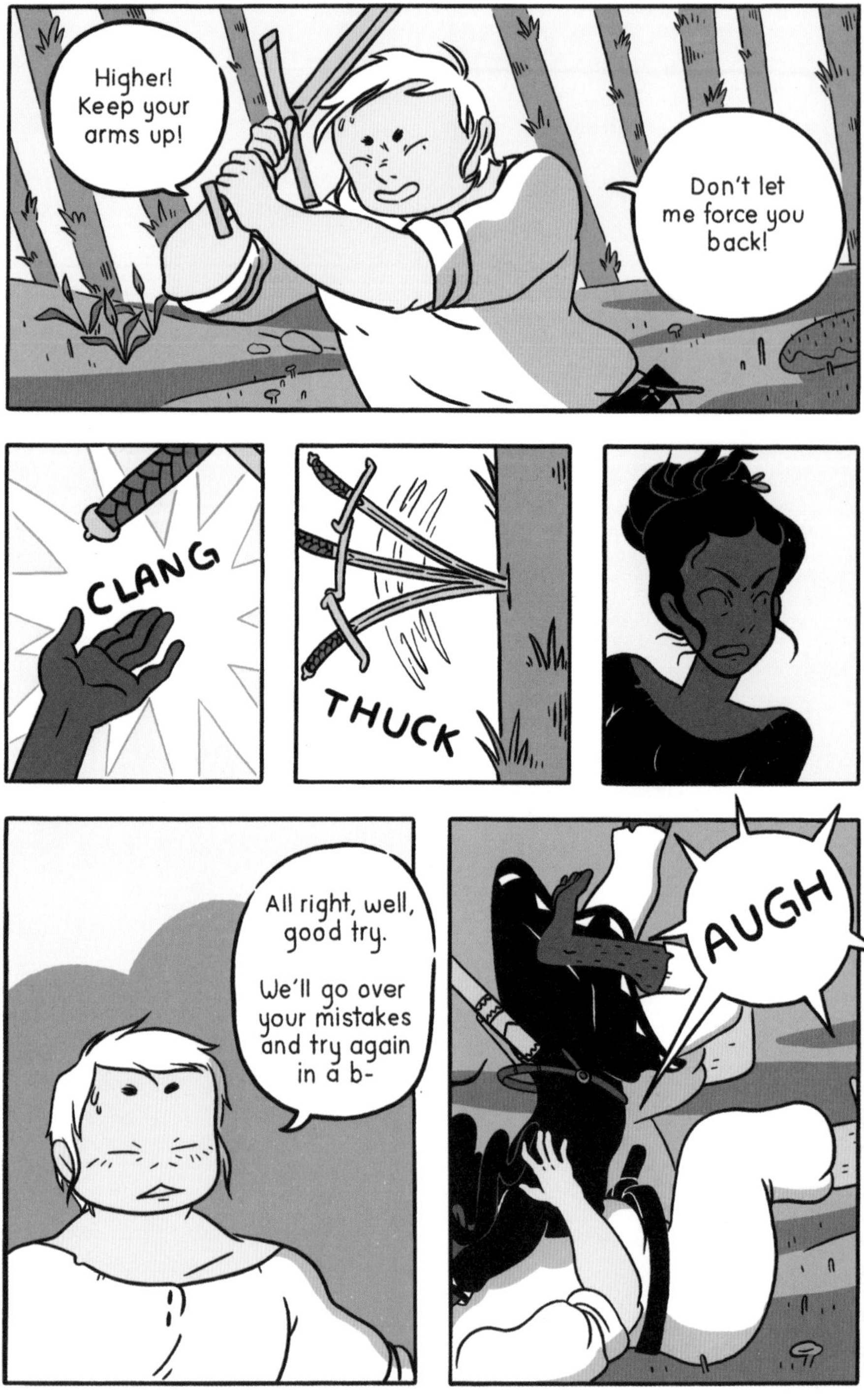
Higher! Keep your arms up!
Don't let me force you back!
CLANG
THUCK
All right, well, good try.
We'll go over your mistakes and try again in a b-
AUGH

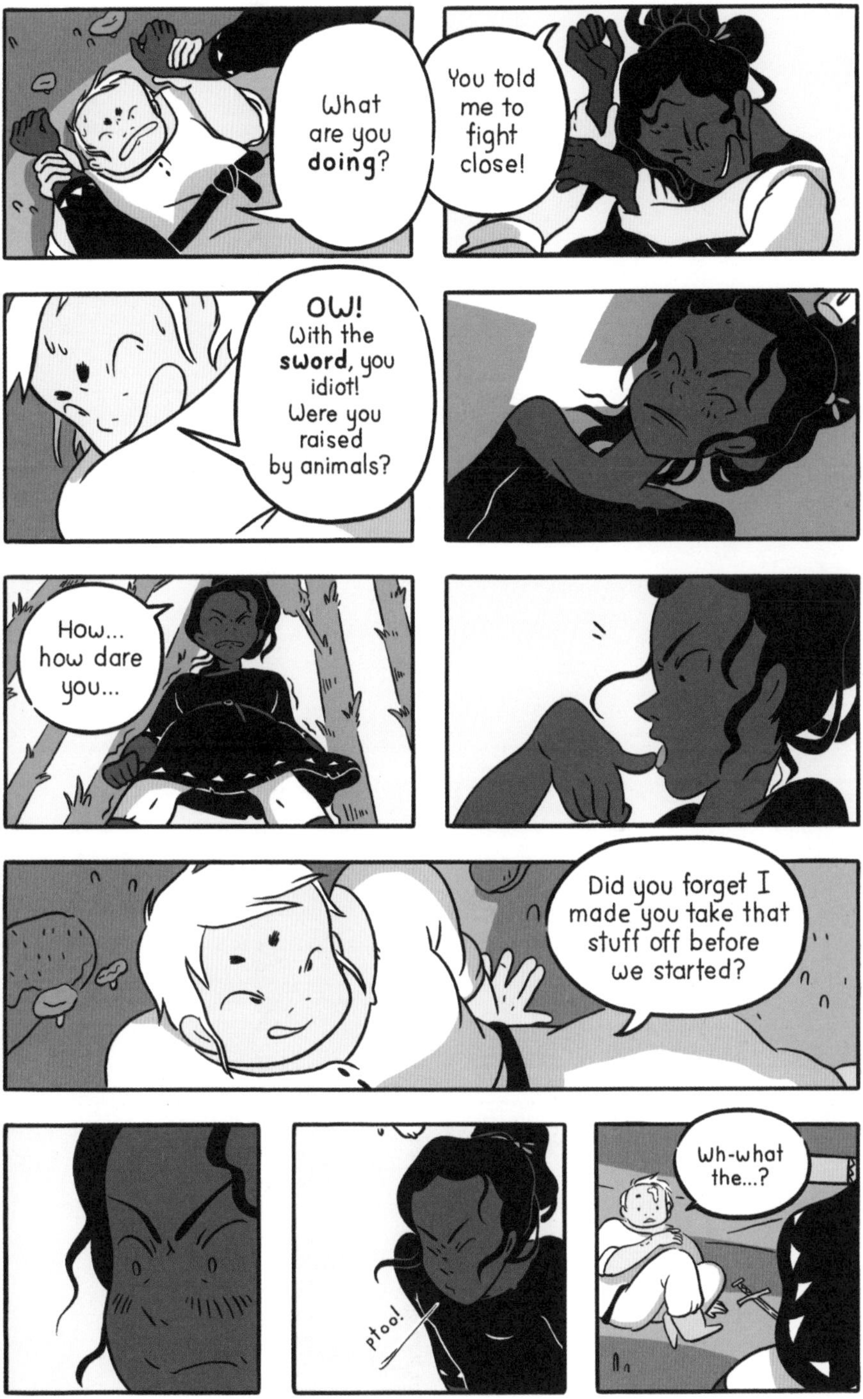

What are you doing?
You told me to fight close!
OW! With the sword, you idiot! Were you raised by animals?
How... how dare you...
Did you forget I made you take that stuff off before we started?
ptoo!
Wh-what the...?

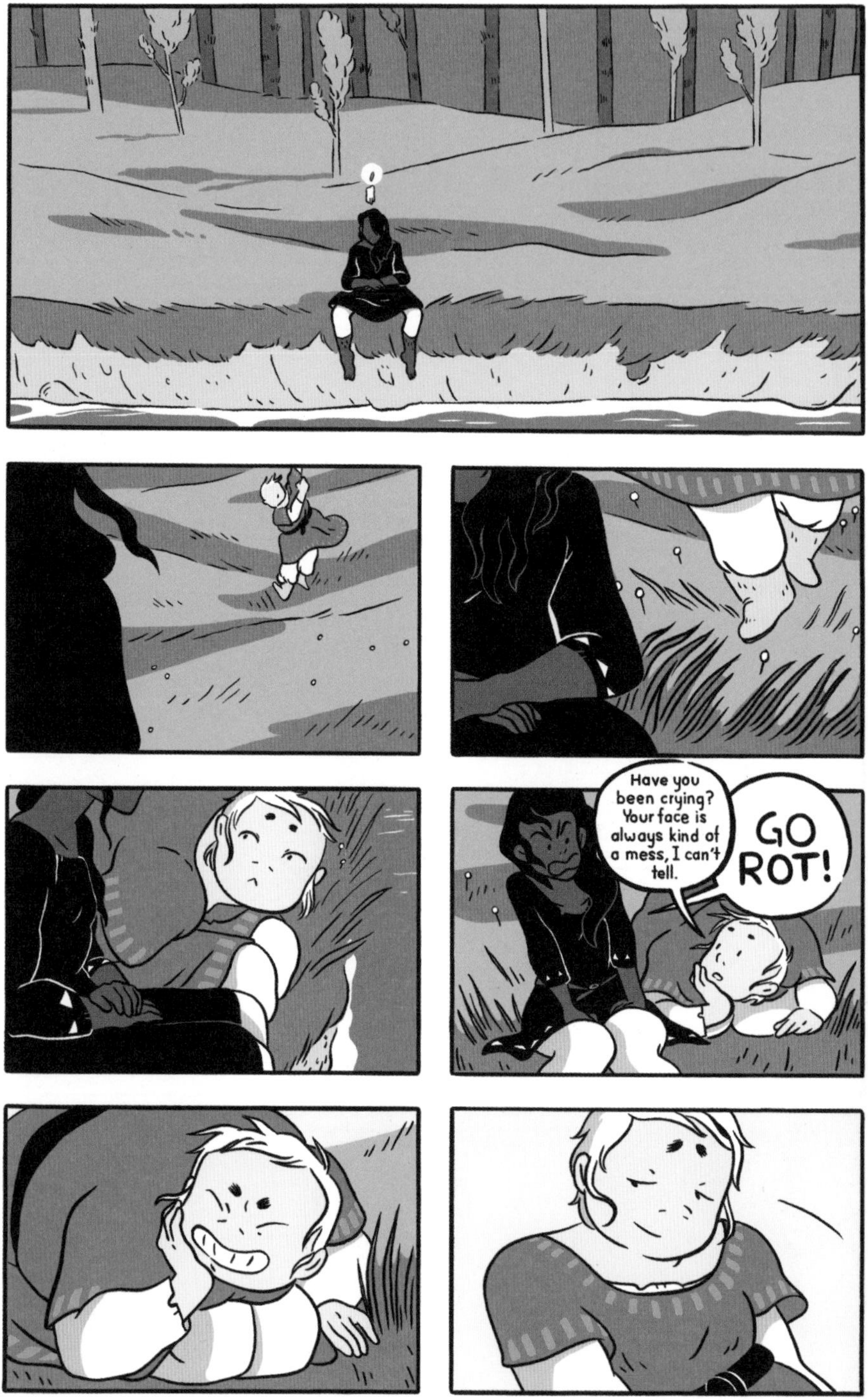
Have you been crying? Your face is always kind of a mess, I can't tell.
GO ROT!

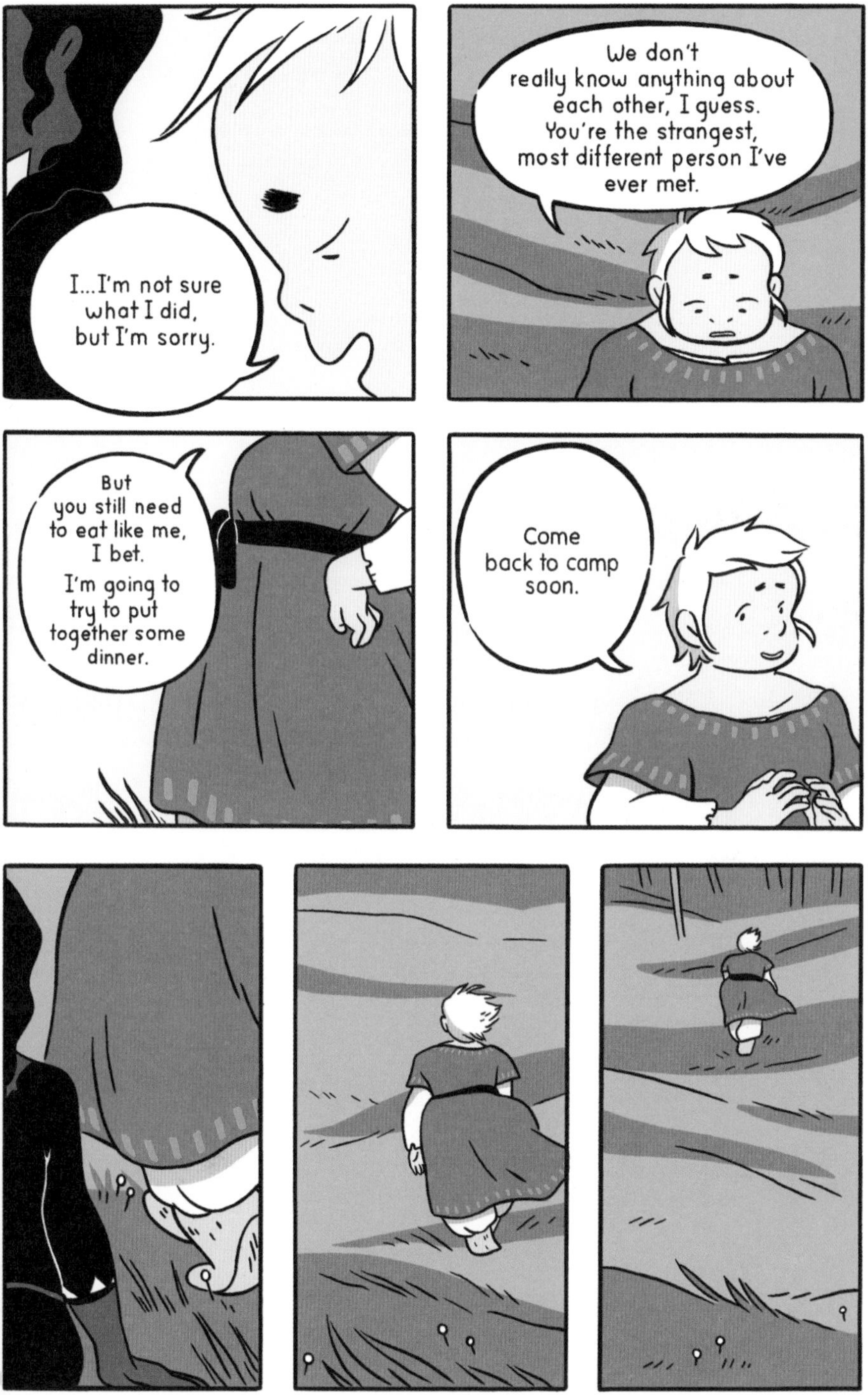
I...I'm not sure what I did, but I'm sorry.
We don't really know anything about each other, I guess. You're the strangest, most different person I've ever met.
But you still need to eat like me, I bet.
I'm going to try to put together some dinner.
Come back to camp soon.

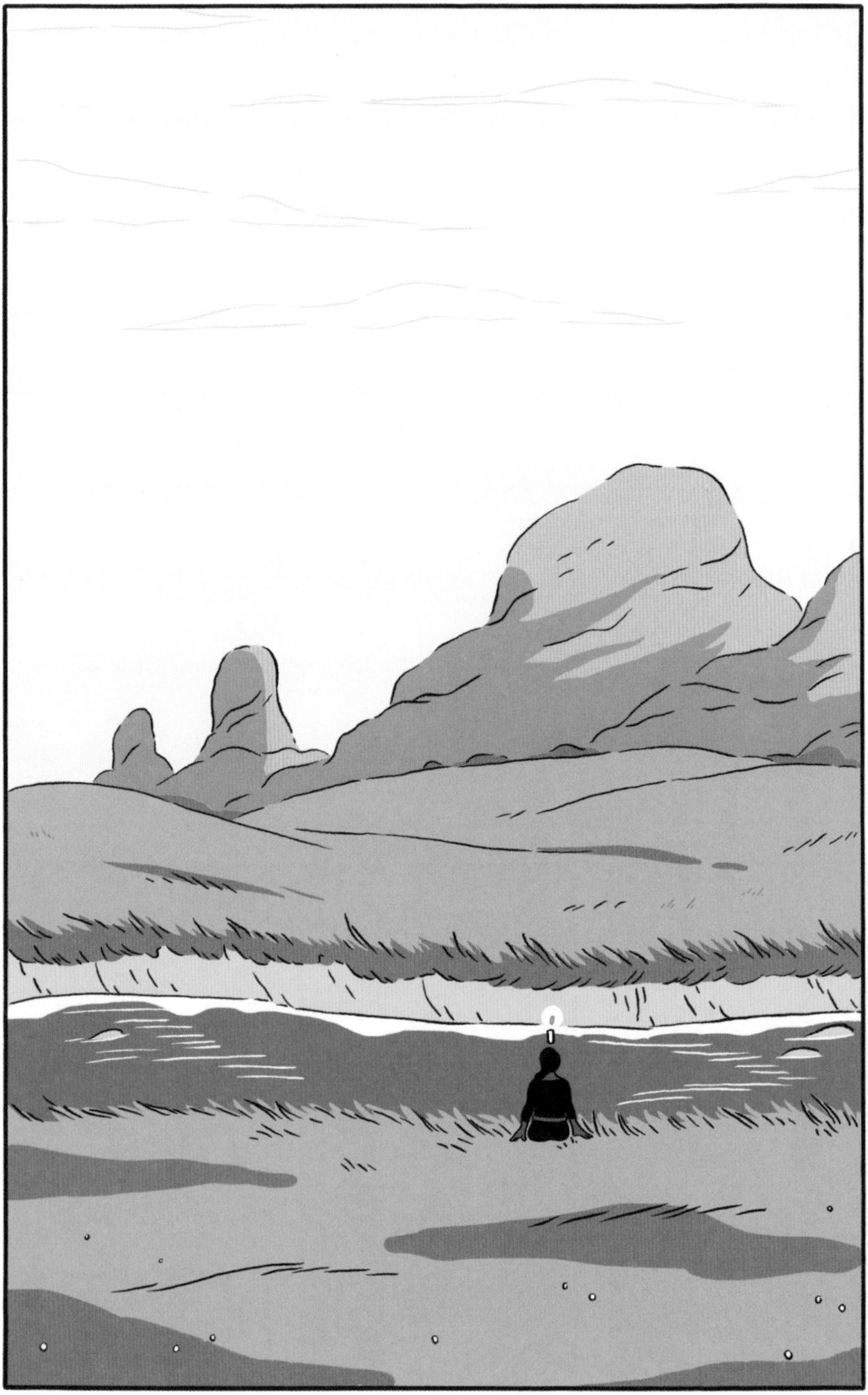

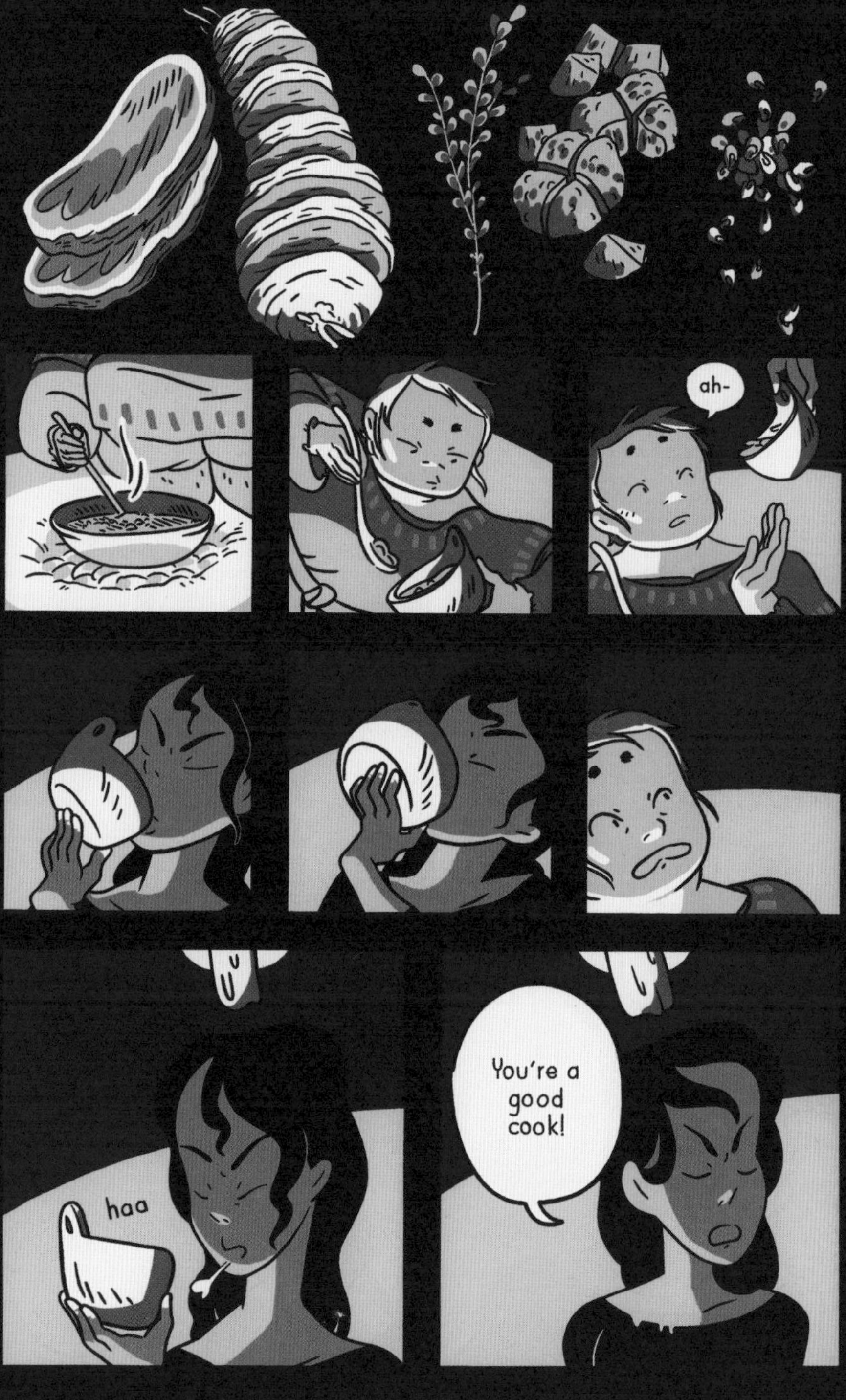

ah-
haa
You're a good cook!

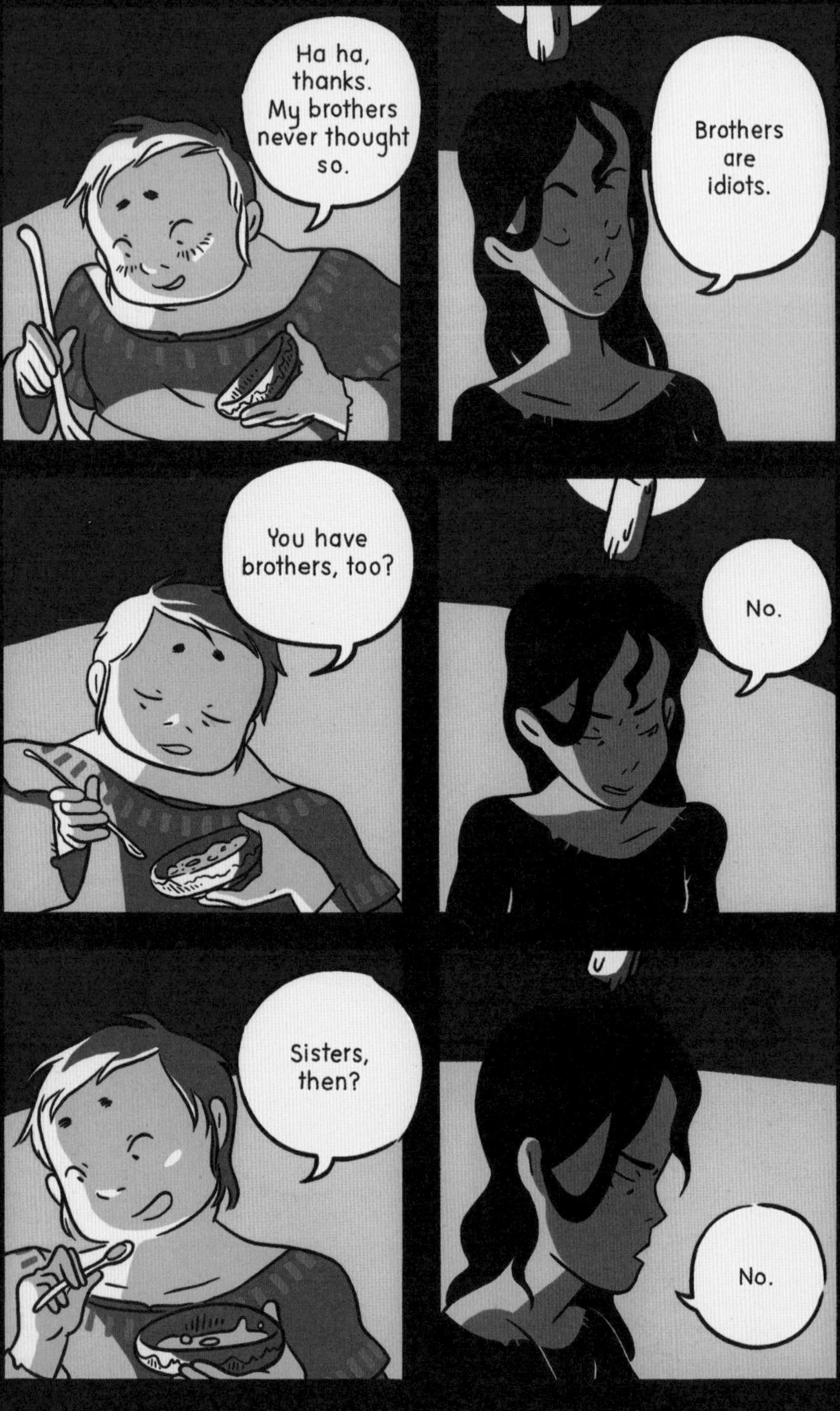
Ha ha, thanks. My brothers never thought so.
Brothers are idiots.
You have brothers, too?
No.
Sisters, then?
No.

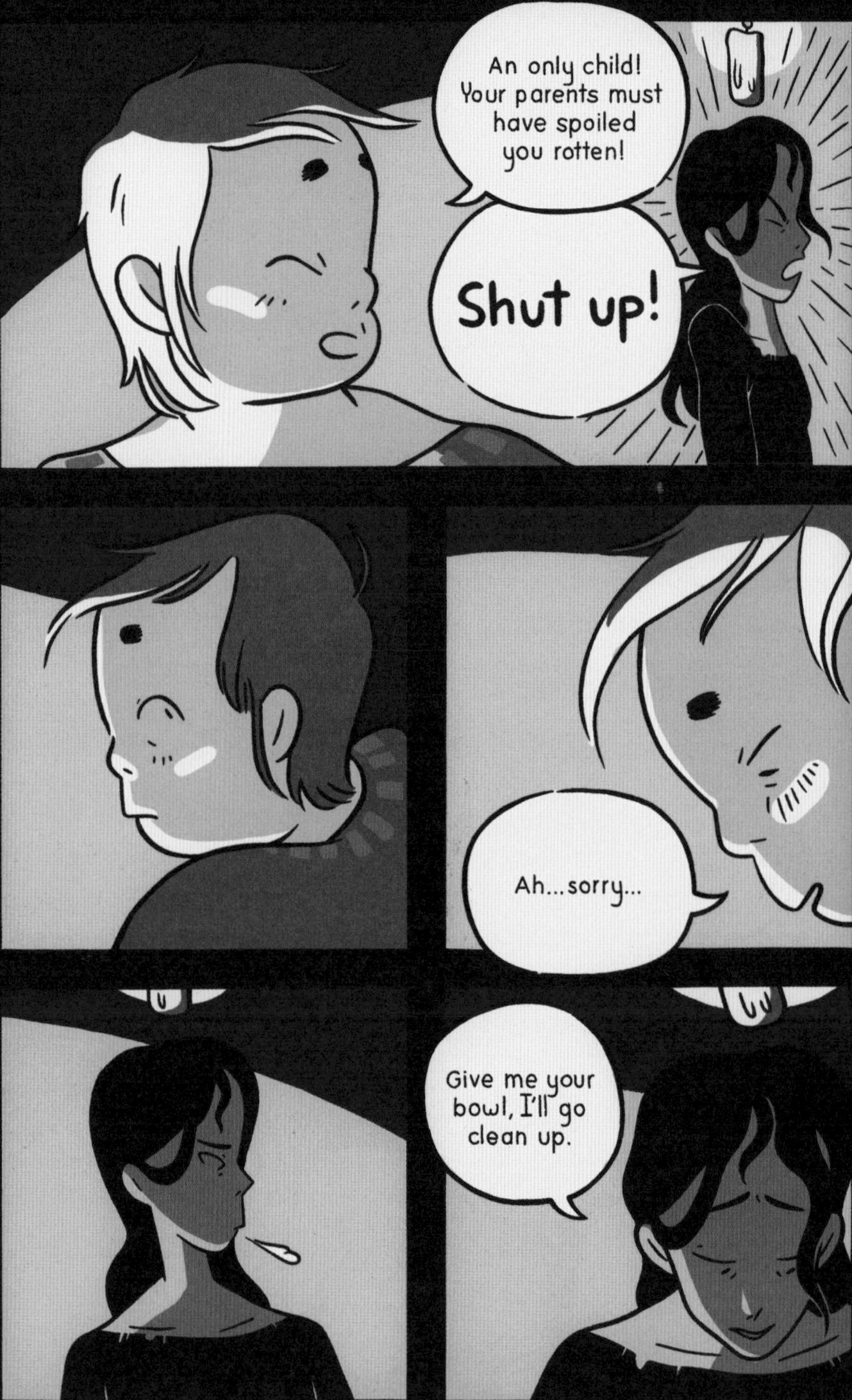
An only child! Your parents must have spoiled you rotten!
Shut up!
Ah...sorry...
Give me your bowl, I'll go clean up.

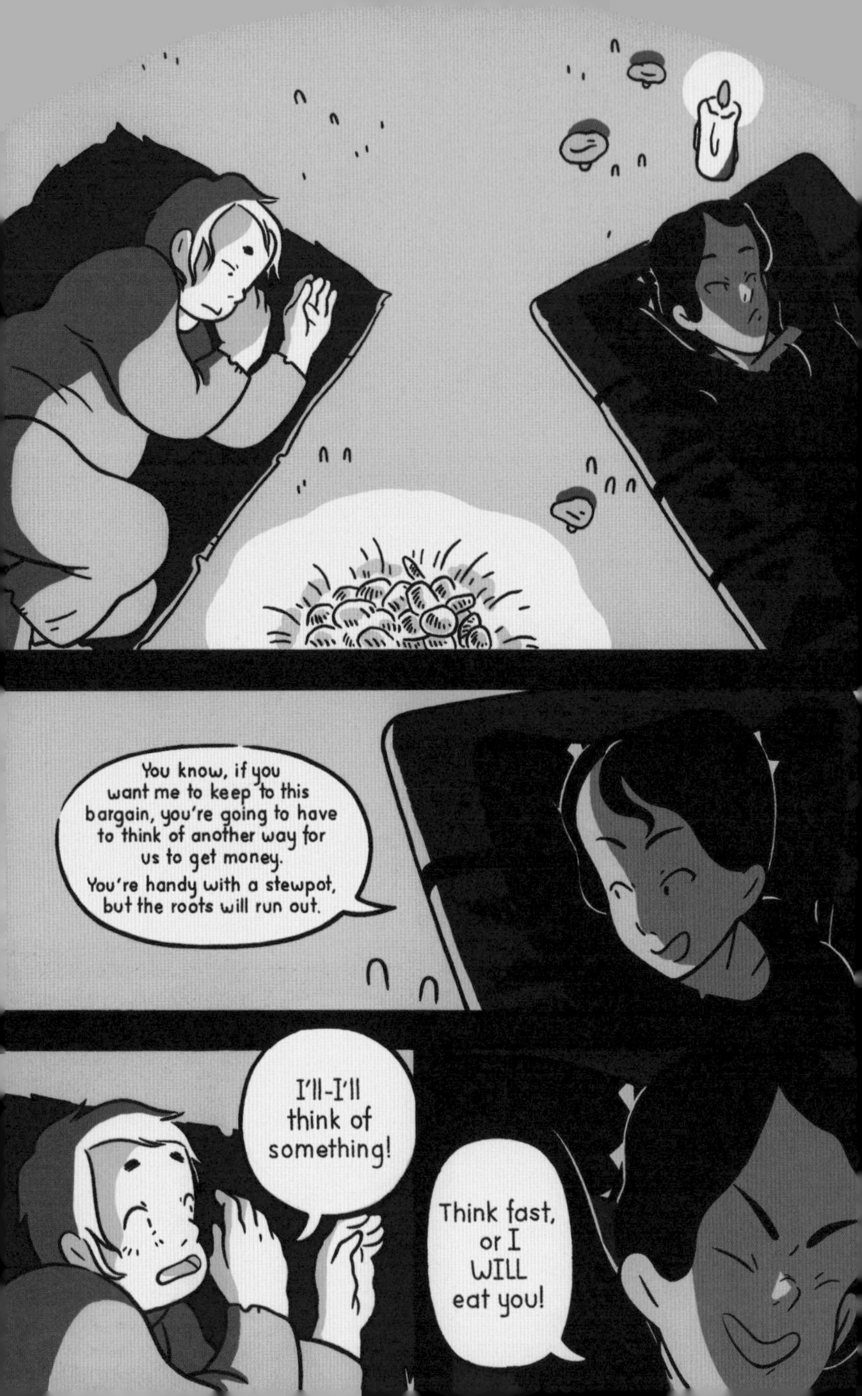
You know, if you want me to keep to this bargain, you're going to have to think of another way for us to get money.
You're handy with a stewpot, but the roots will run out.
I'll-I'll think of something!
Think fast, or I WILL eat you!

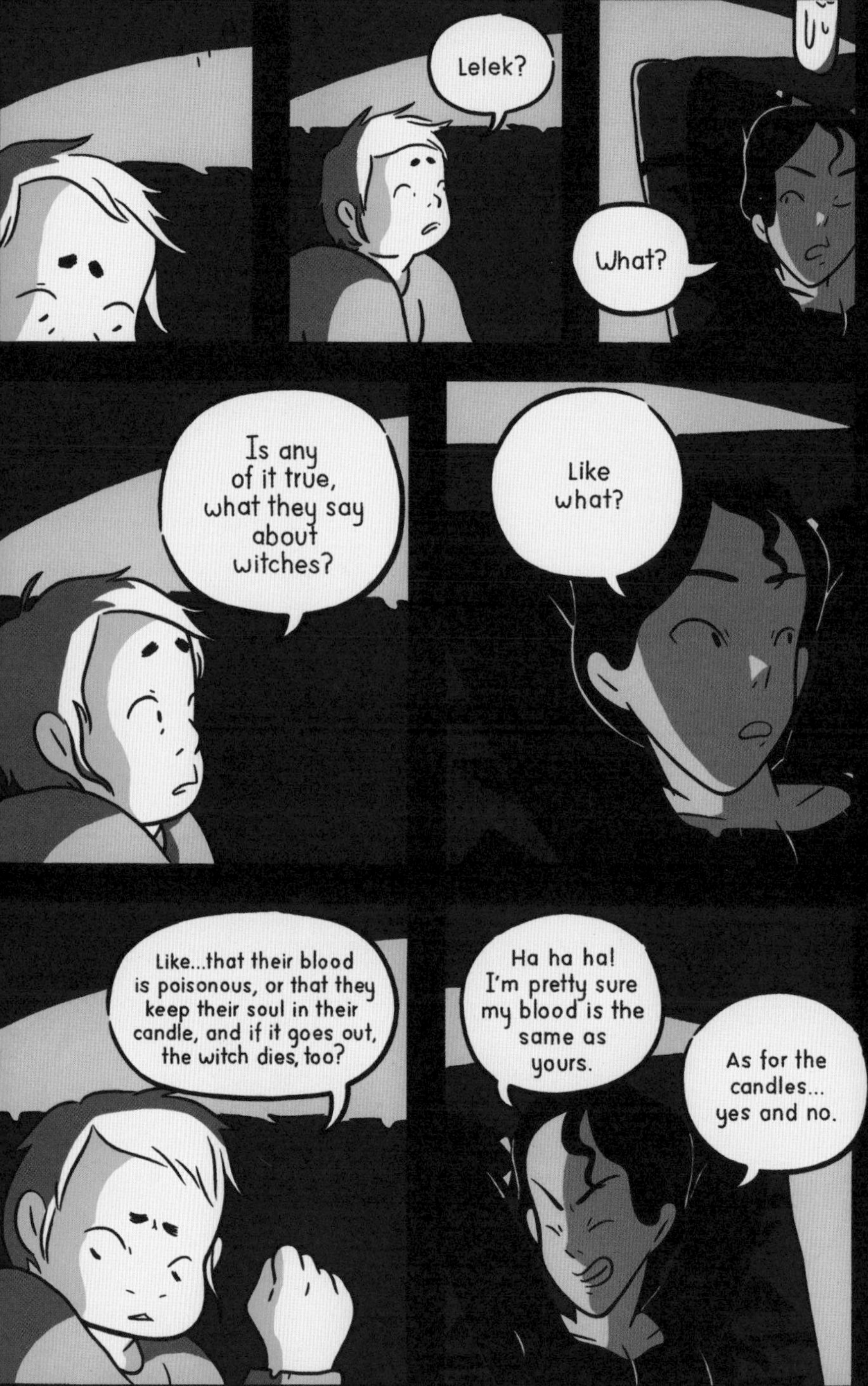
Lelek?
What?
Is any of it true, what they say about witches?
Like what?
Like...that their blood is poisonous, or that they keep their soul in their candle, and if it goes out, the witch dies, too?
Ha ha ha! I'm pretty sure my blood is the same as yours.
As for the candles... yes and no.

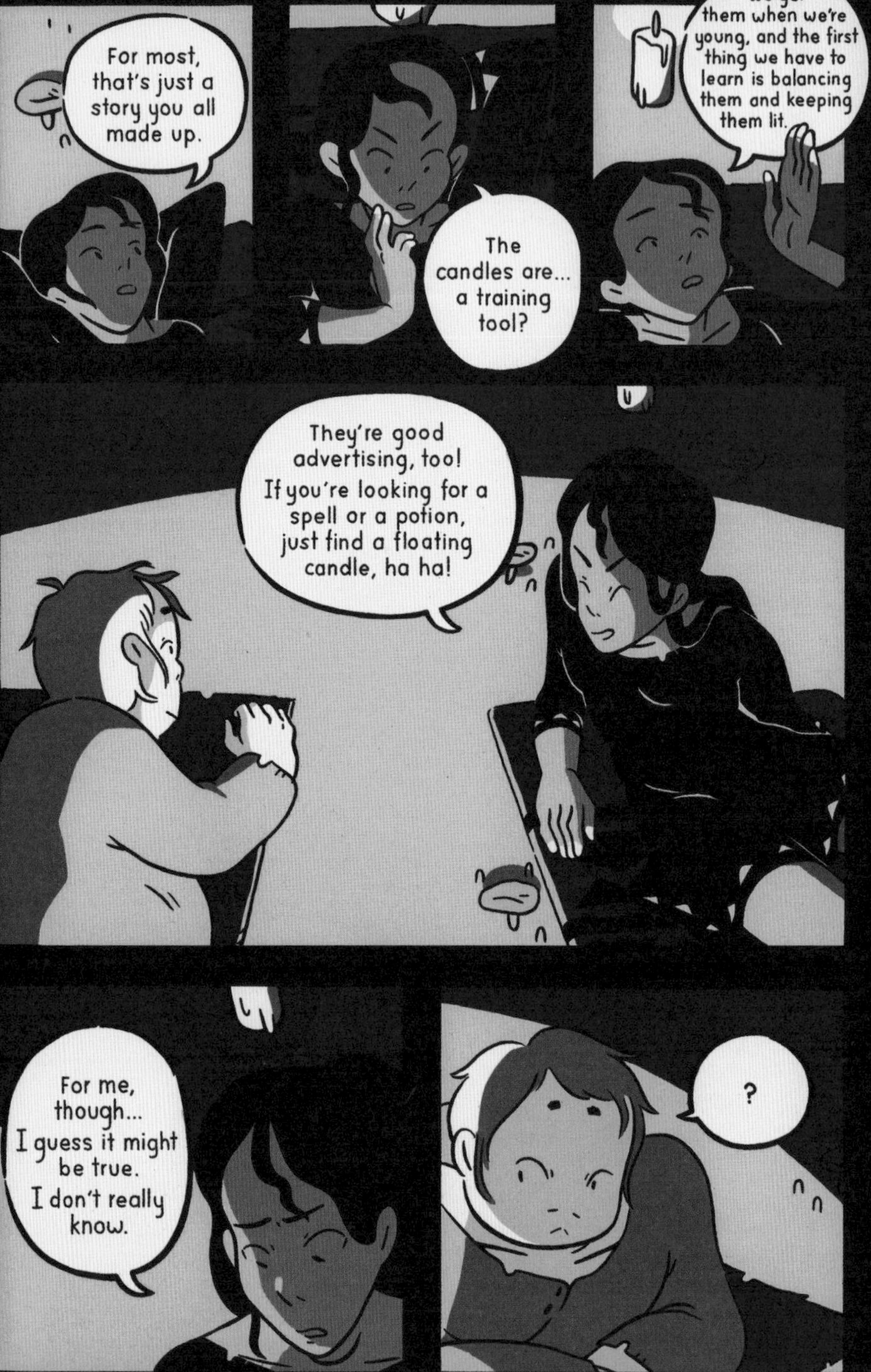
For most, that's just a story you all made up.
The candles are... a training tool?
We get them when we're young, and the first thing we have to learn is balancing them and keeping them lit.
They're good advertising, too! If you're looking for a spell or a potion, just find a floating candle, ha ha!
For me, though... I guess it might be true. I don't really know.
?

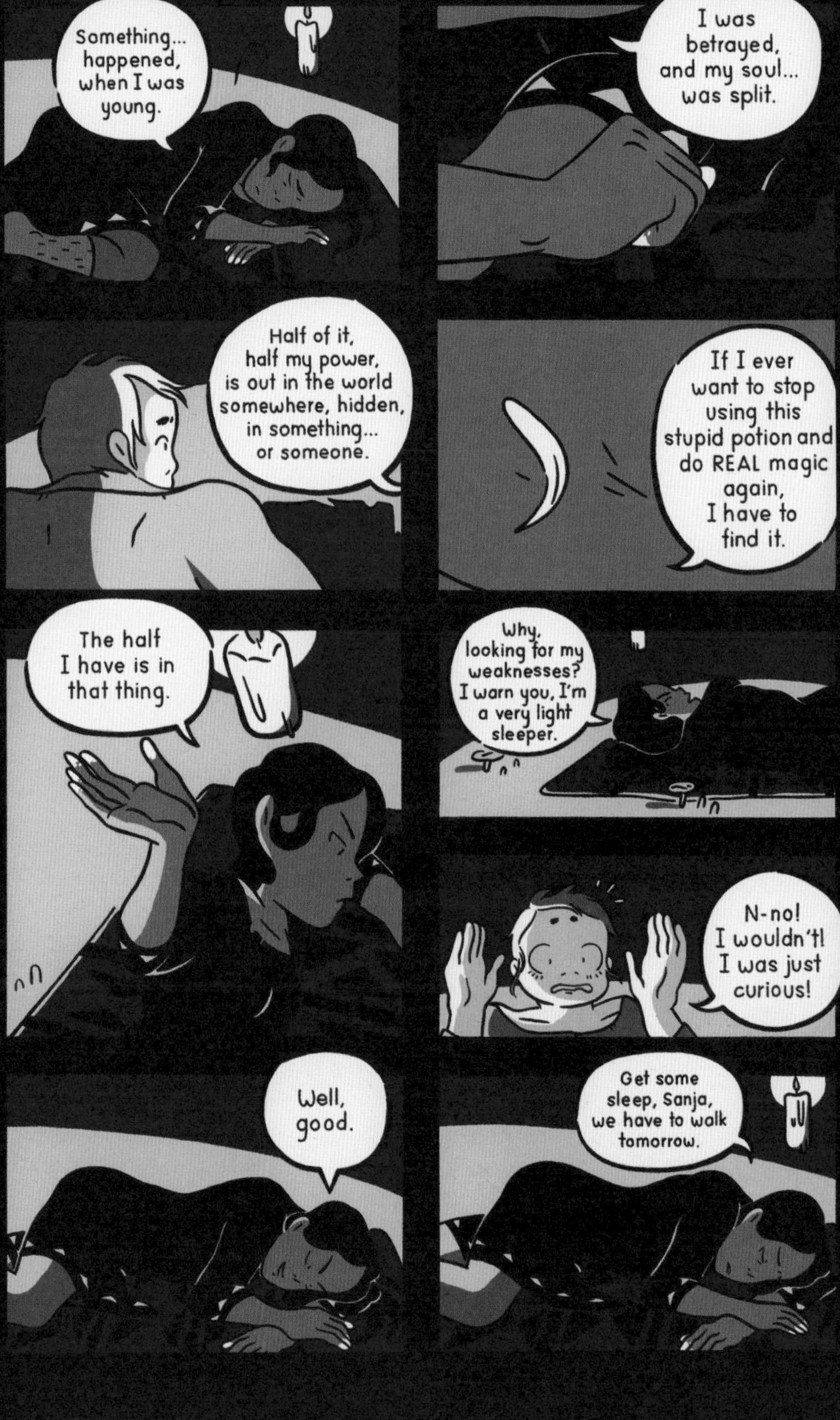
Something... happened, when I was young.
I was betrayed, and my soul... was split.
Half of it, half my power, is out in the world somewhere, hidden, in something... or someone.
If I ever want to stop using this stupid potion and do REAL magic again, I have to find it.
The half I have is in that thing.
Why, looking for my weaknesses? I warn you, I'm a very light sleeper.
N-no! I wouldn't! I was just curious!
Well, good.
Get some sleep, Sanja, we have to walk tomorrow.

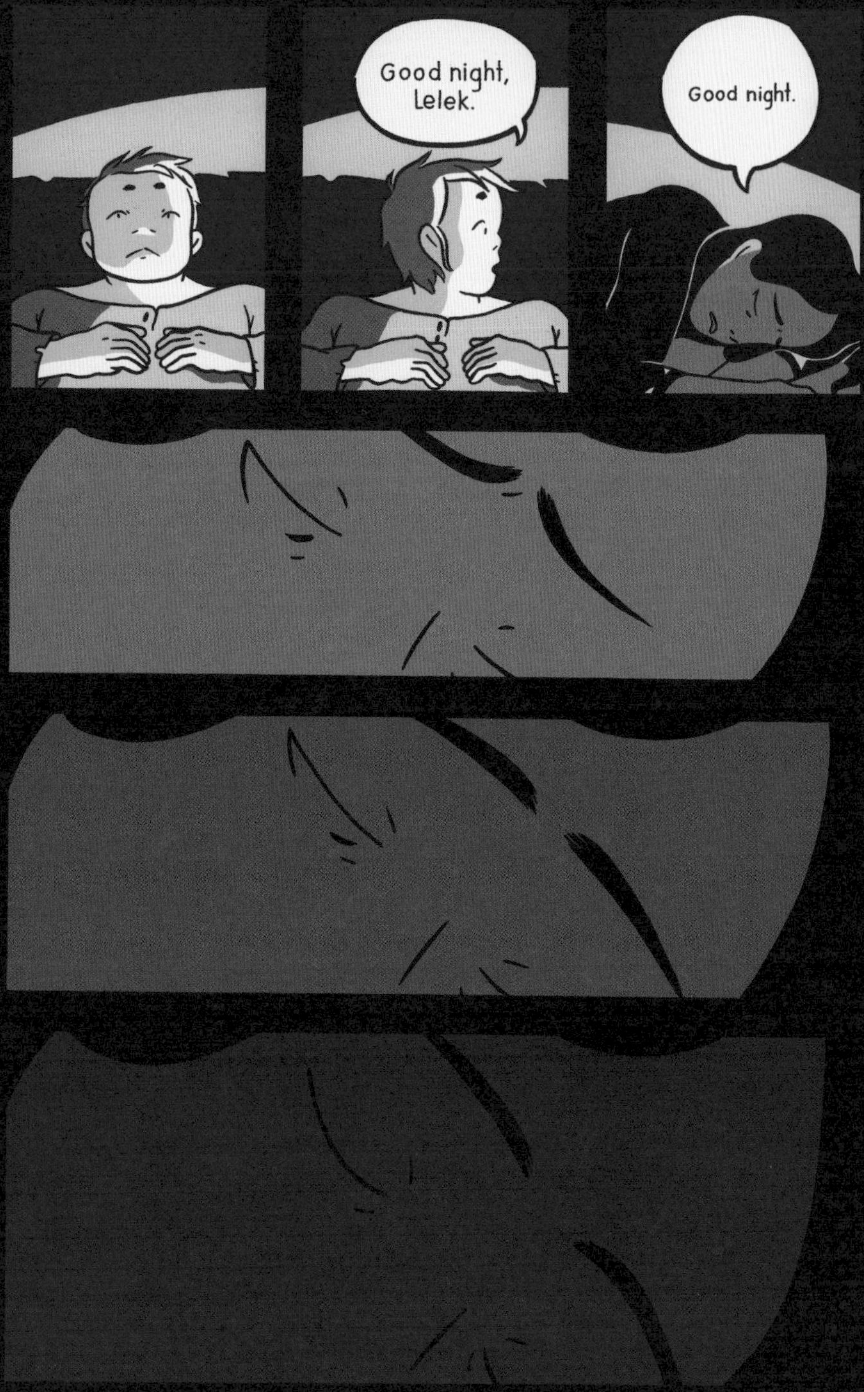
Good night, Lelek.
Good night.

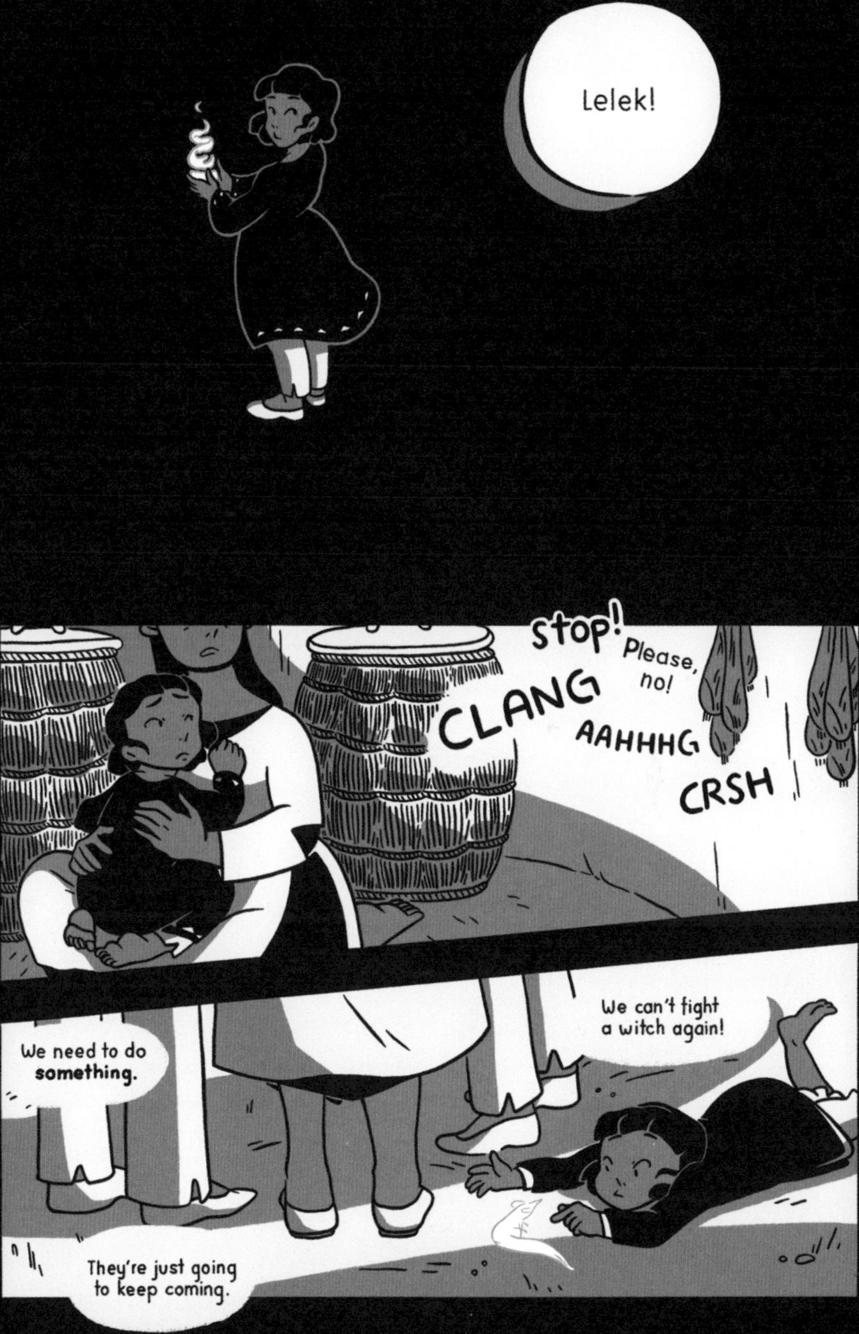
Lelek!
Stop!
Please, no!
CLANG
AAHHHG
CRSH
We need to do **something.**
We can't fight a witch again!
They're just going to keep coming.

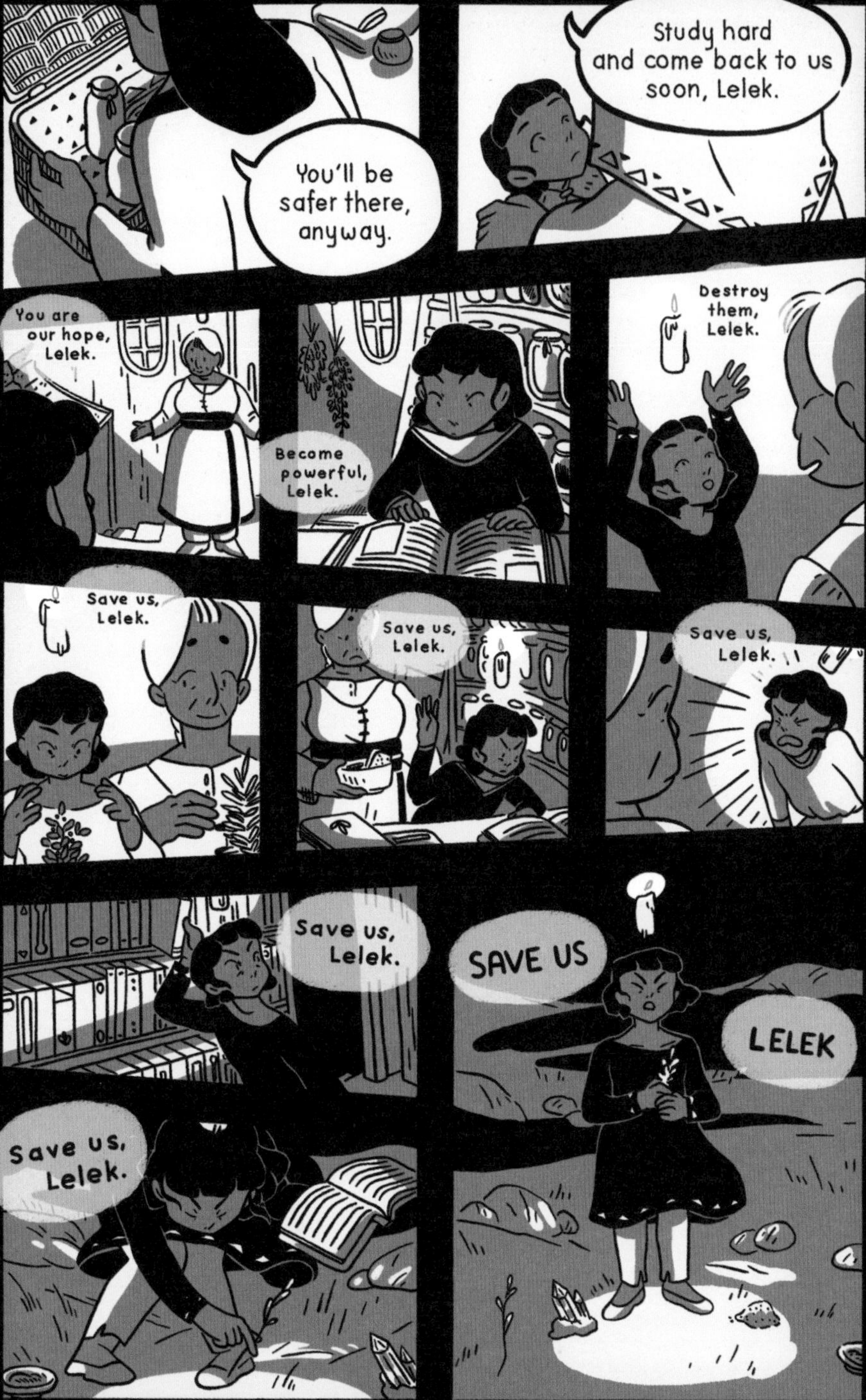
You'll be safer there, anyway.
Study hard and come back to us soon, Lelek.
You are our hope, Lelek.
Become powerful, Lelek.
Destroy them, Lelek.
Save us, Lelek.
Save us, Lelek.
Save us, Lelek.
Save us, Lelek.
Save us, Lelek.
SAVE US
LELEK

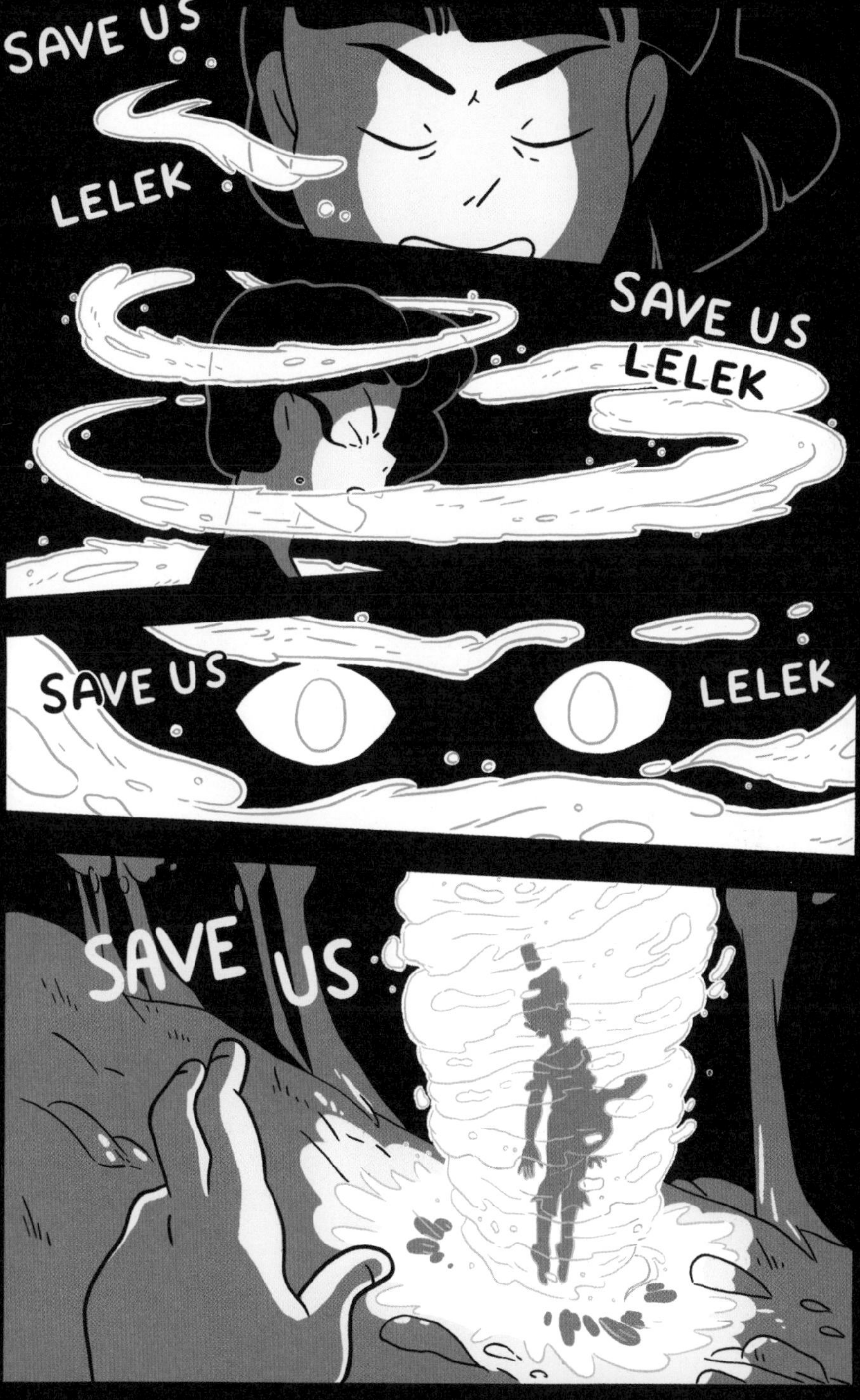
SAVE US
LELEK
SAVE US
LELEK
SAVE US
LELEK
SAVE US

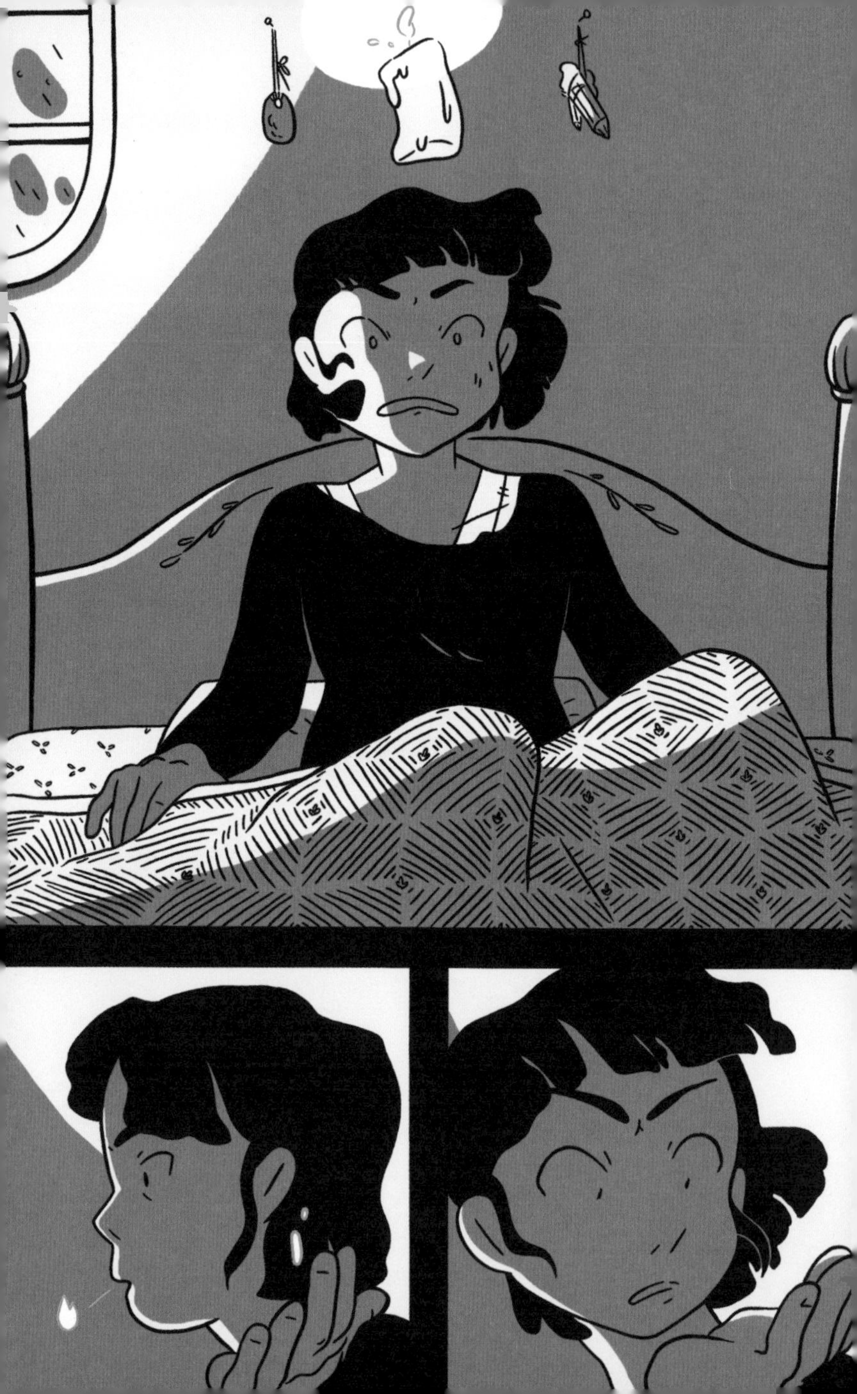

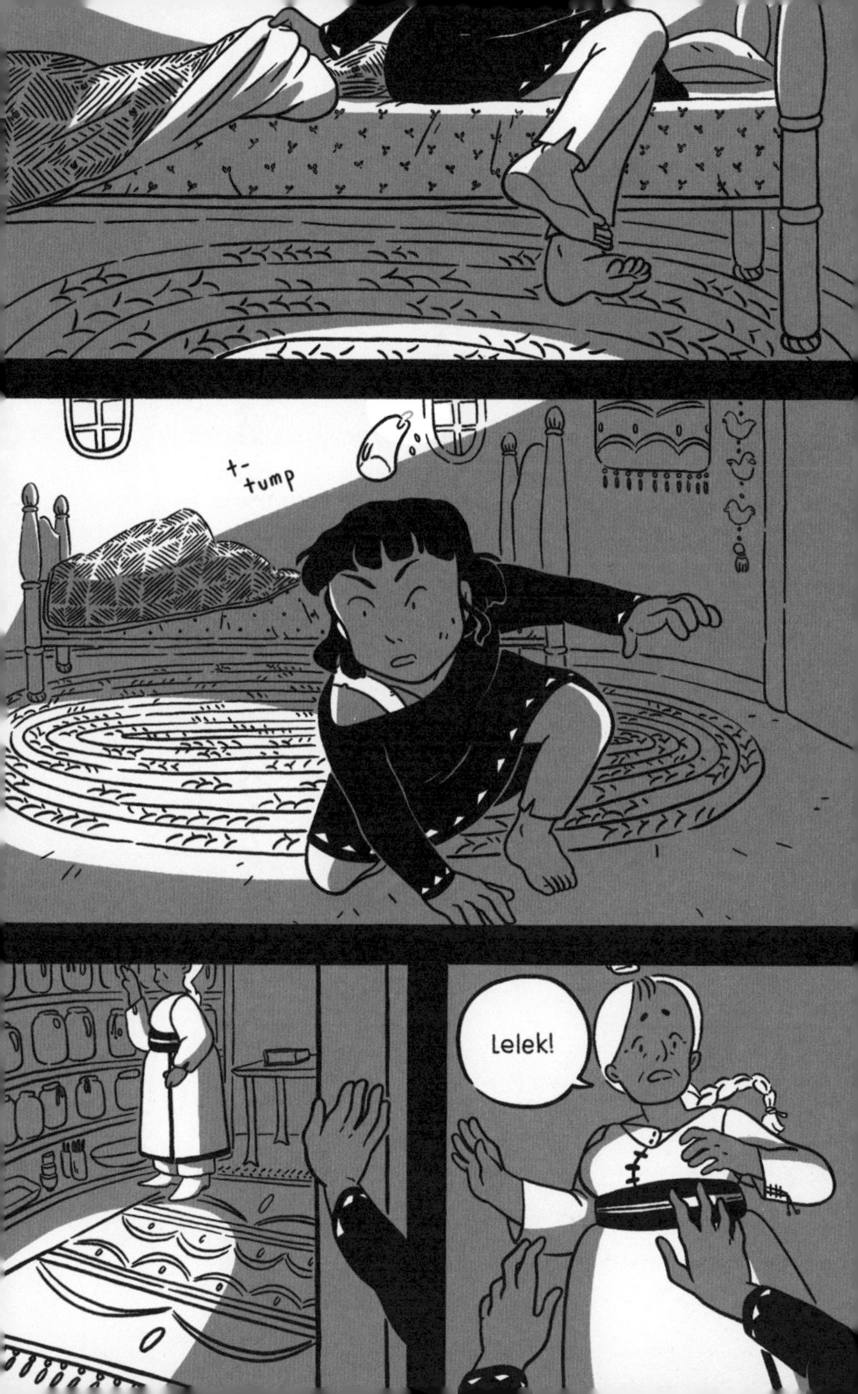

t-
tump
Lelek!

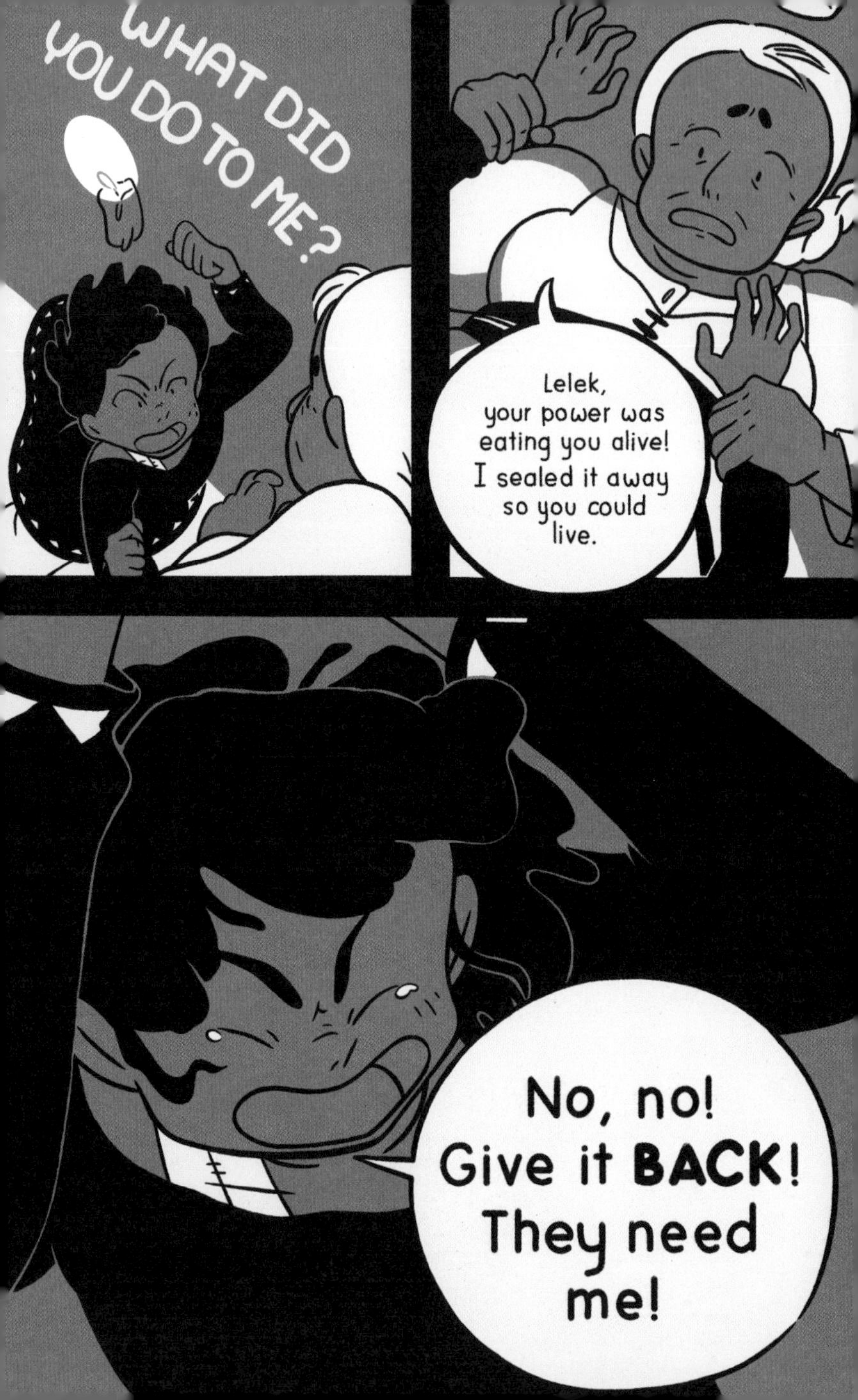
WHAT DID YOU DO TO ME?
Lelek, your power was eating you alive! I sealed it away so you could live.
No, no! Give it **BACK**! They need me!

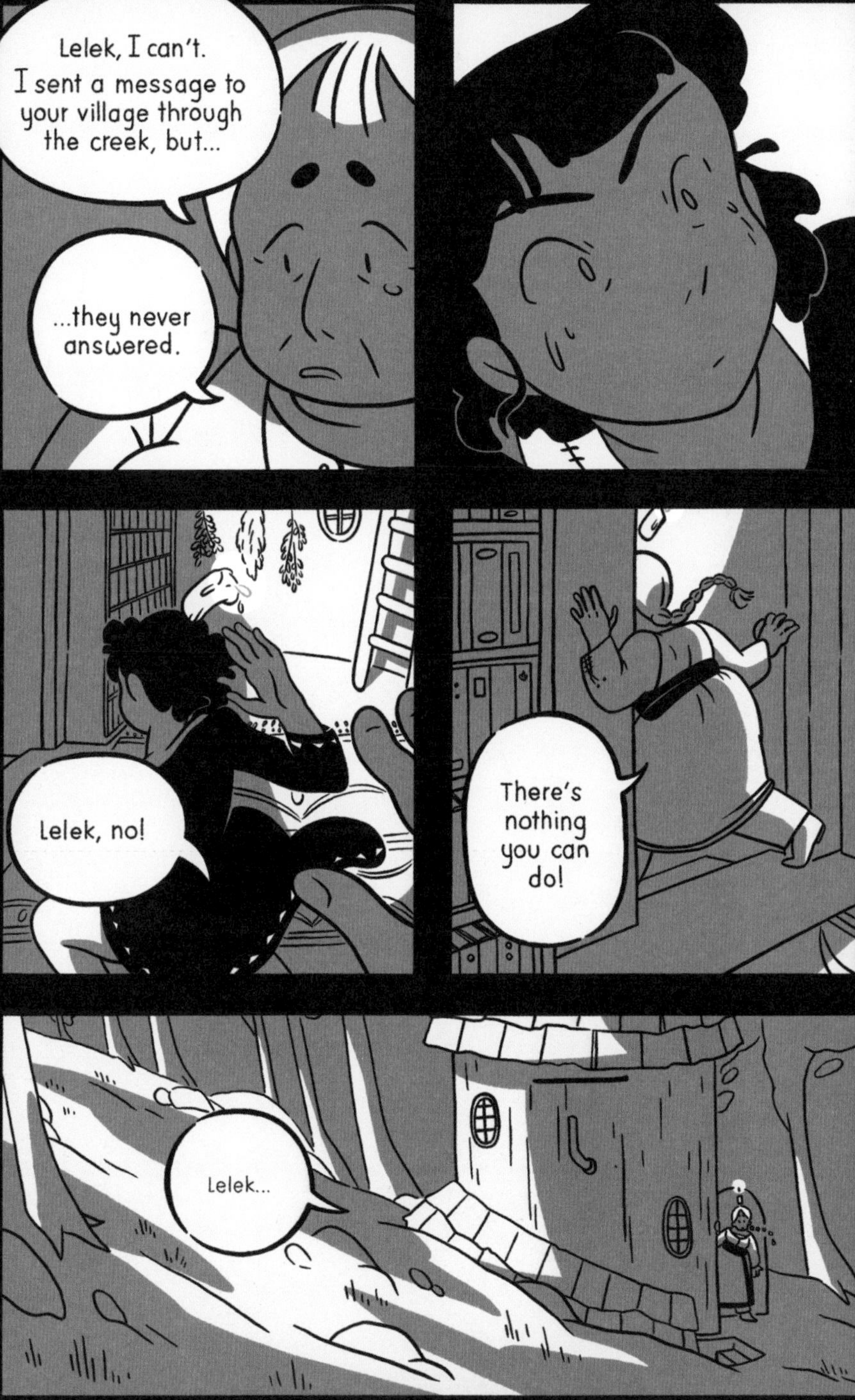
Lelek, I can't.
I sent a message to your village through the creek, but...
...they never answered.
Lelek, no!
There's nothing you can do!
Lelek...

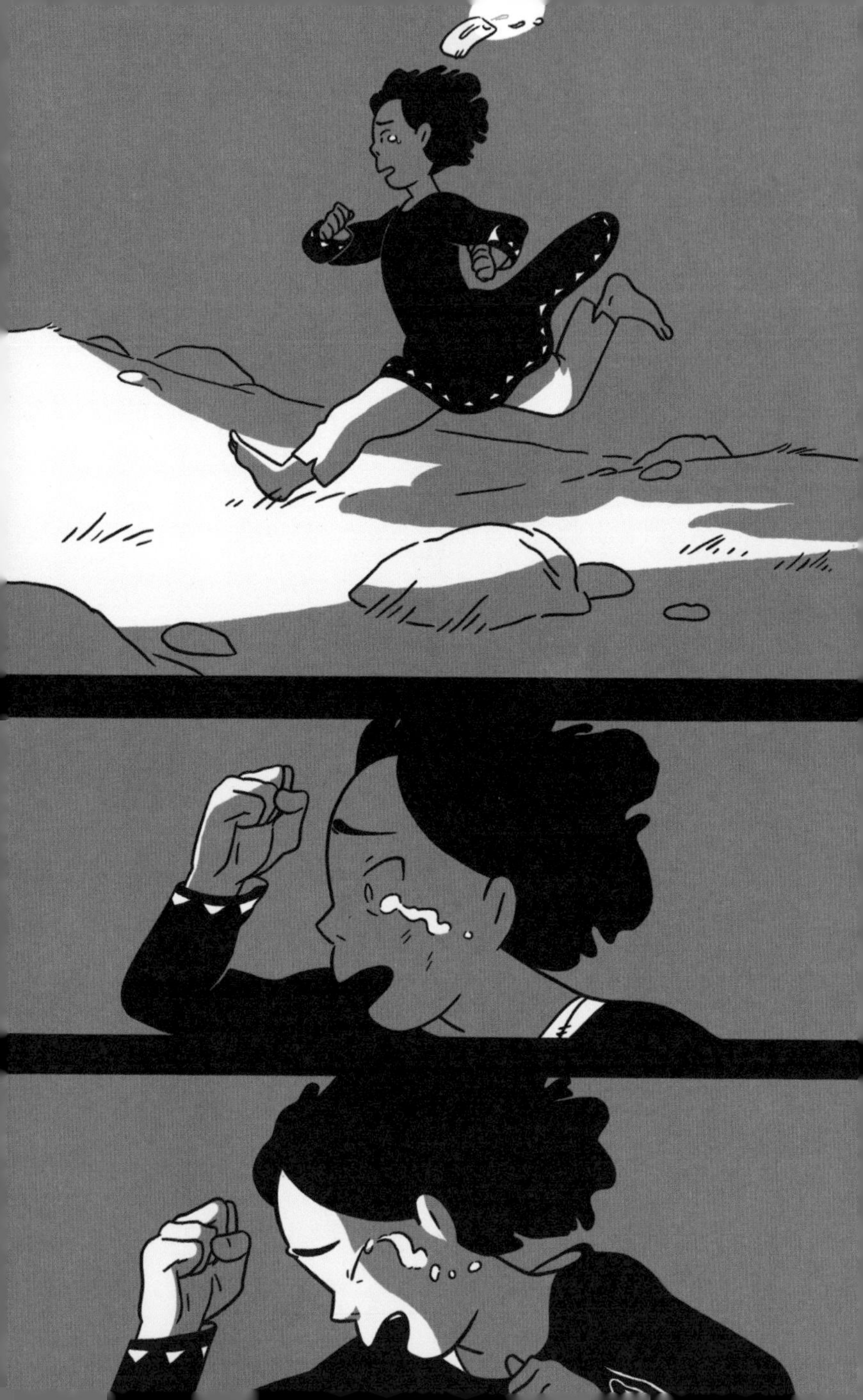

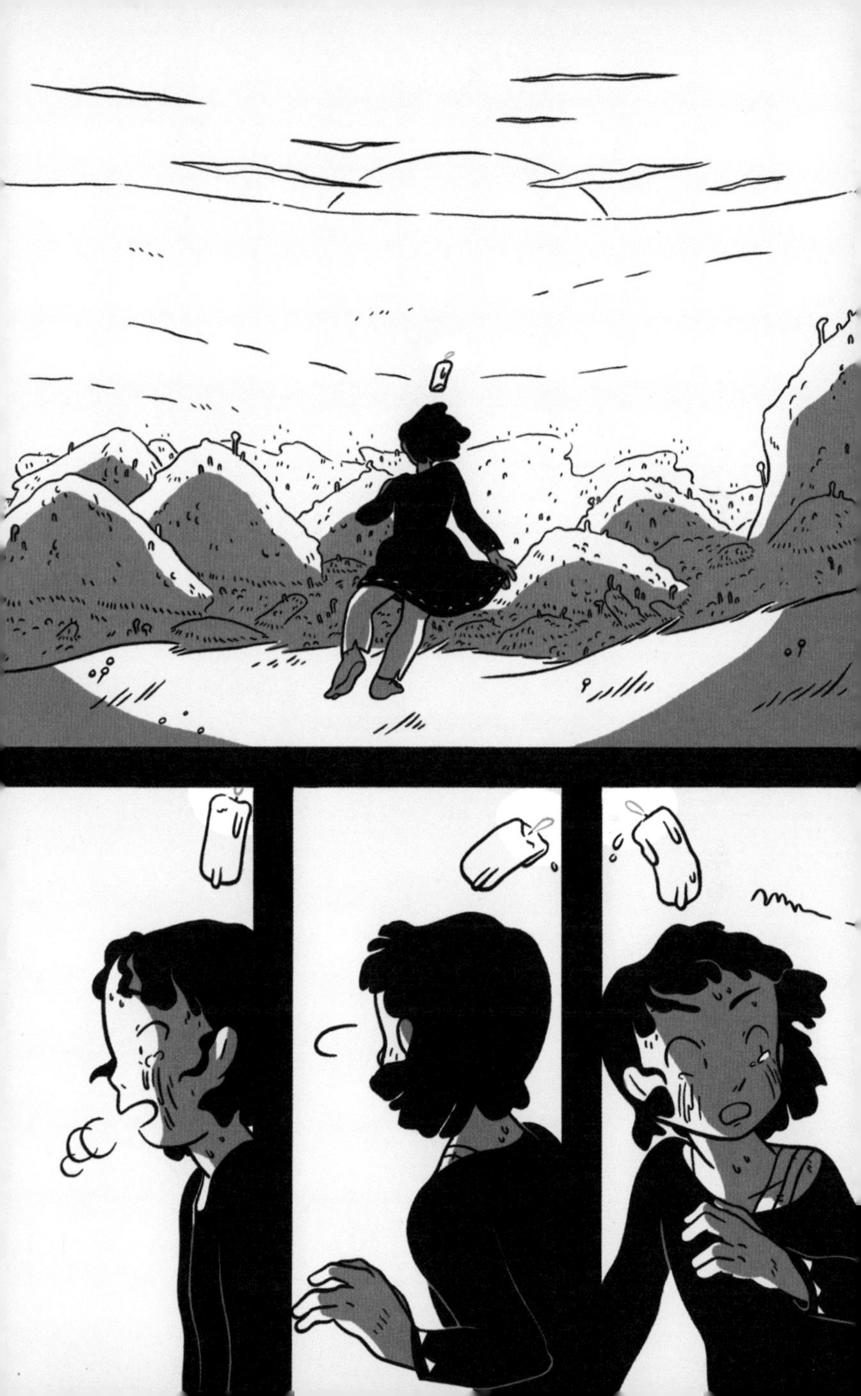

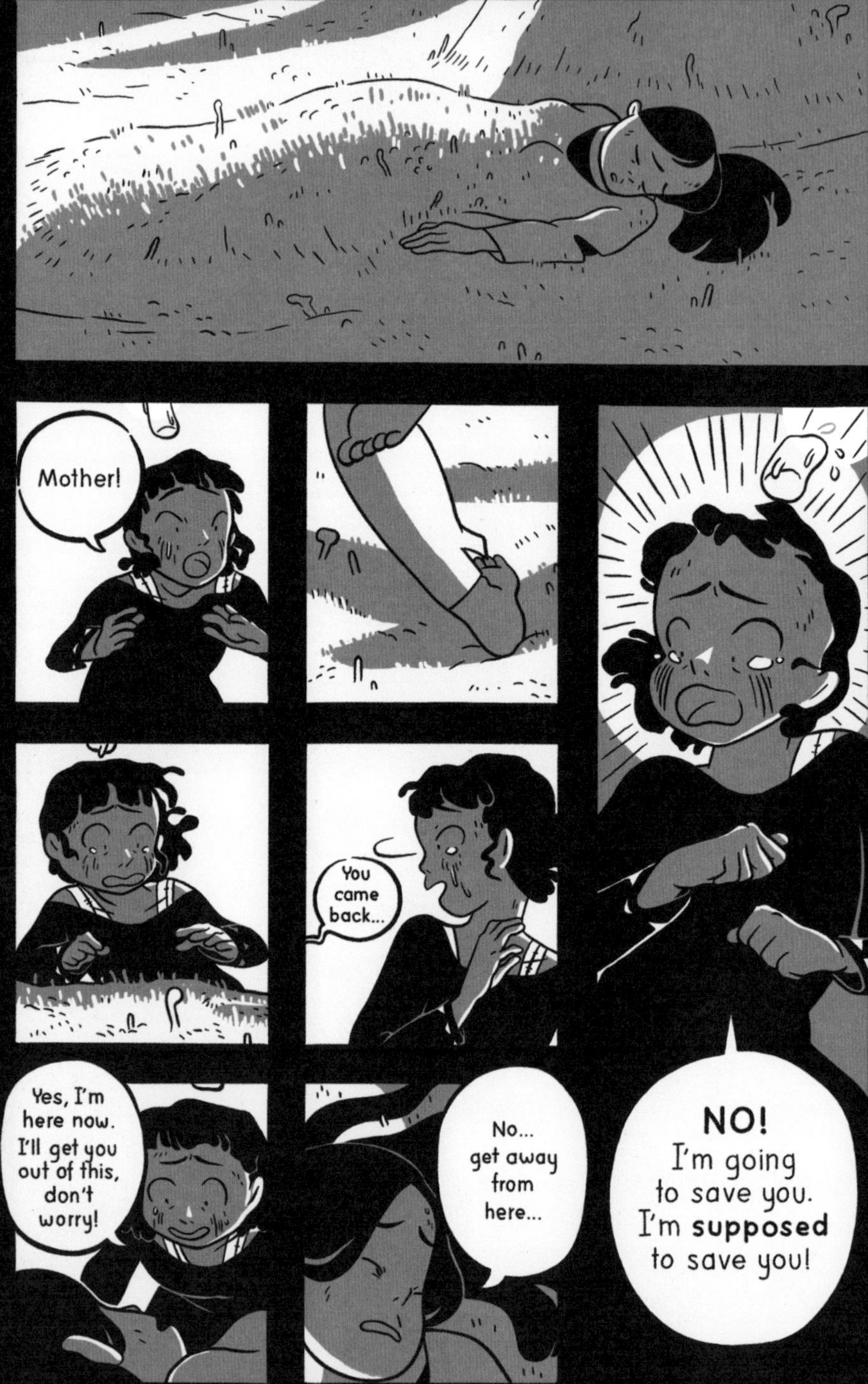
Mother!
You came back...
Yes, I'm here now. I'll get you out of this, don't worry!
No... get away from here...
NO! I'm going to save you. I'm **supposed** to save you!

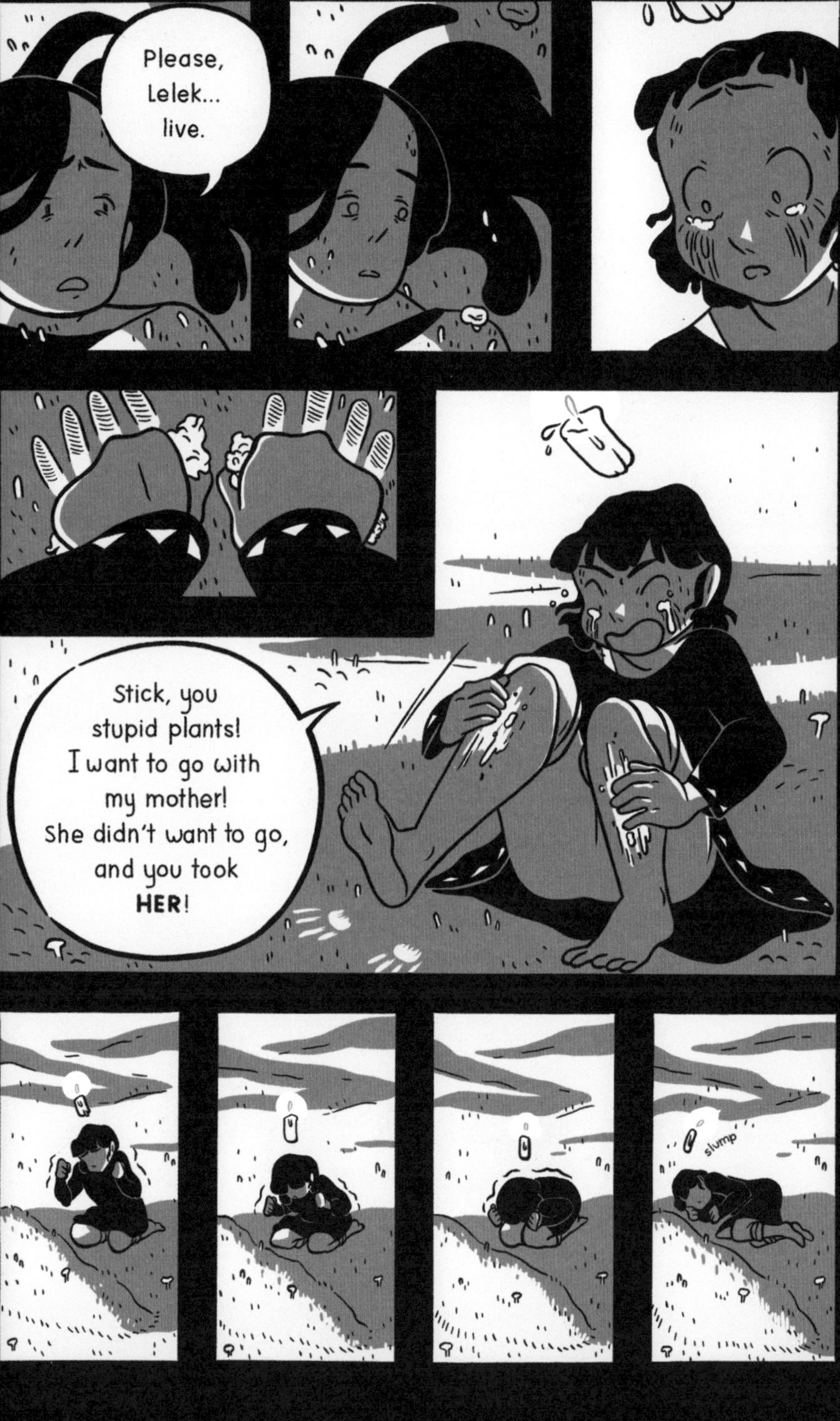
Please, Lelek... live.
Stick, you stupid plants! I want to go with my mother! She didn't want to go, and you took **HER**!
slump

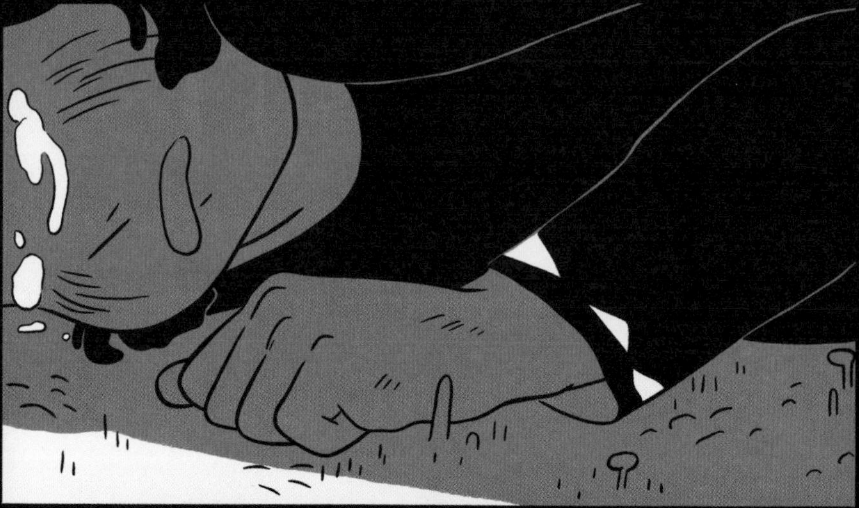

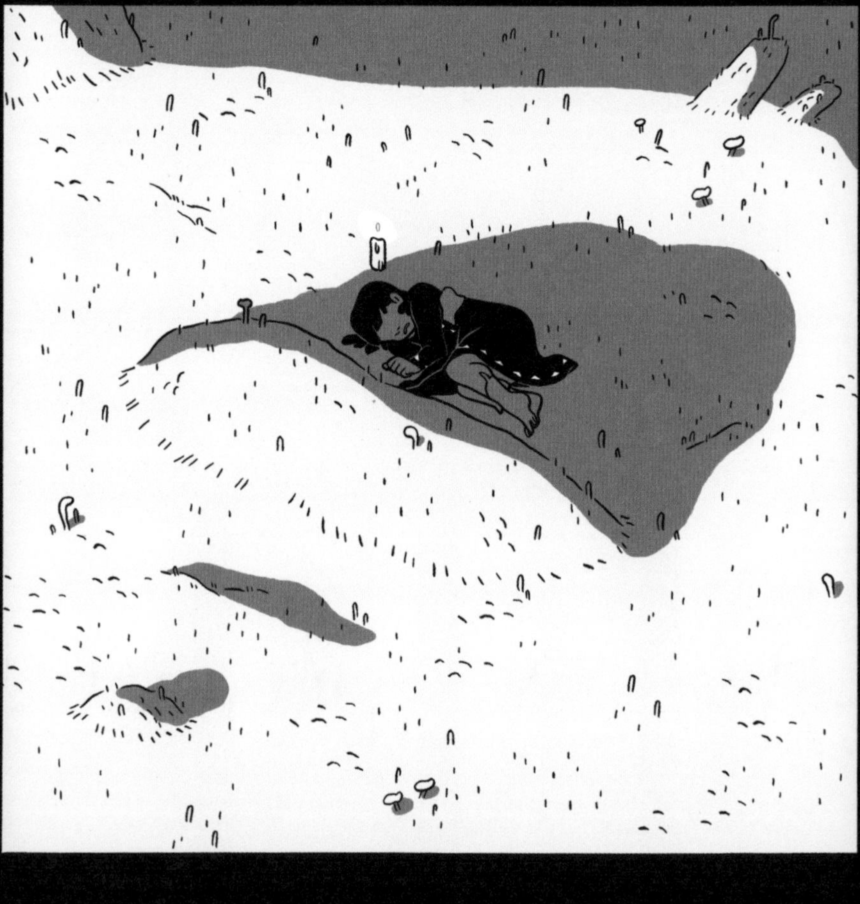

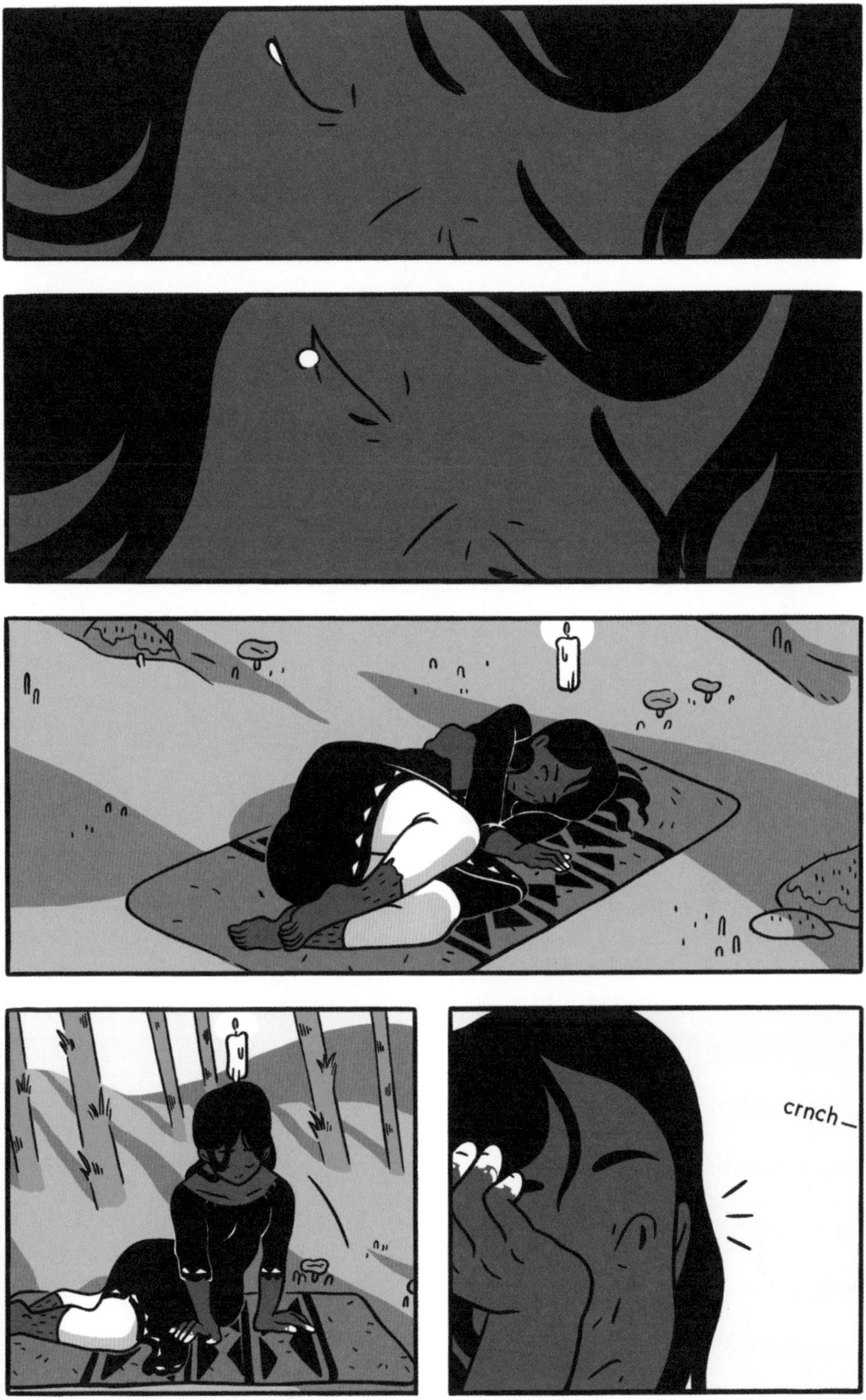
crnch—

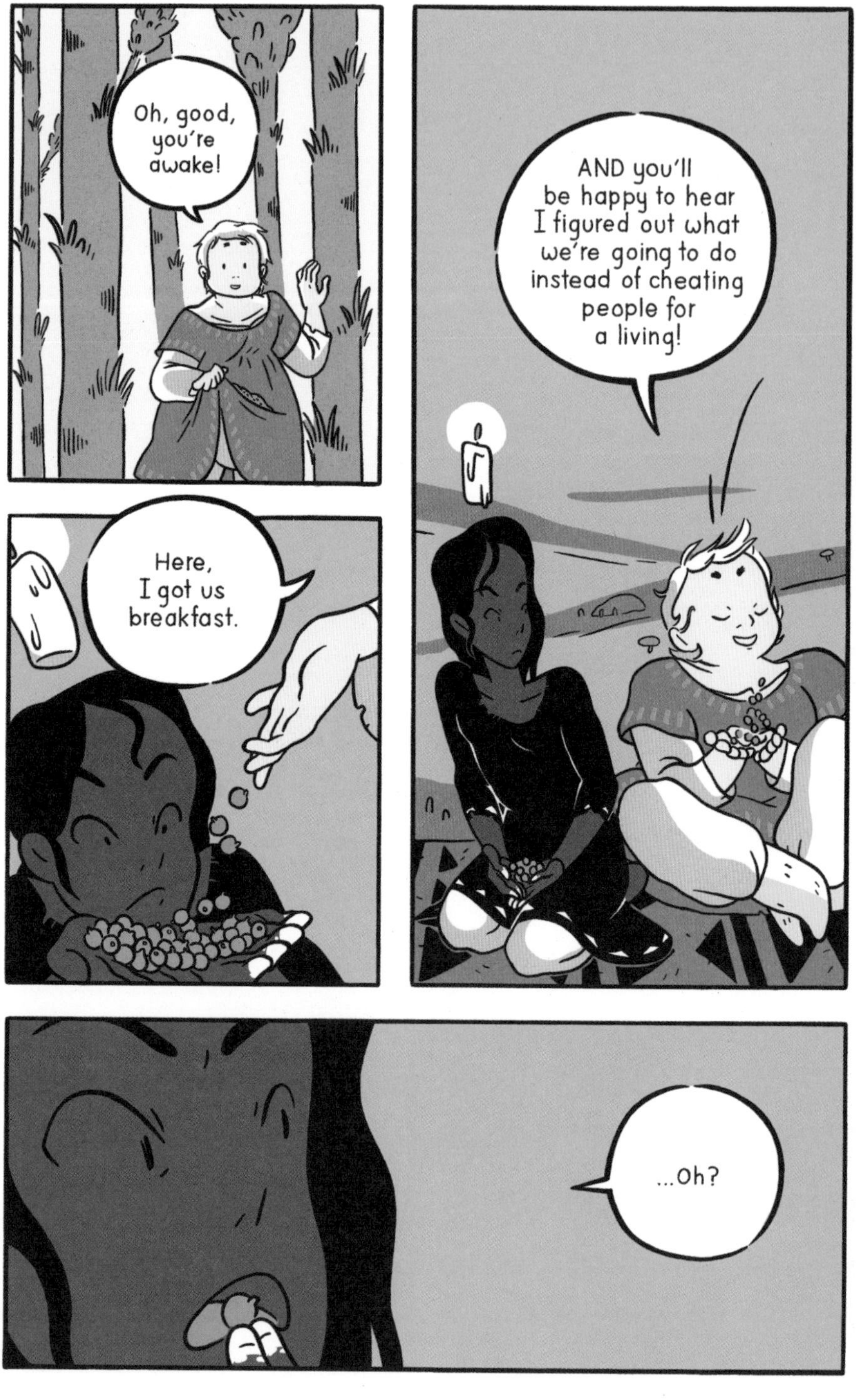
Oh, good, you're awake!
AND you'll be happy to hear I figured out what we're going to do instead of cheating people for a living!
Here, I got us breakfast.
...Oh?

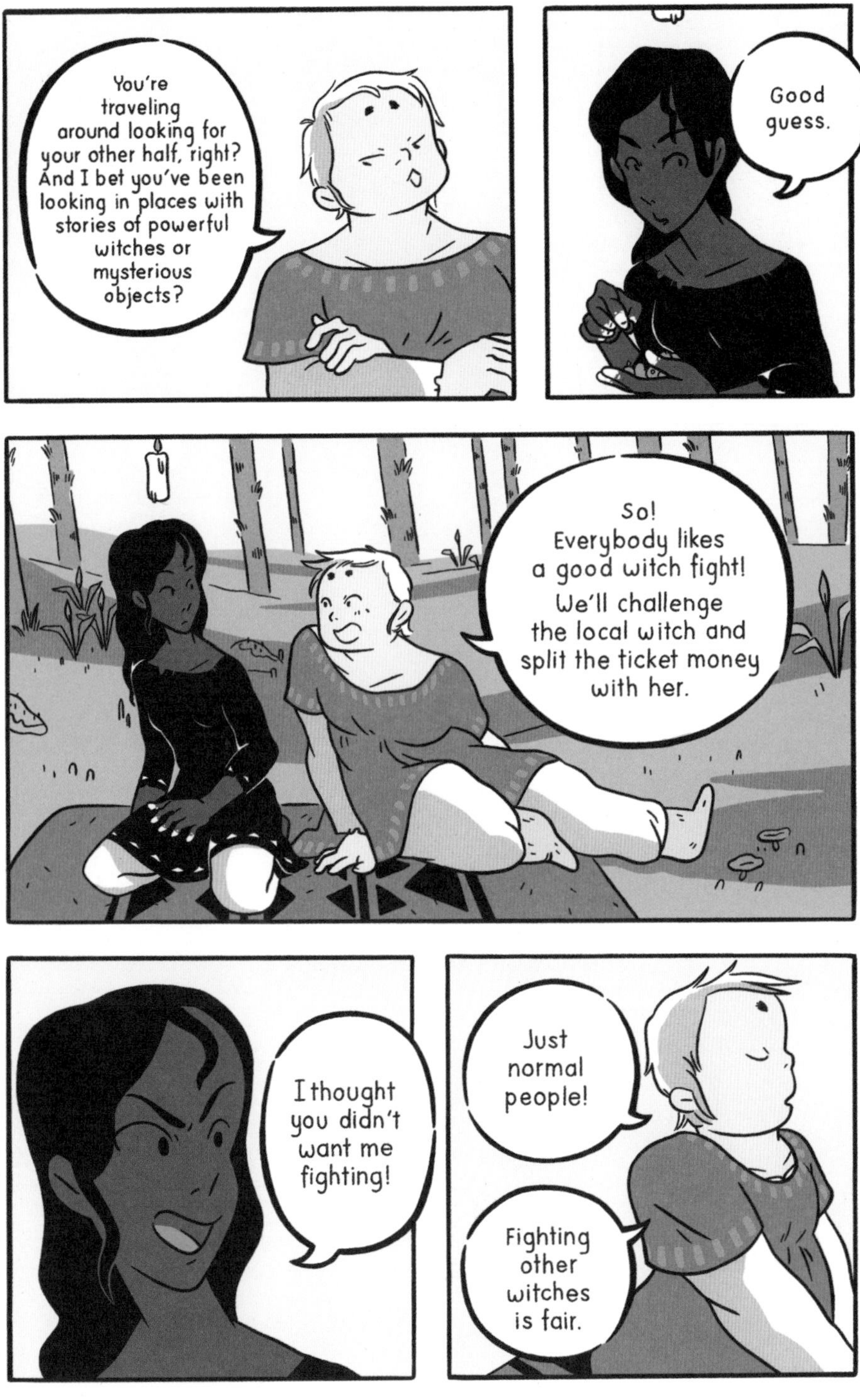

You're traveling around looking for your other half, right? And I bet you've been looking in places with stories of powerful witches or mysterious objects?
Good guess.
So! Everybody likes a good witch fight!
We'll challenge the local witch and split the ticket money with her.
I thought you didn't want me fighting!
Just normal people!
Fighting other witches is fair.

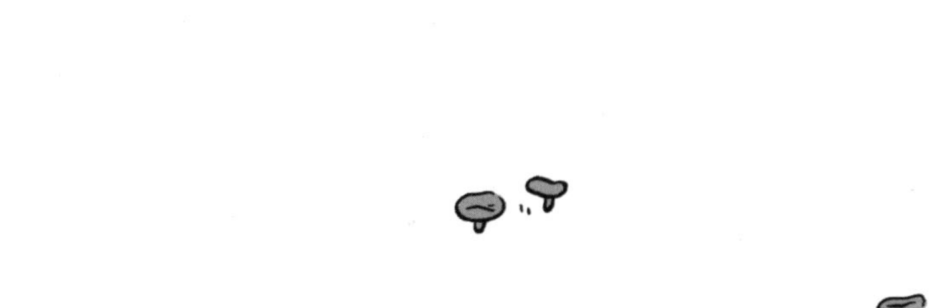

Part 3

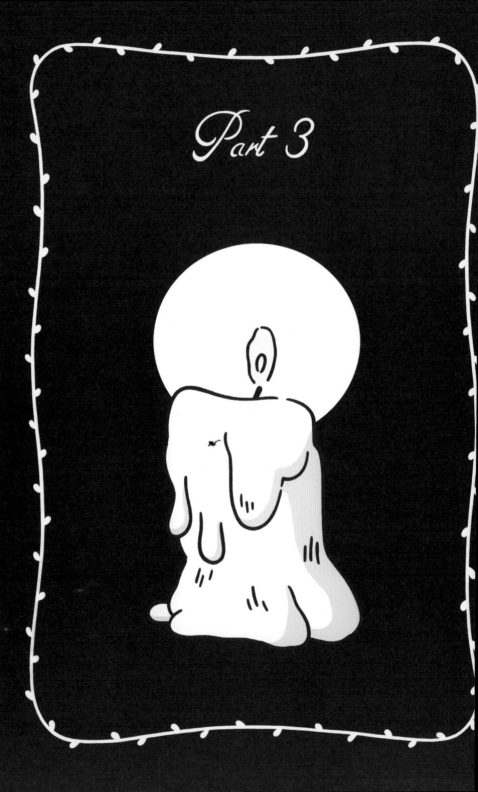

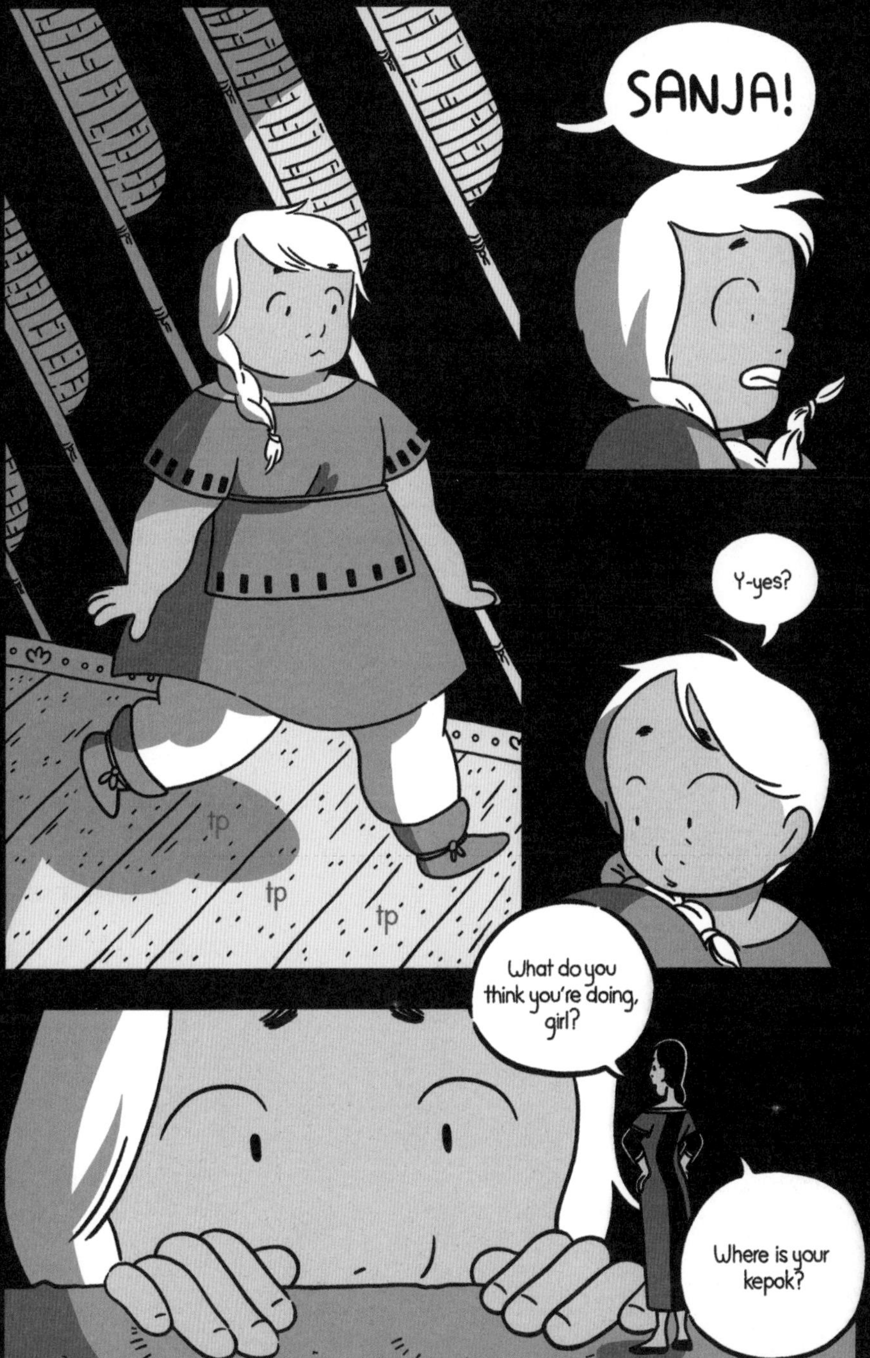
SANJA!
tp
tp
tp
Y-yes?
What do you think you're doing, girl?
Where is your kepok?

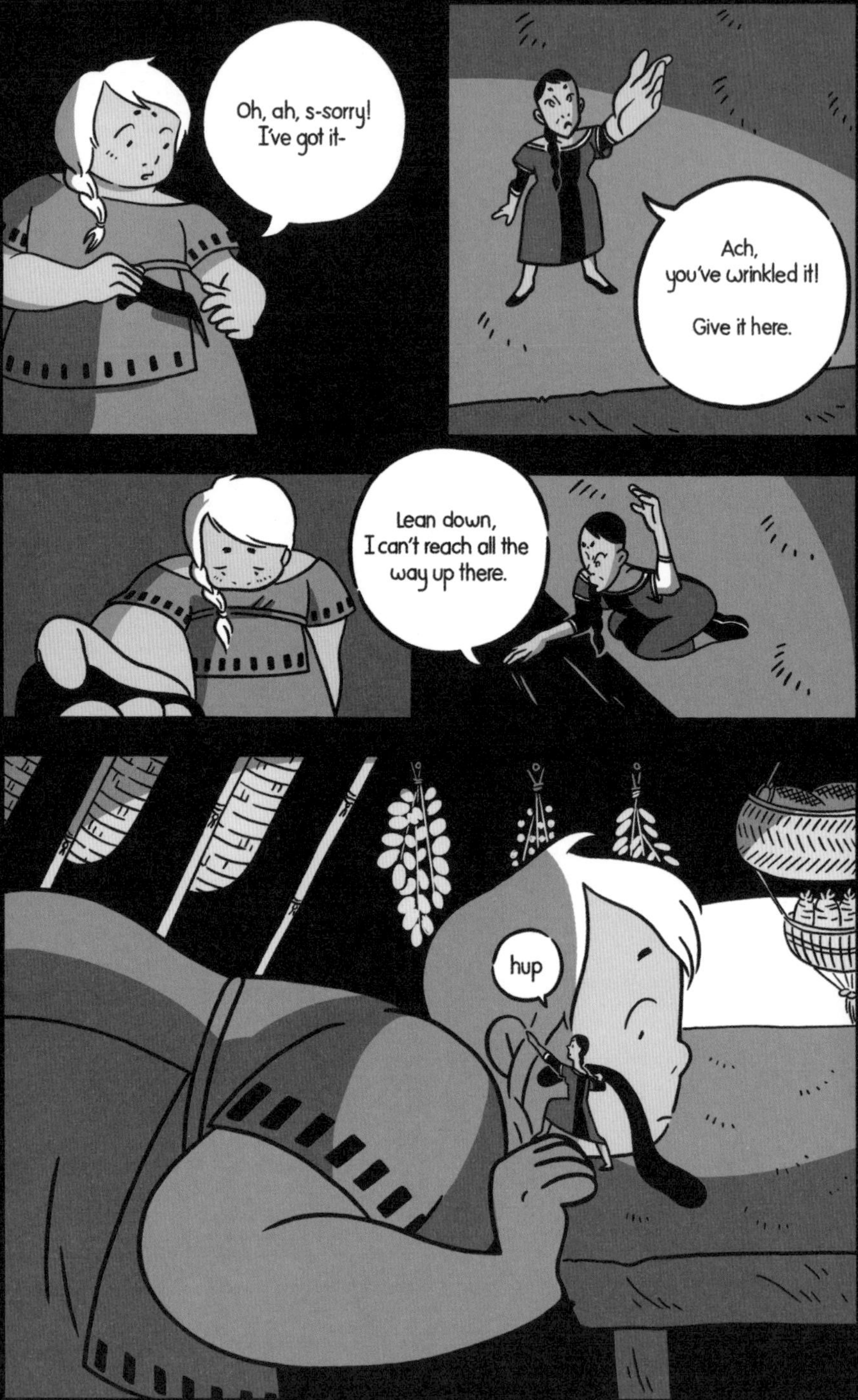
Oh, ah, s-sorry! I've got it-
Ach, you've wrinkled it!
Give it here.
Lean down, I can't reach all the way up there.
hup

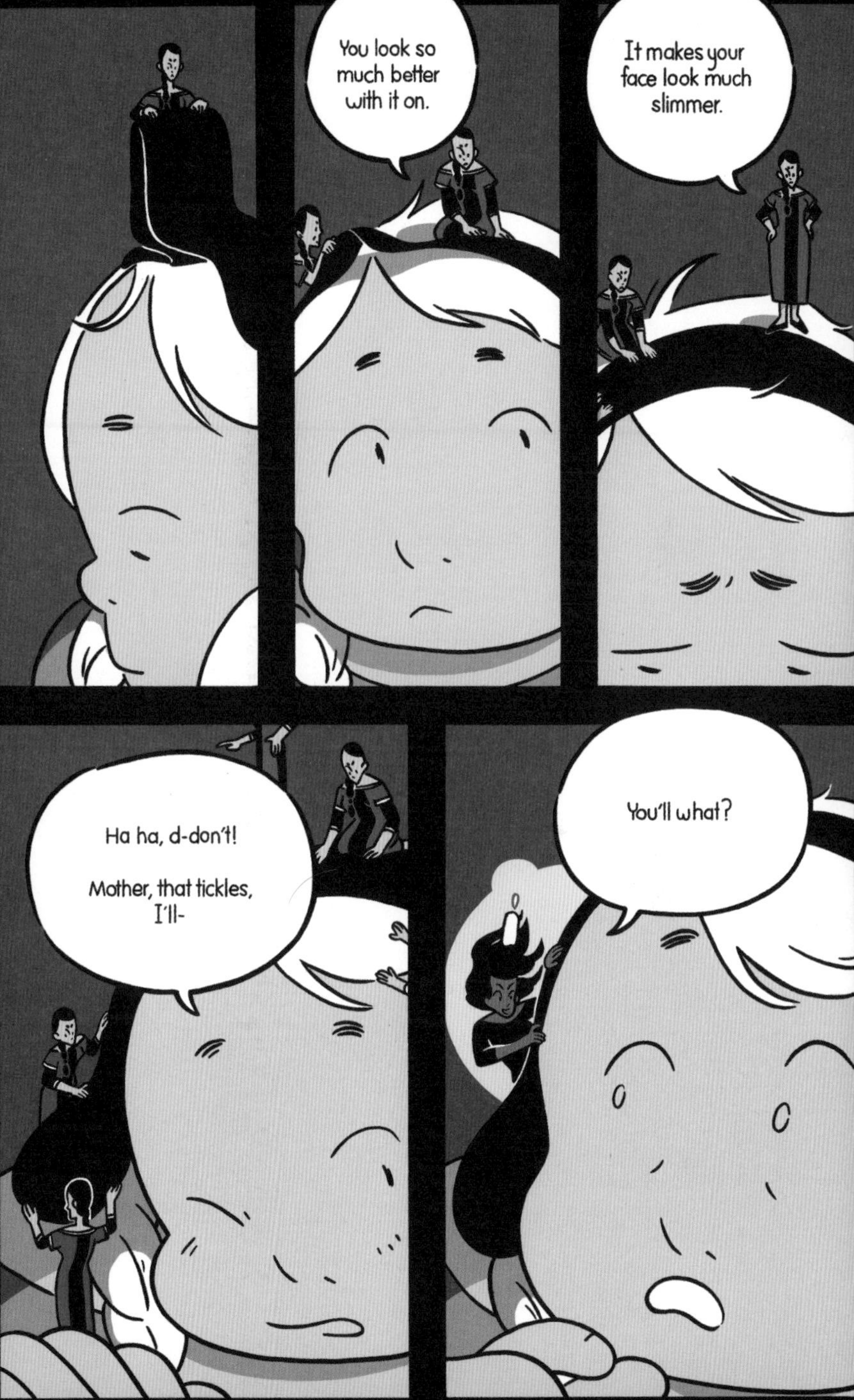
You look so much better with it on.
It makes your face look much slimmer.
Ha ha, d-don't! Mother, that tickles, I'll-
You'll what?

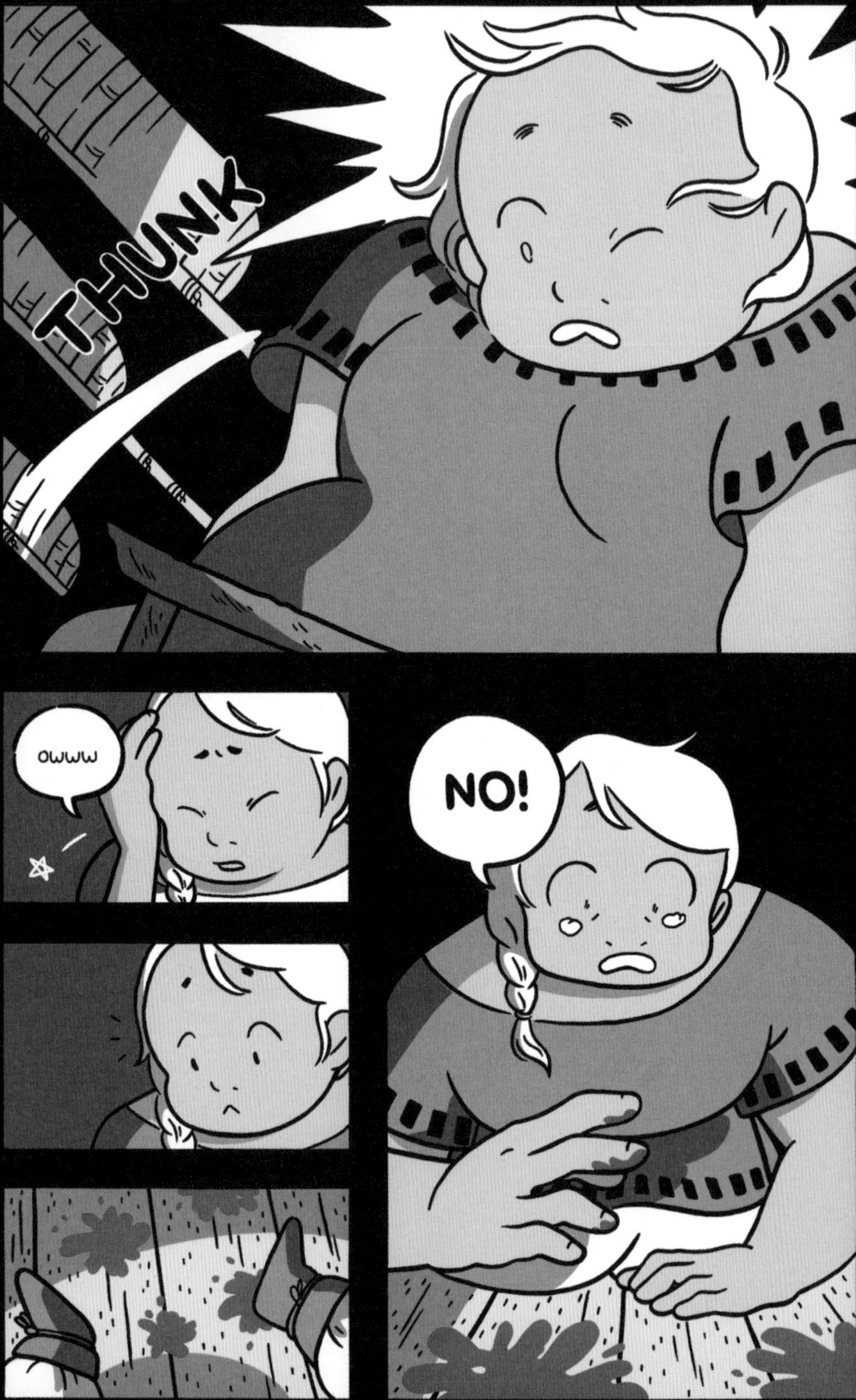
THUNK
OWWW
NO!

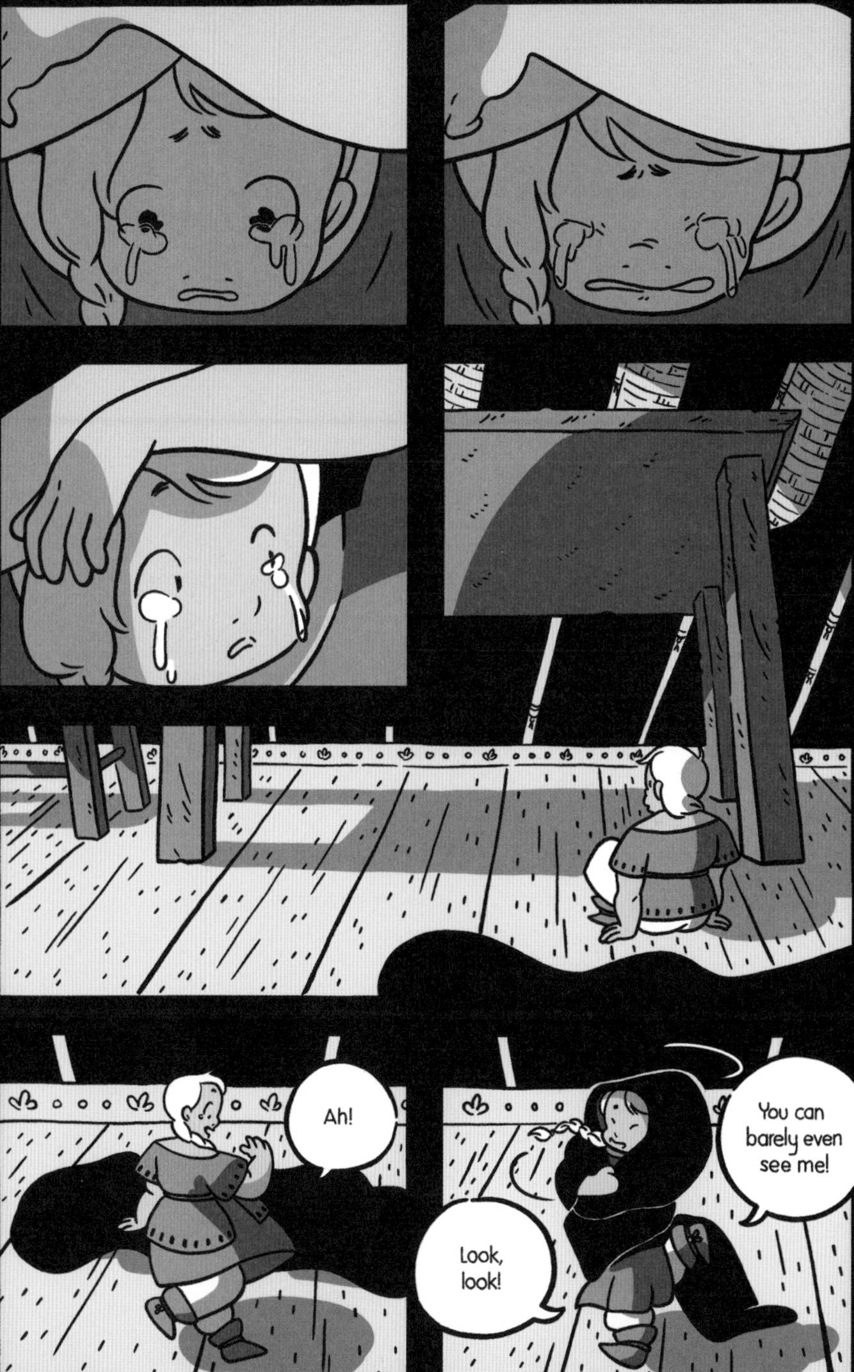
Ah!
You can barely even see me!
Look, look!

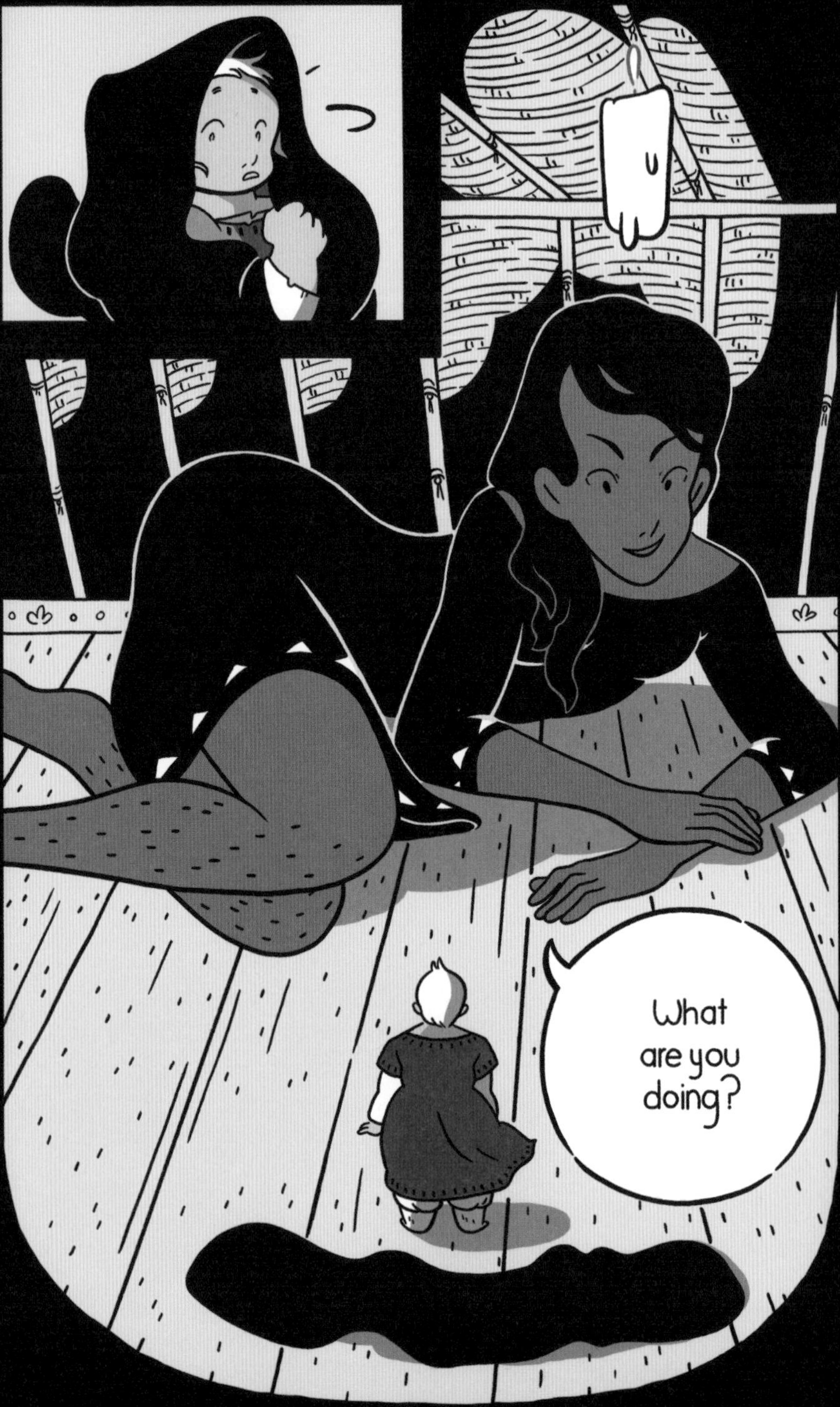
What are you doing?

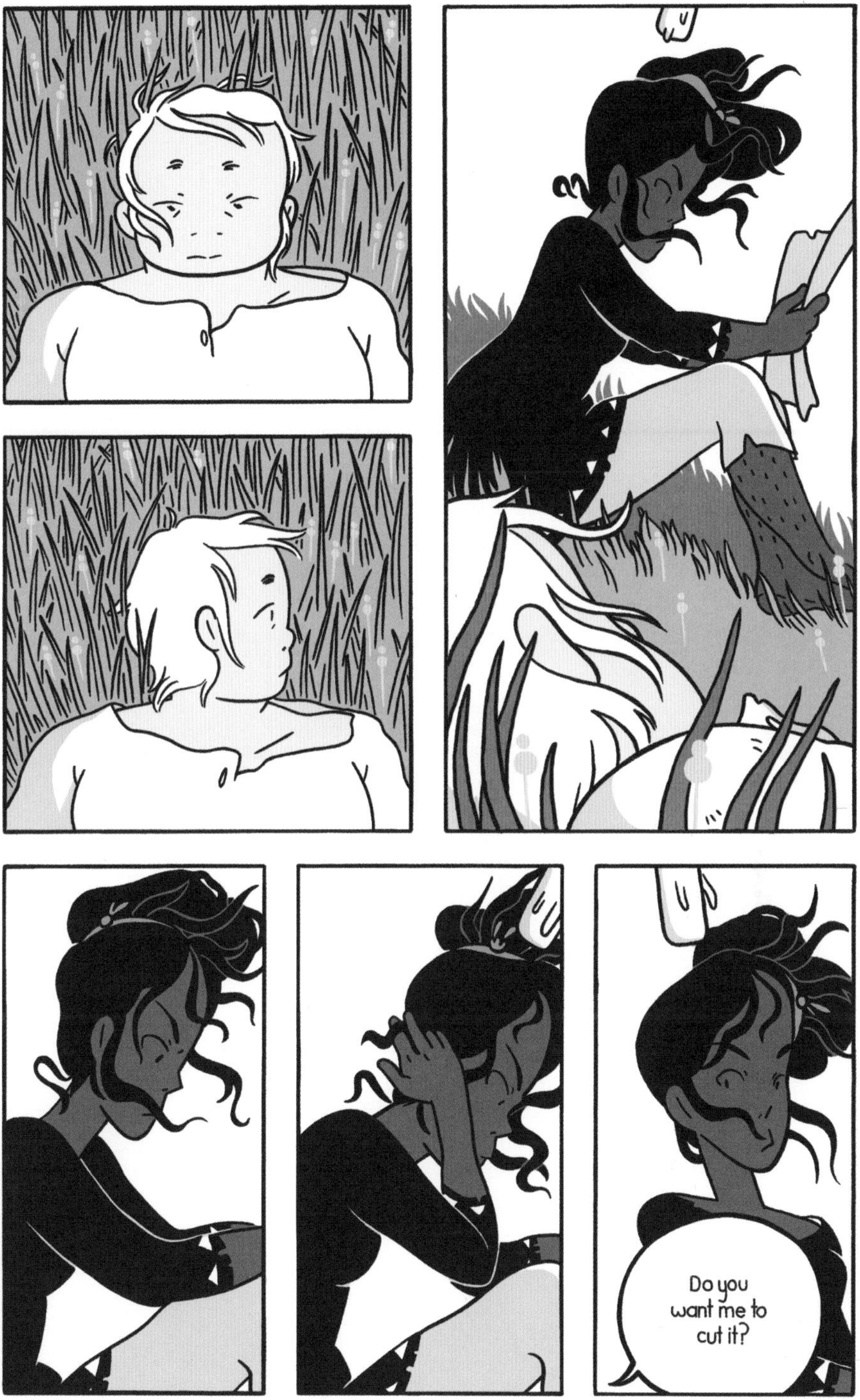
Do you
want me to
cut it?

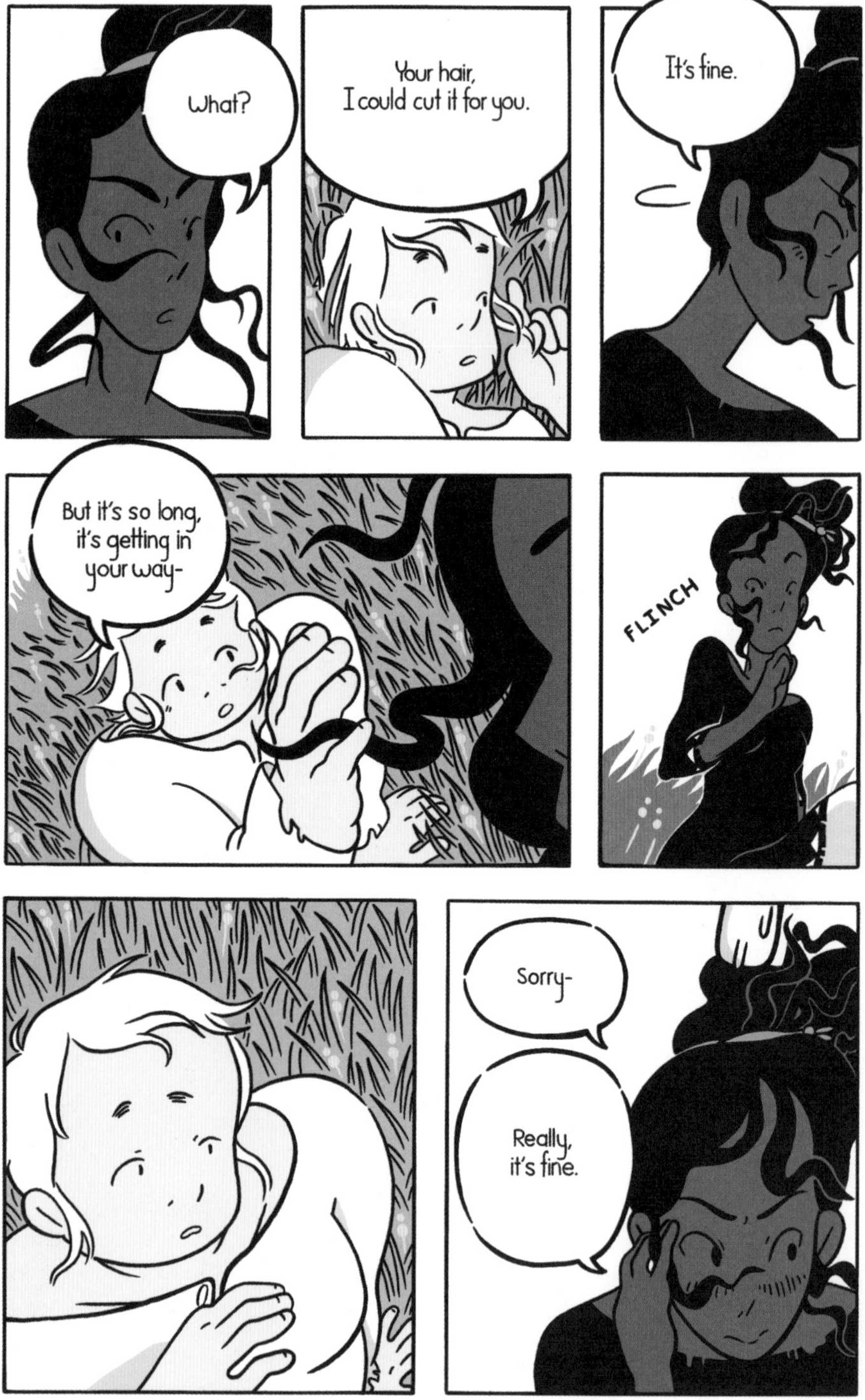
What?
Your hair, I could cut it for you.
It's fine.
But it's so long, it's getting in your way-
FLINCH
Sorry-
Really, it's fine.

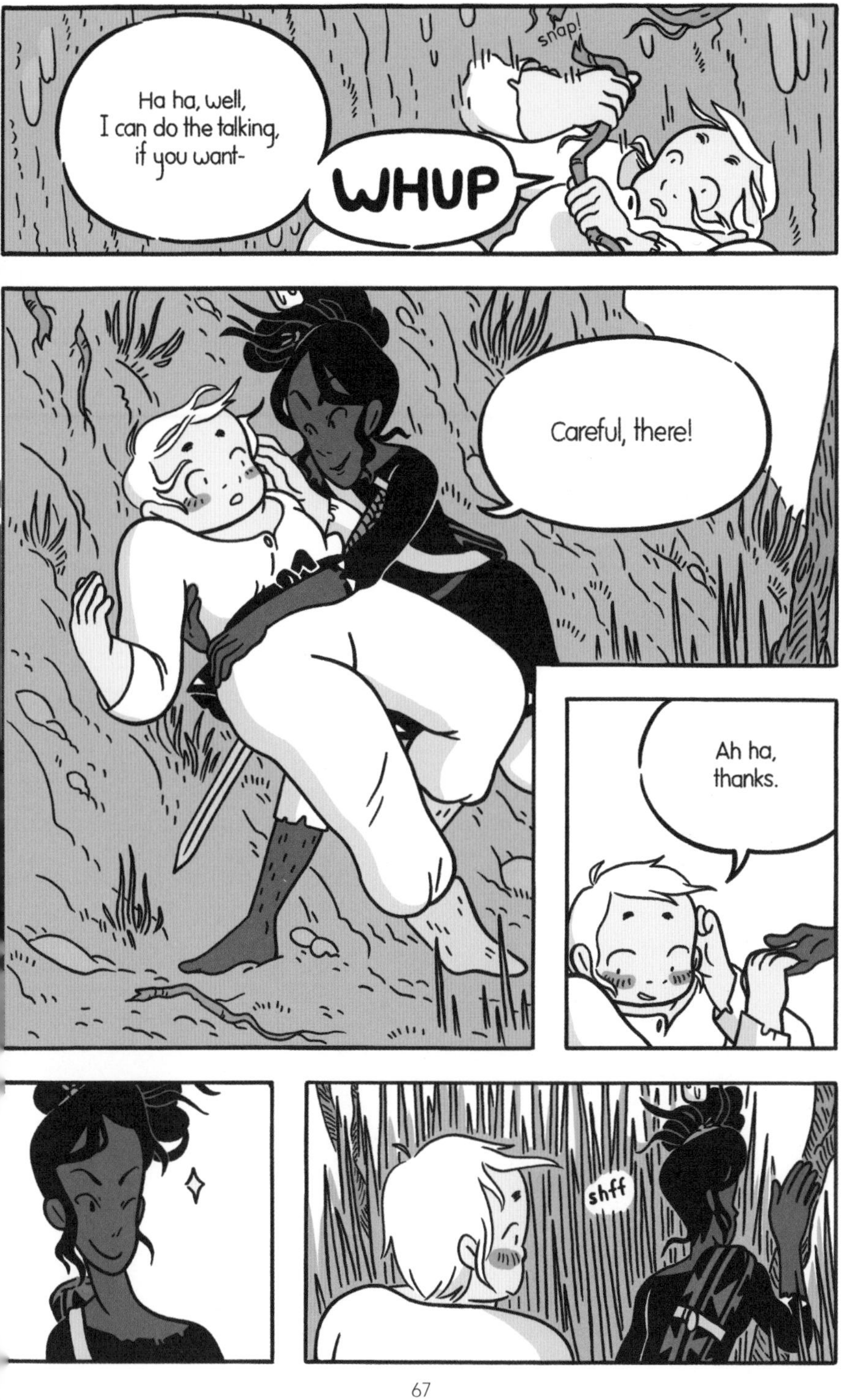
snap!
Ha ha, well,
I can do the talking,
if you want-
WHUP
Careful, there!
Ah ha,
thanks.
shff

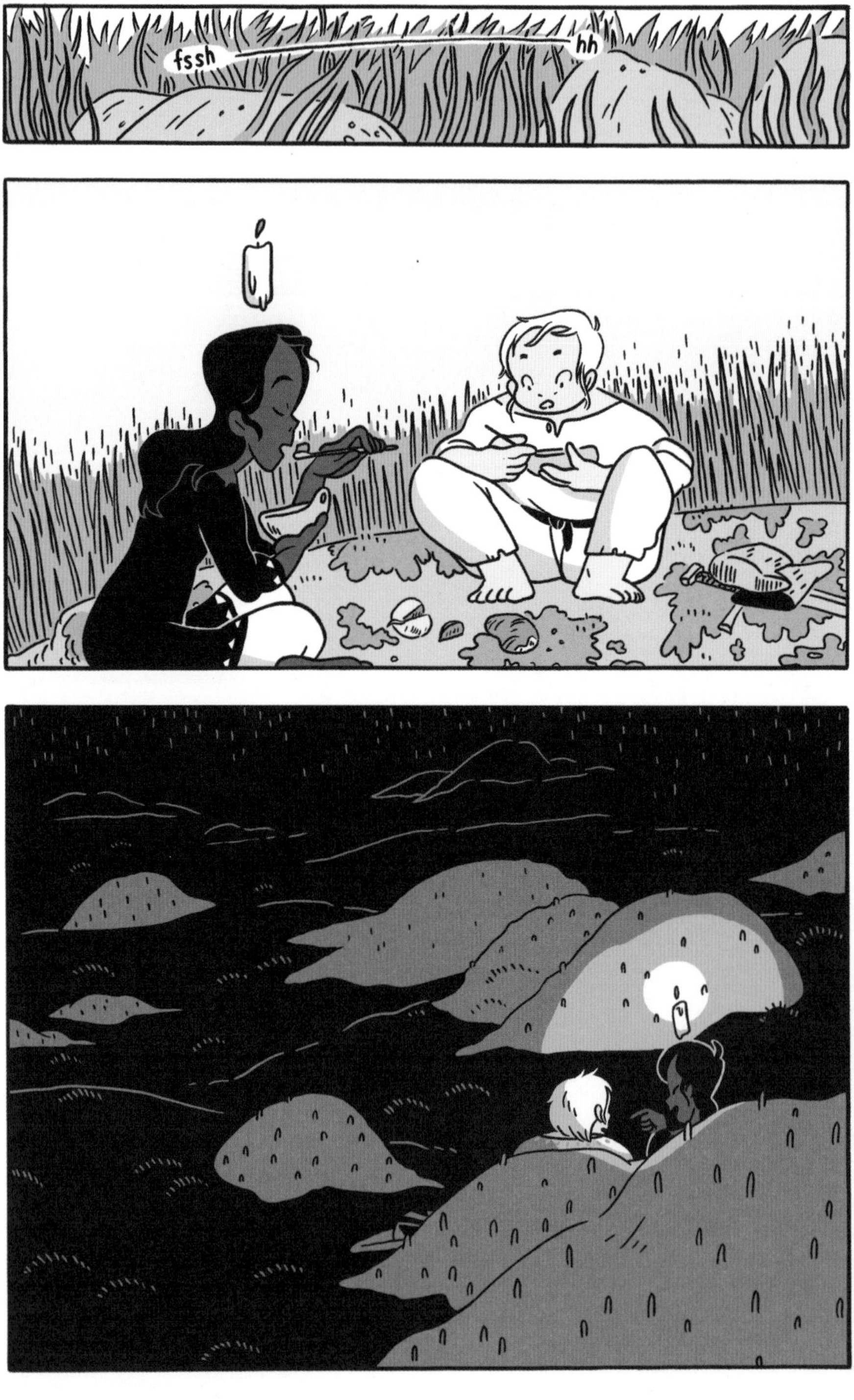
fssh
hh

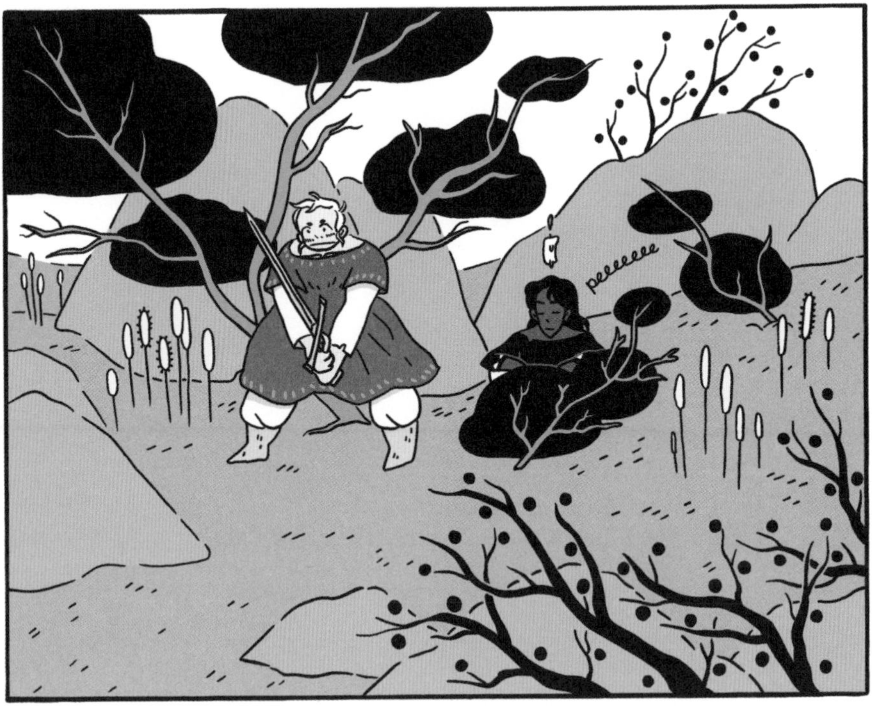
peeeeeee

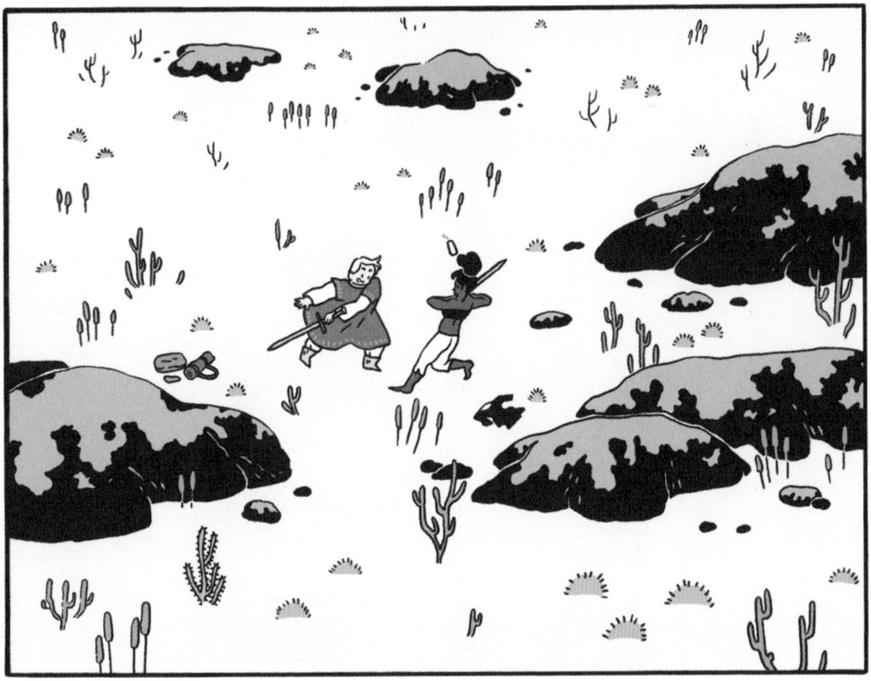

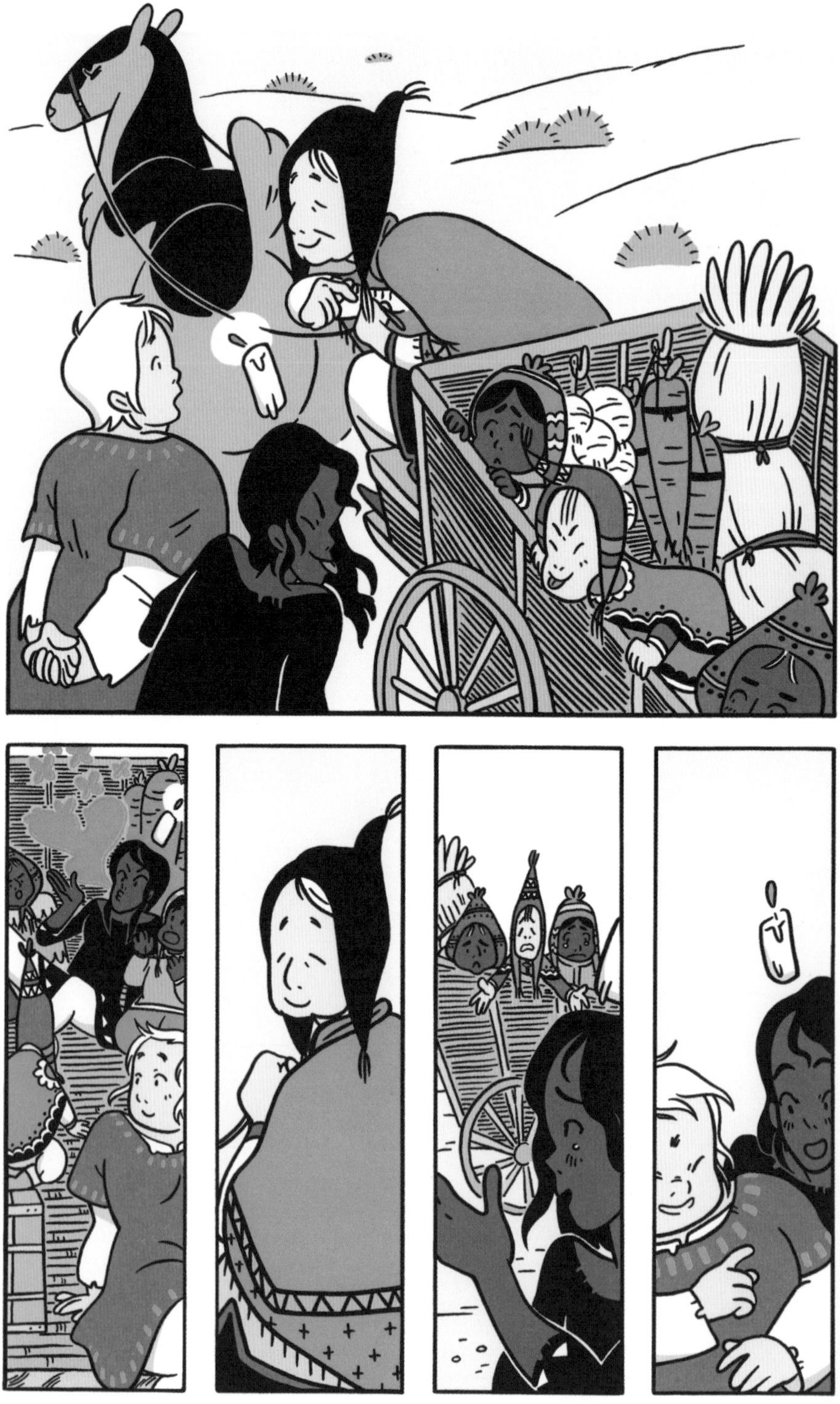

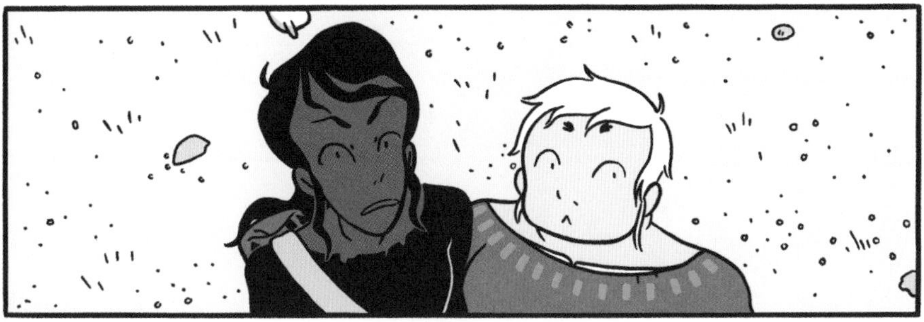

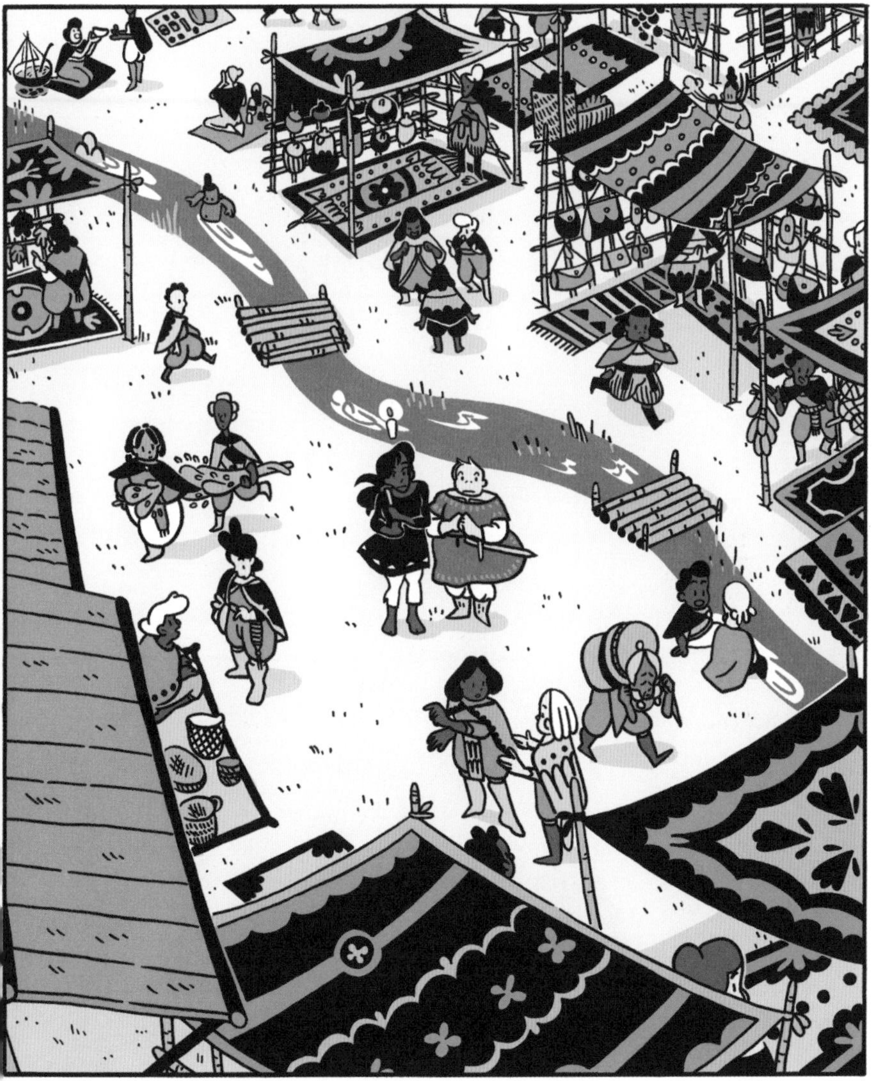

73

74

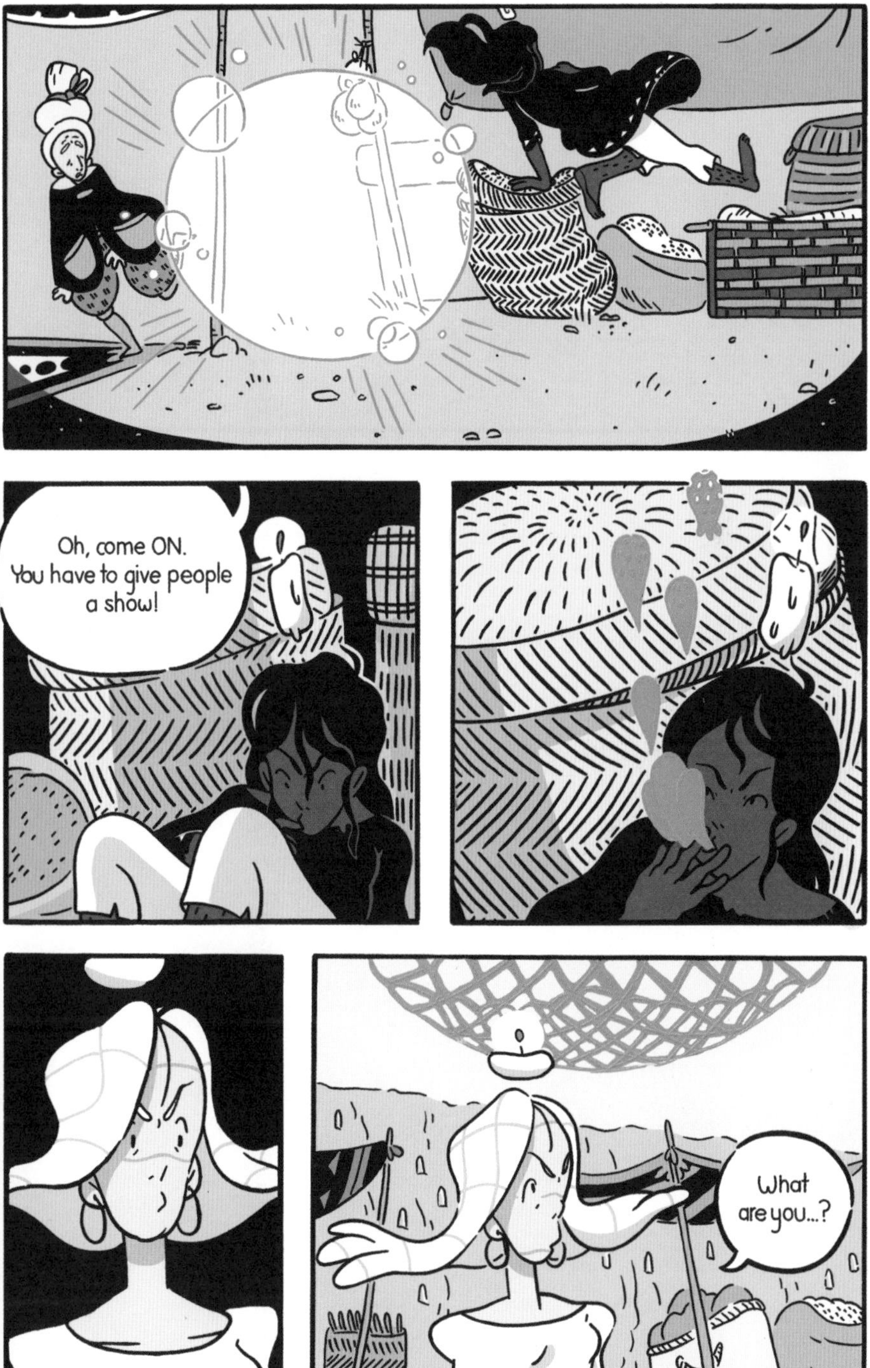
Oh, come ON.
You have to give people a show!
What are you...?

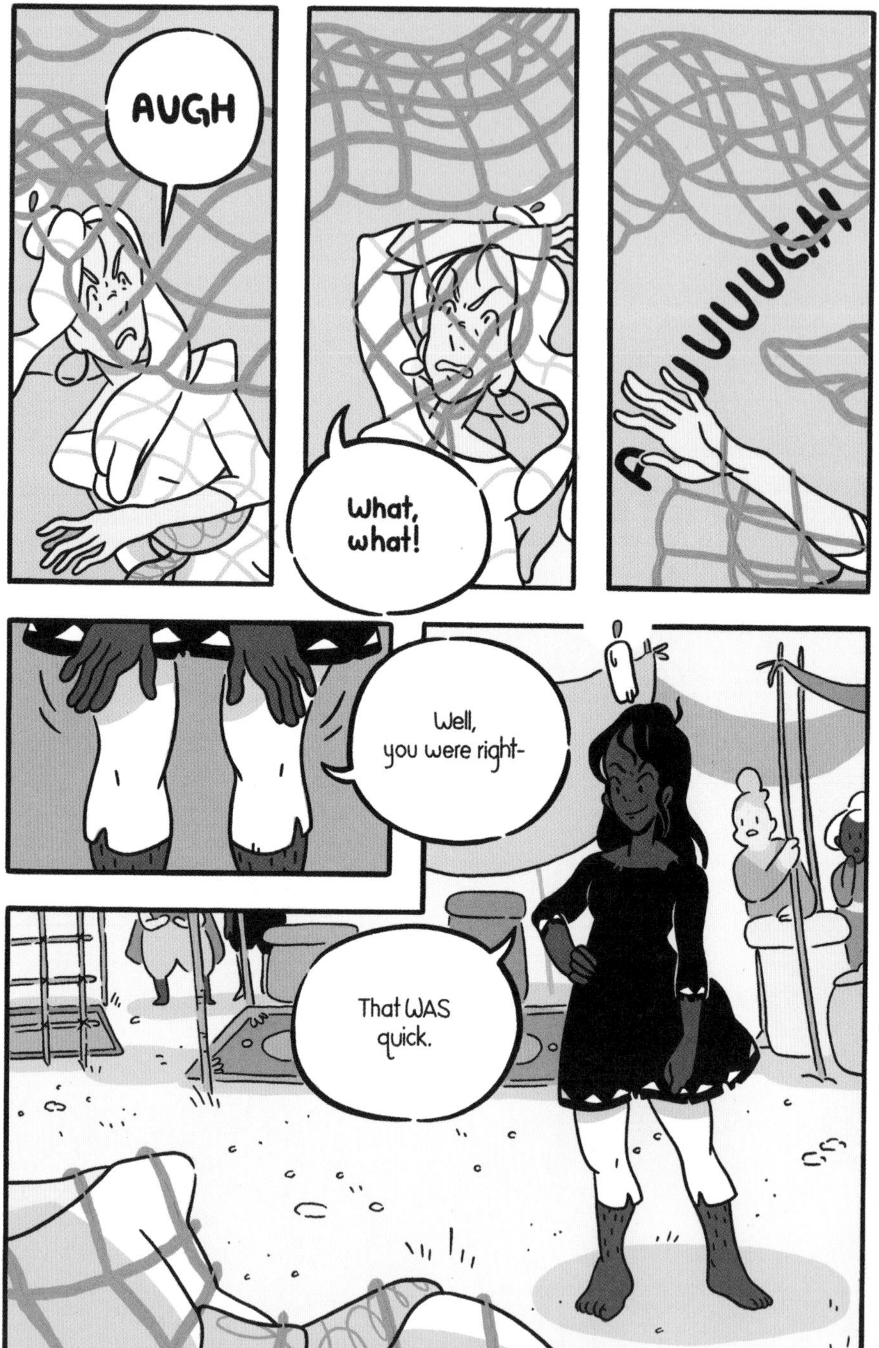
AUGH
What, what!
AUUUUGH
Well, you were right-
That WAS quick.

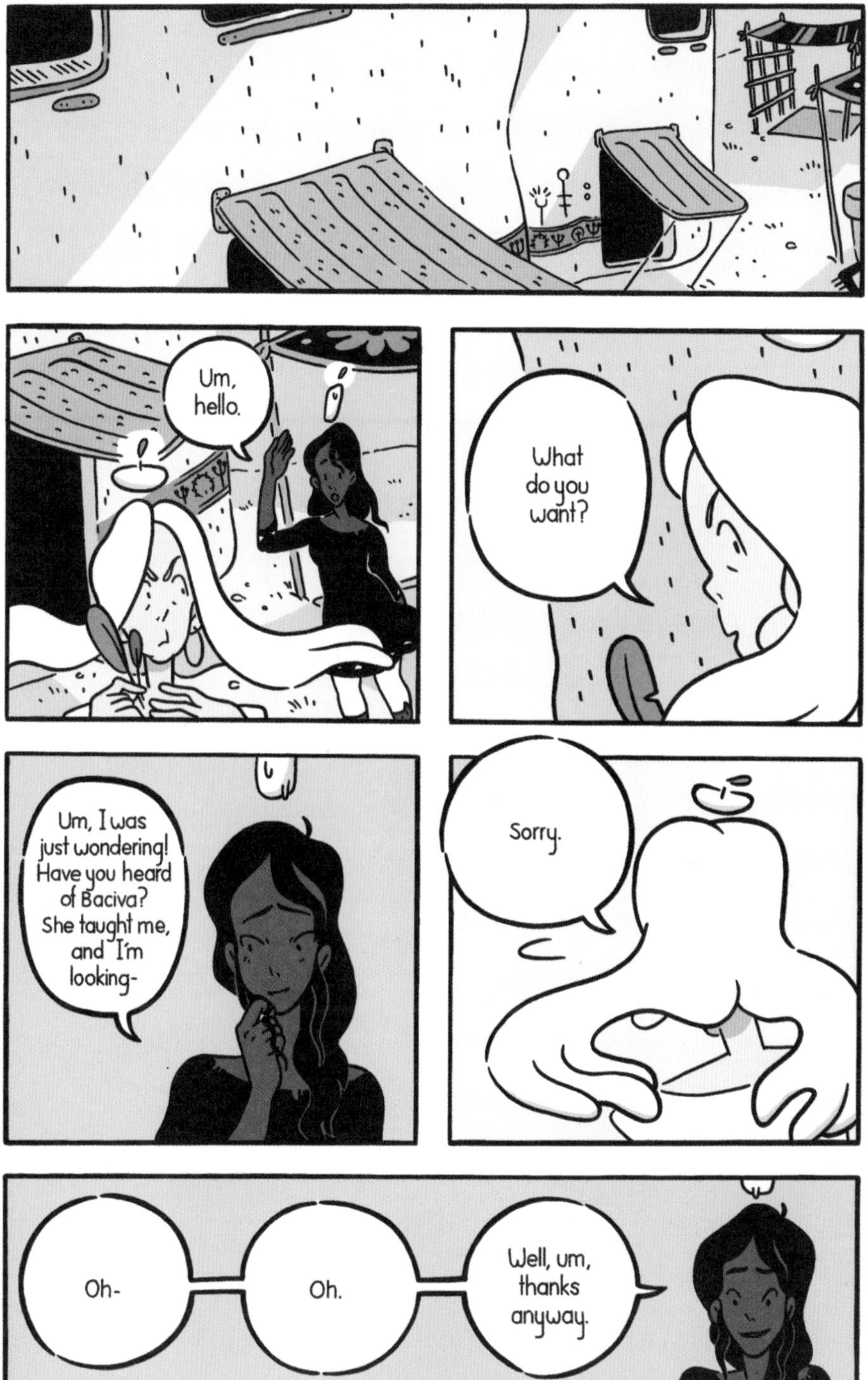
Um,
hello.
What
do you
want?
Um, I was
just wondering!
Have you heard
of Baciva?
She taught me,
and I'm
looking-
Sorry.
Oh-
Oh.
Well, um,
thanks
anyway.

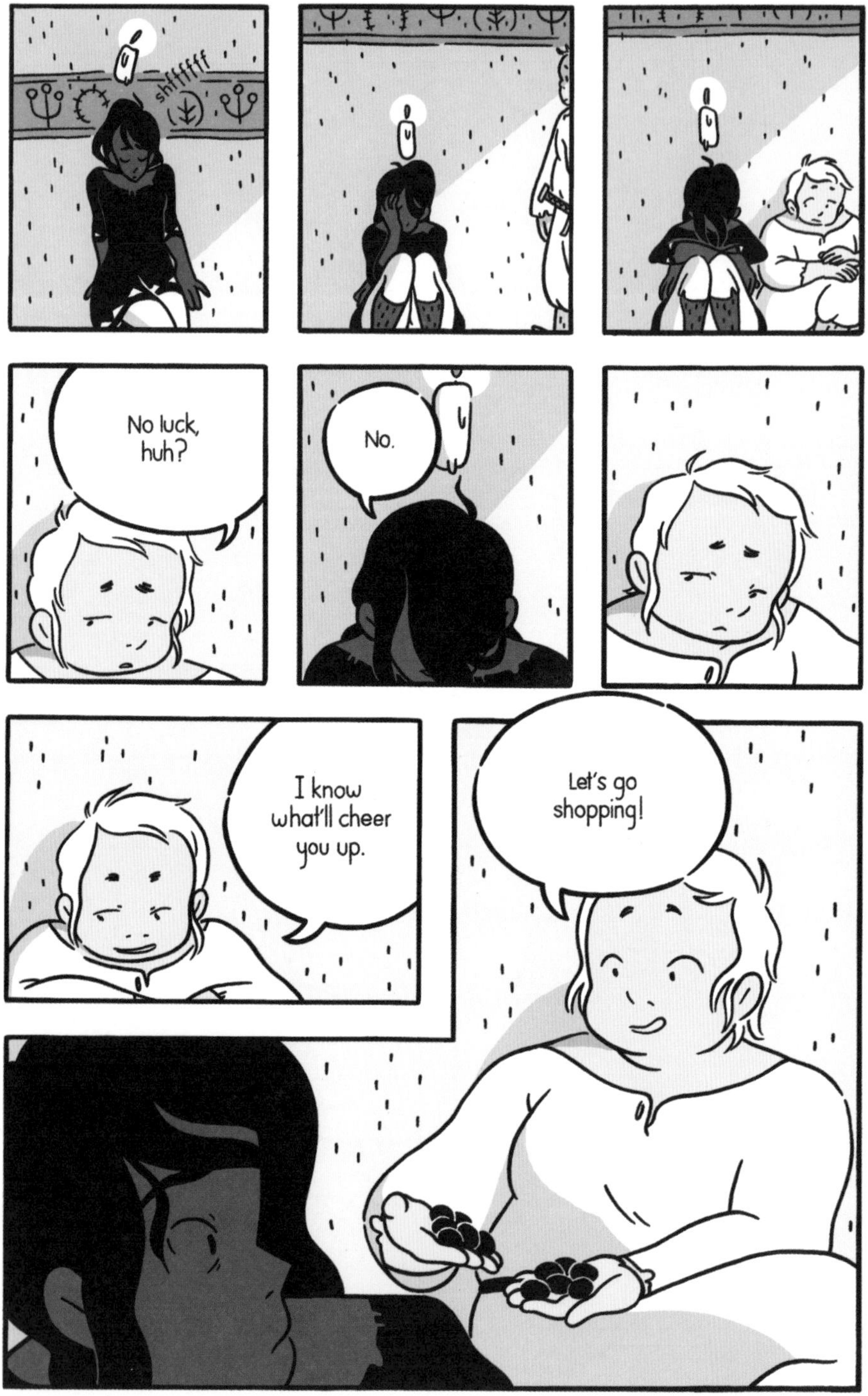
shffffff
No luck, huh?
No.
I know what'll cheer you up.
Let's go shopping!

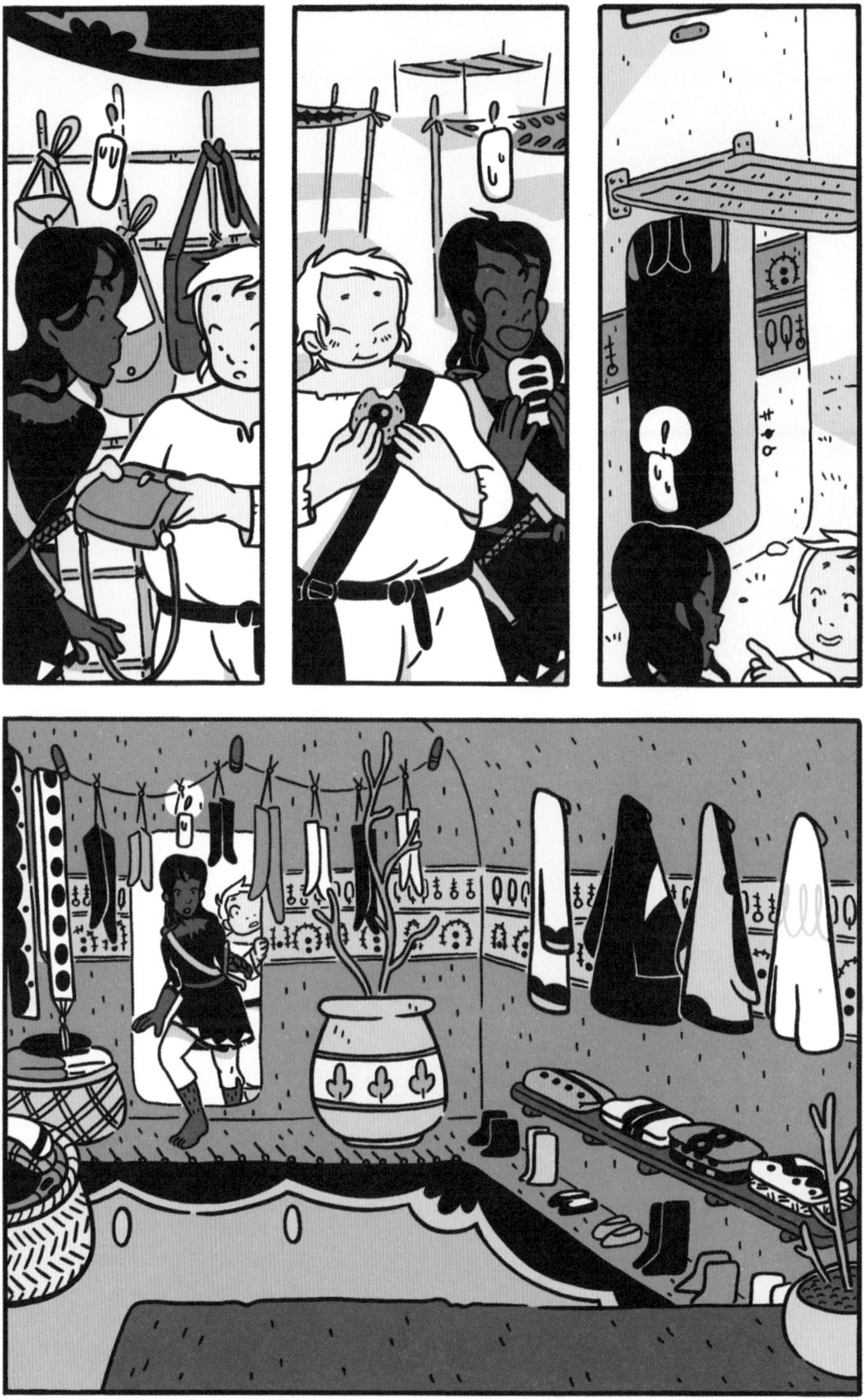

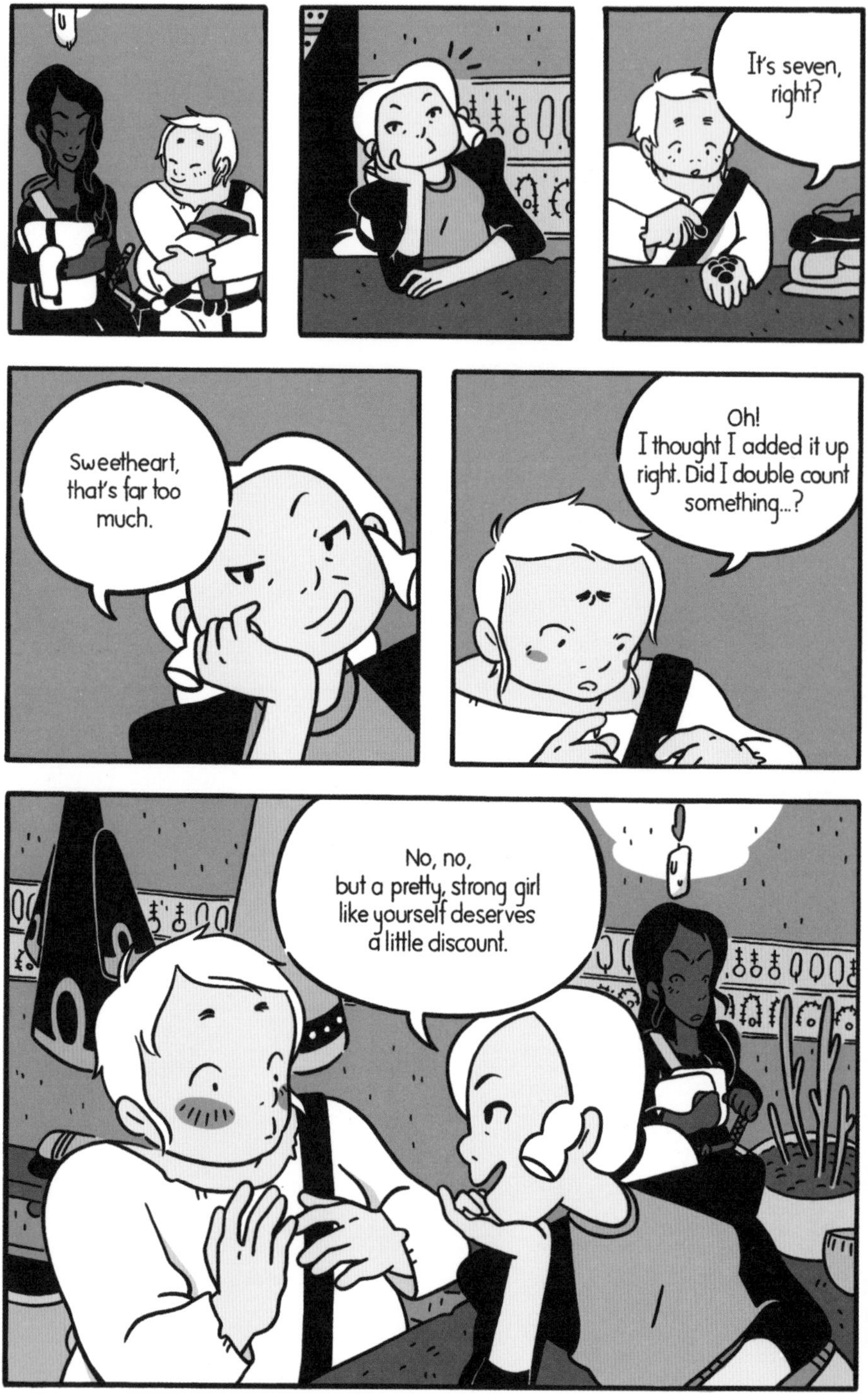
It's seven, right?
Sweetheart, that's far too much.
Oh! I thought I added it up right. Did I double count something...?
No, no, but a pretty, strong girl like yourself deserves a little discount.

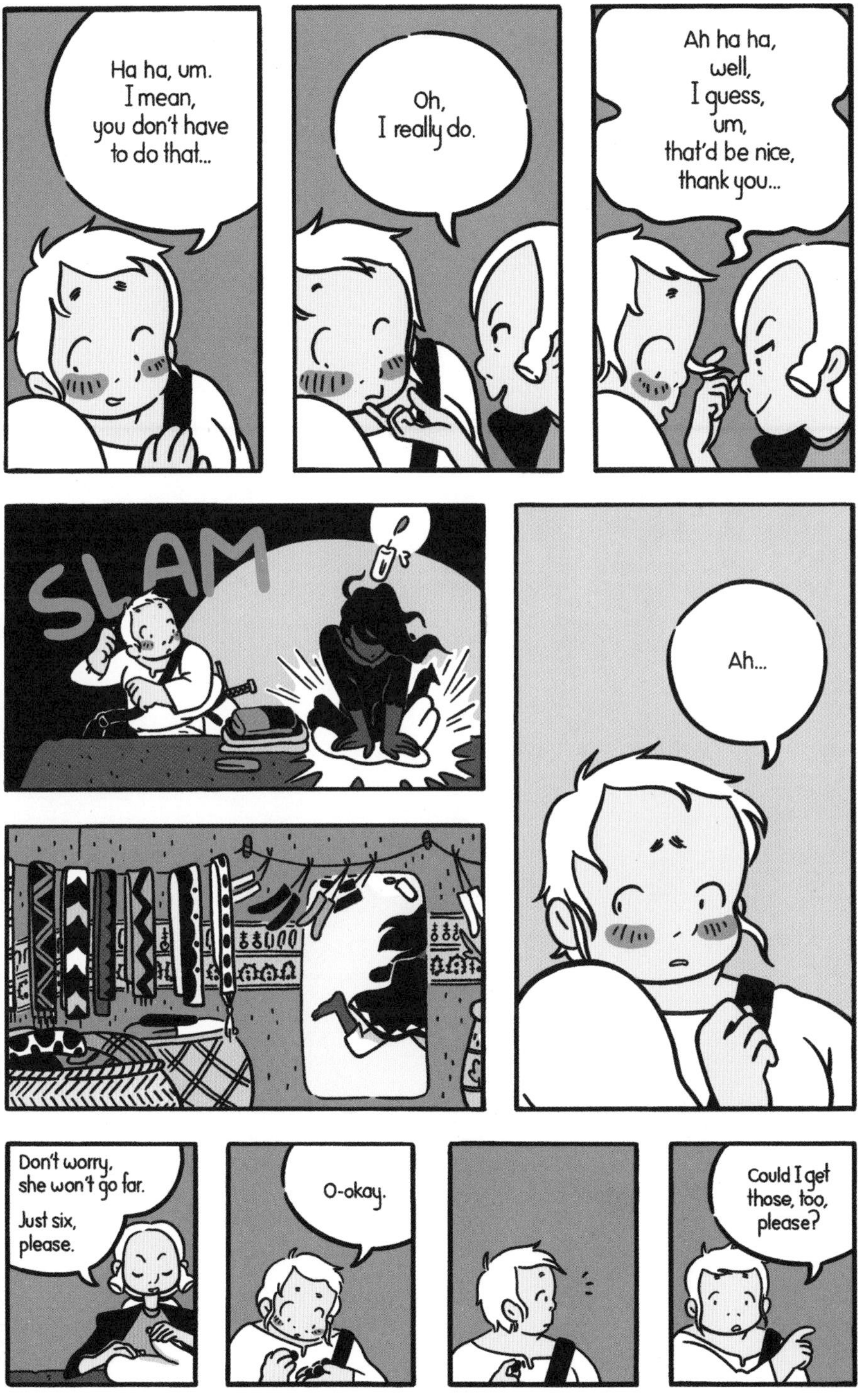
Ha ha, um. I mean, you don't have to do that...
Oh, I really do.
Ah ha ha, well, I guess, um, that'd be nice, thank you...
SLAM
Ah...
Don't worry, she won't go far.
Just six, please.
O-okay.
Could I get those, too, please?

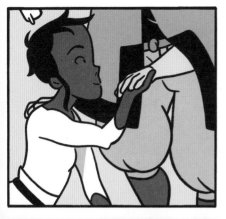

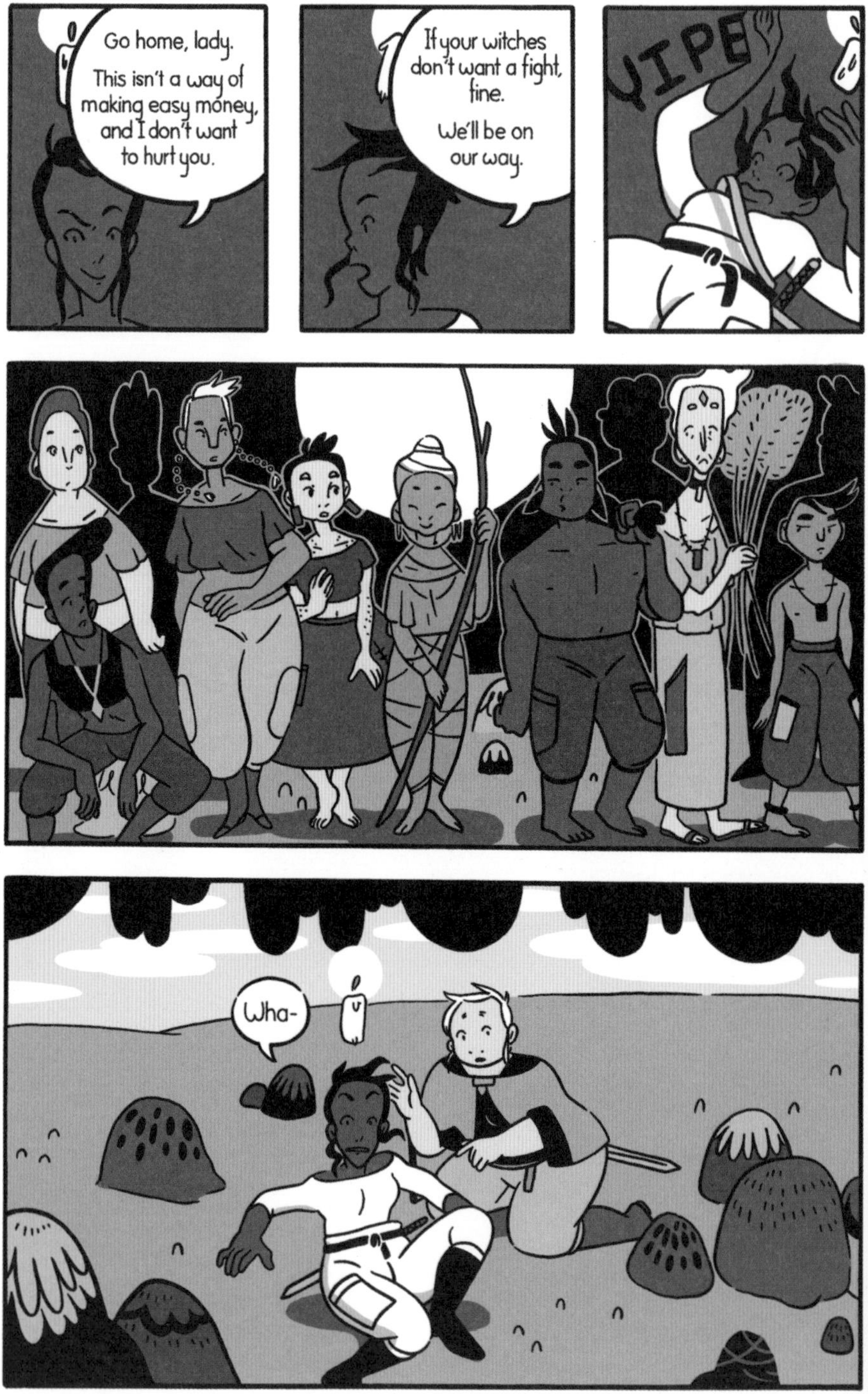
Go home, lady.
This isn't a way of making easy money, and I don't want to hurt you.
If your witches don't want a fight, fine.
We'll be on our way.
YIPE
Wha-

Part 4

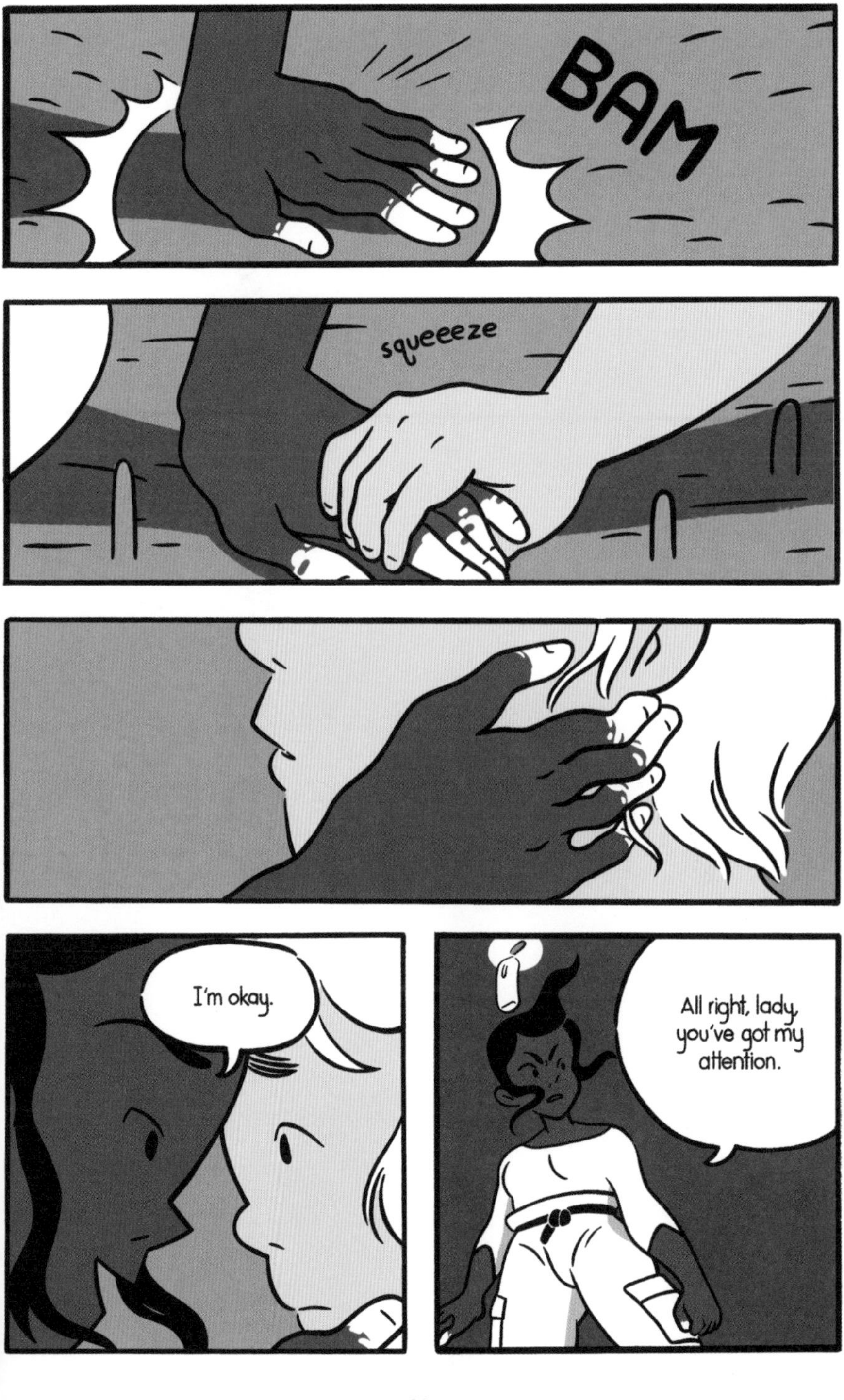
BAM
squeeeze
I'm okay.
All right, lady, you've got my attention.

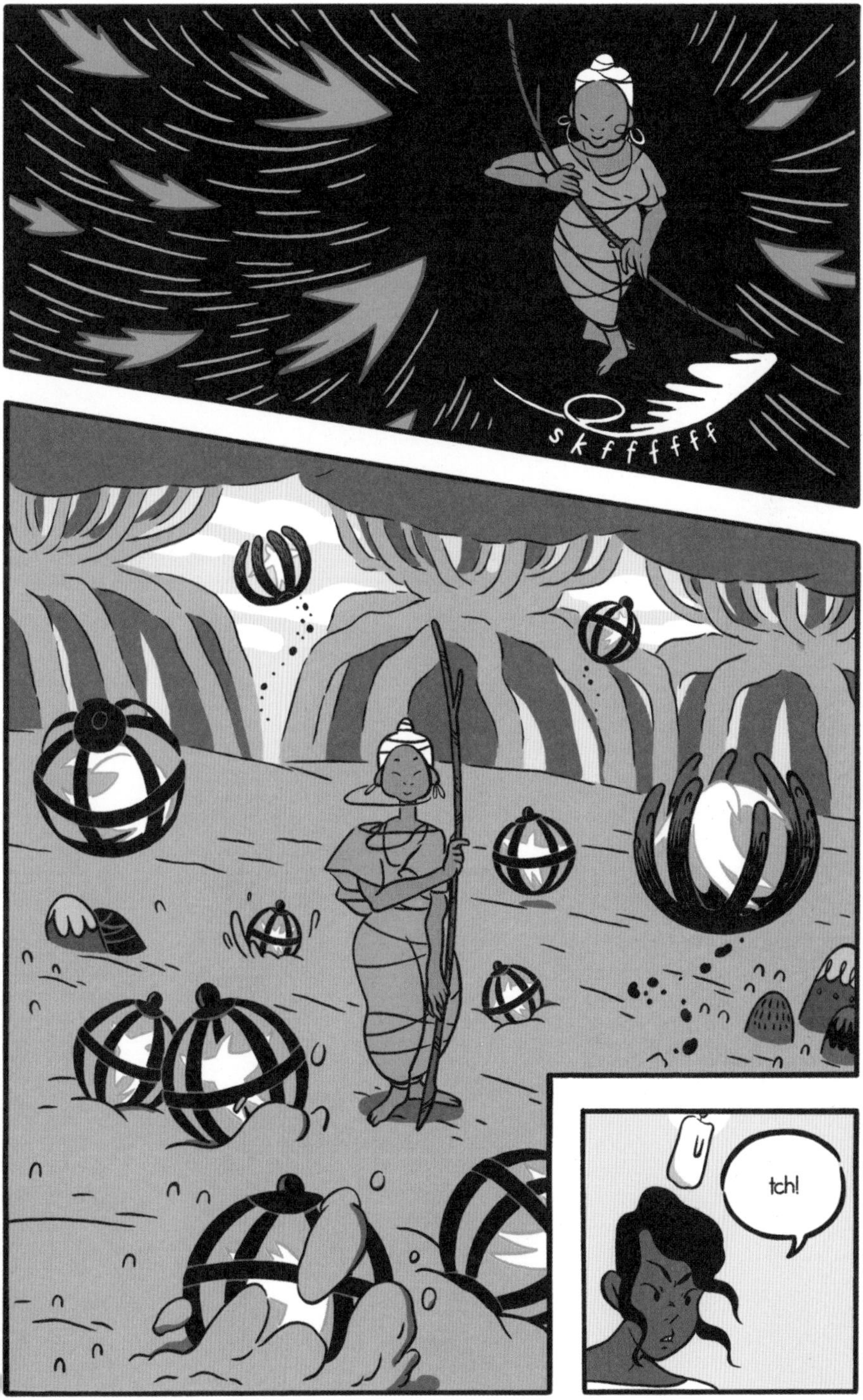
skfffffff
tch!

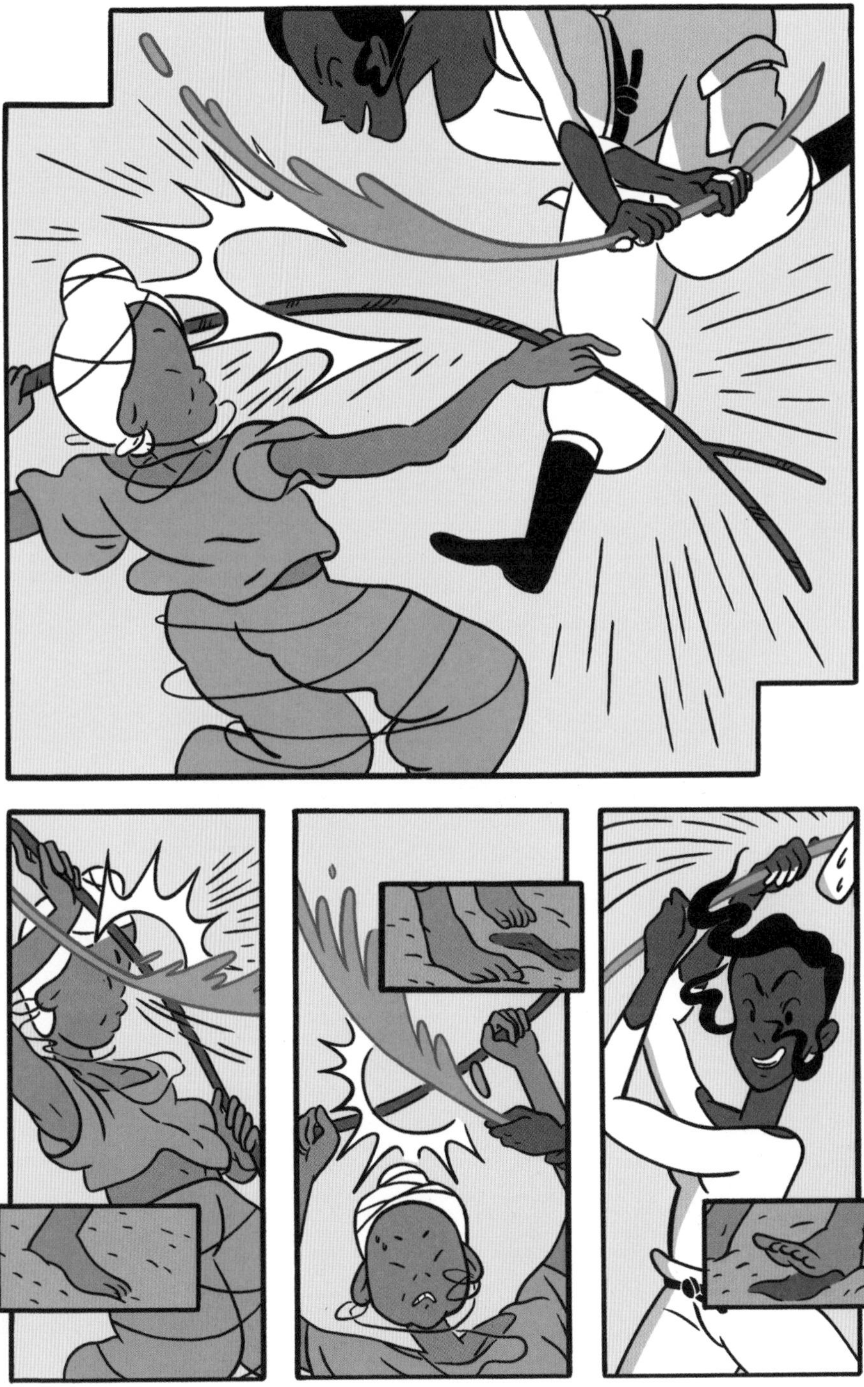

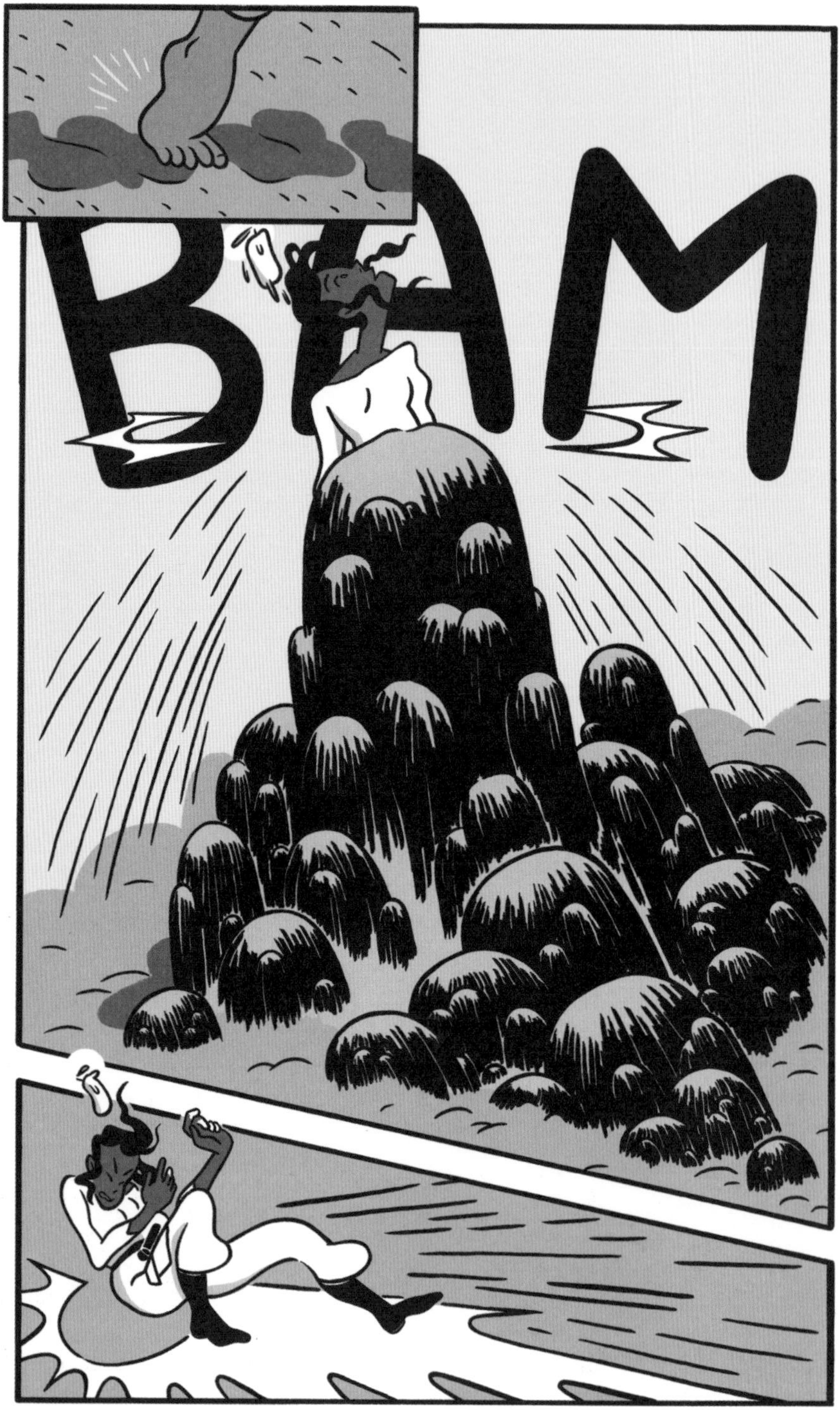
BAM

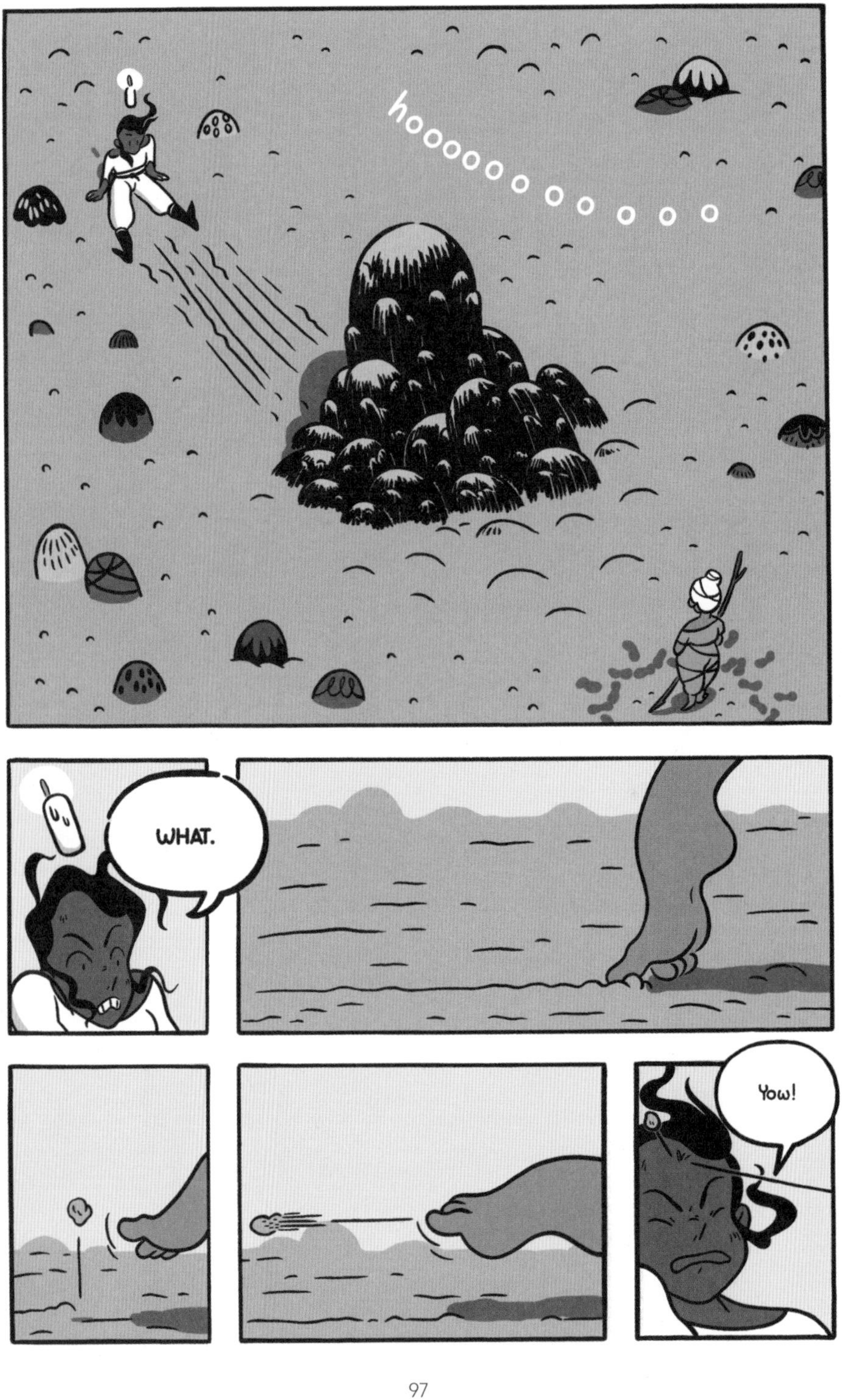
hoooooooooo
WHAT.
Yow!

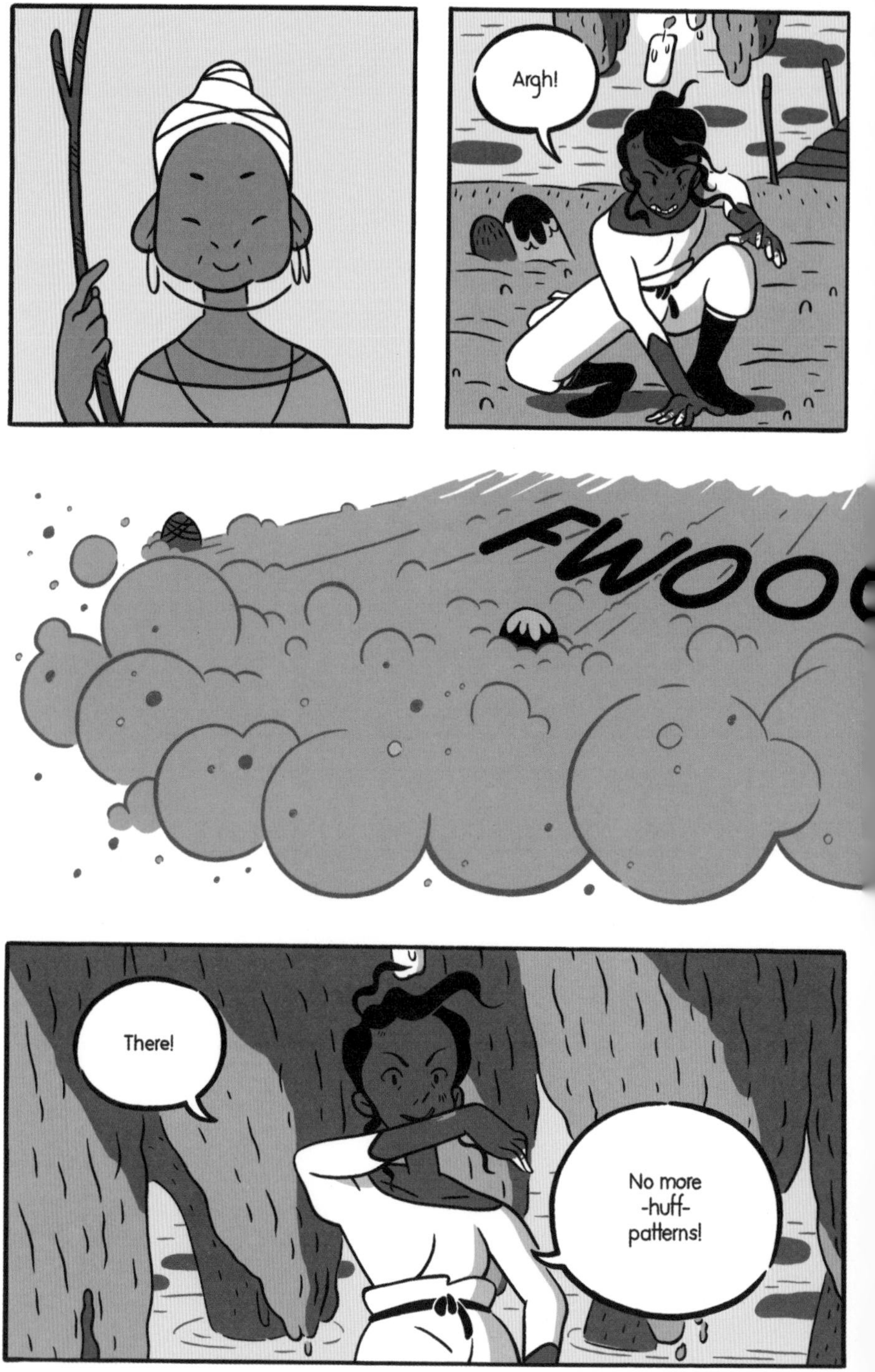

Argh!
FWOOO
There!
No more
-huff-
patterns!

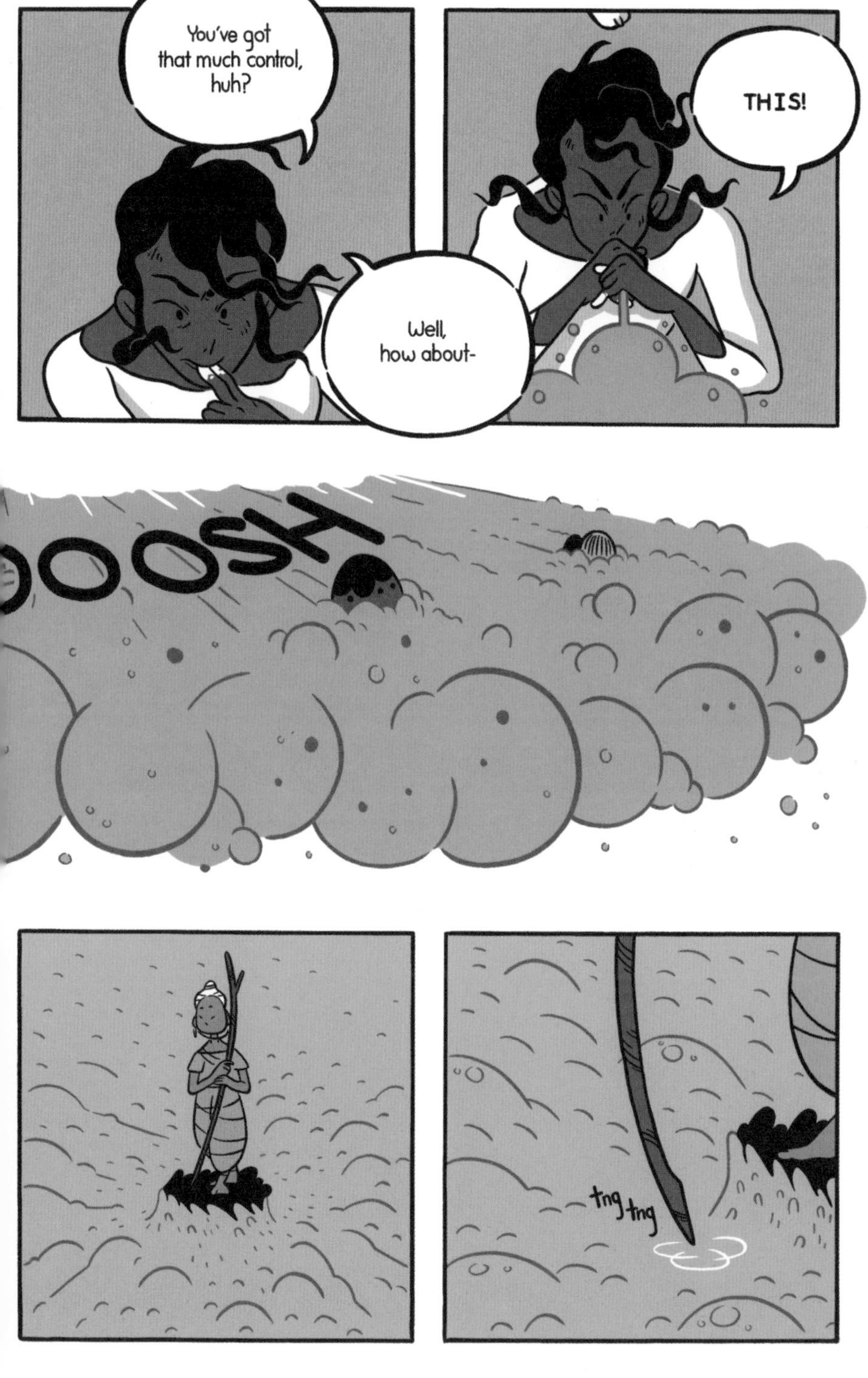
You've got
that much control,
huh?
Well,
how about-
THIS!
OOSH
tng tng

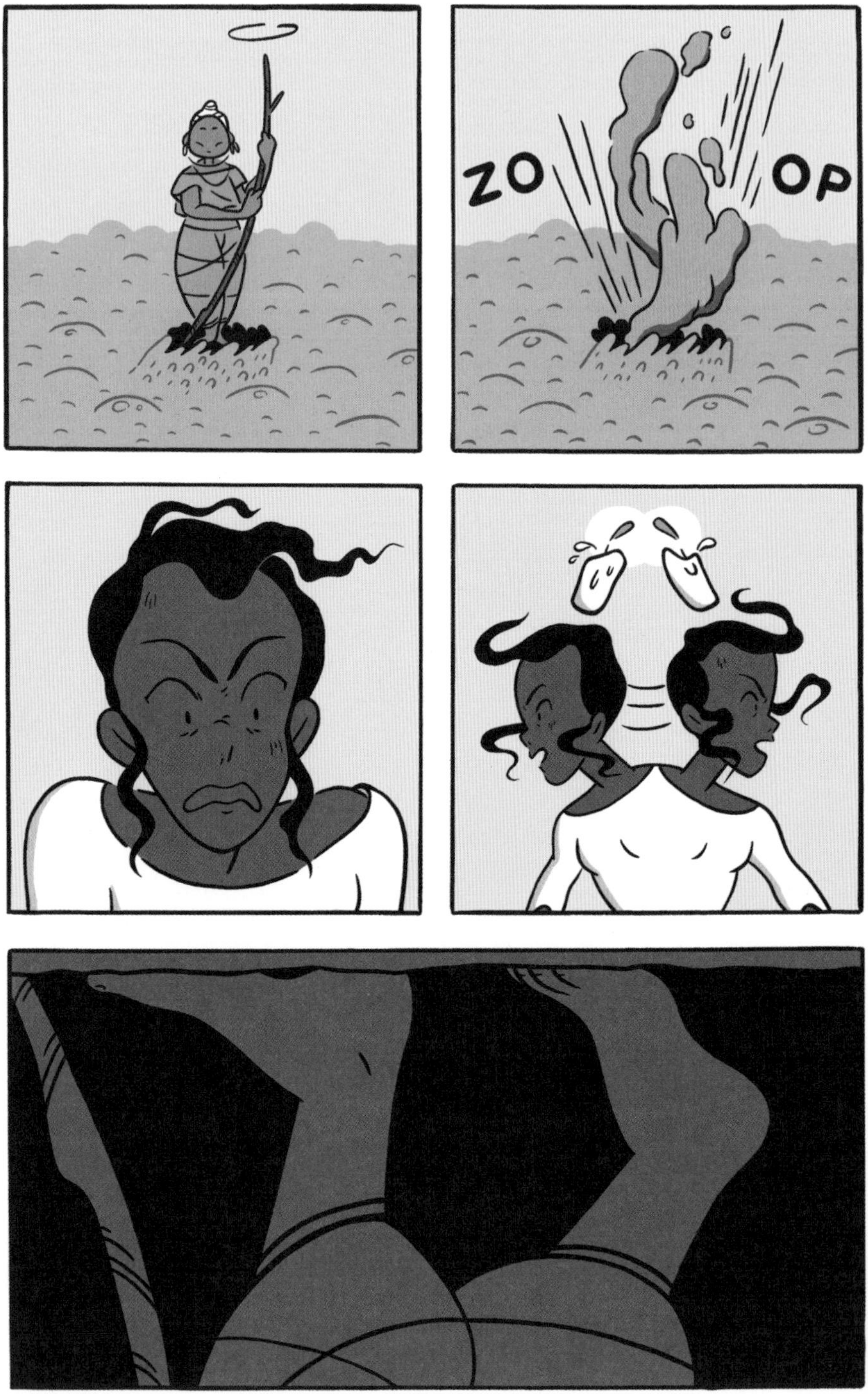
ZO
OP

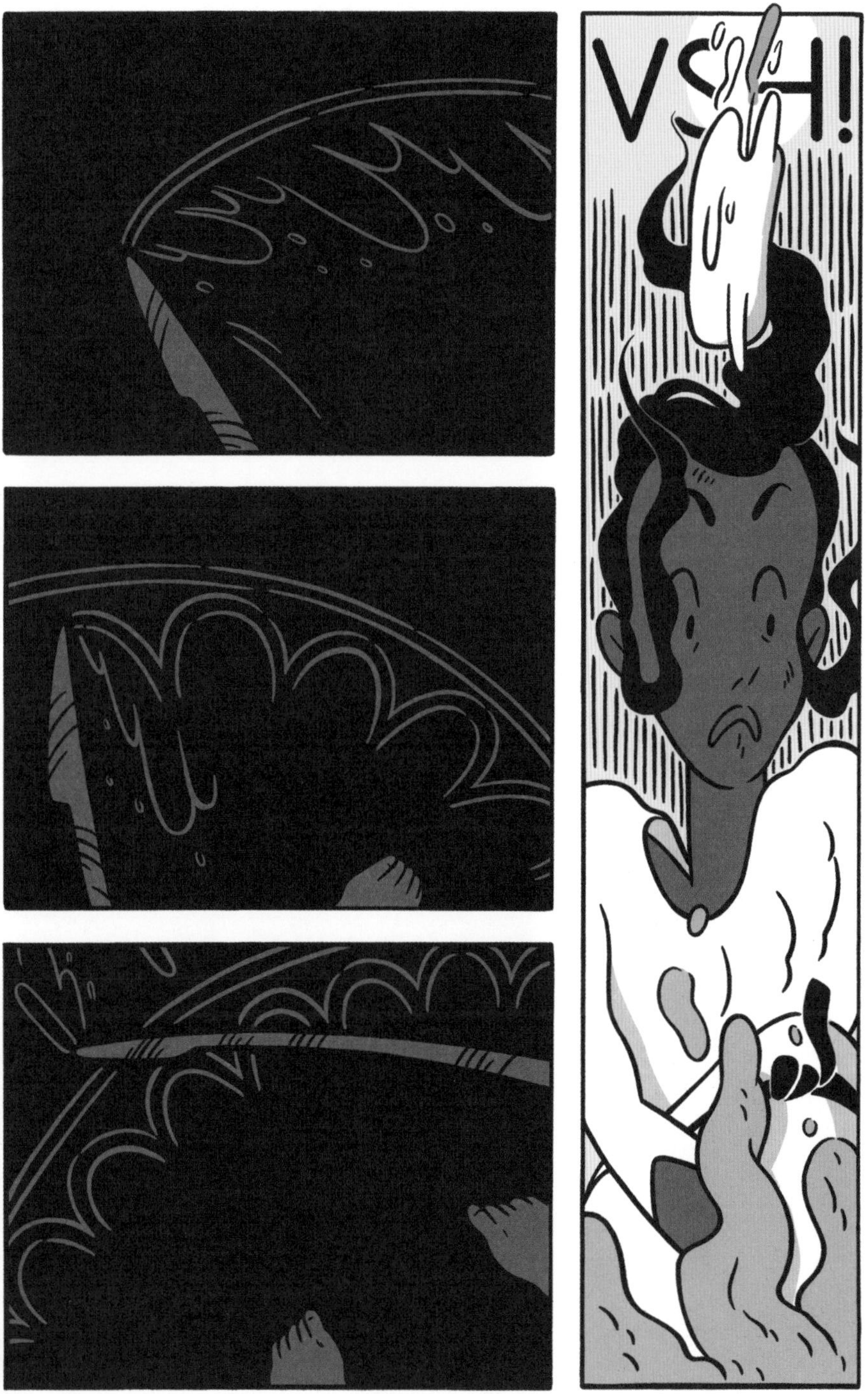
VSH!

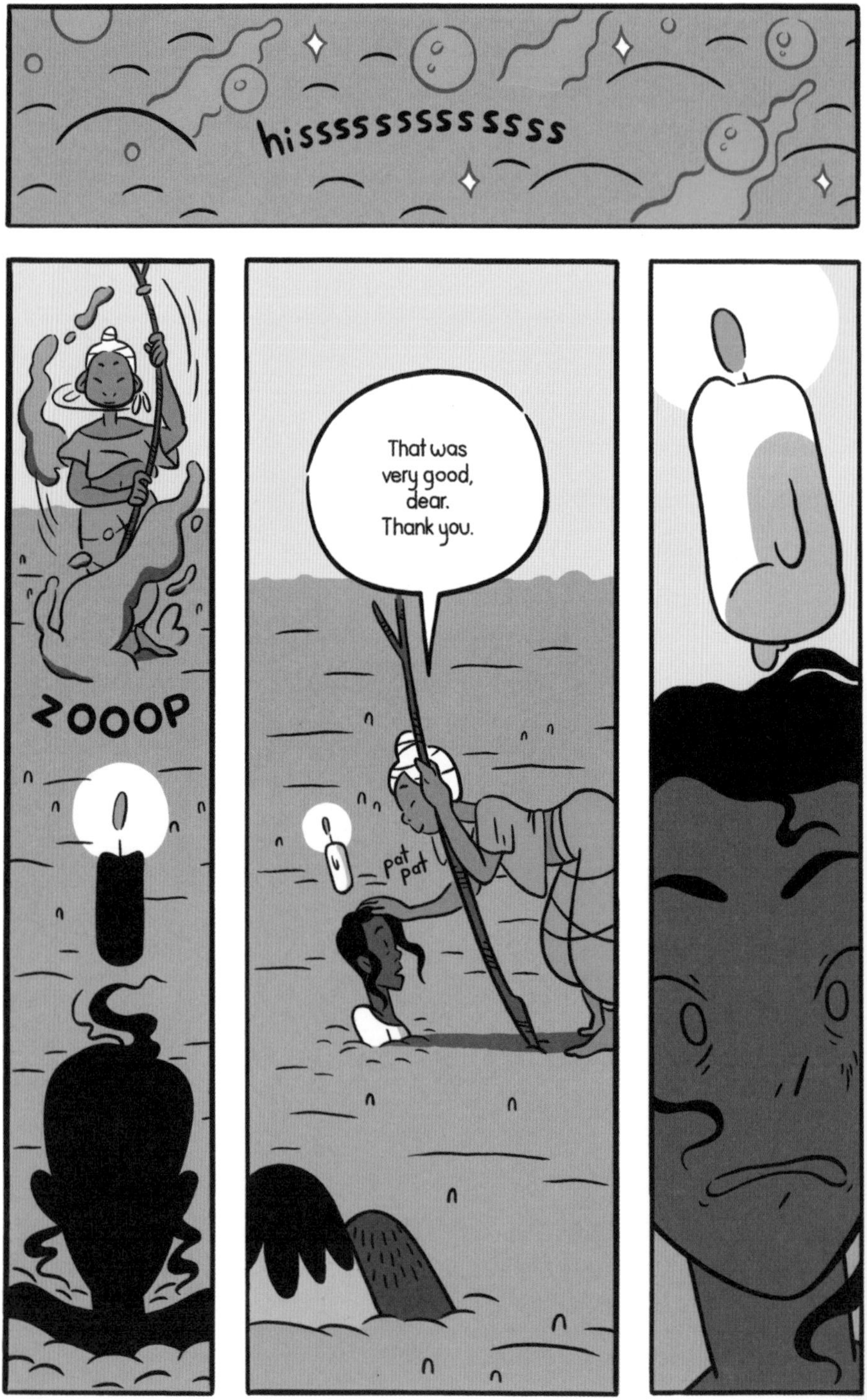
hissssssssssss
ZOOOP
That was very good, dear. Thank you.
pat pat

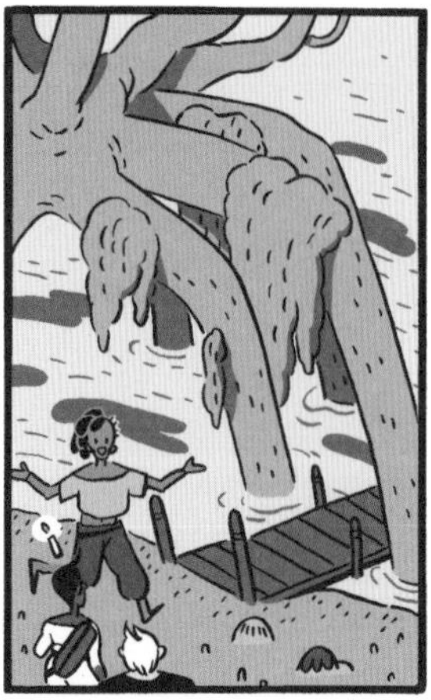
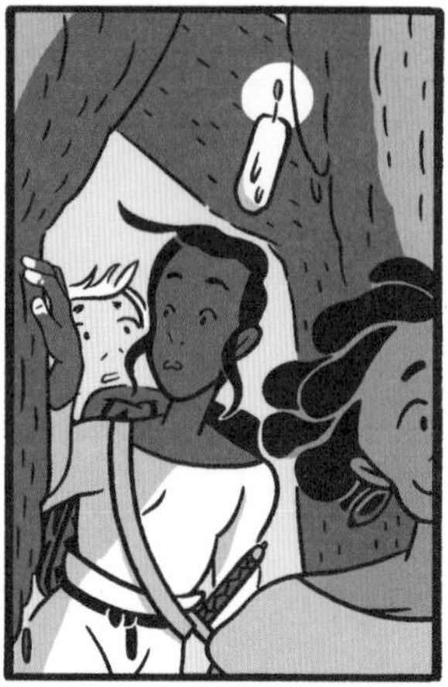
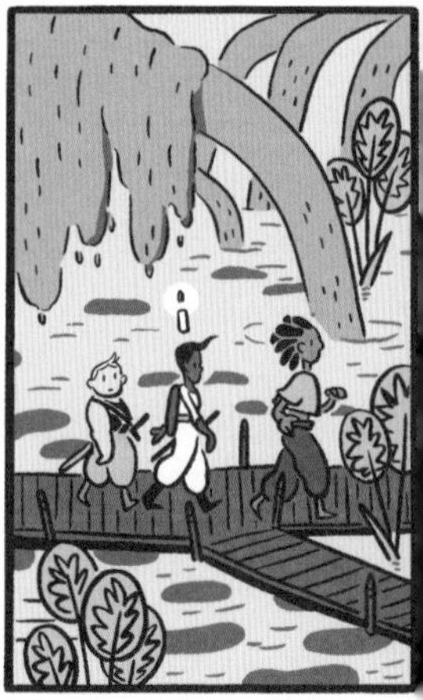
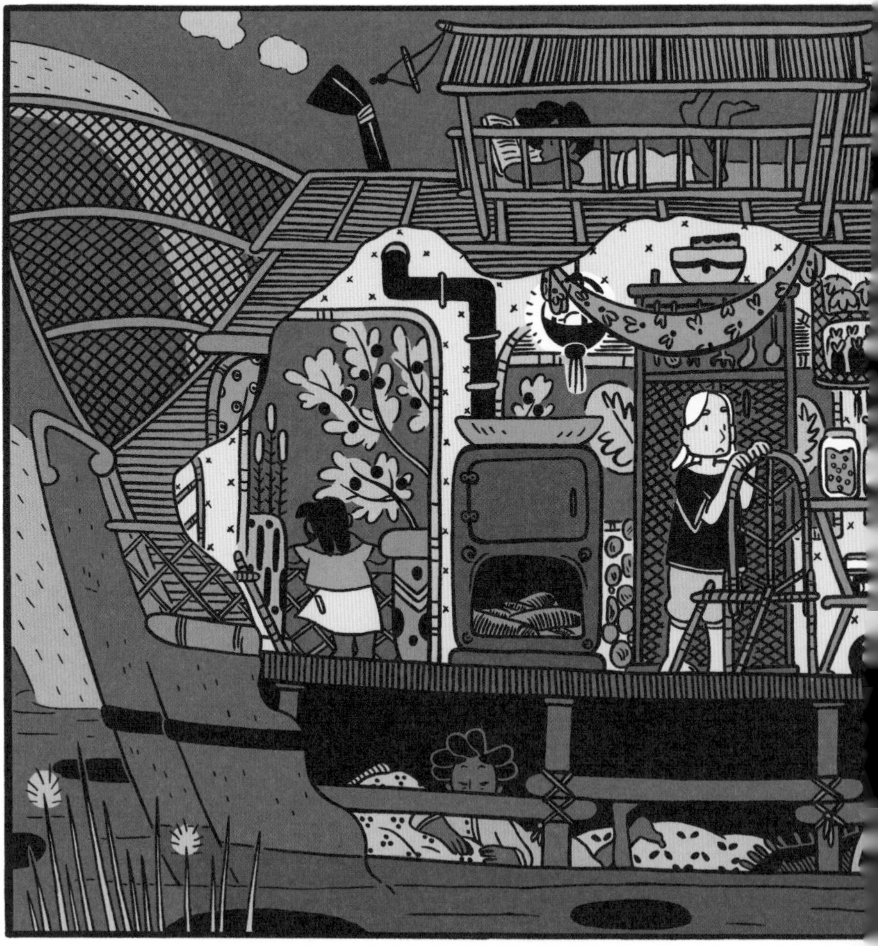

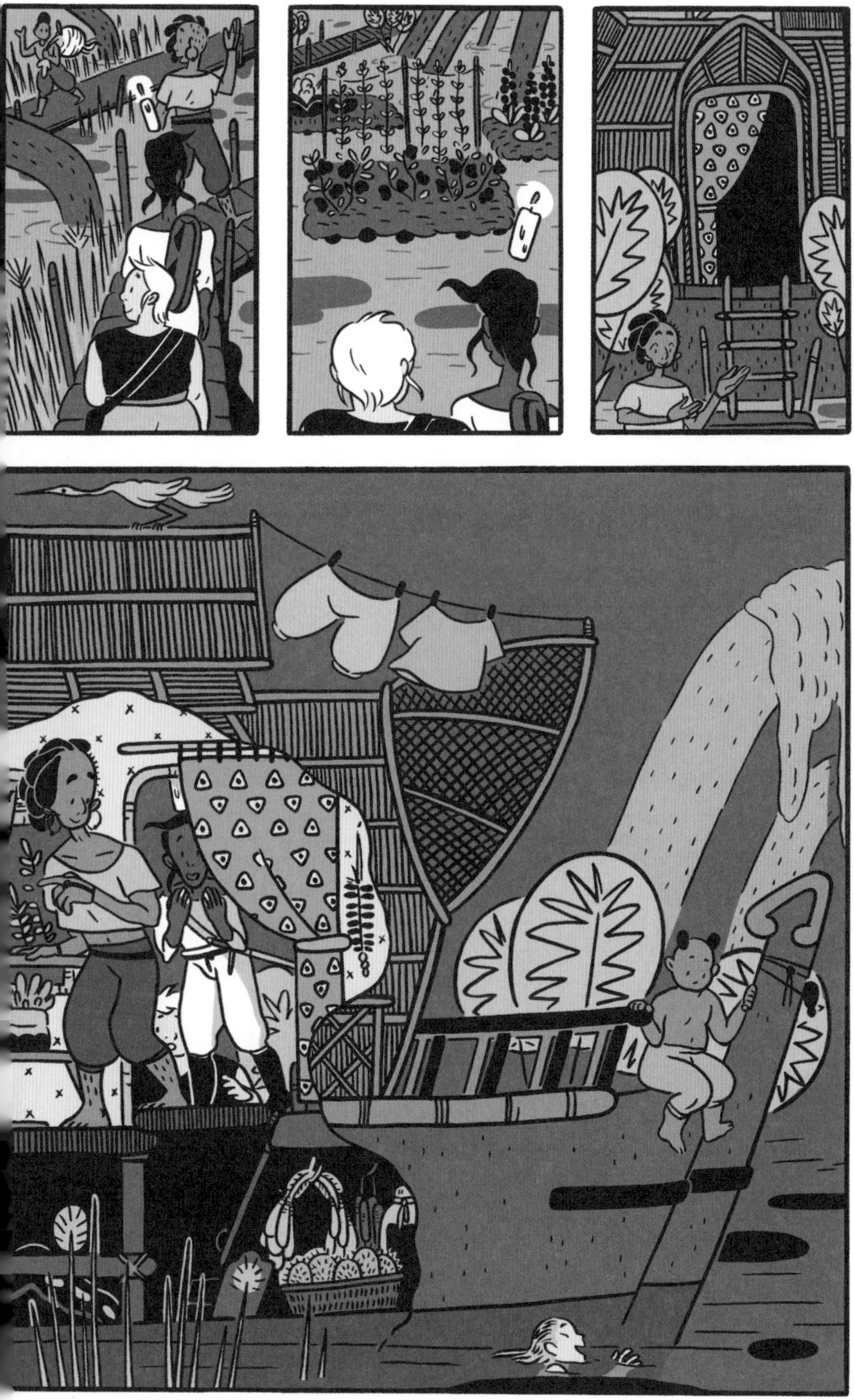

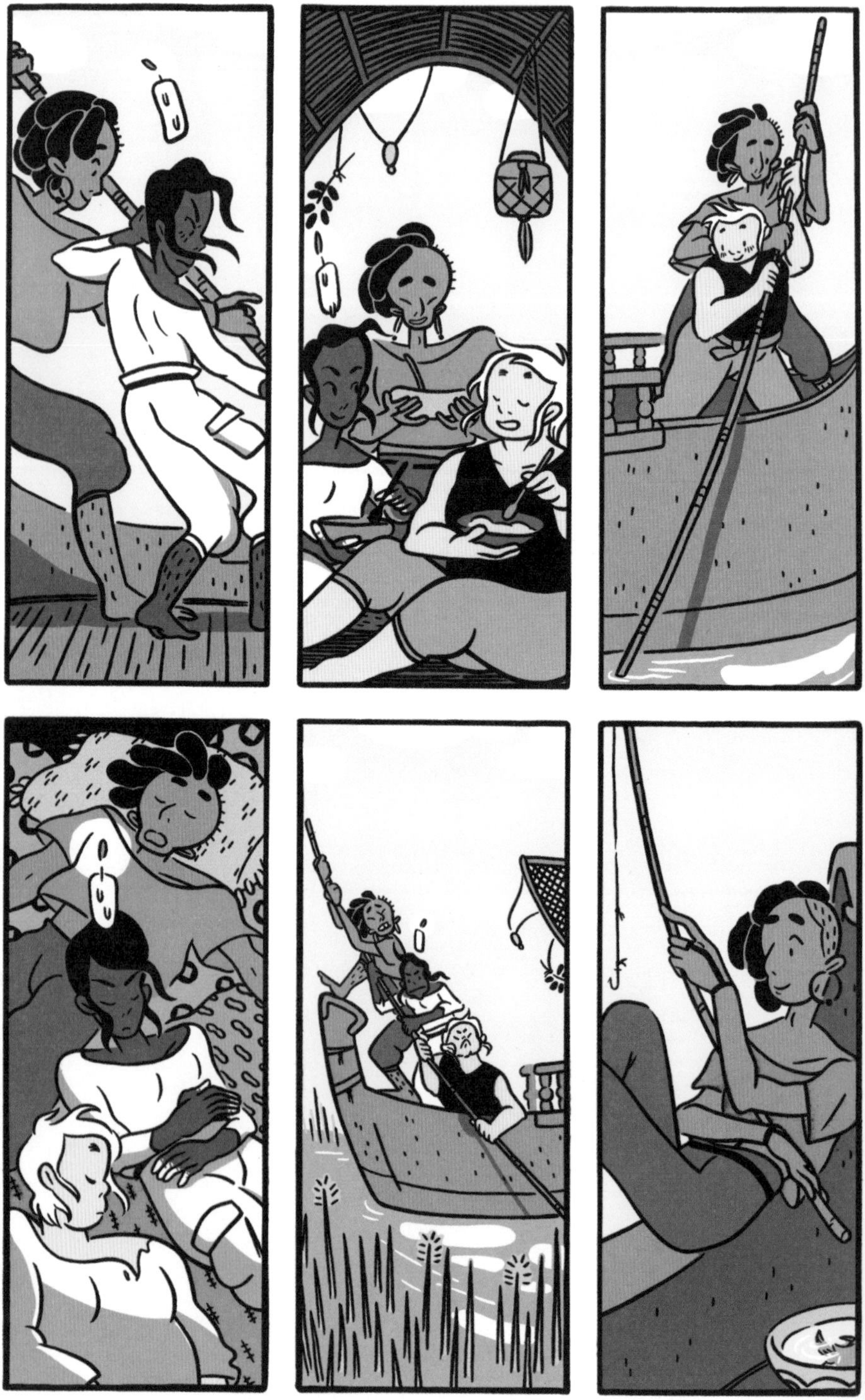

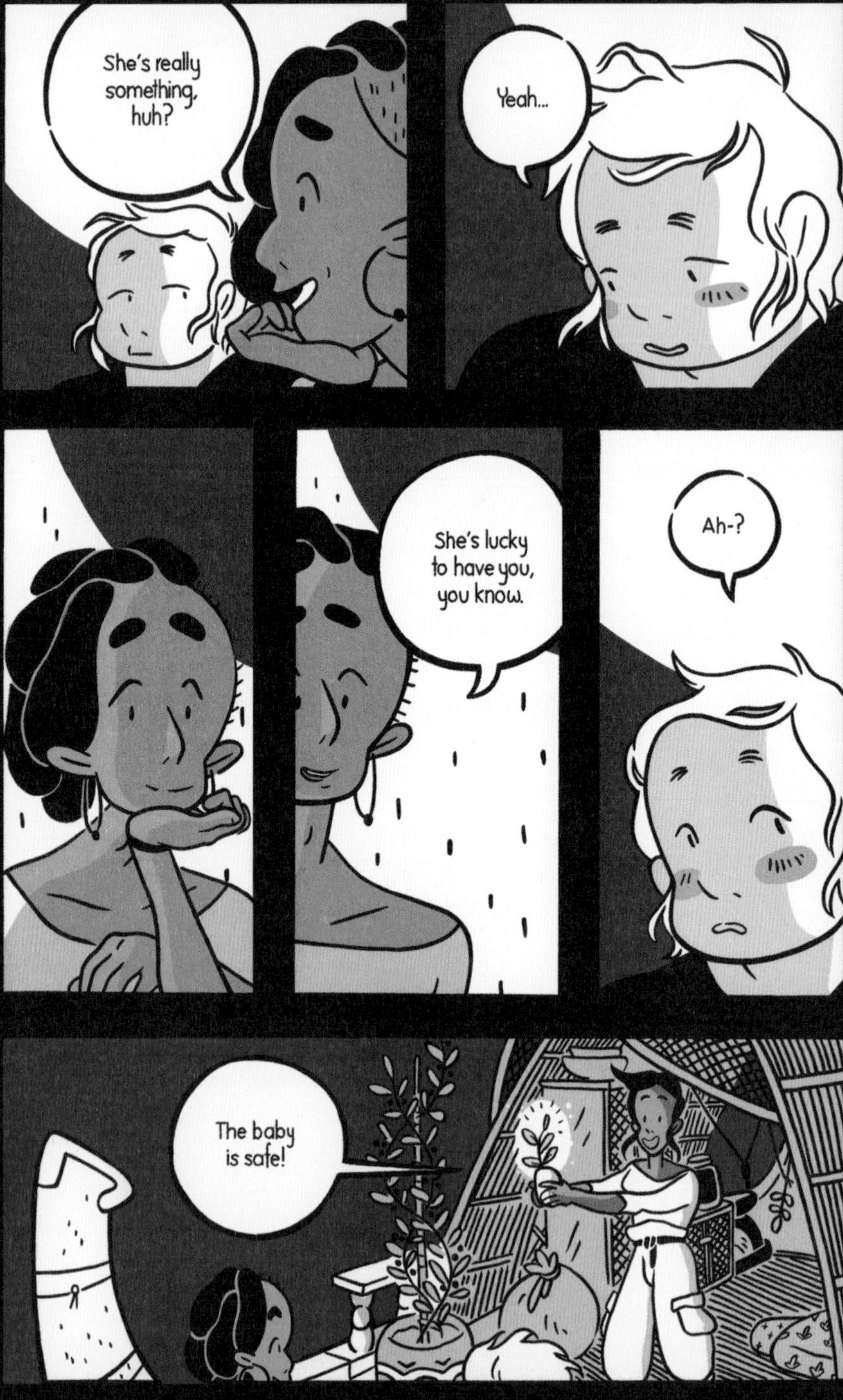
She's really something, huh?
Yeah...
She's lucky to have you, you know.
Ah-?
The baby is safe!

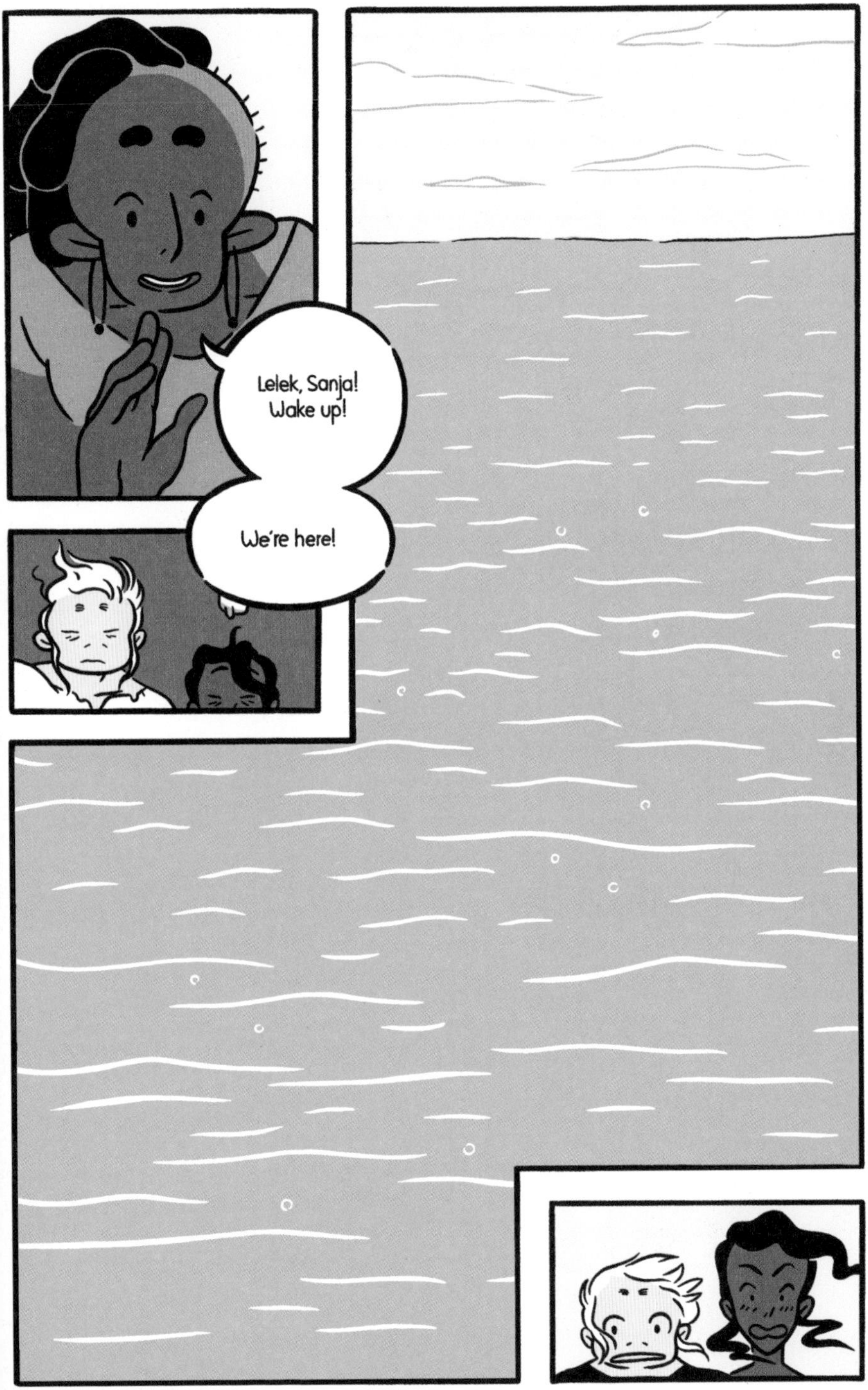
Lelek, Sanja! Wake up!
We're here!

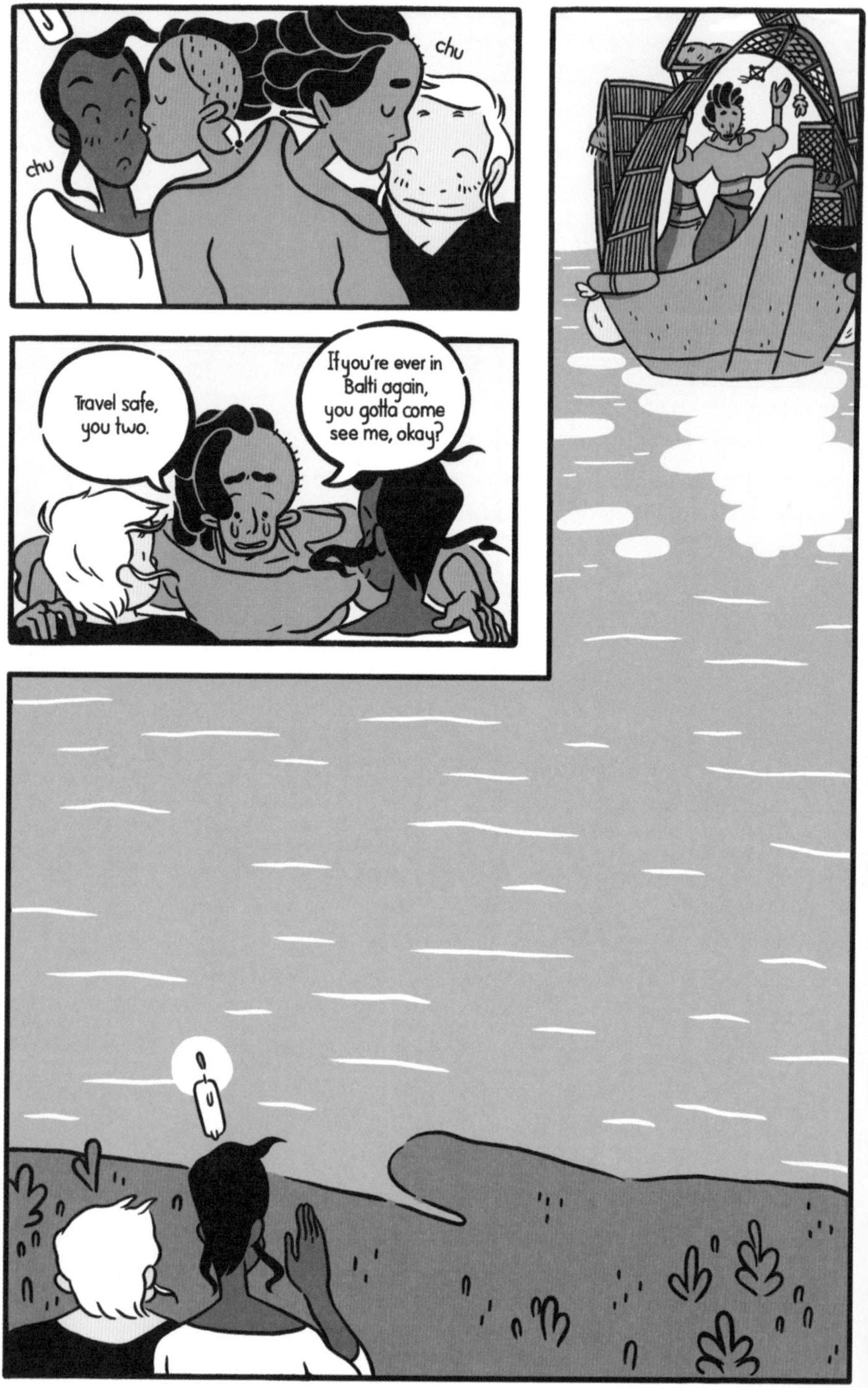
chu
chu
Travel safe, you two.
If you're ever in Balti again, you gotta come see me, okay?

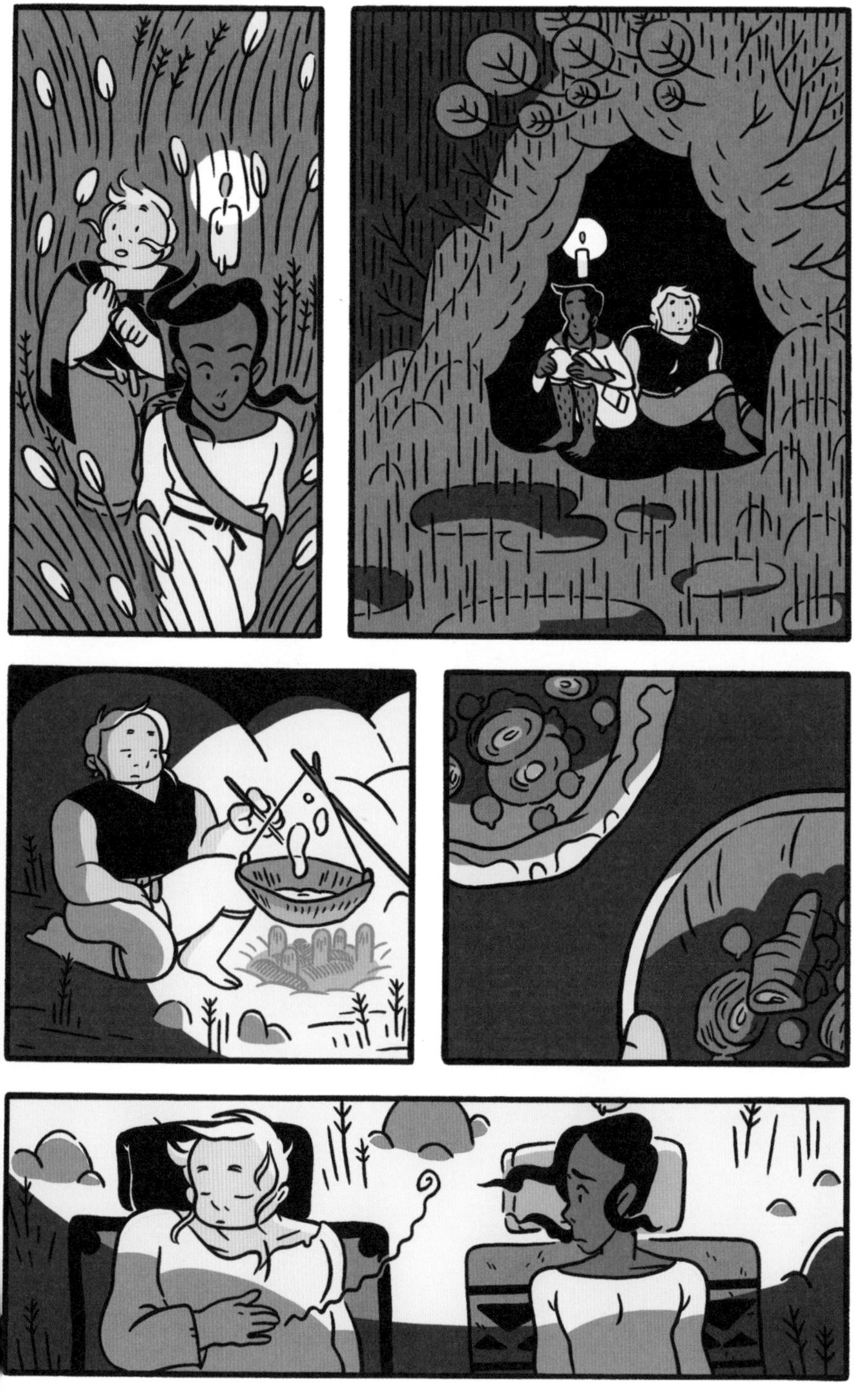

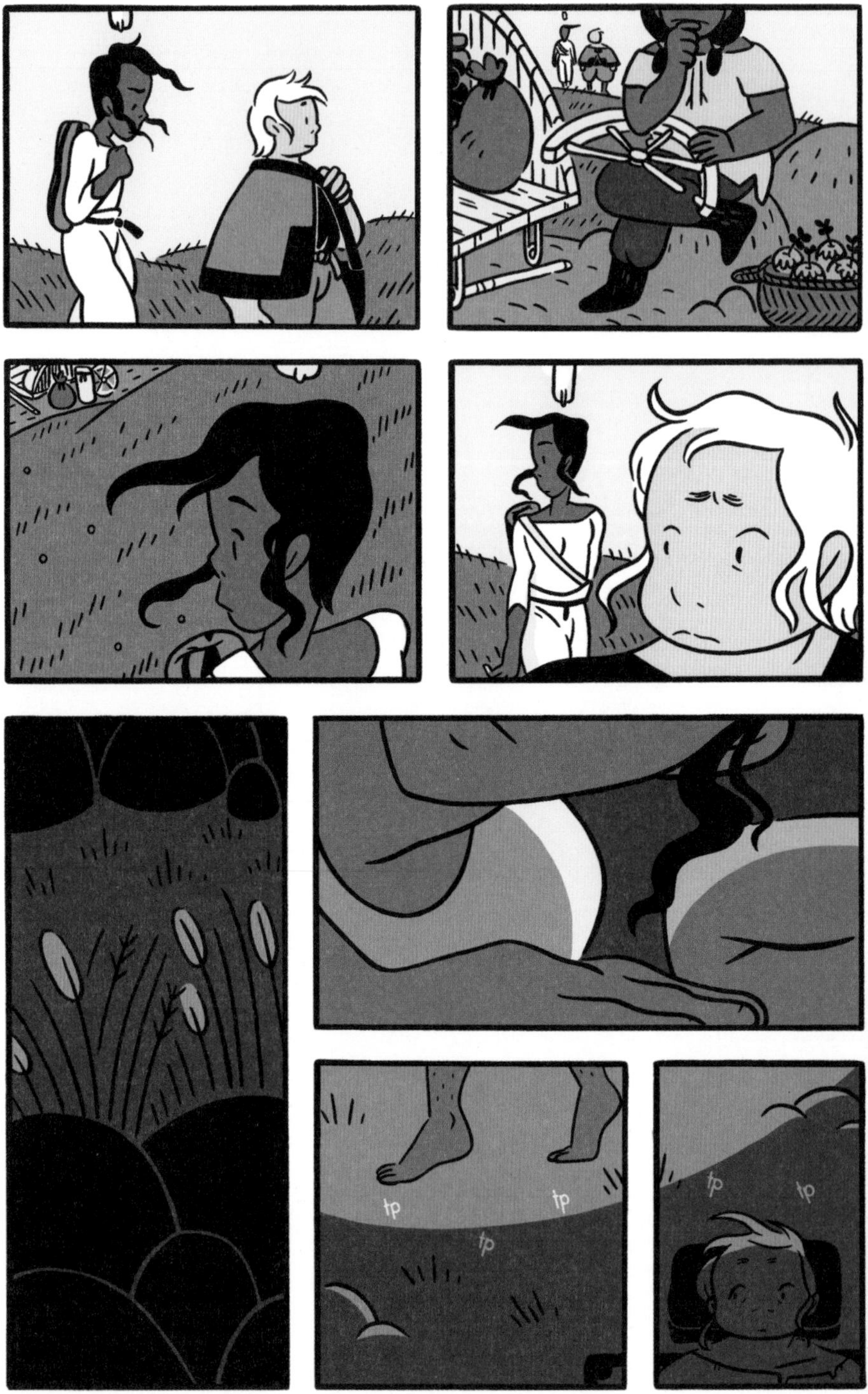
tp
tp
tp
tp
tp

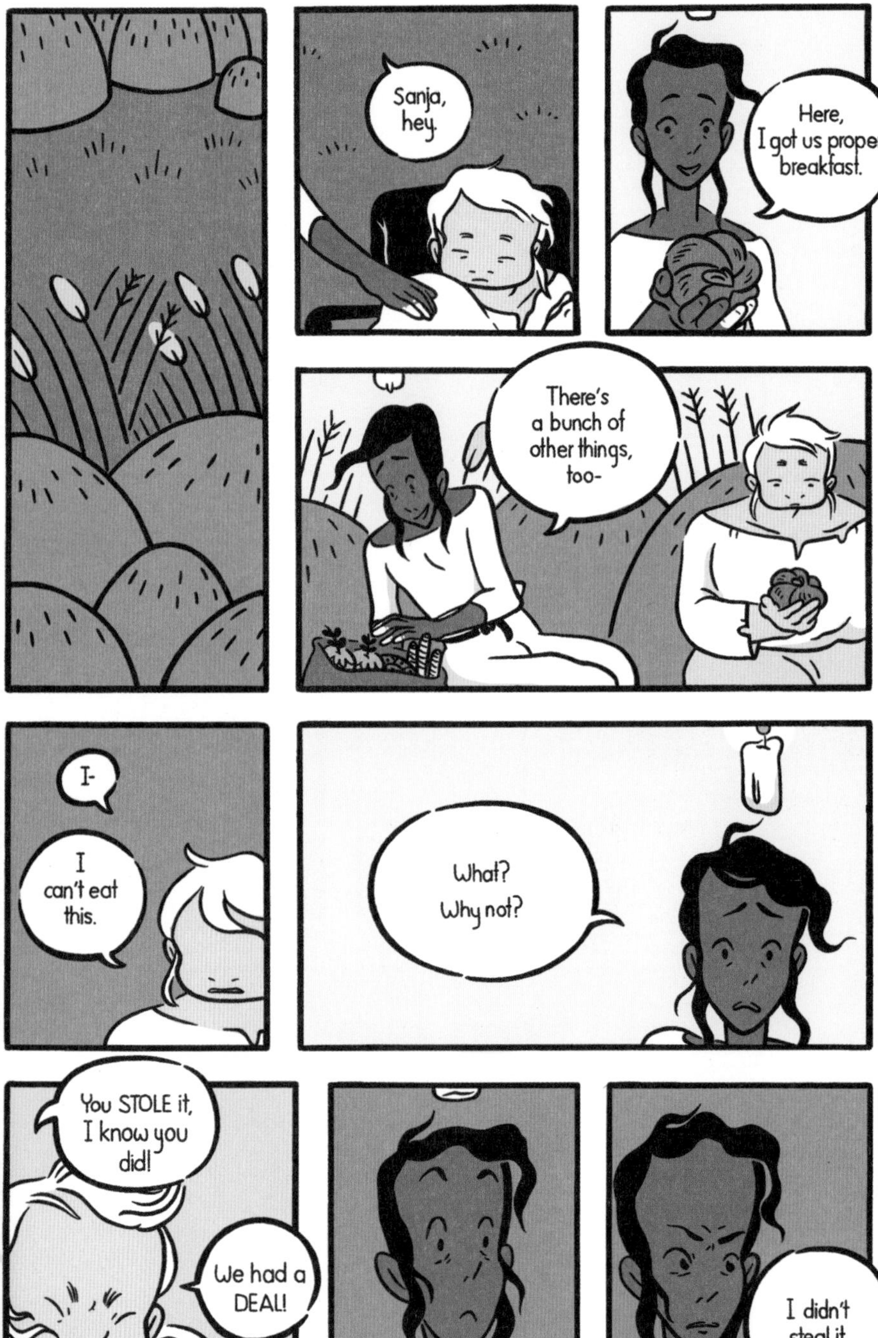
Sanja, hey.
Here, I got us proper breakfast.
There's a bunch of other things, too-
I-
I can't eat this.
What? Why not?
You STOLE it, I know you did!
We had a DEAL!
I didn't steal it.

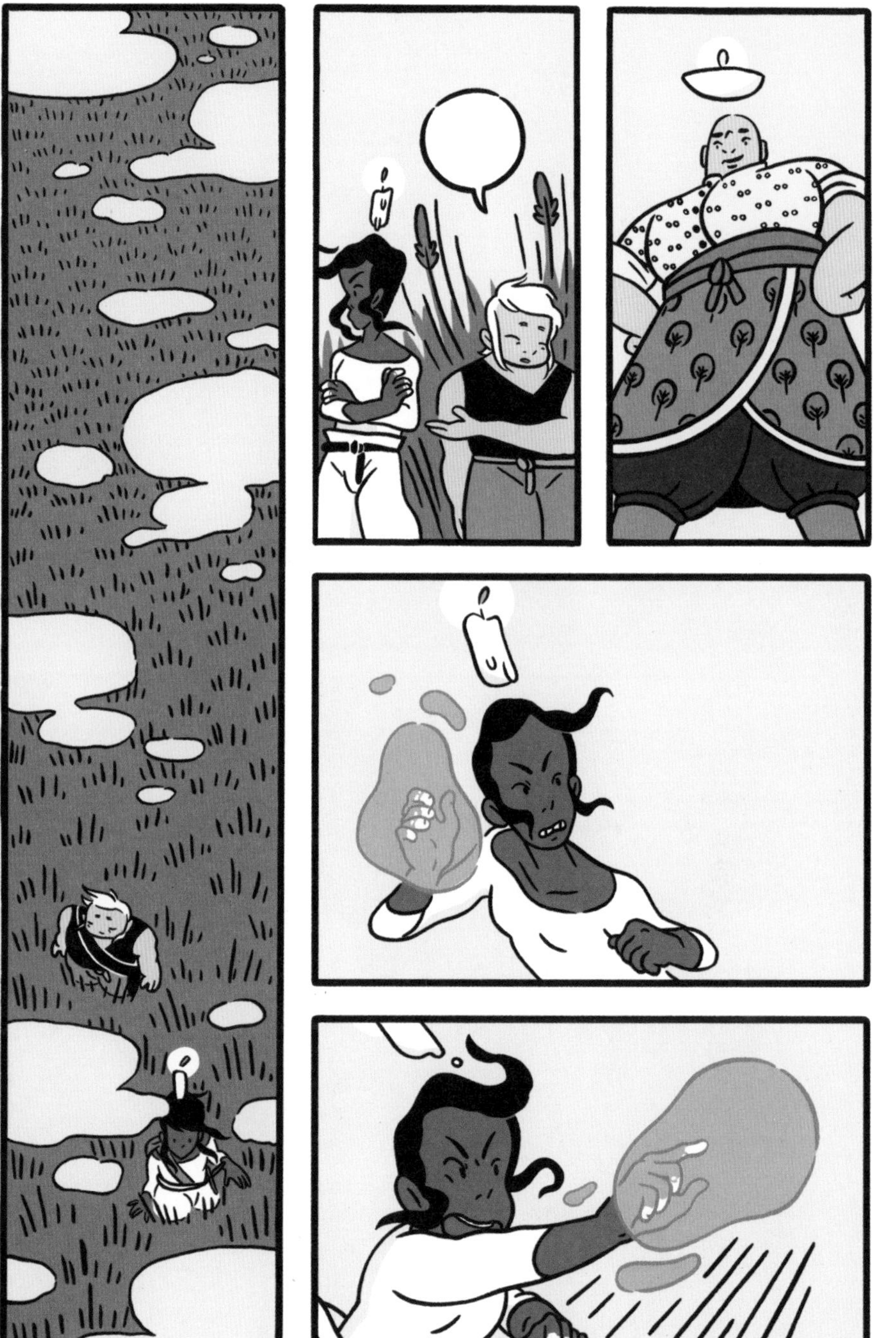

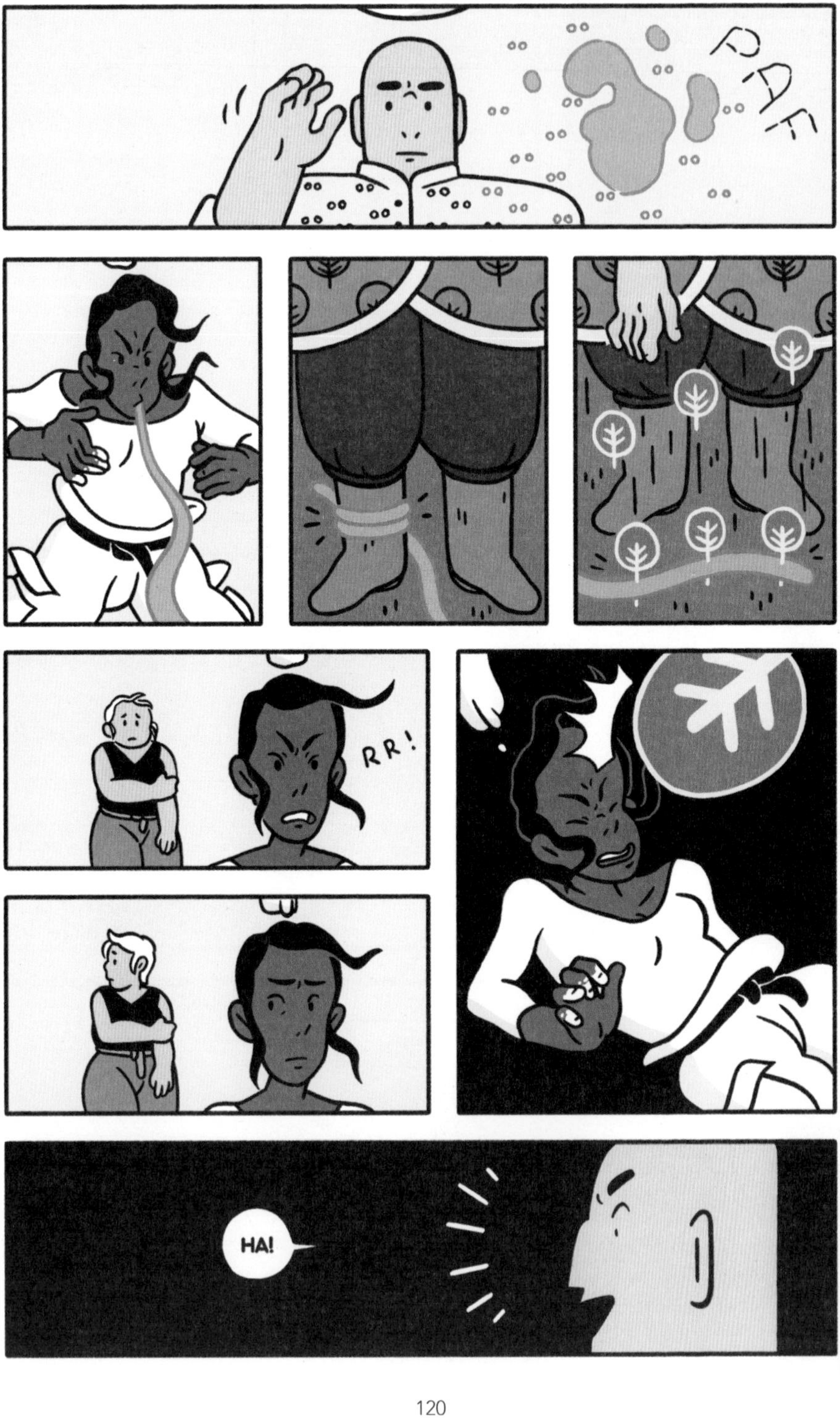
PAF
RR!
HA!

121

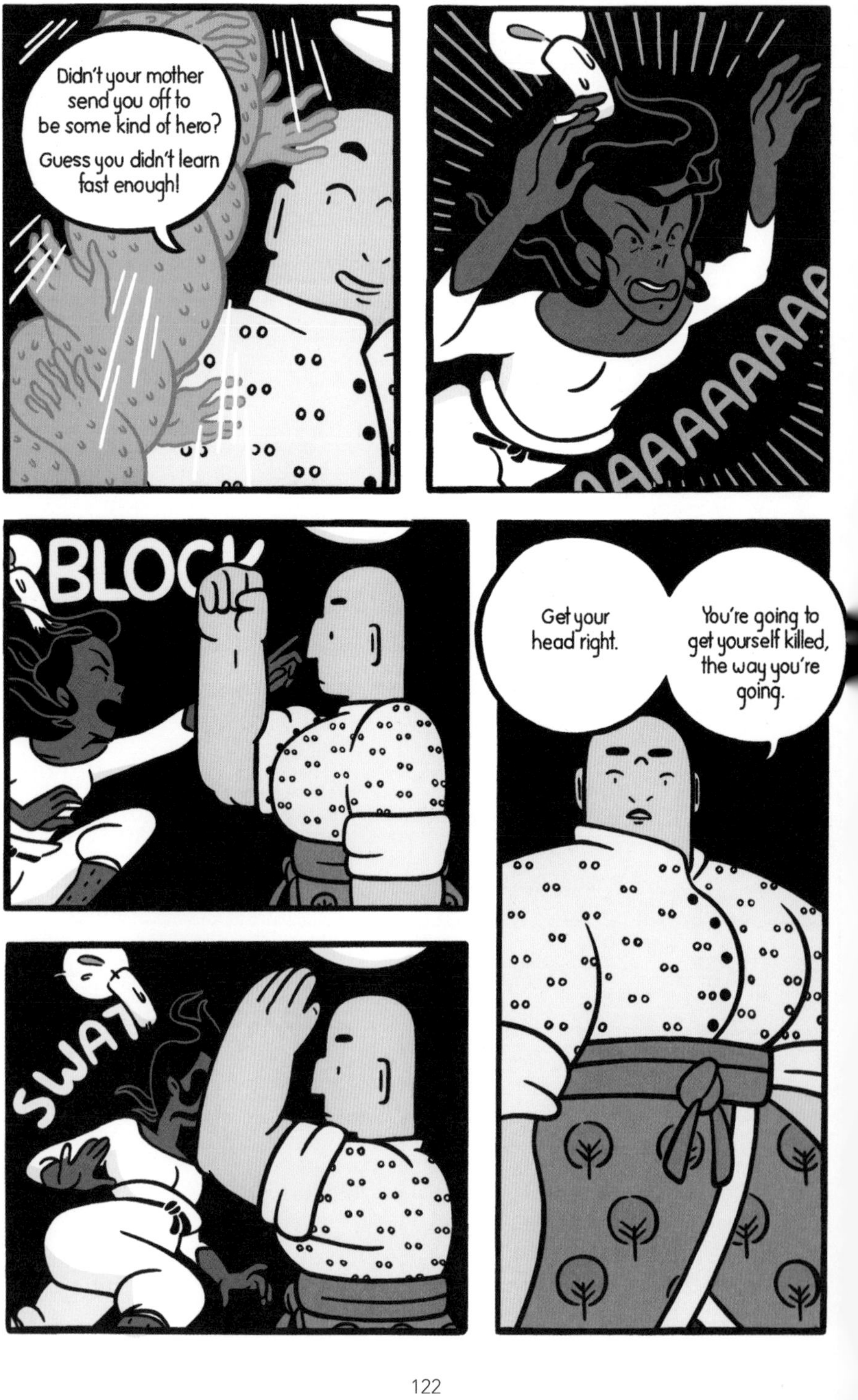
Didn't your mother send you off to be some kind of hero?
Guess you didn't learn fast enough!
AAAAAAAAAA
BLOC
Get your head right.
You're going to get yourself killed, the way you're going.
SWAT

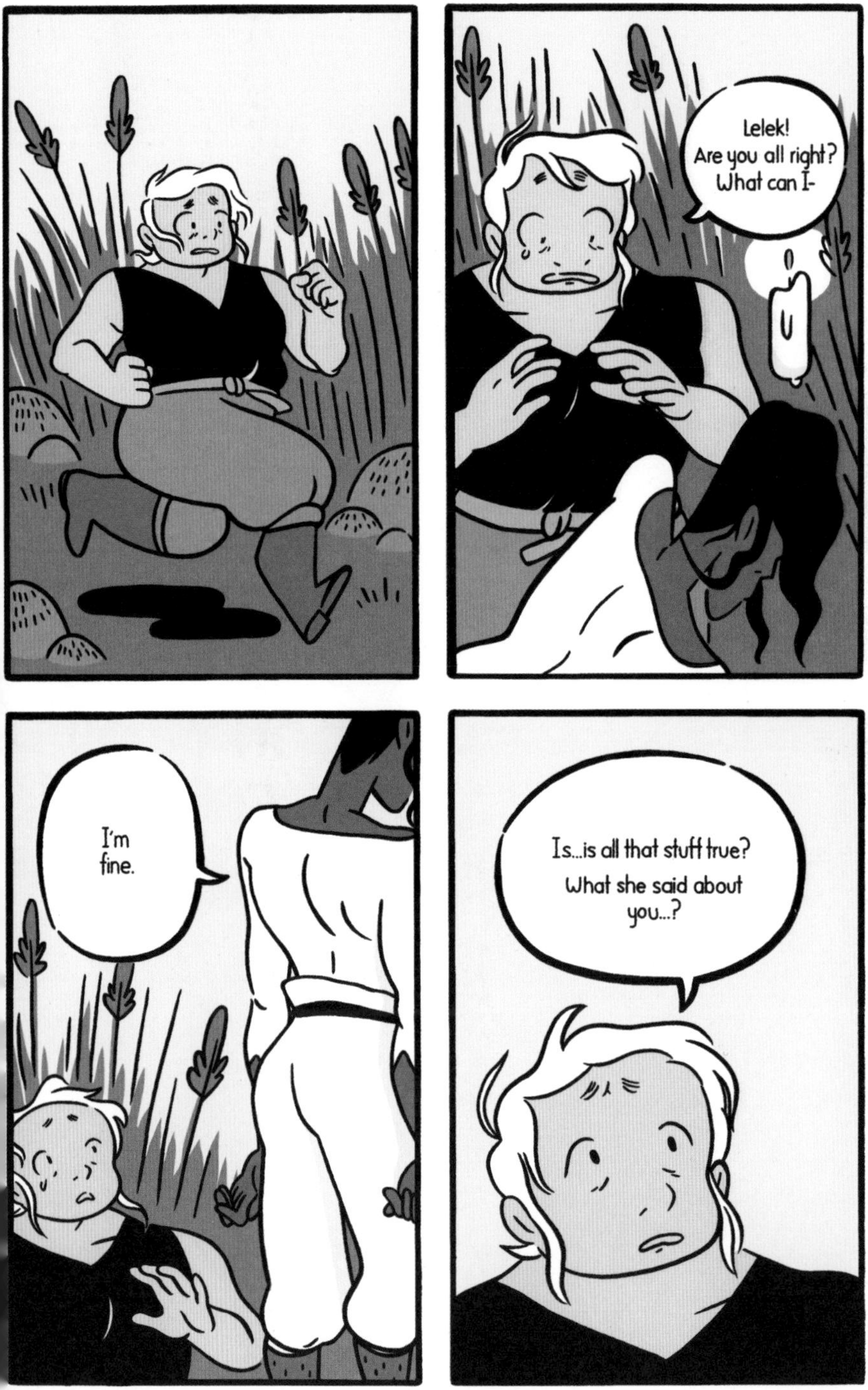
Lelek!
Are you all right?
What can I-
I'm fine.
Is...is all that stuff true?
What she said about you...?

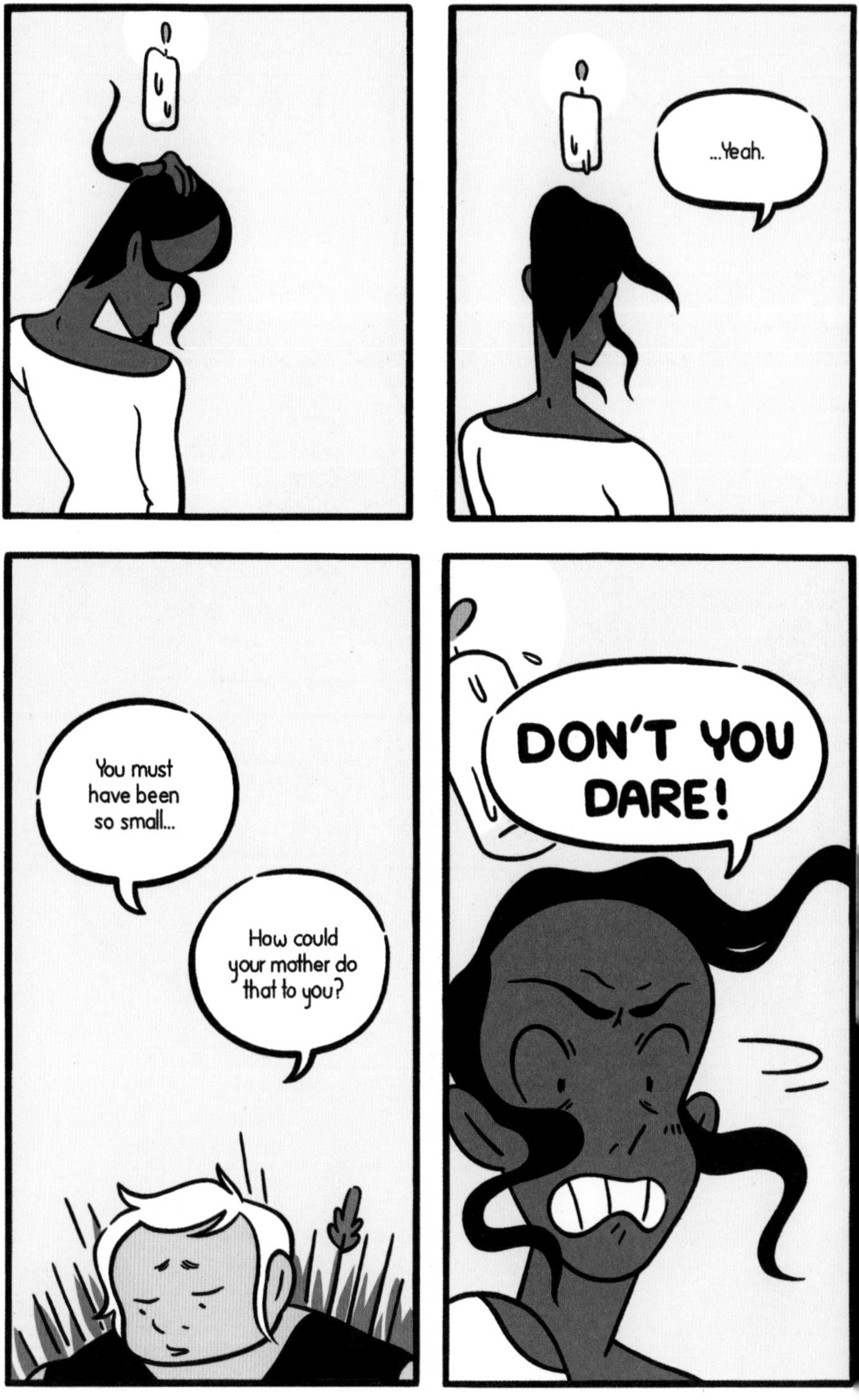
...Yeah.
You must have been so small...
How could your mother do that to you?
DON'T YOU DARE!

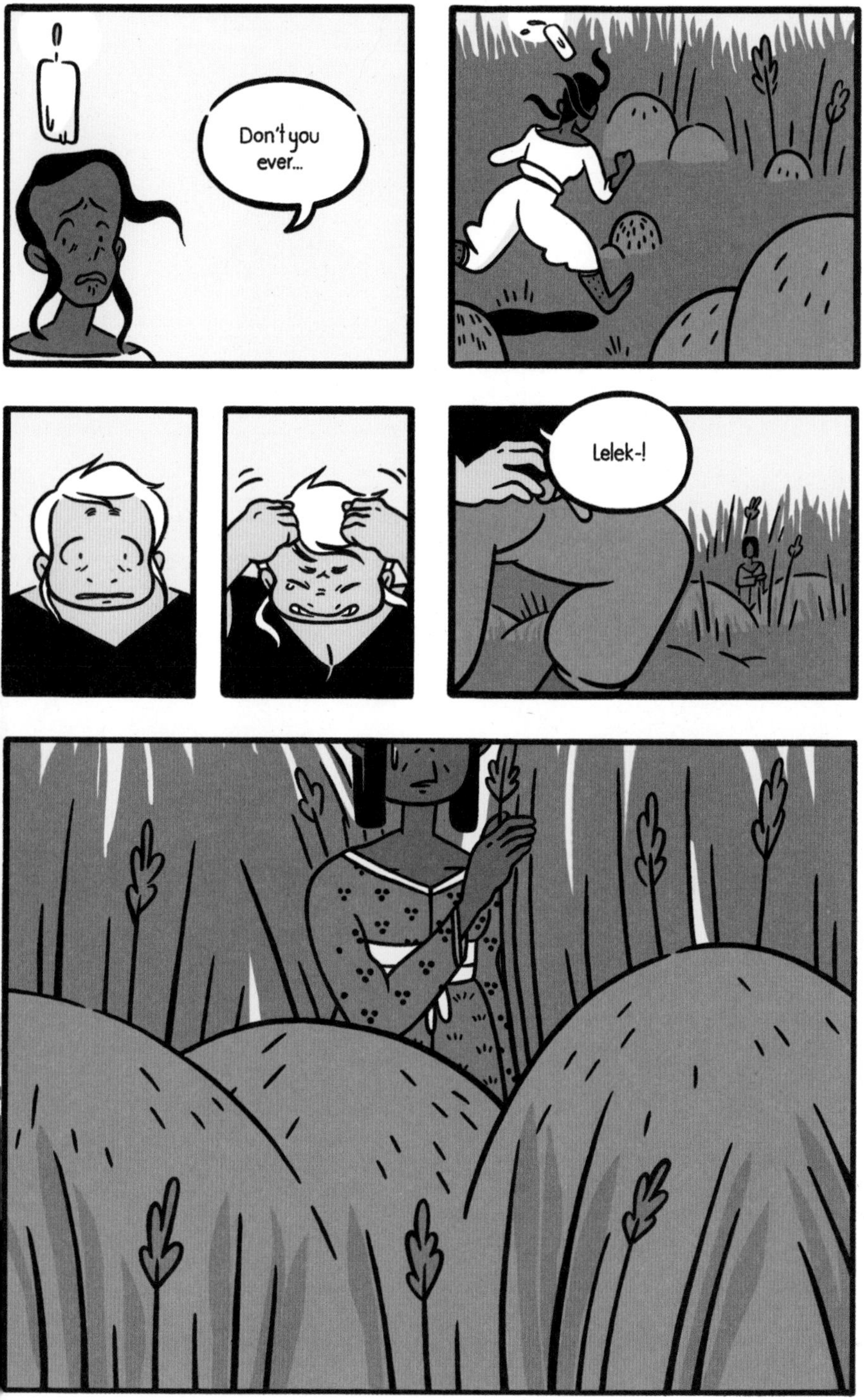
Don't you ever...
Lelek-!

Part 5

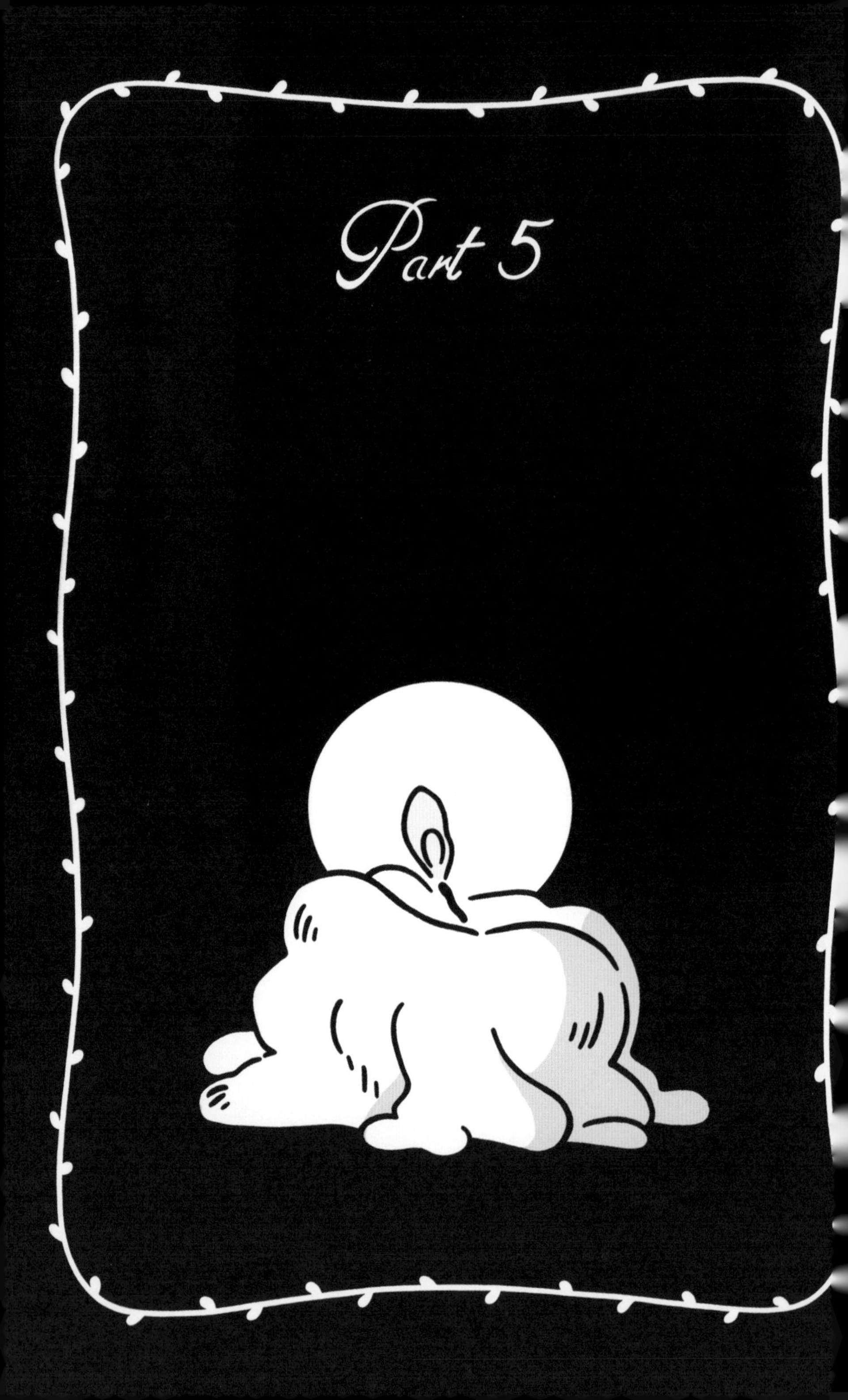

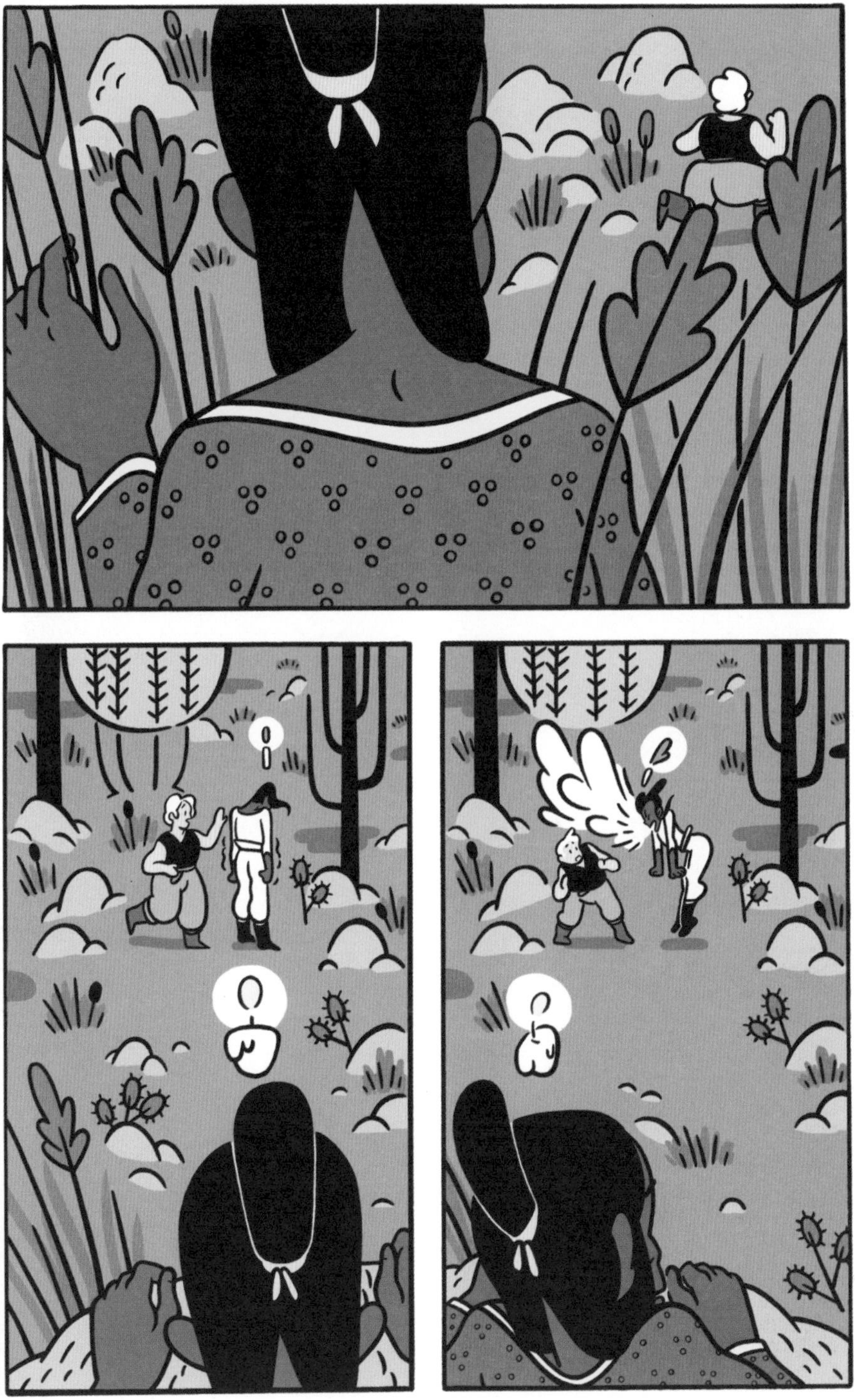

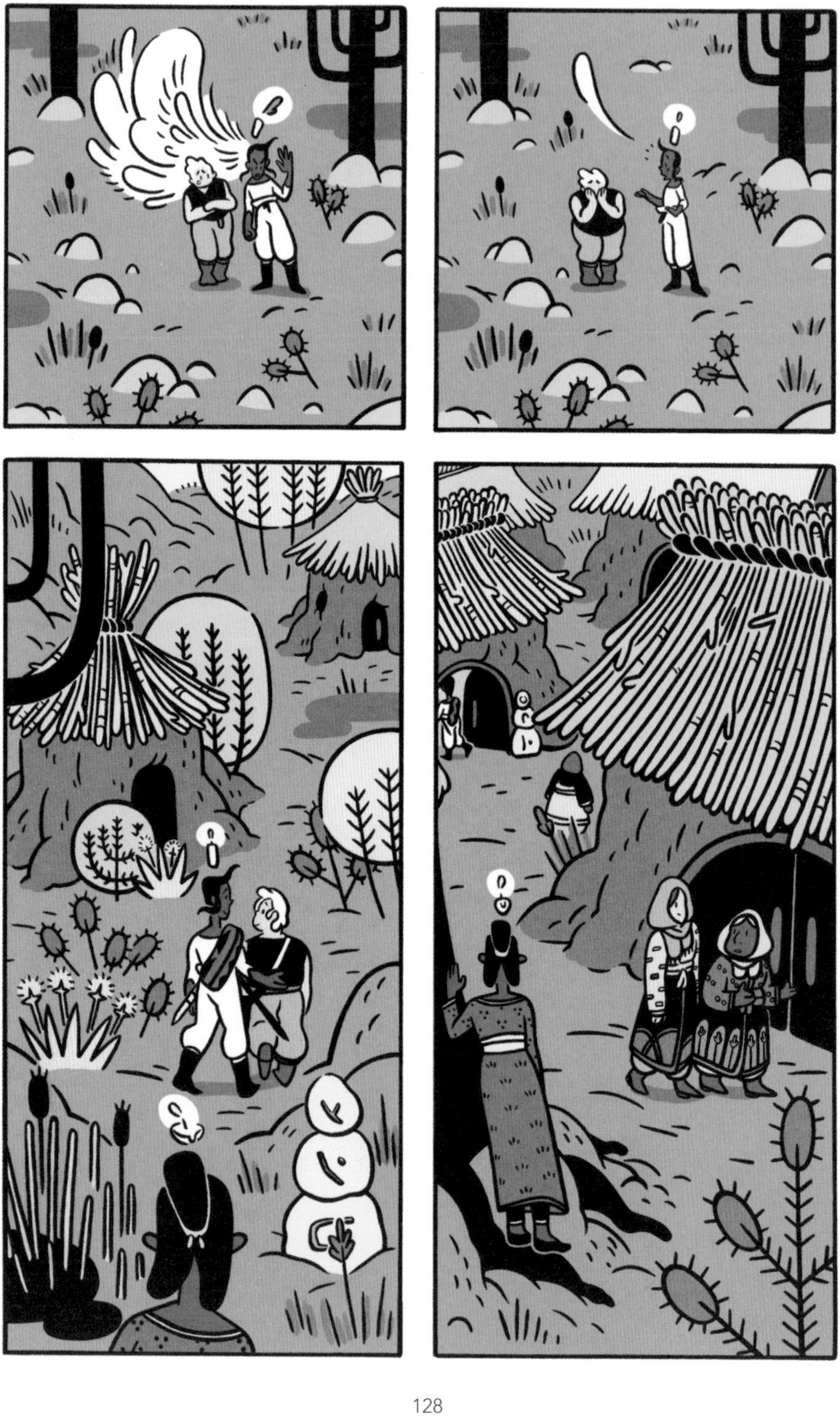

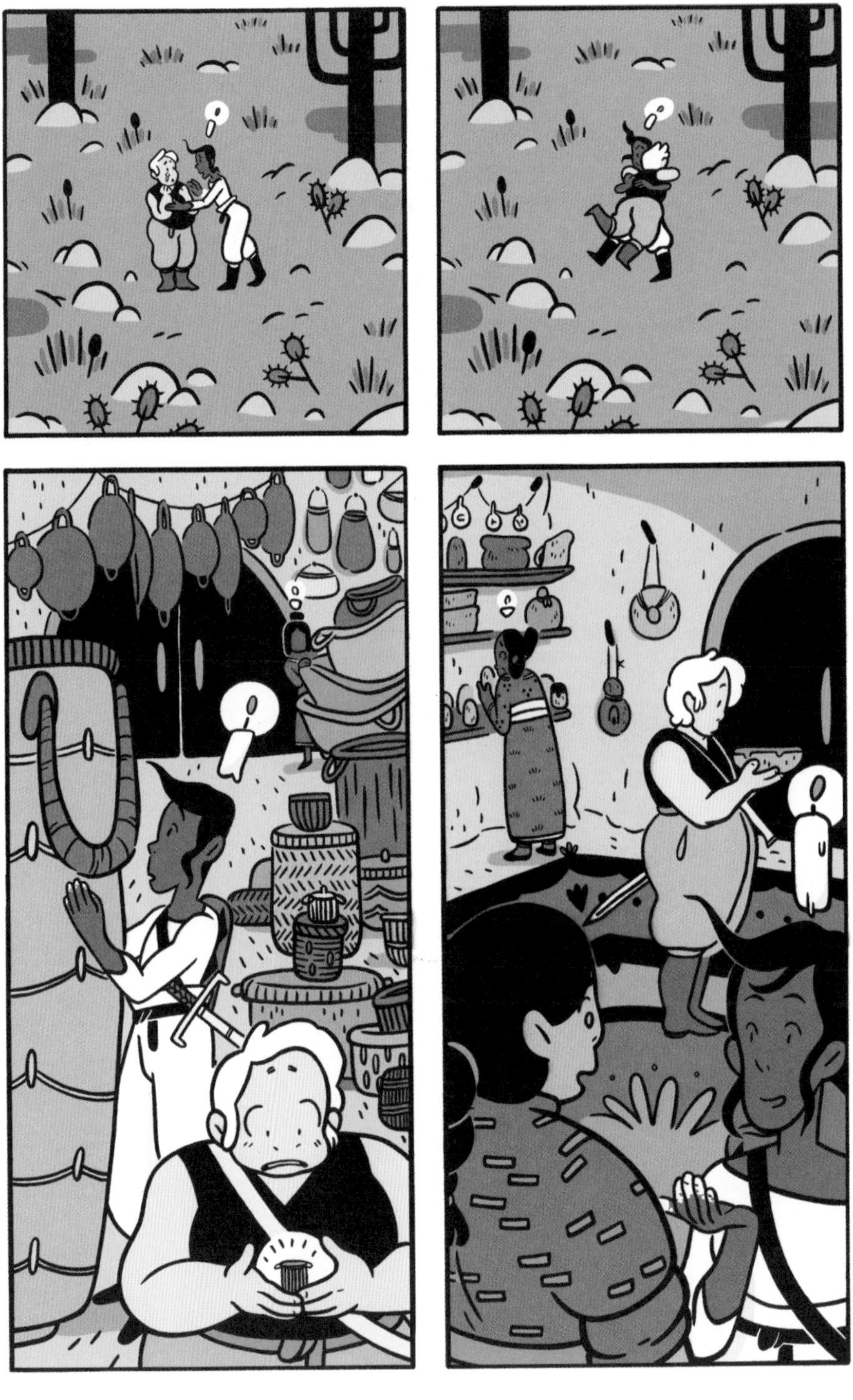

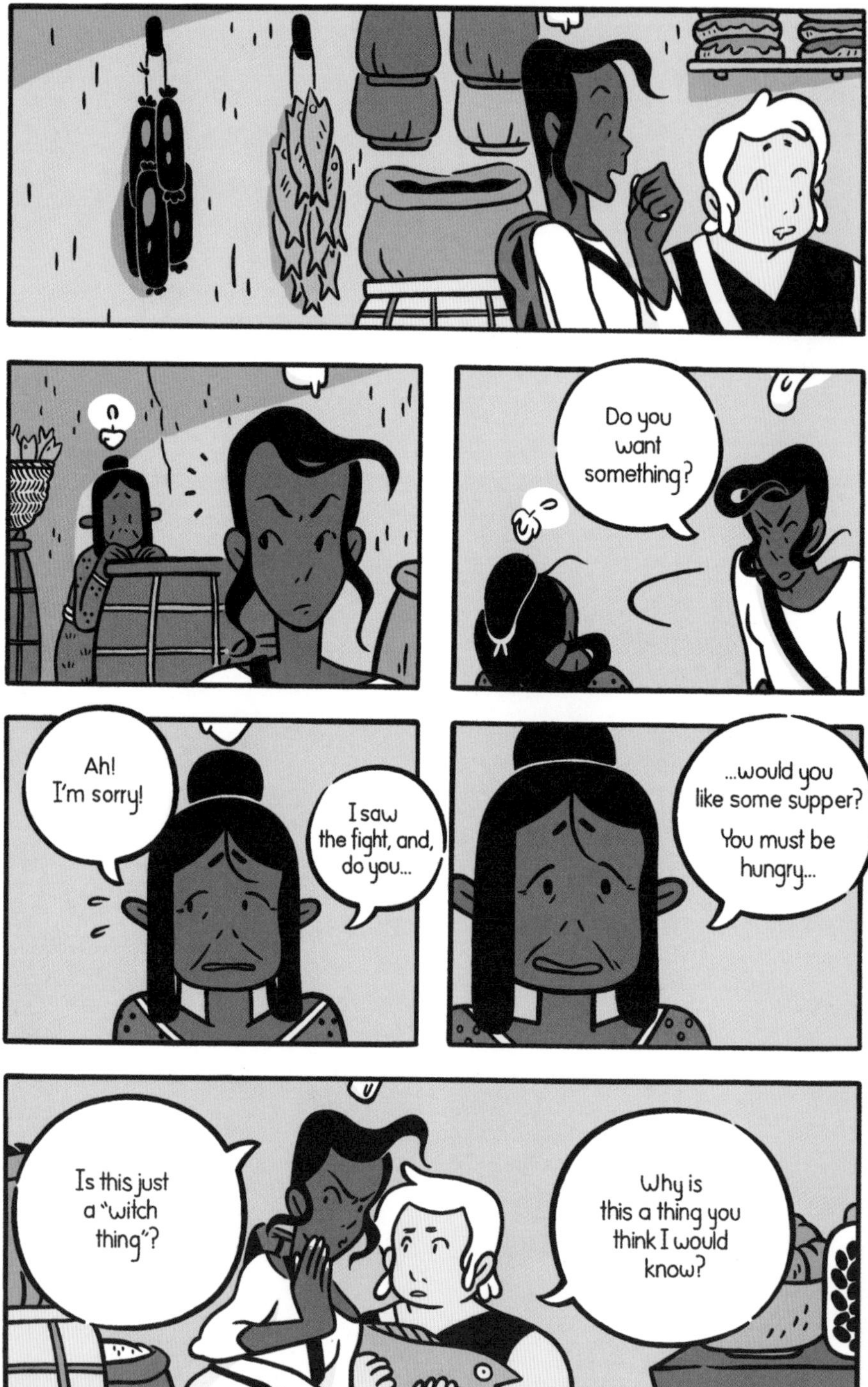
Do you want something?
Ah! I'm sorry!
I saw the fight, and, do you...
...would you like some supper?
You must be hungry...
Is this just a "witch thing"?
Why is this a thing you think I would know?

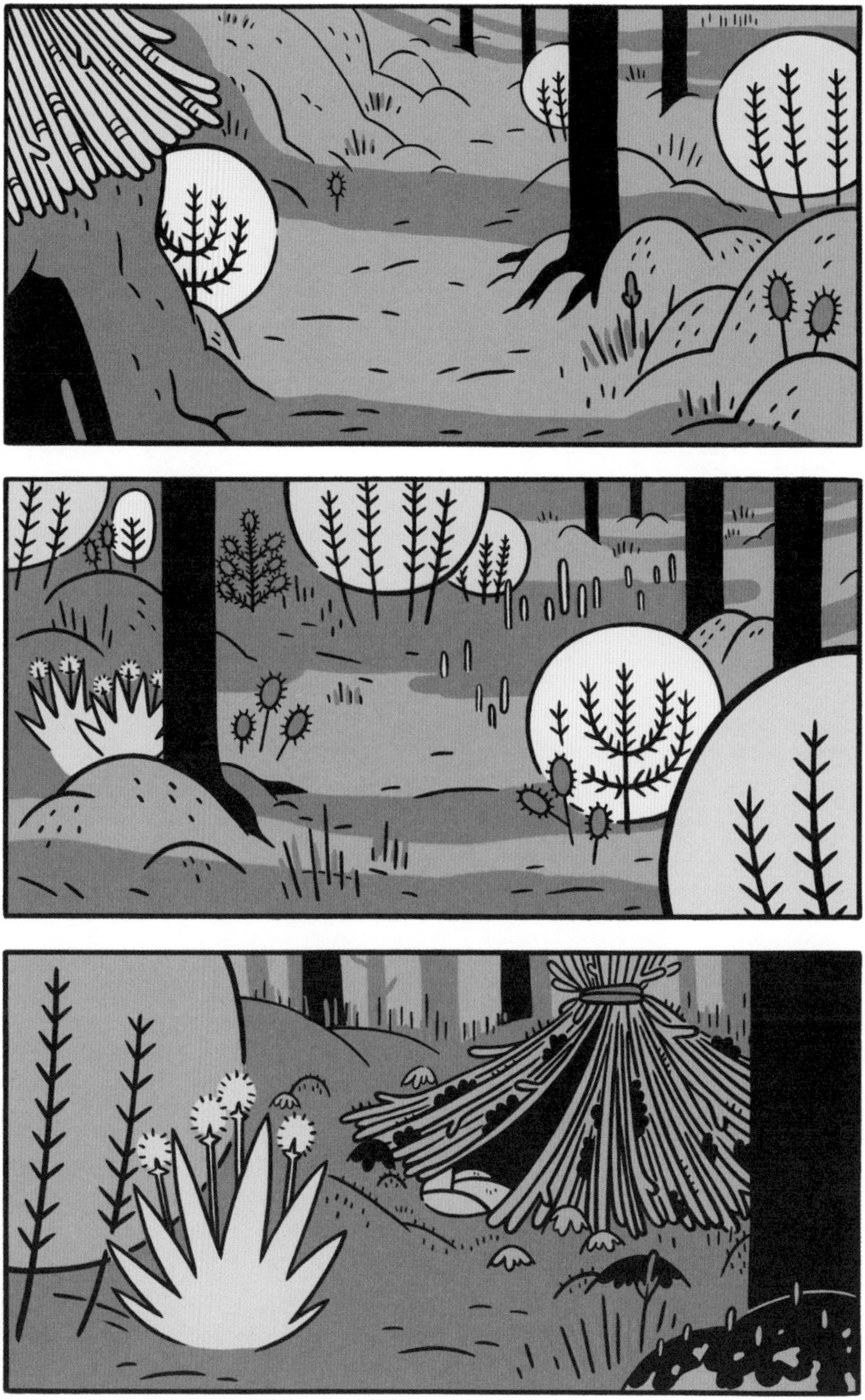

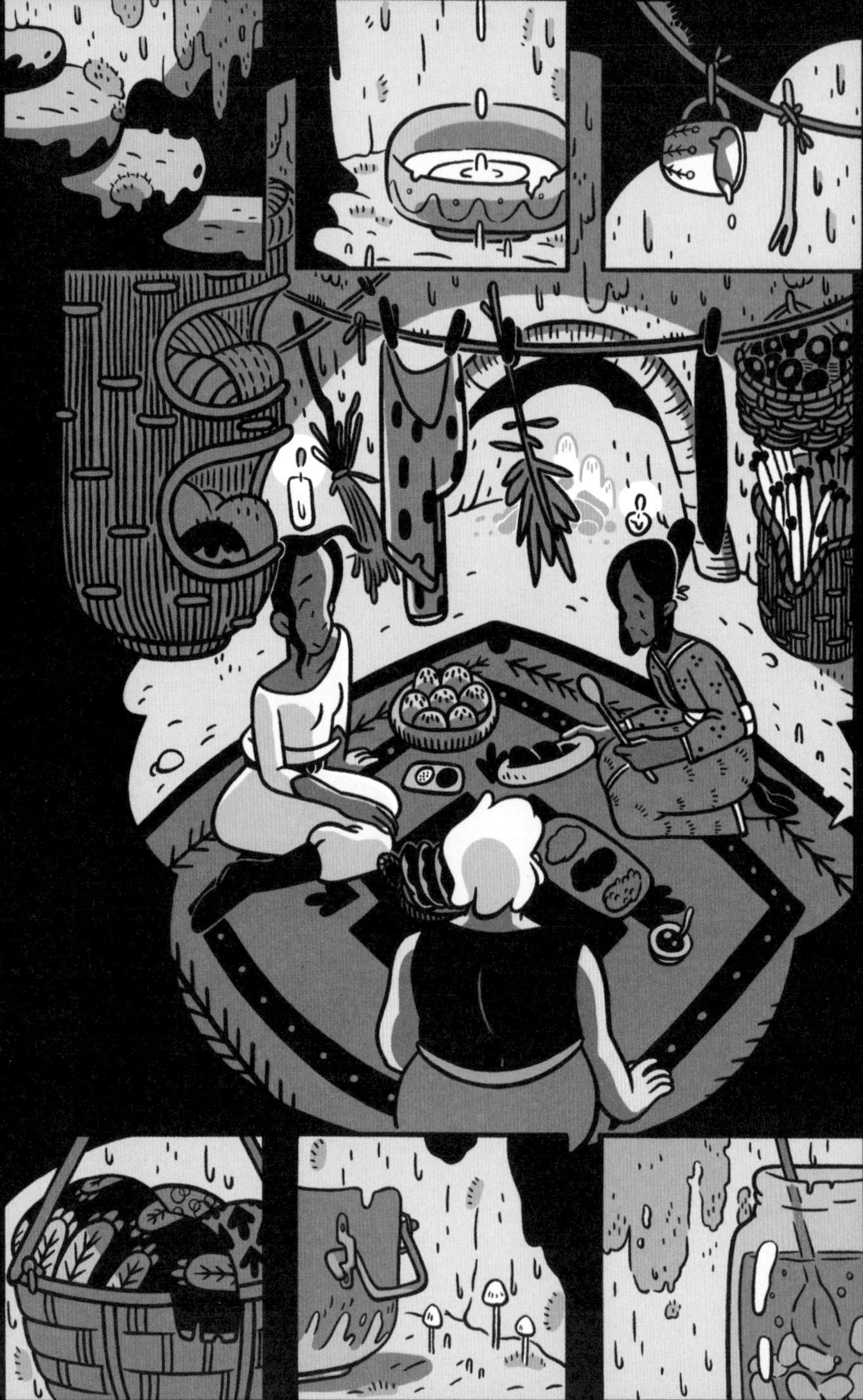

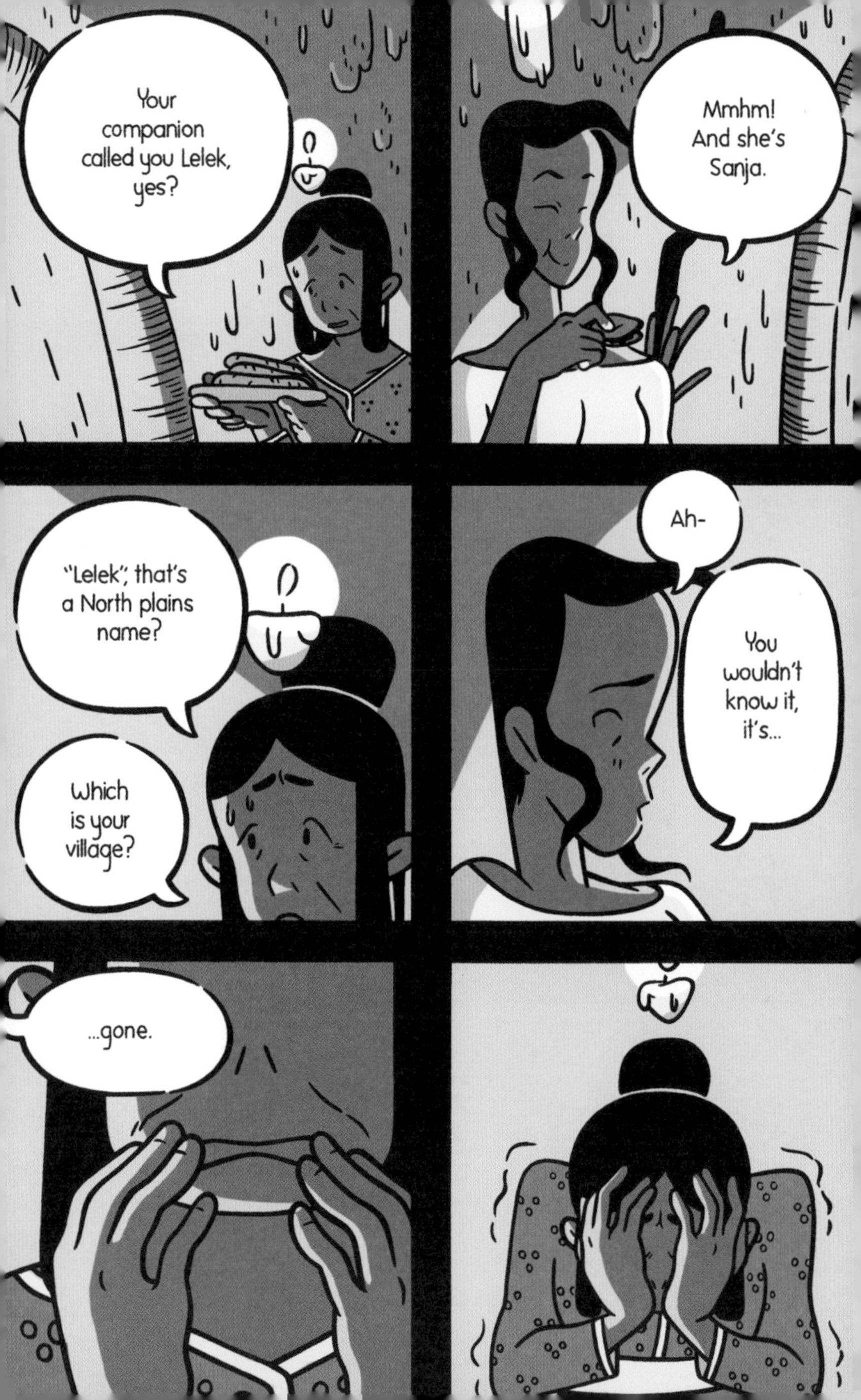
Your companion called you Lelek, yes?
Mmhm! And she's Sanja.
"Lelek"; that's a North plains name?
Which is your village?
Ah-
You wouldn't know it, it's...
...gone.

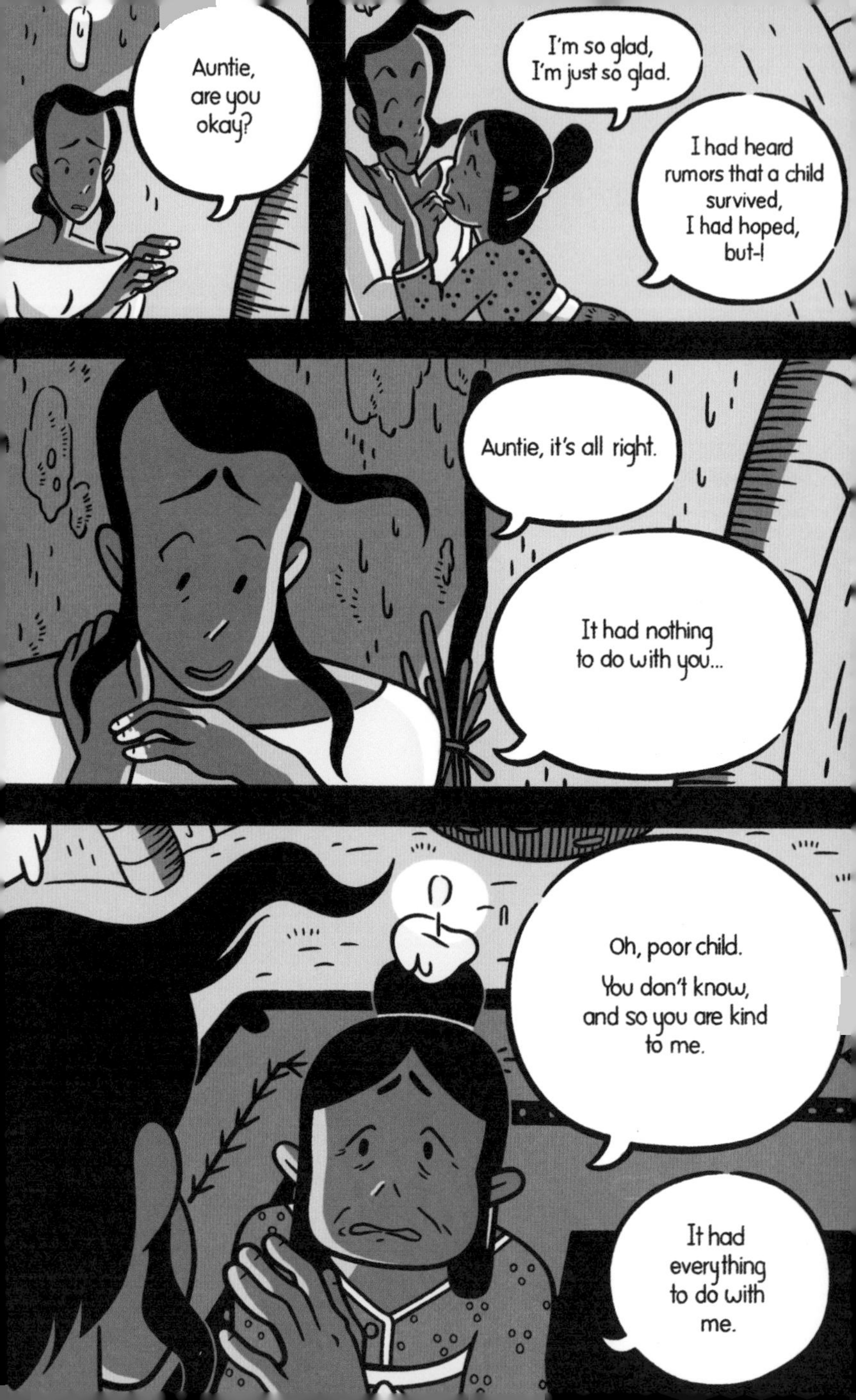
Auntie,
are you
okay?
I'm so glad,
I'm just so glad.
I had heard
rumors that a child
survived,
I had hoped,
but-!
Auntie, it's all right.
It had nothing
to do with you...
Oh, poor child.
You don't know,
and so you are kind
to me.
It had
everything
to do with
me.

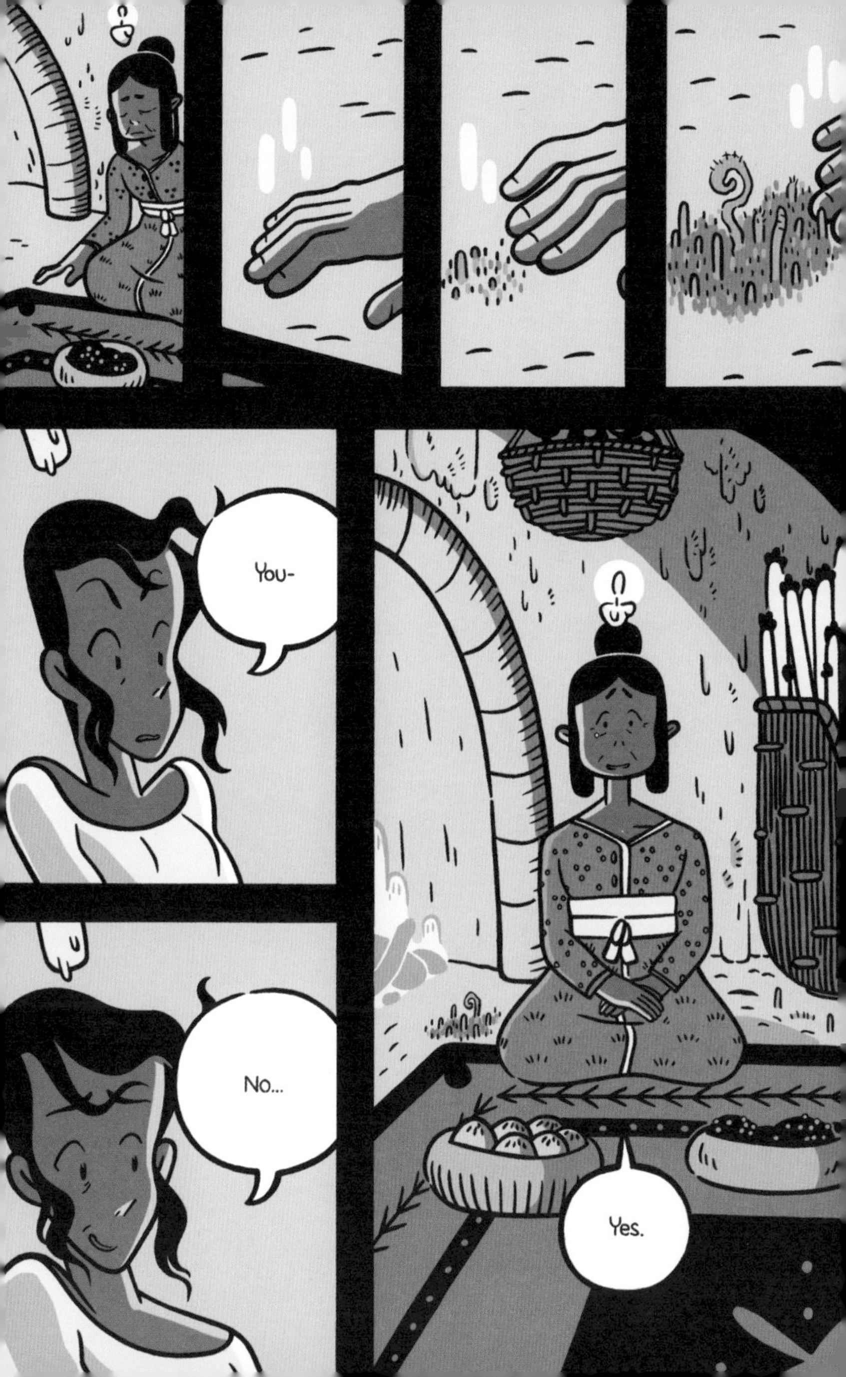
You-
No...
Yes.

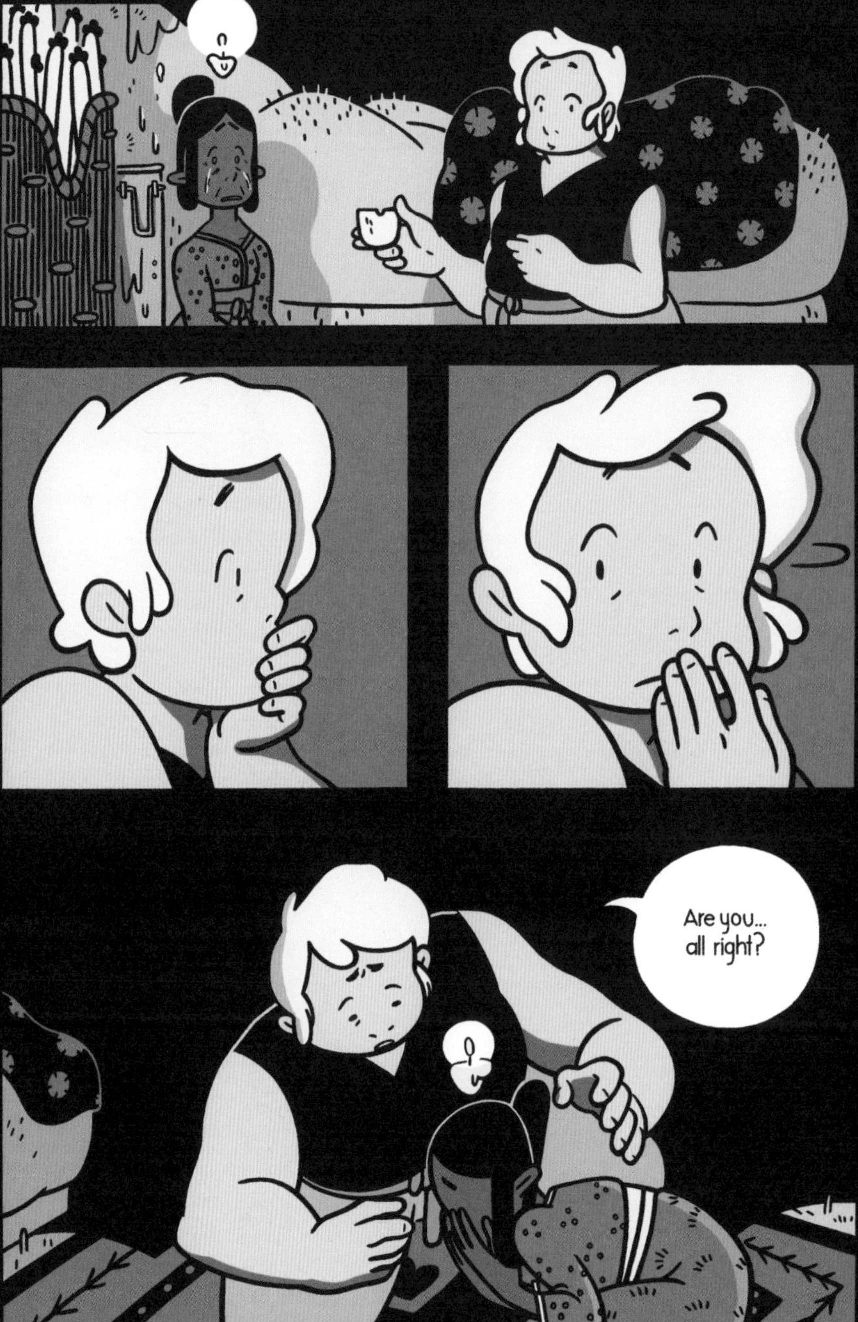
Are you...
all right?

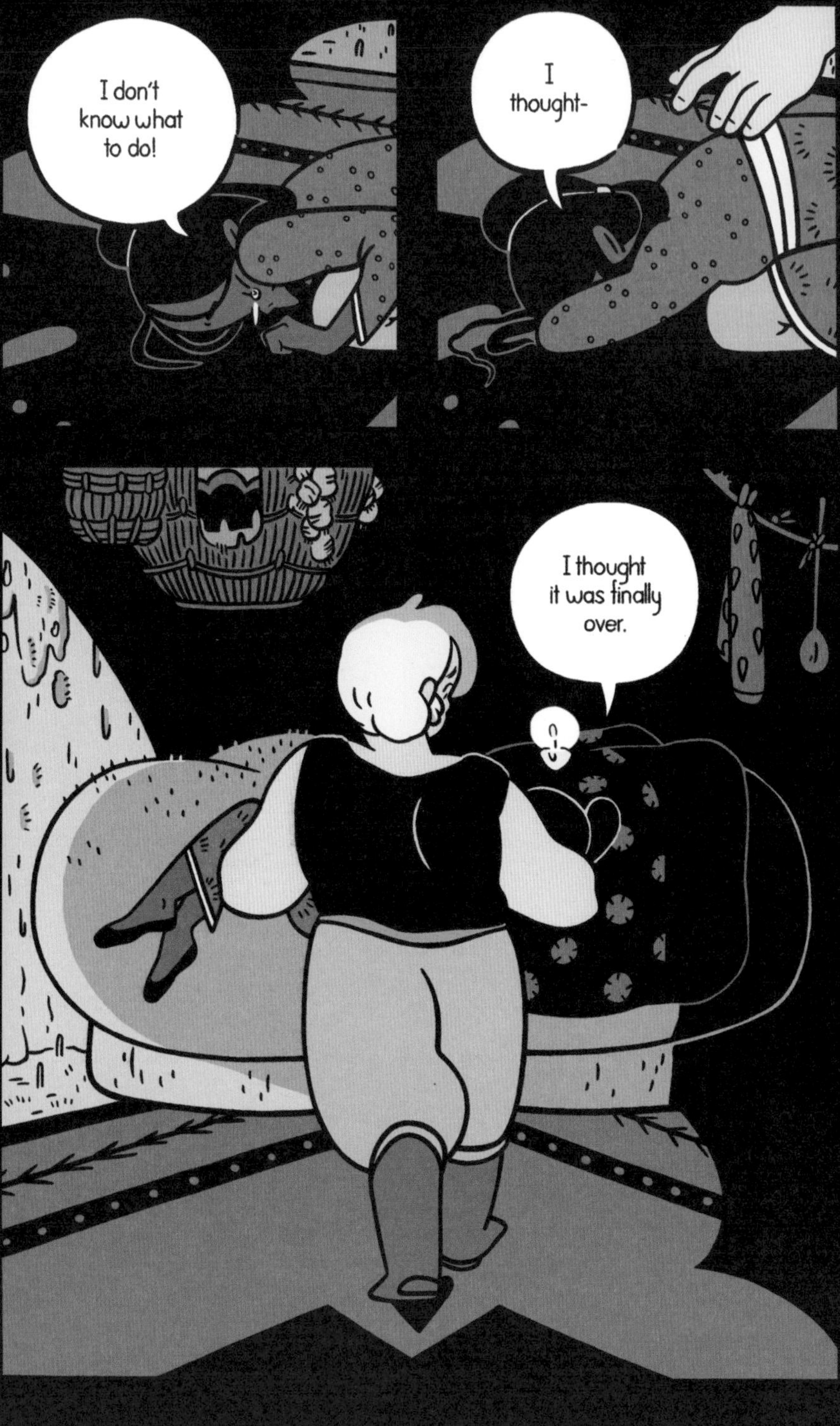
I don't know what to do!
I thought-
I thought it was finally over.

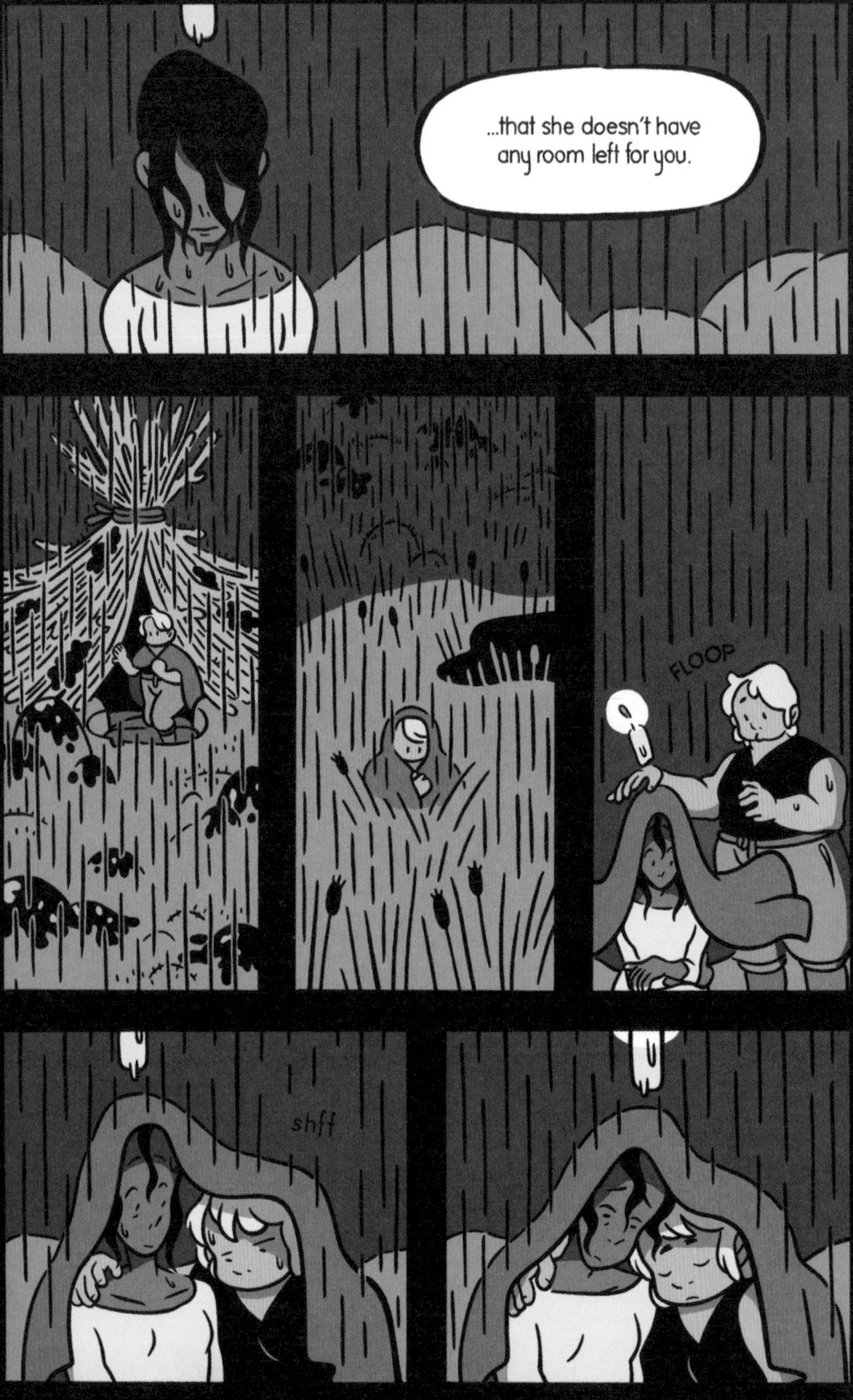

...that she doesn't have any room left for you.
FLOOP
shff

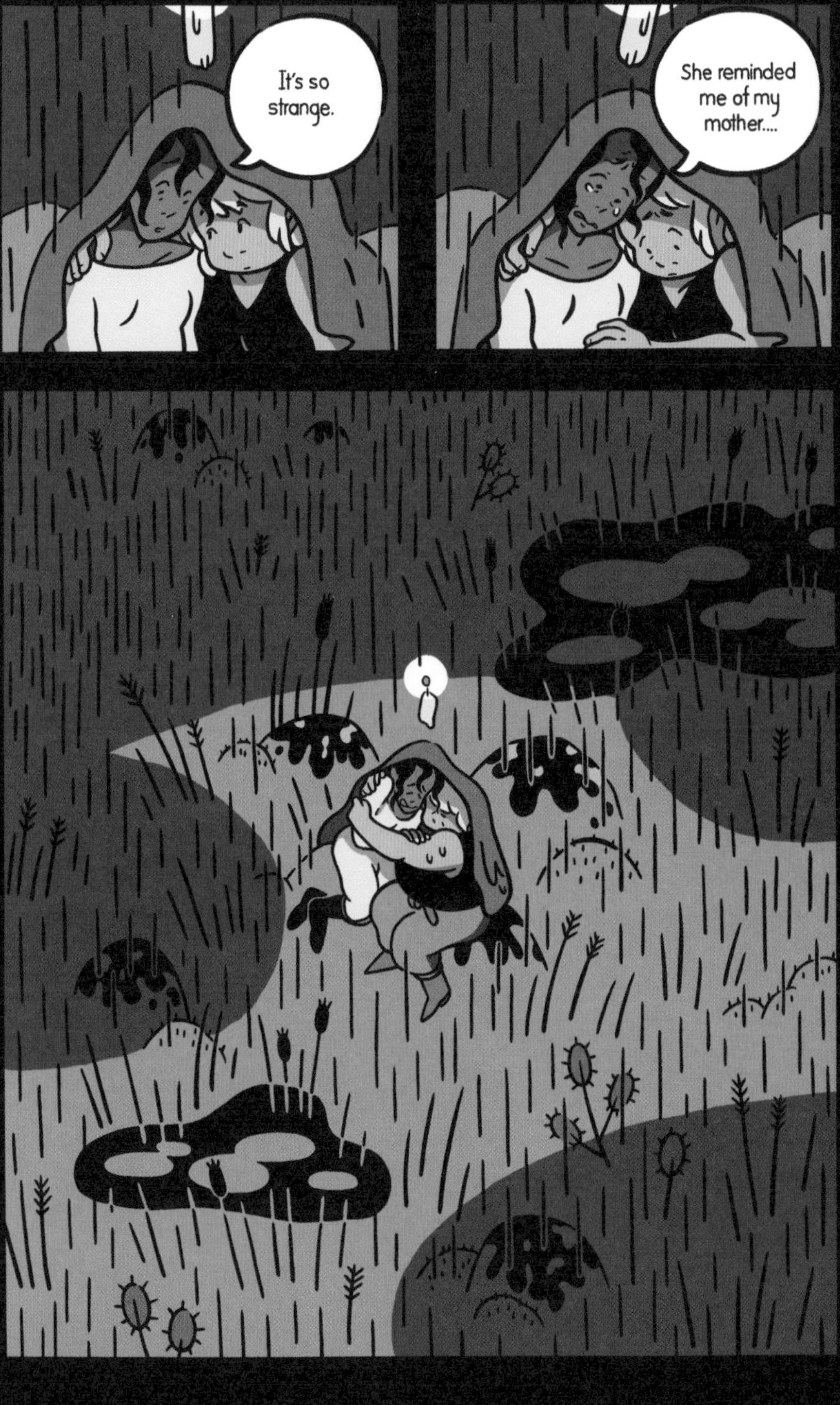
It's so strange.
She reminded me of my mother....

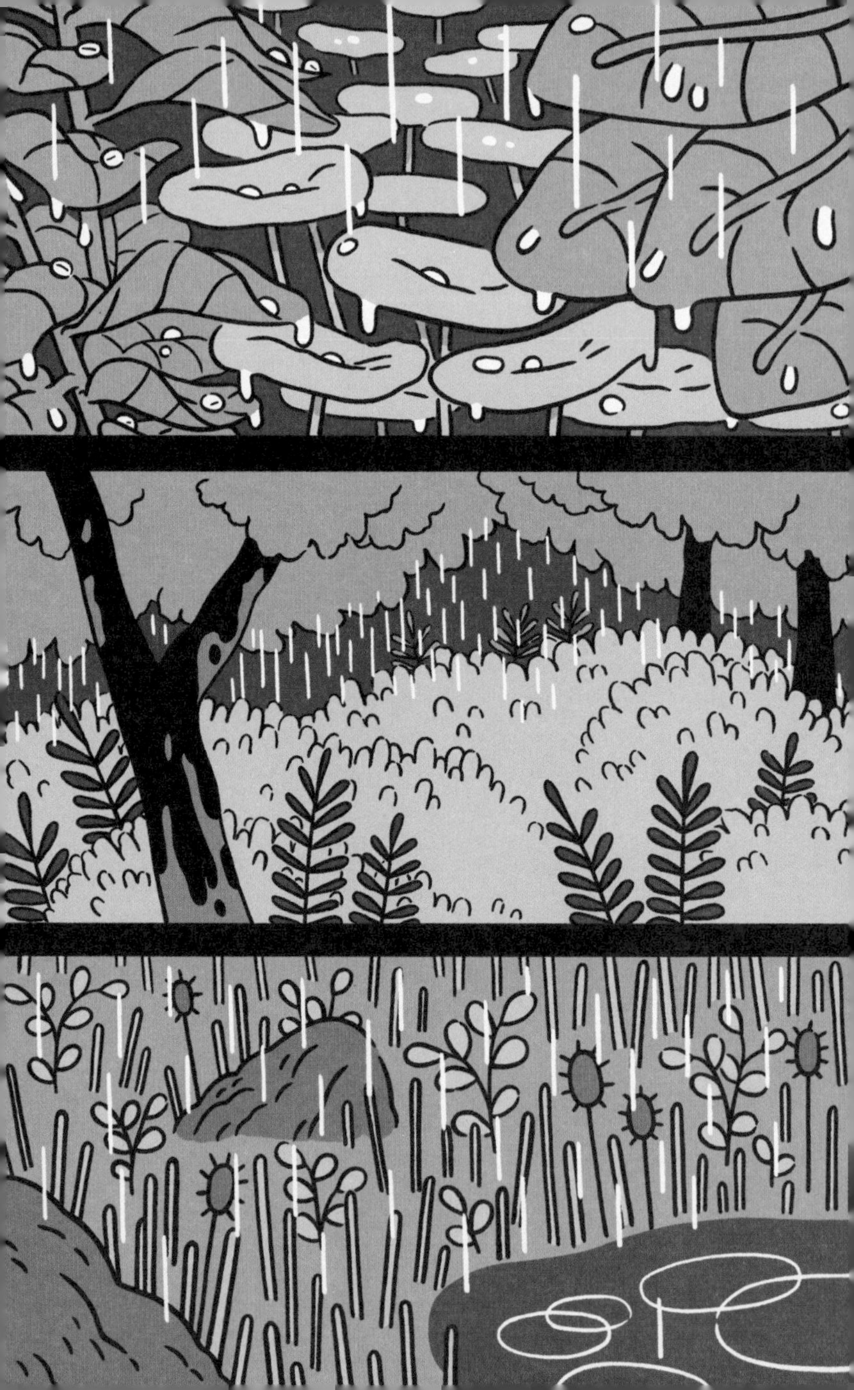

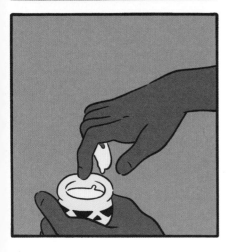

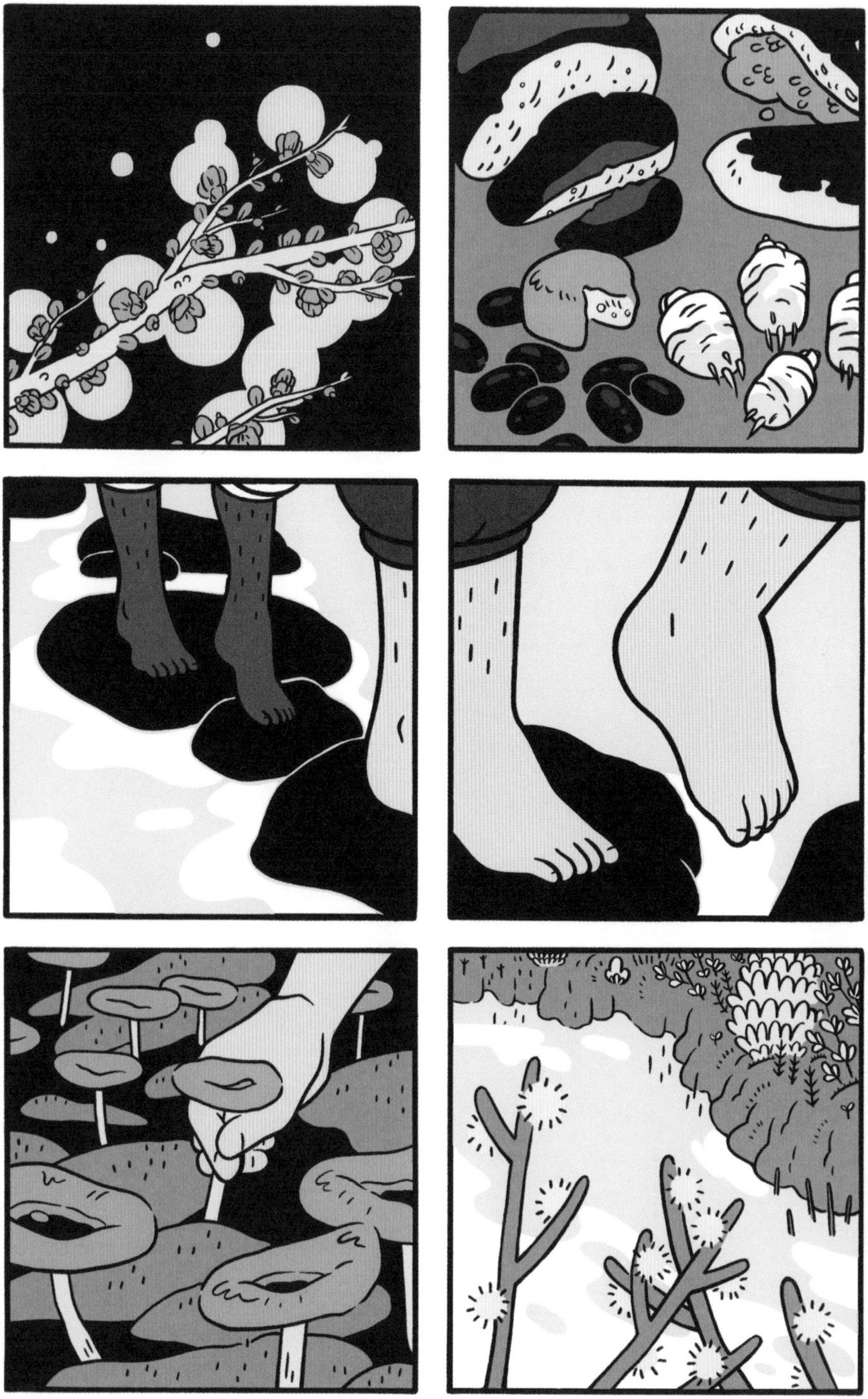

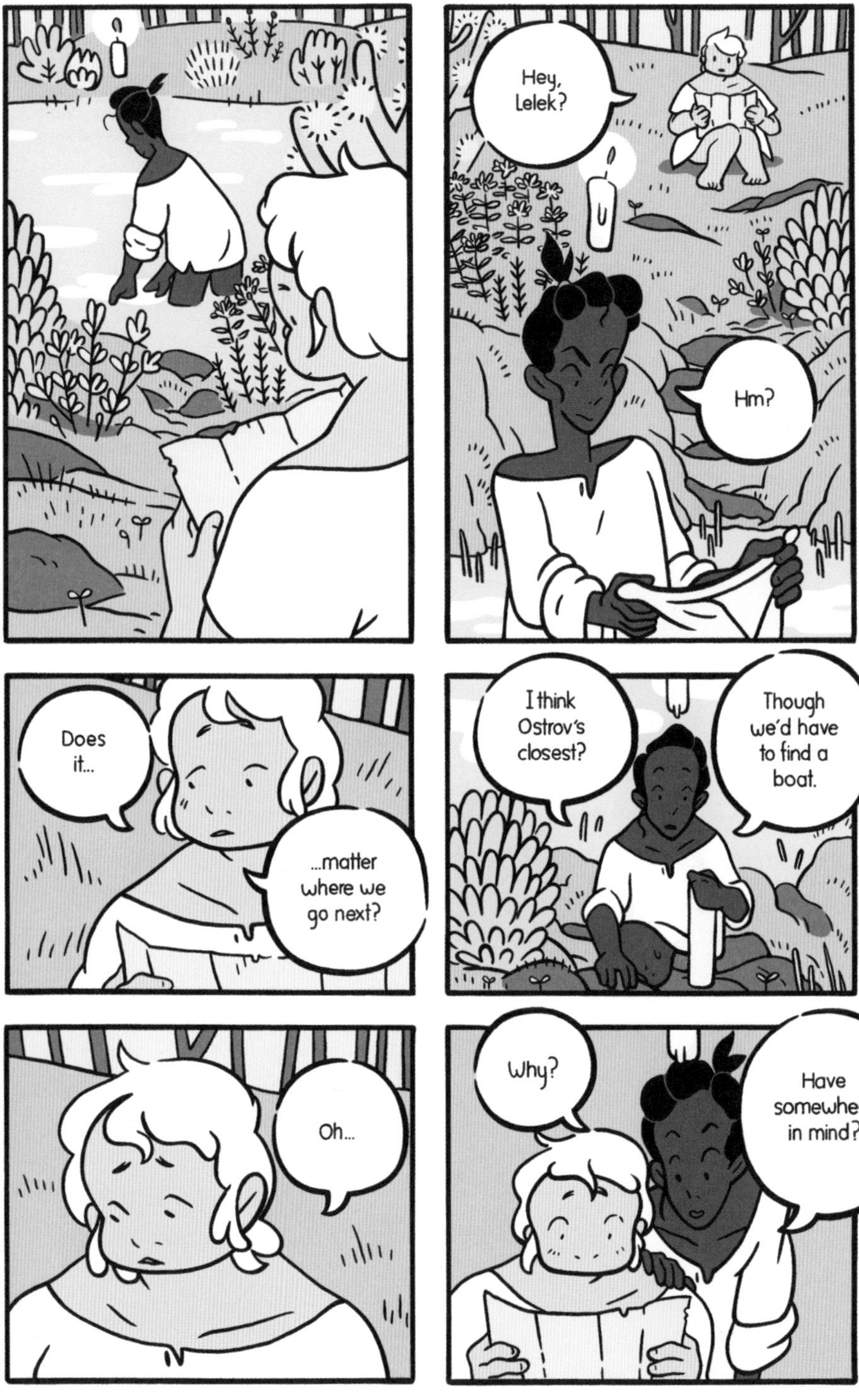
Hey, Lelek?
Hm?
Does it...
...matter where we go next?
I think Ostrov's closest?
Though we'd have to find a boat.
Oh...
Why?
Have somewhere in mind?

148

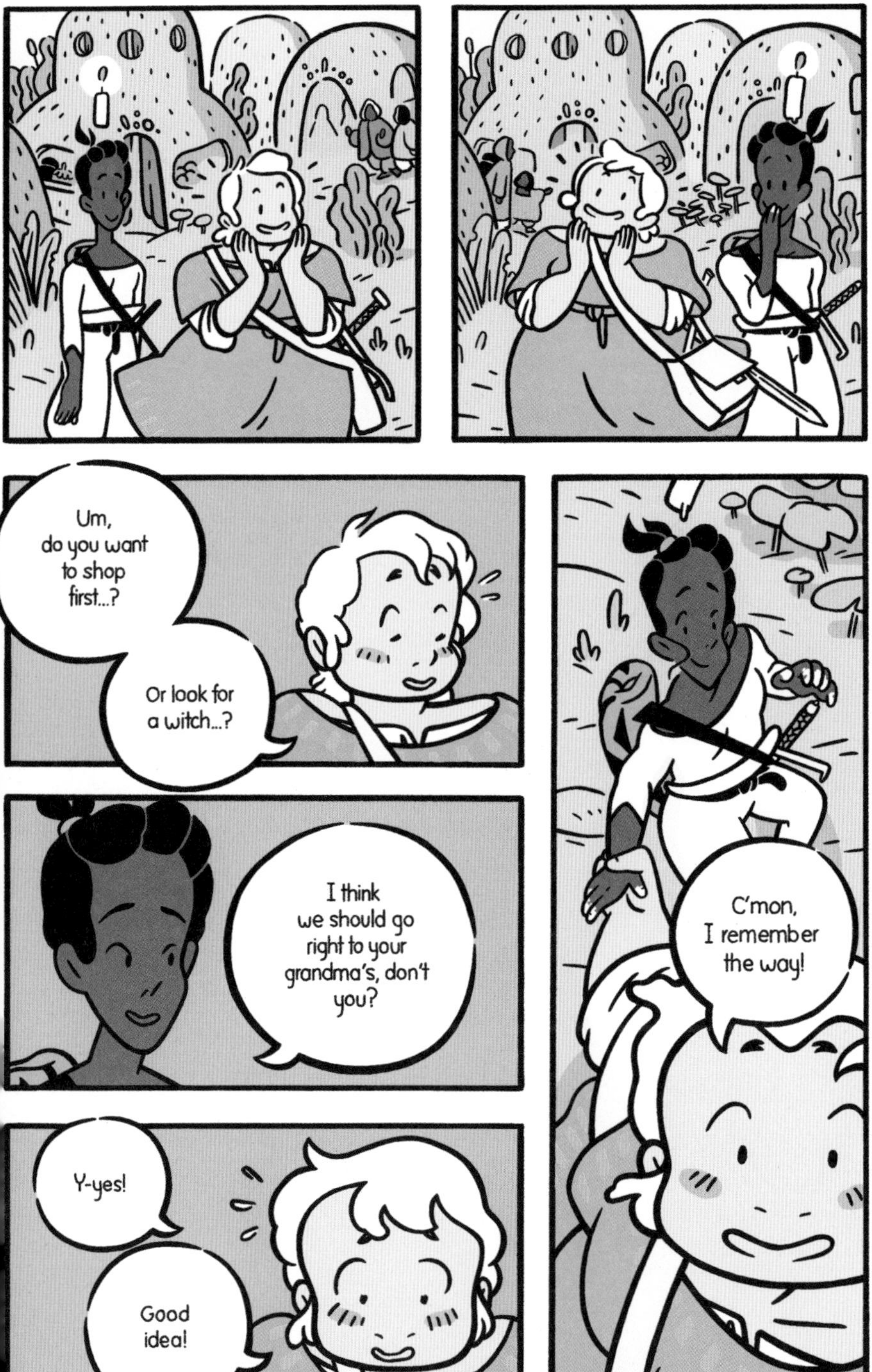
Um, do you want to shop first...?
Or look for a witch...?
I think we should go right to your grandma's, don't you?
Y-yes!
Good idea!
C'mon, I remember the way!

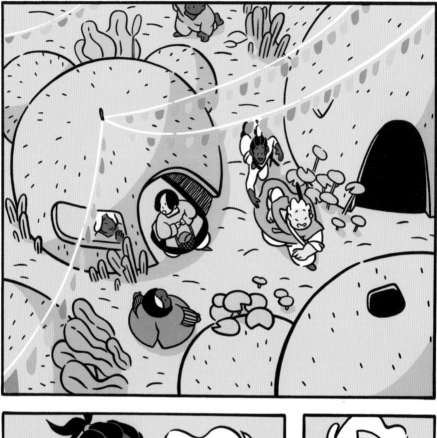

OOF

ha ha
ha ha
ha

Now, who could these two silly girls in my garden be?

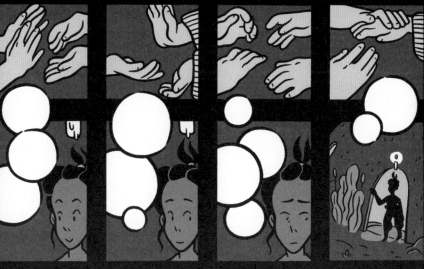

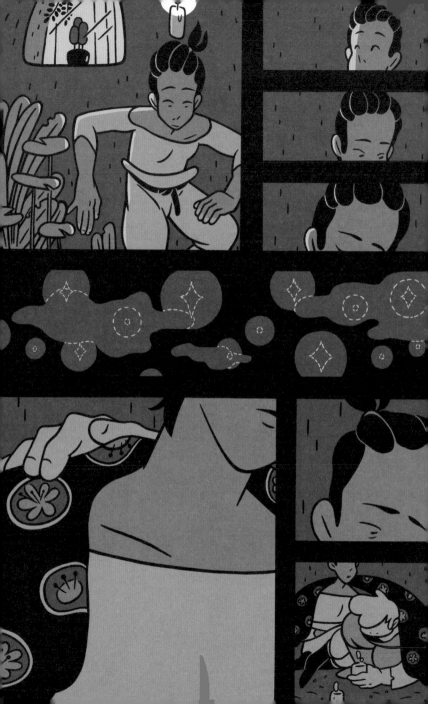

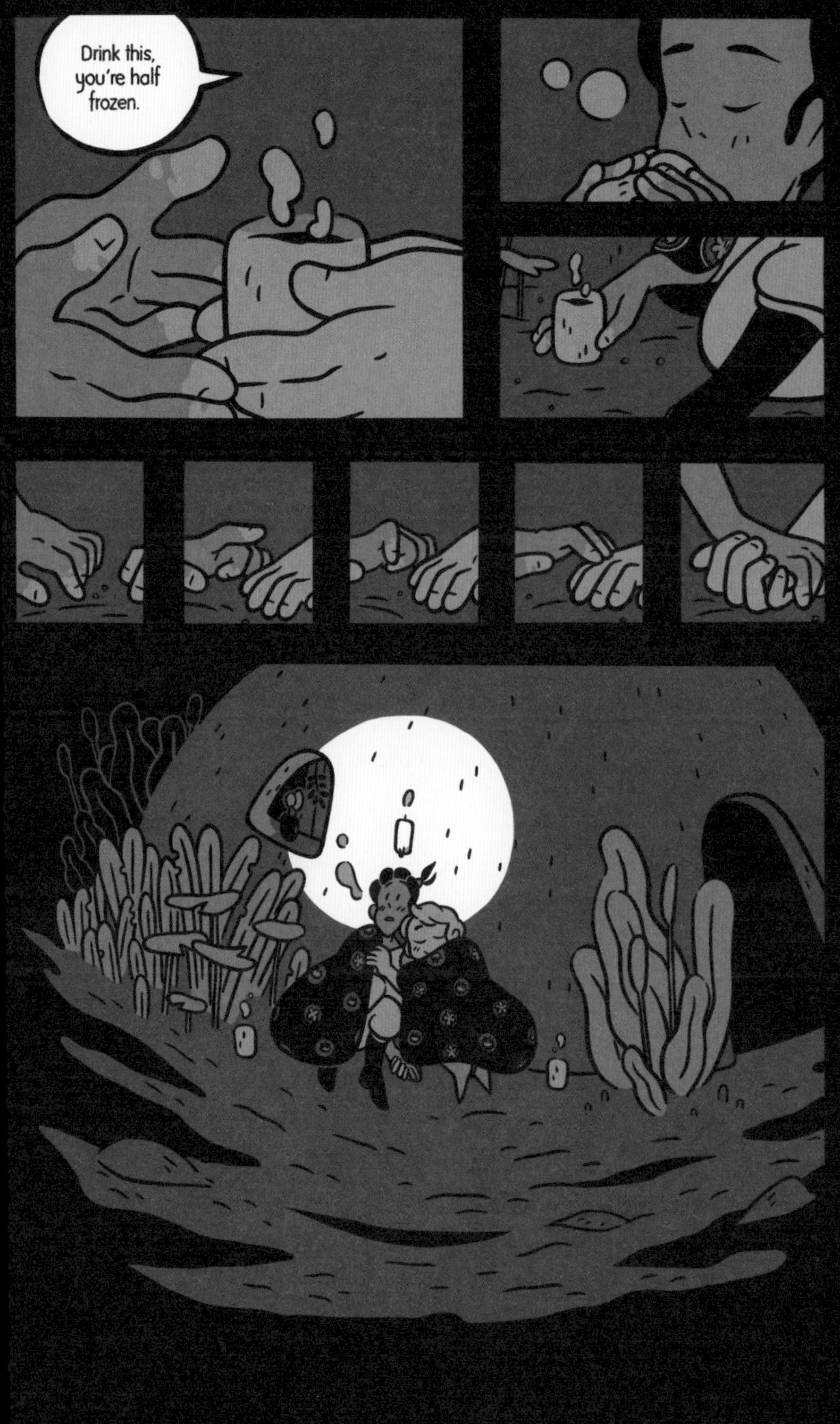
Drink this, you're half frozen.

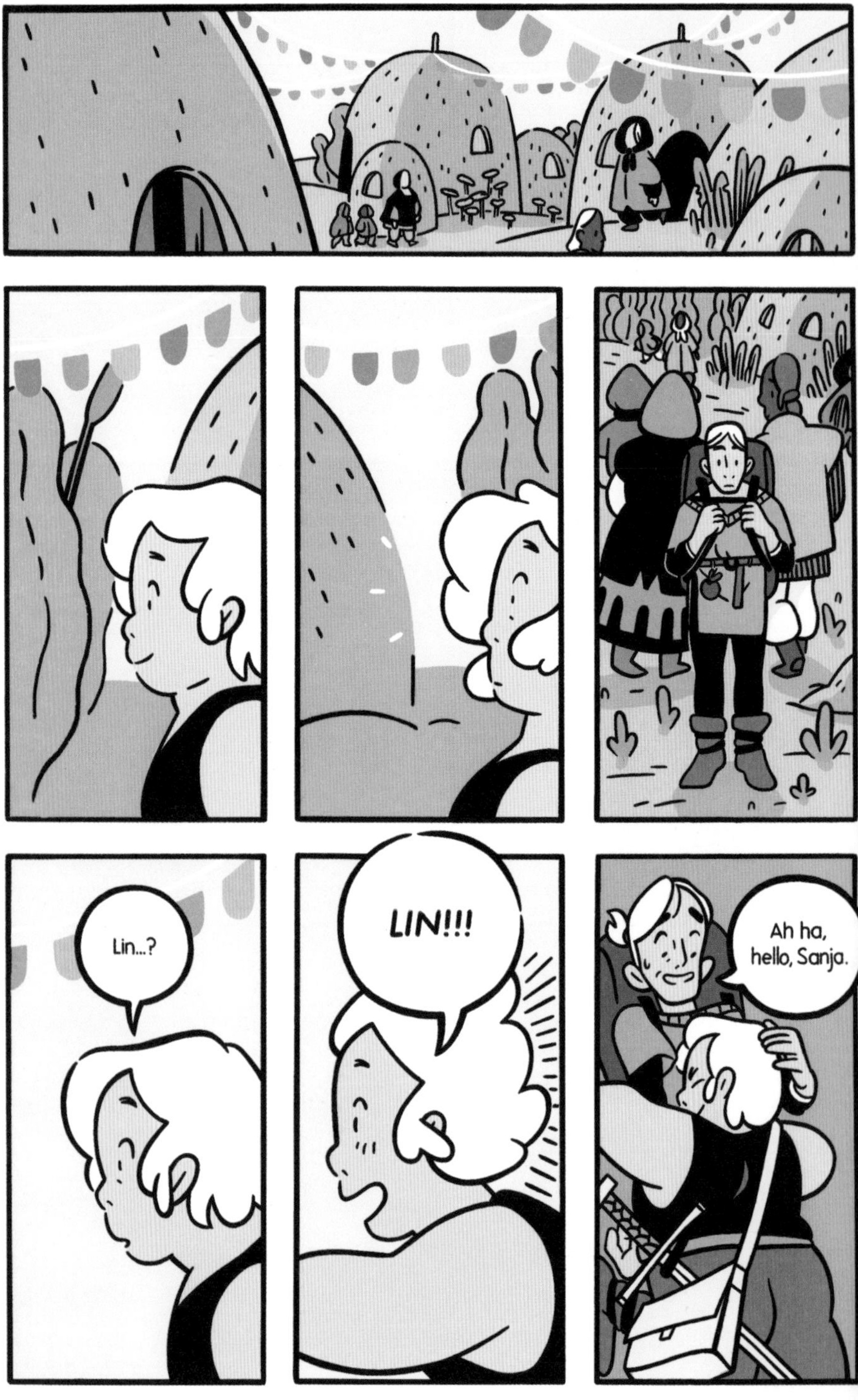
Lin...?
LIN!!!
Ah ha, hello, Sanja.

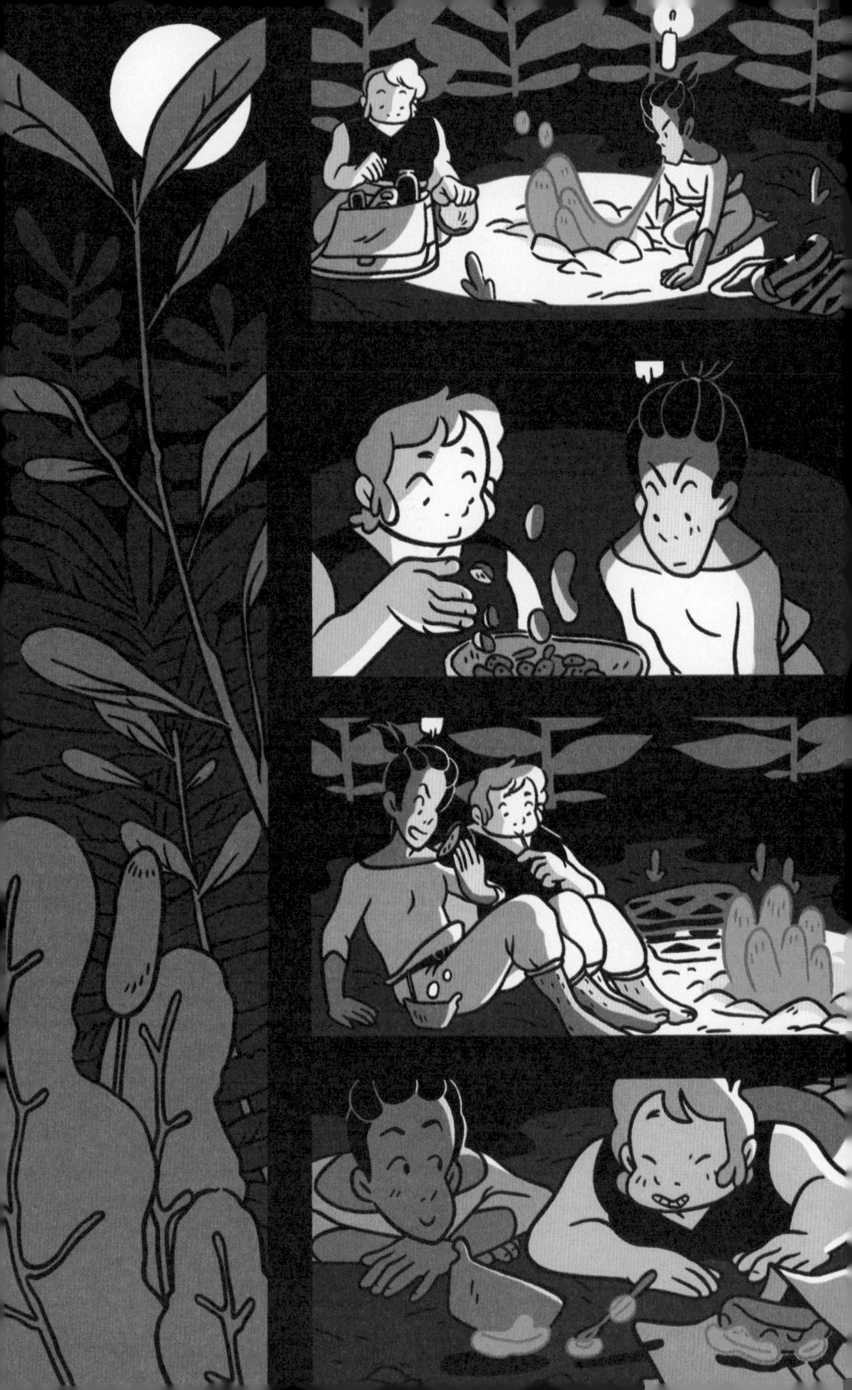

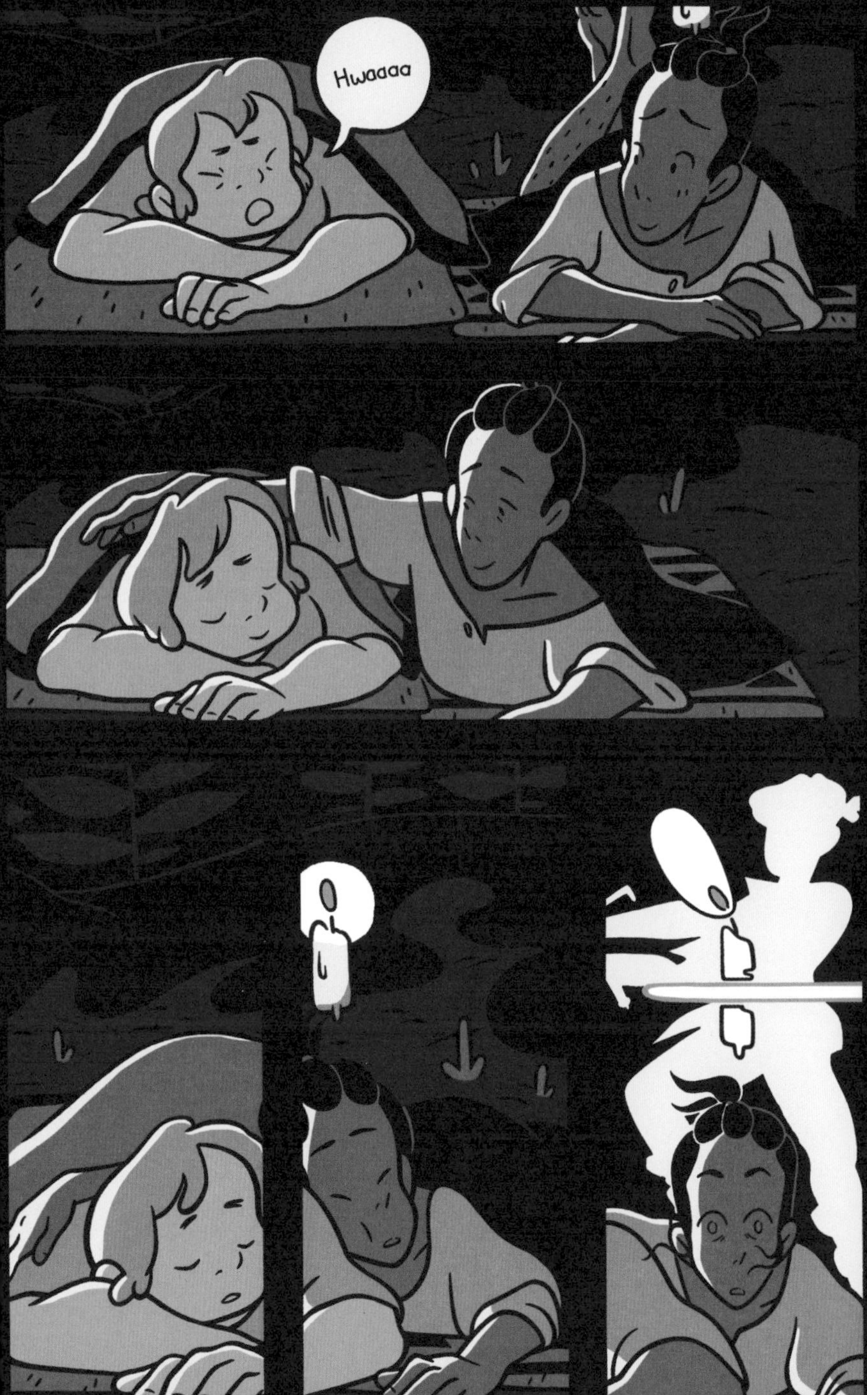
Hwaaaa

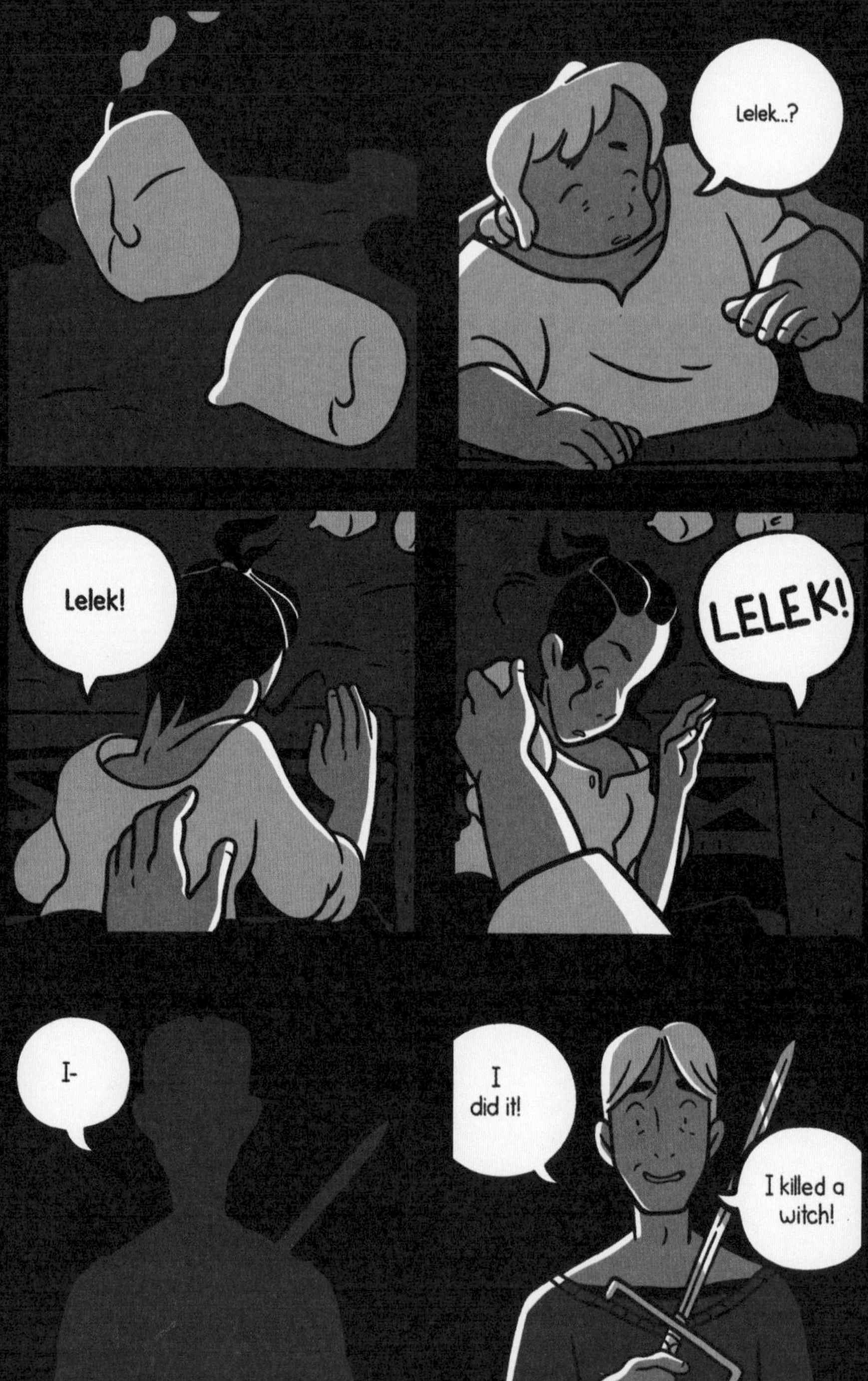
Lelek...?
Lelek!
LELEK!
I-
I did it!
I killed a witch!

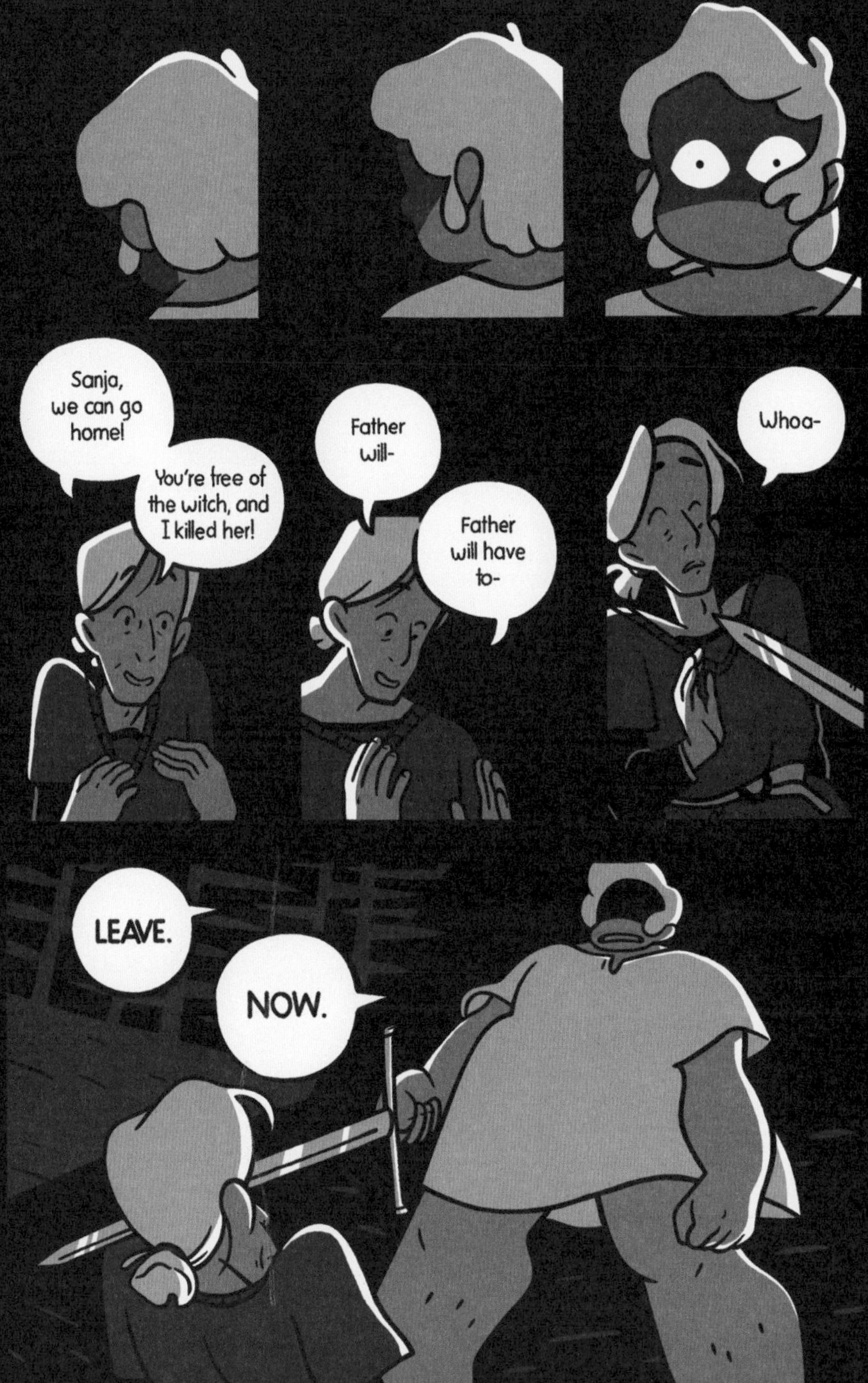
Sanja, we can go home!
You're free of the witch, and I killed her!
Father will-
Father will have to-
Whoa-
LEAVE.
NOW.

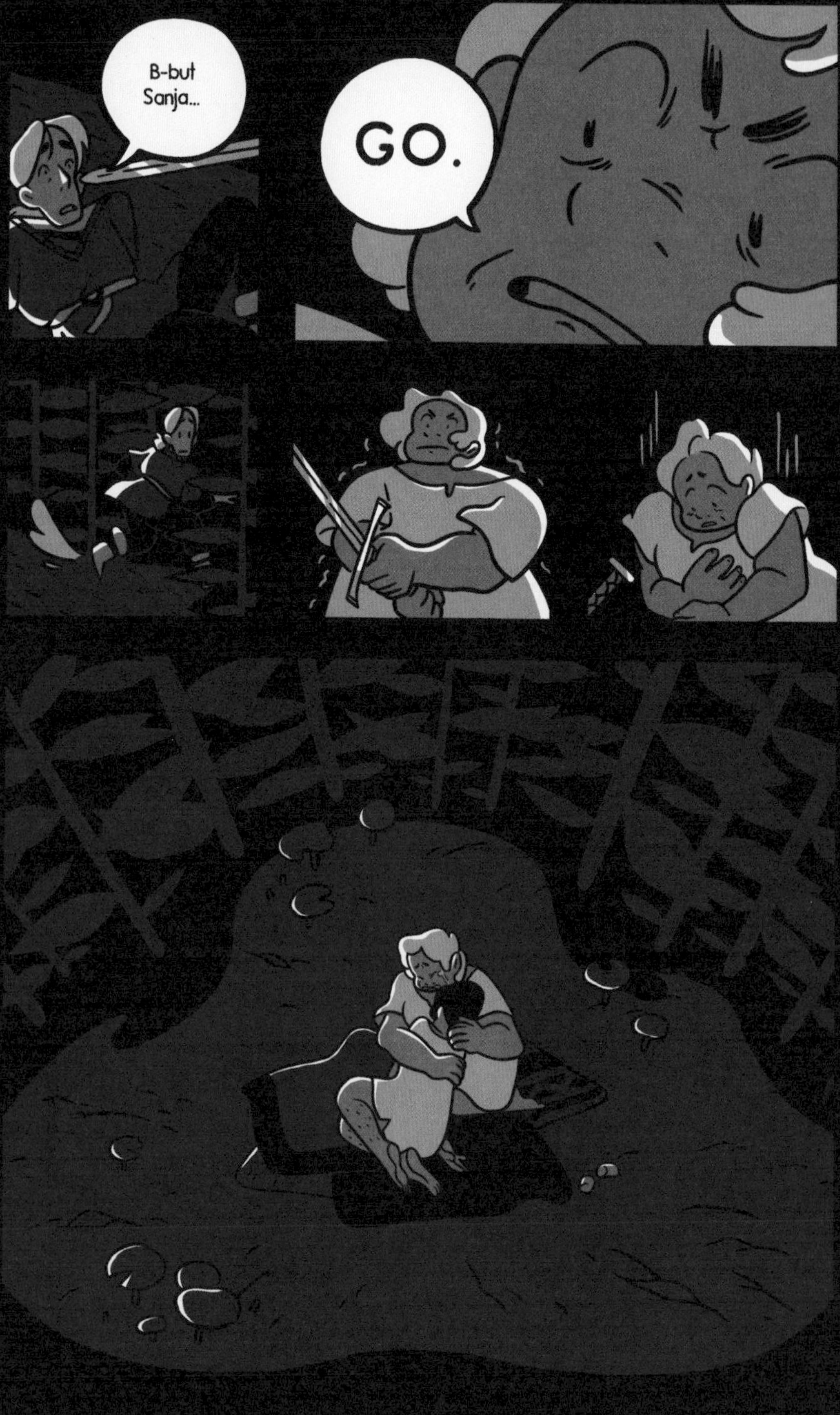
B-but Sanja...
GO.

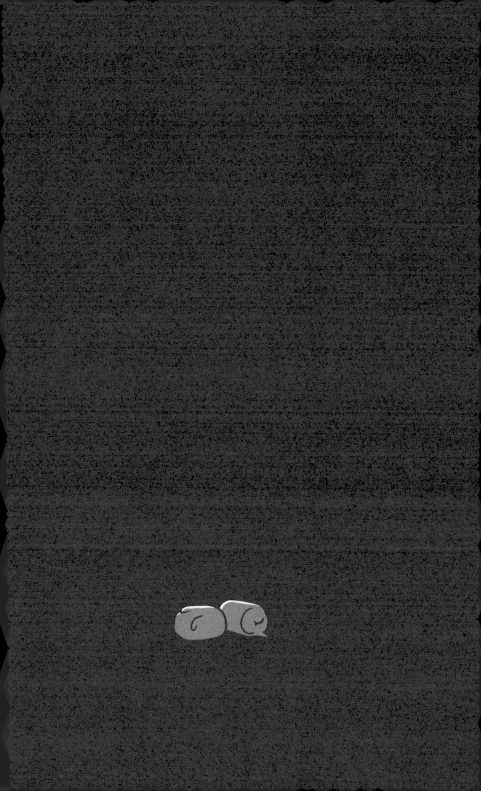

Part 6

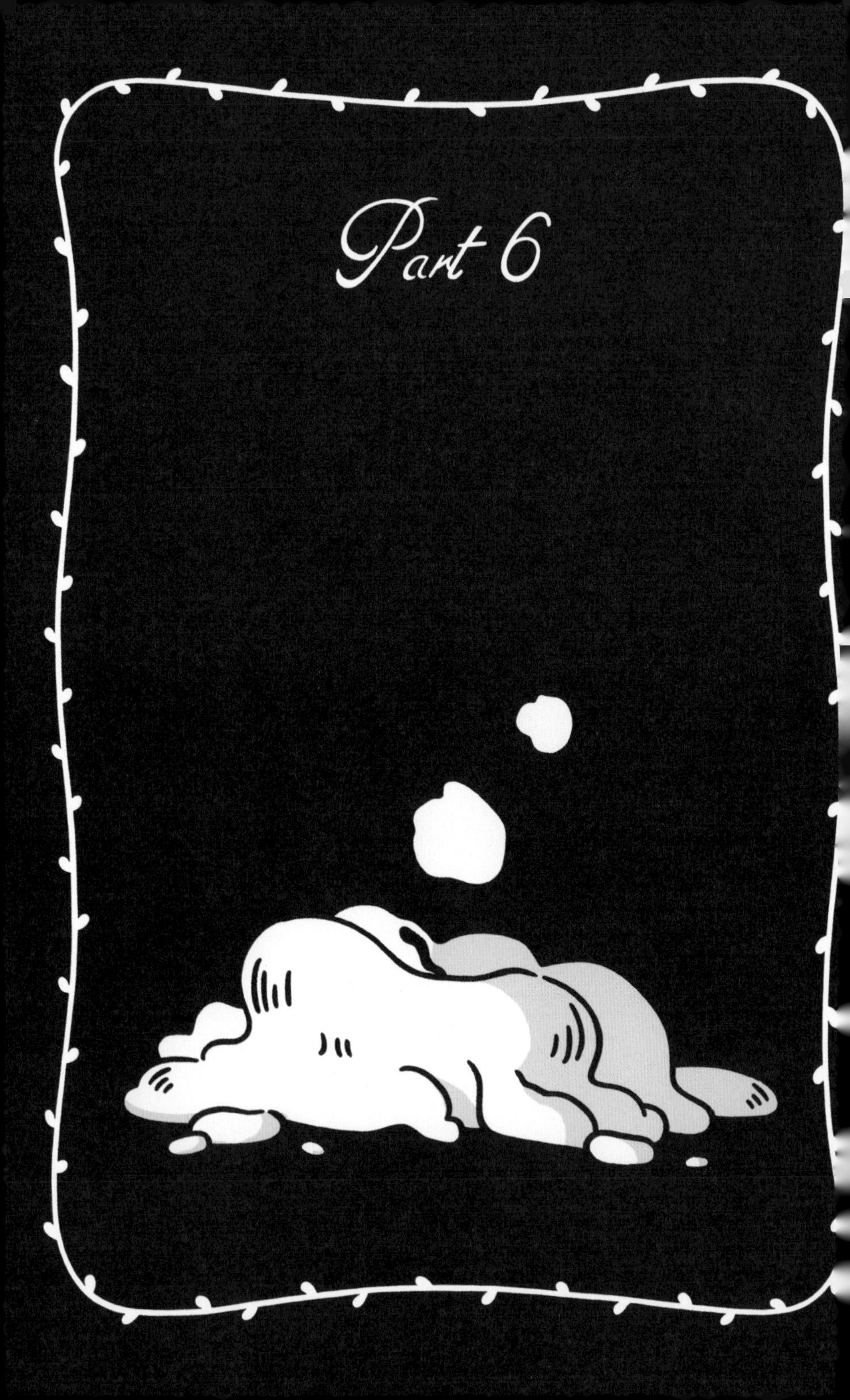

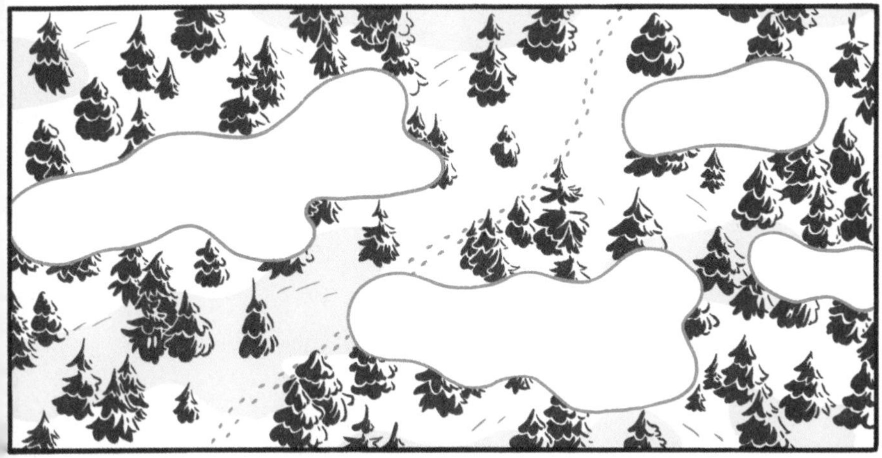

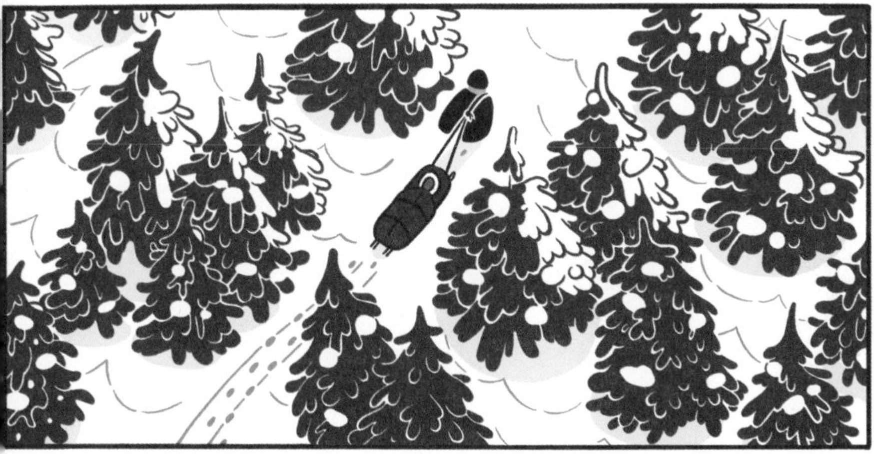

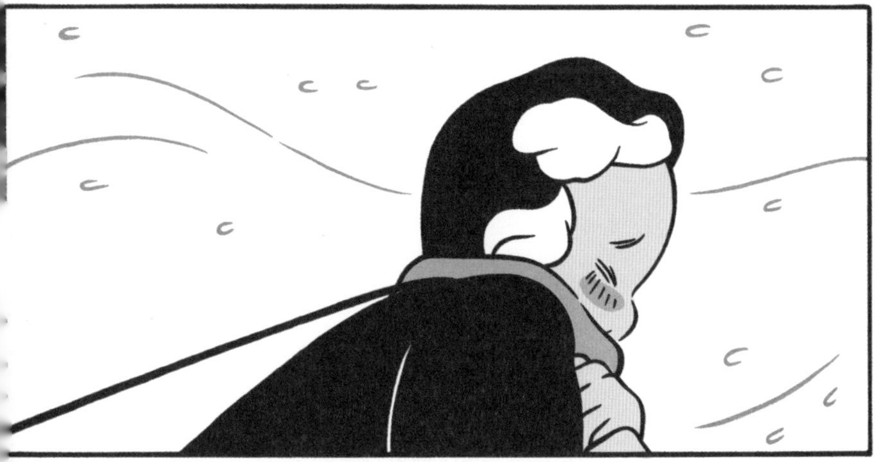

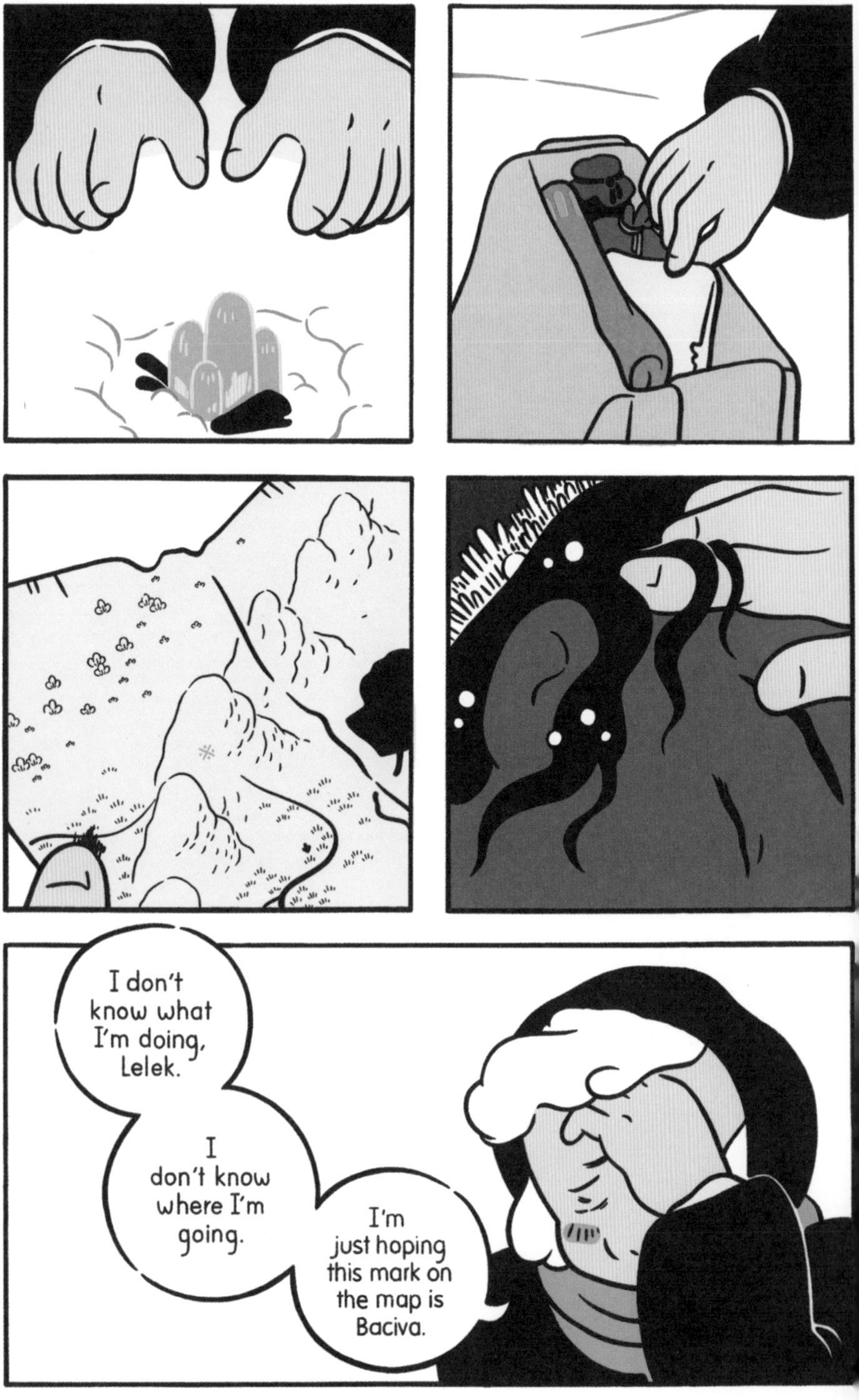
I don't know what I'm doing, Lelek.
I don't know where I'm going.
I'm just hoping this mark on the map is Baciva.

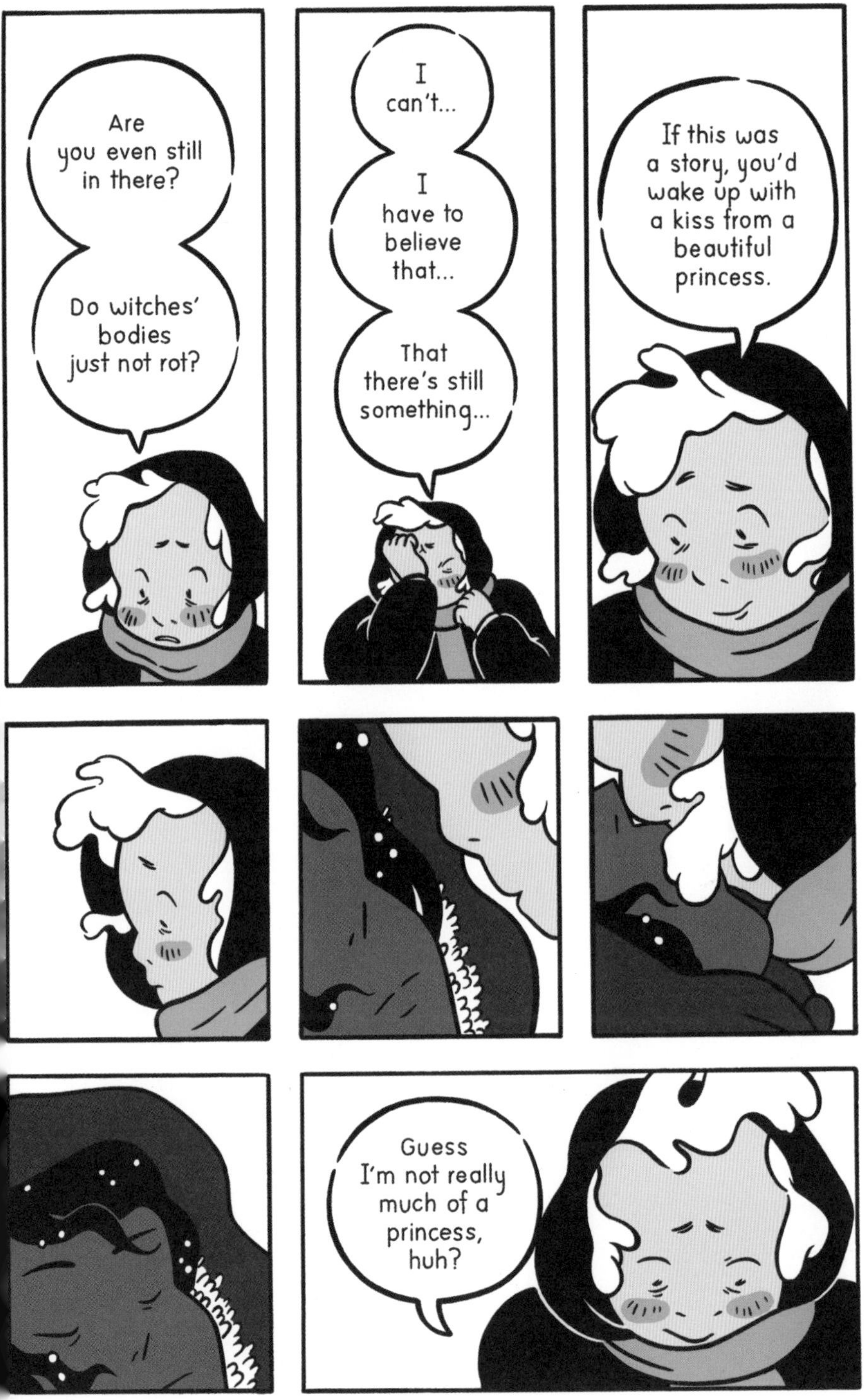
Are you even still in there?
Do witches' bodies just not rot?
I can't...
I have to believe that...
That there's still something...
If this was a story, you'd wake up with a kiss from a beautiful princess.
Guess I'm not really much of a princess, huh?

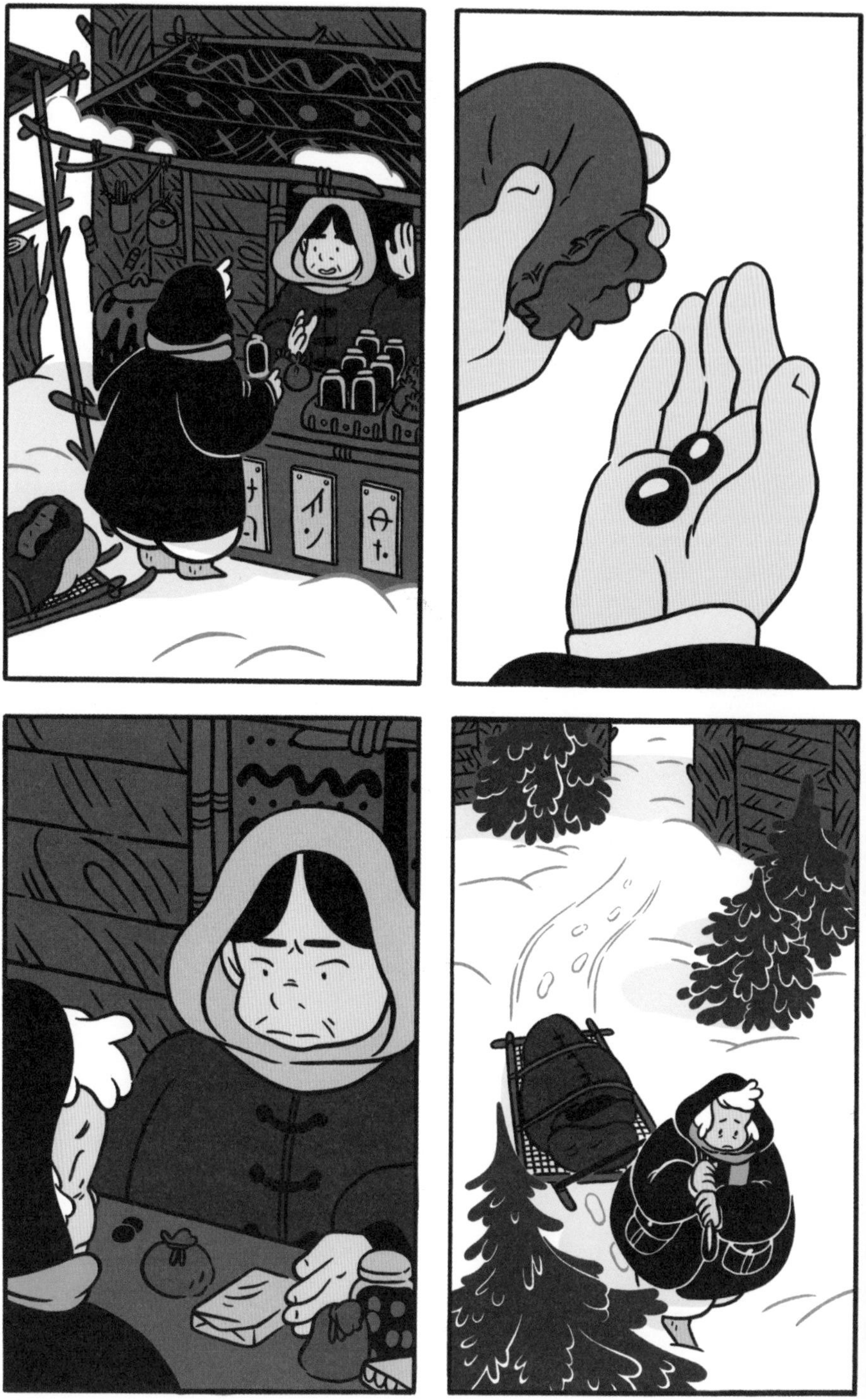

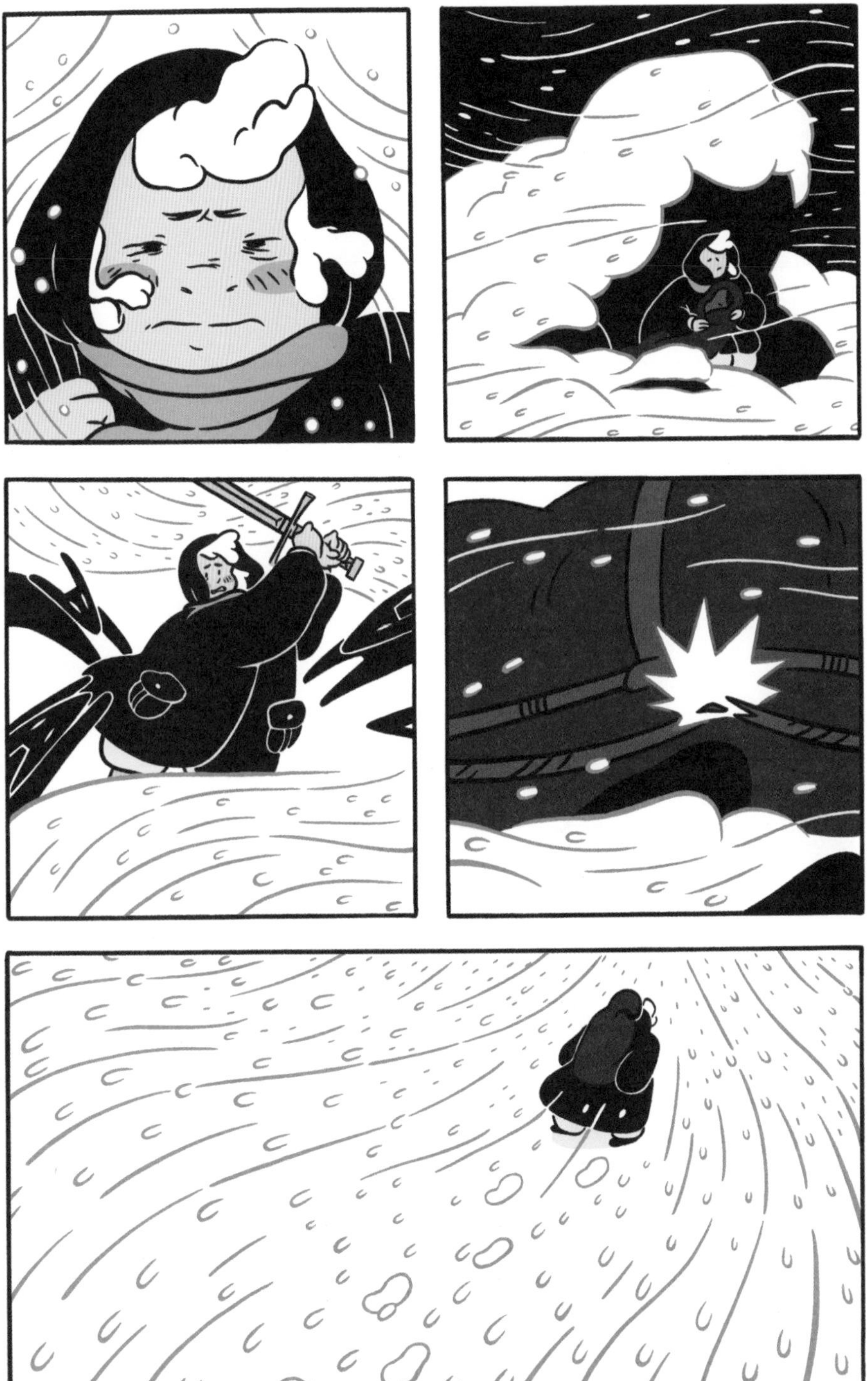

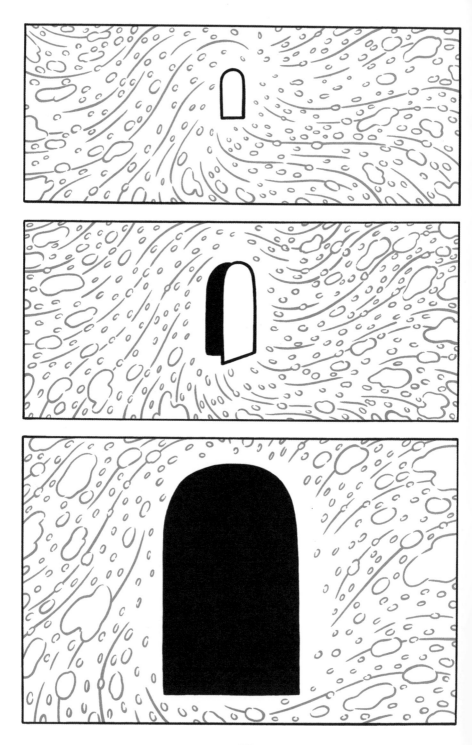

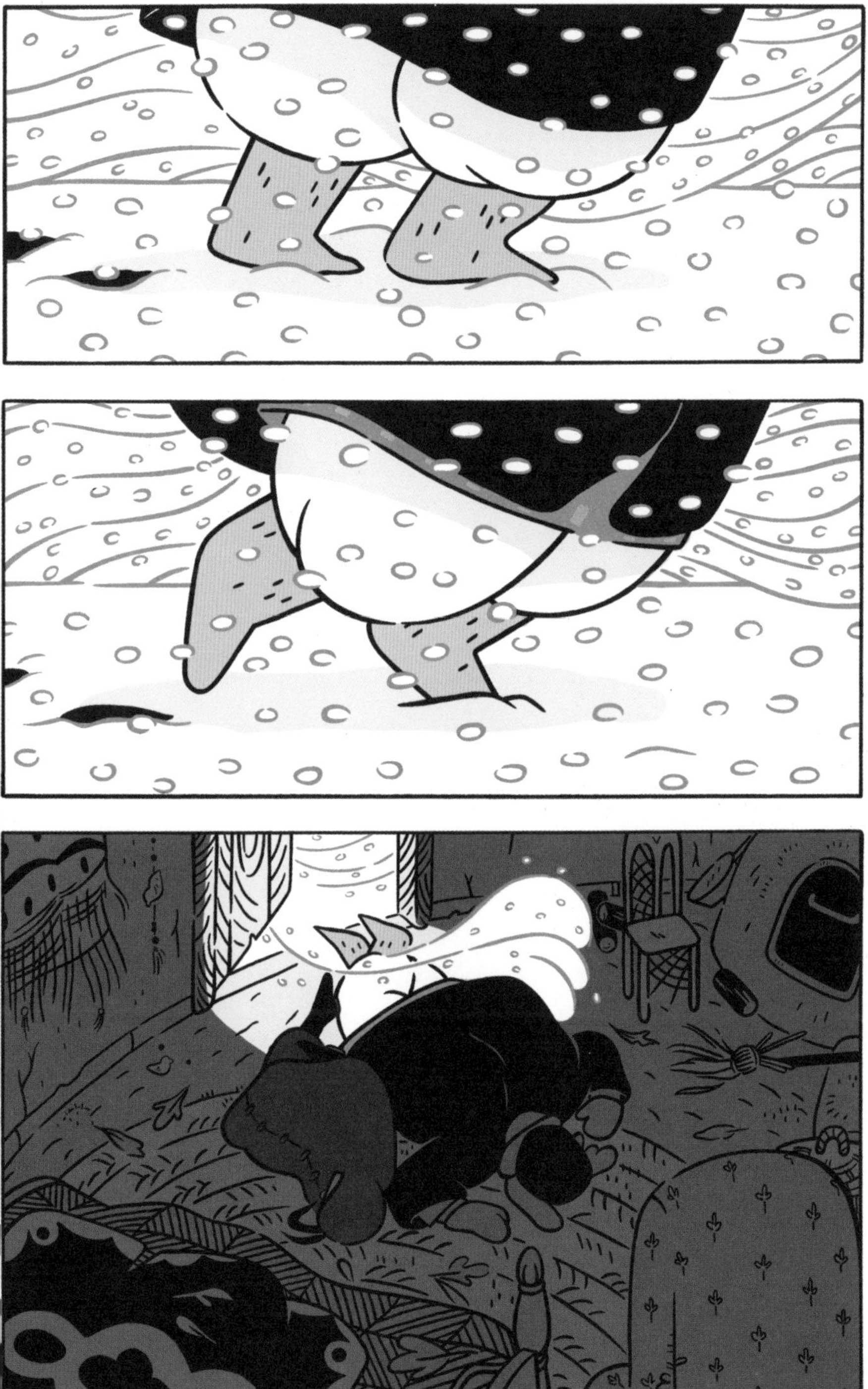

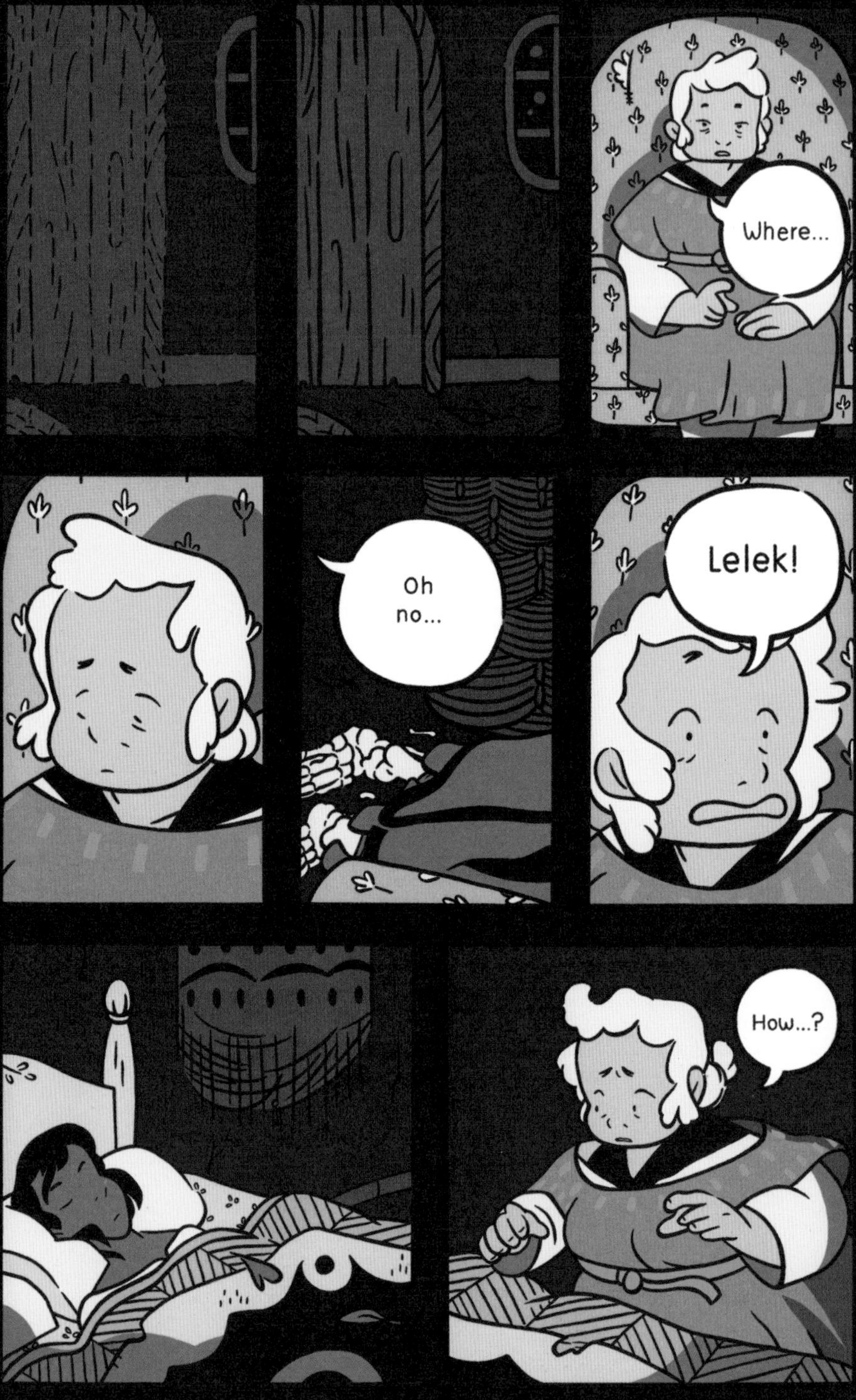
Where...
Oh no...
Lelek!
How...?

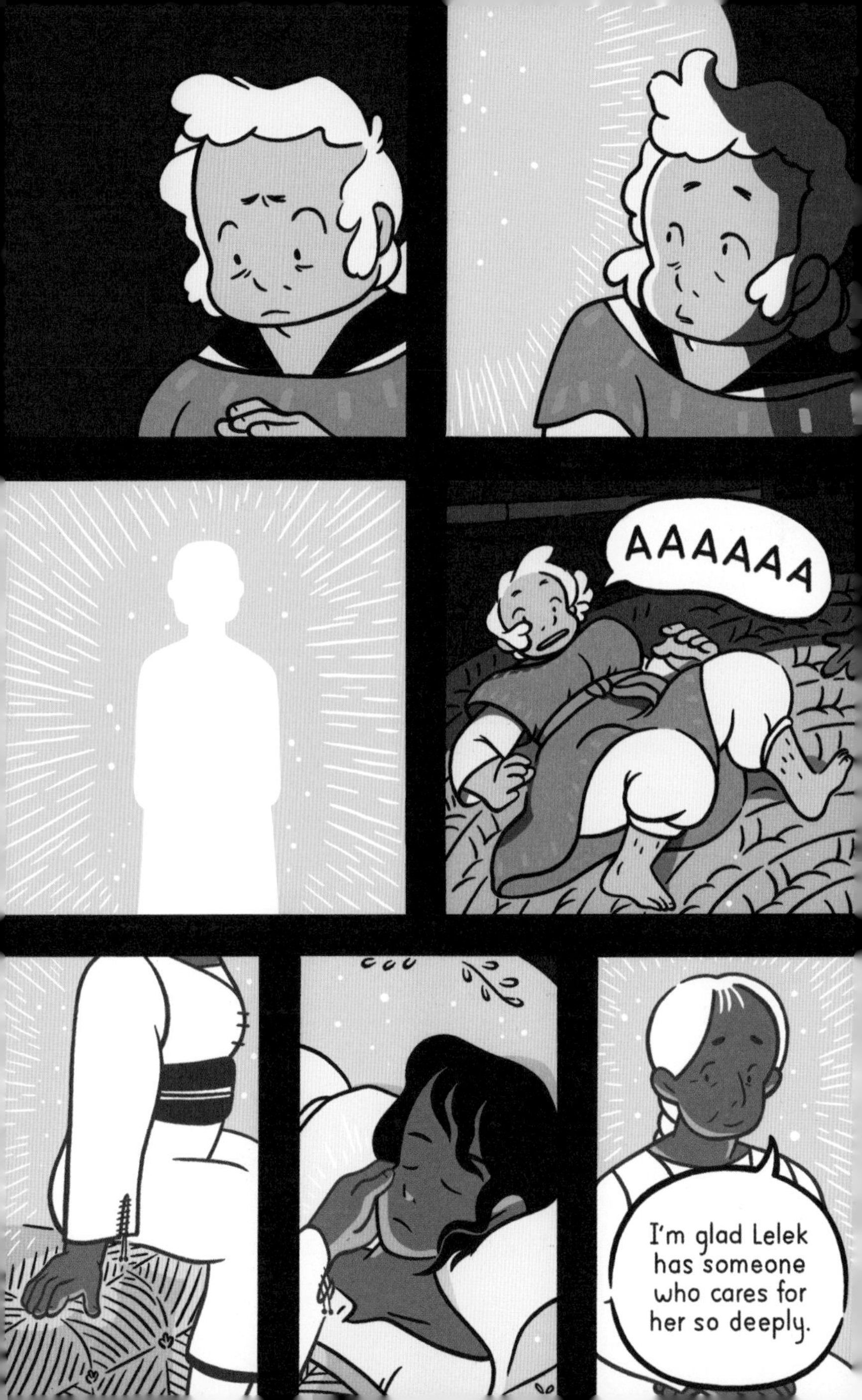
AAAAAA
I'm glad Lelek has someone who cares for her so deeply.

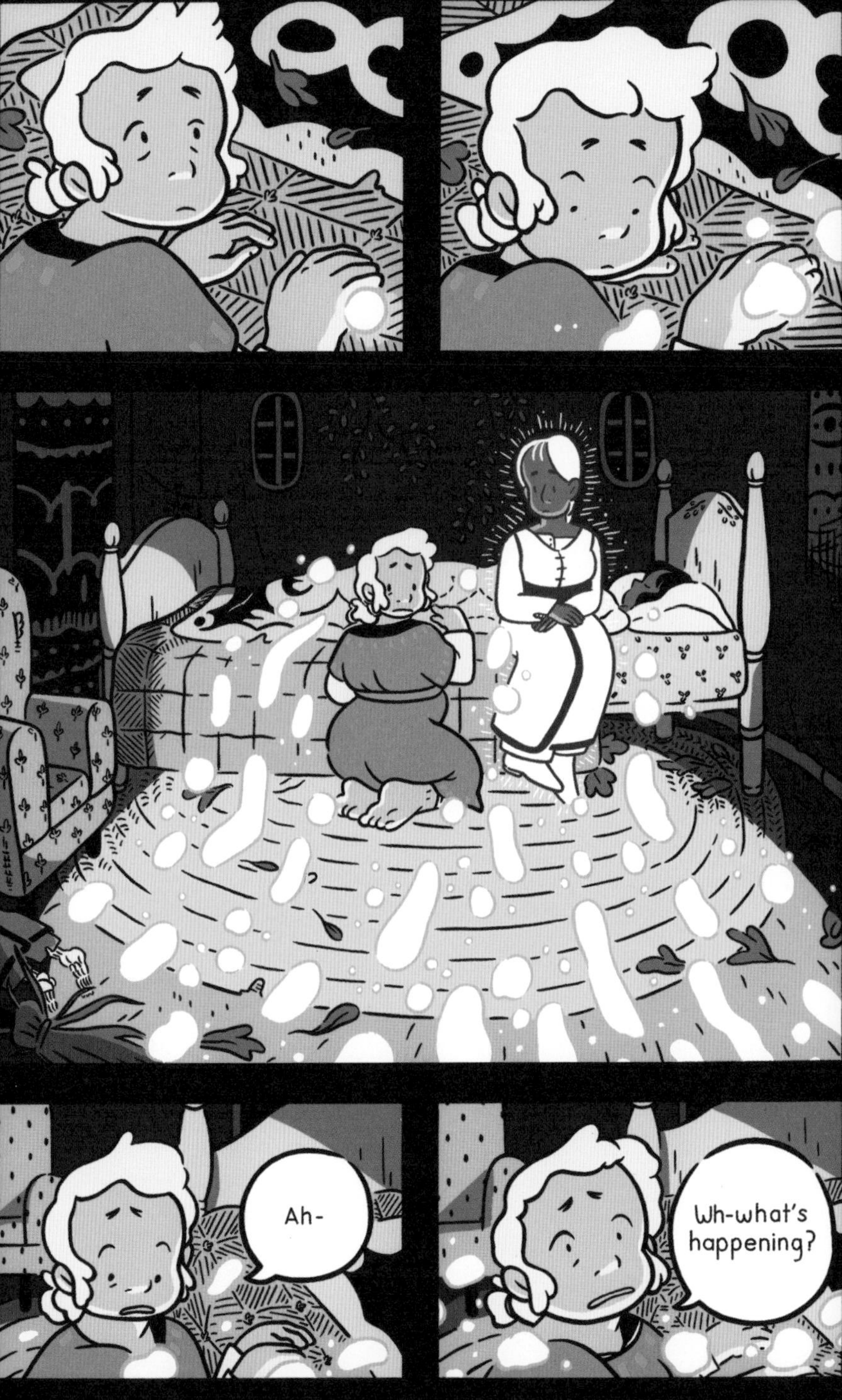
Ah-
Wh-what's happening?

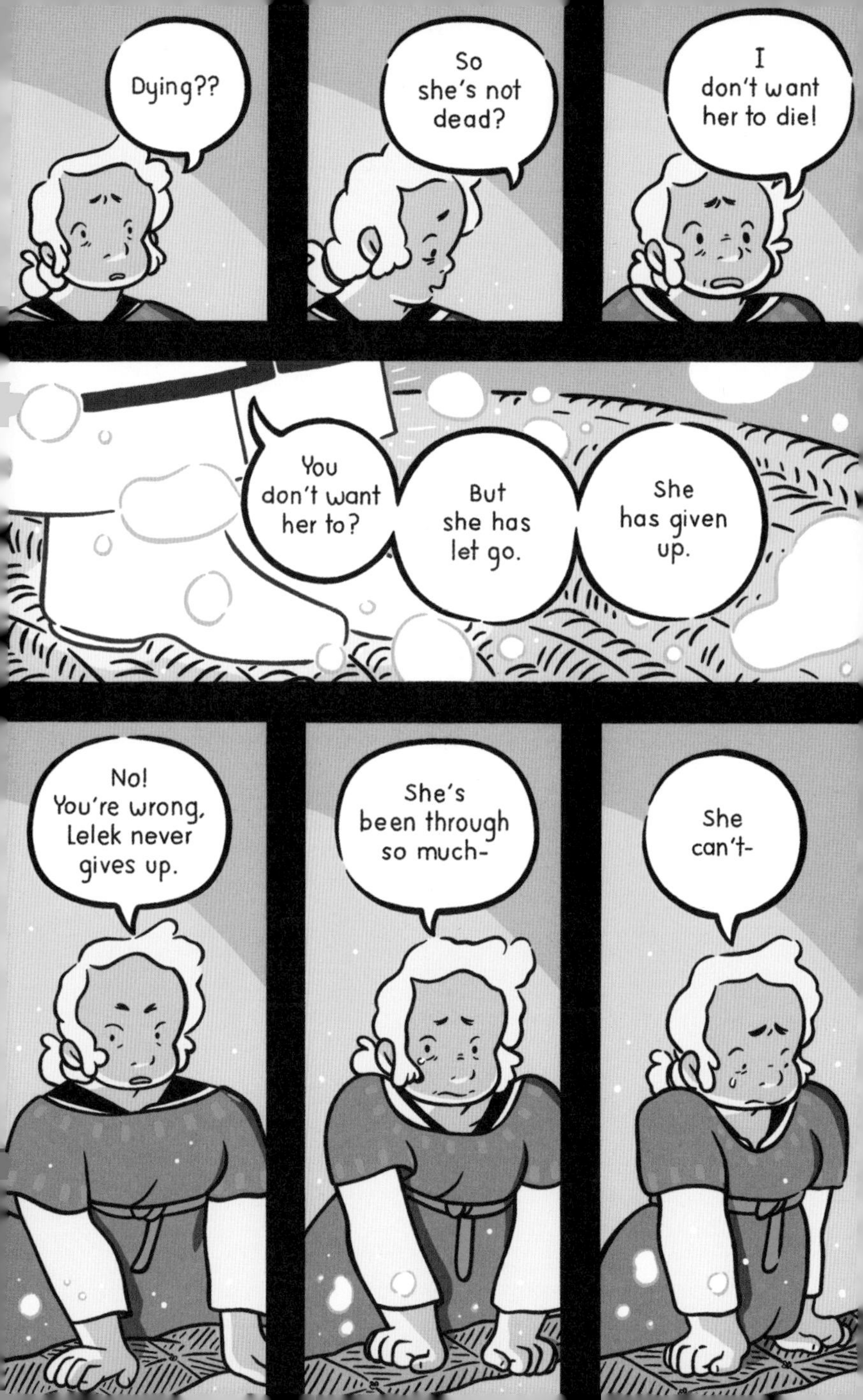
Dying??
So she's not dead?
I don't want her to die!
You don't want her to?
But she has let go.
She has given up.
No! You're wrong, Lelek never gives up.
She's been through so much-
She can't-

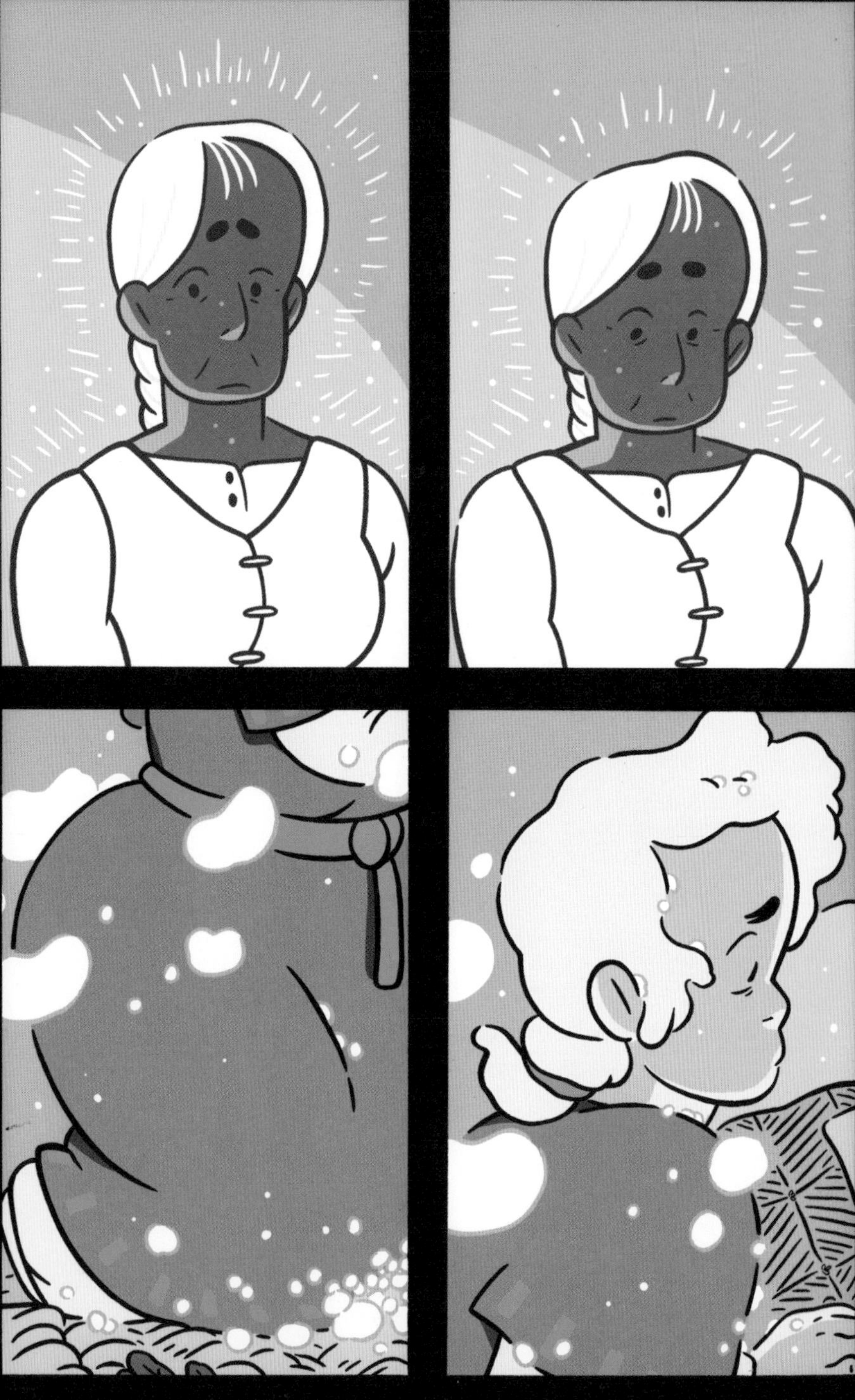

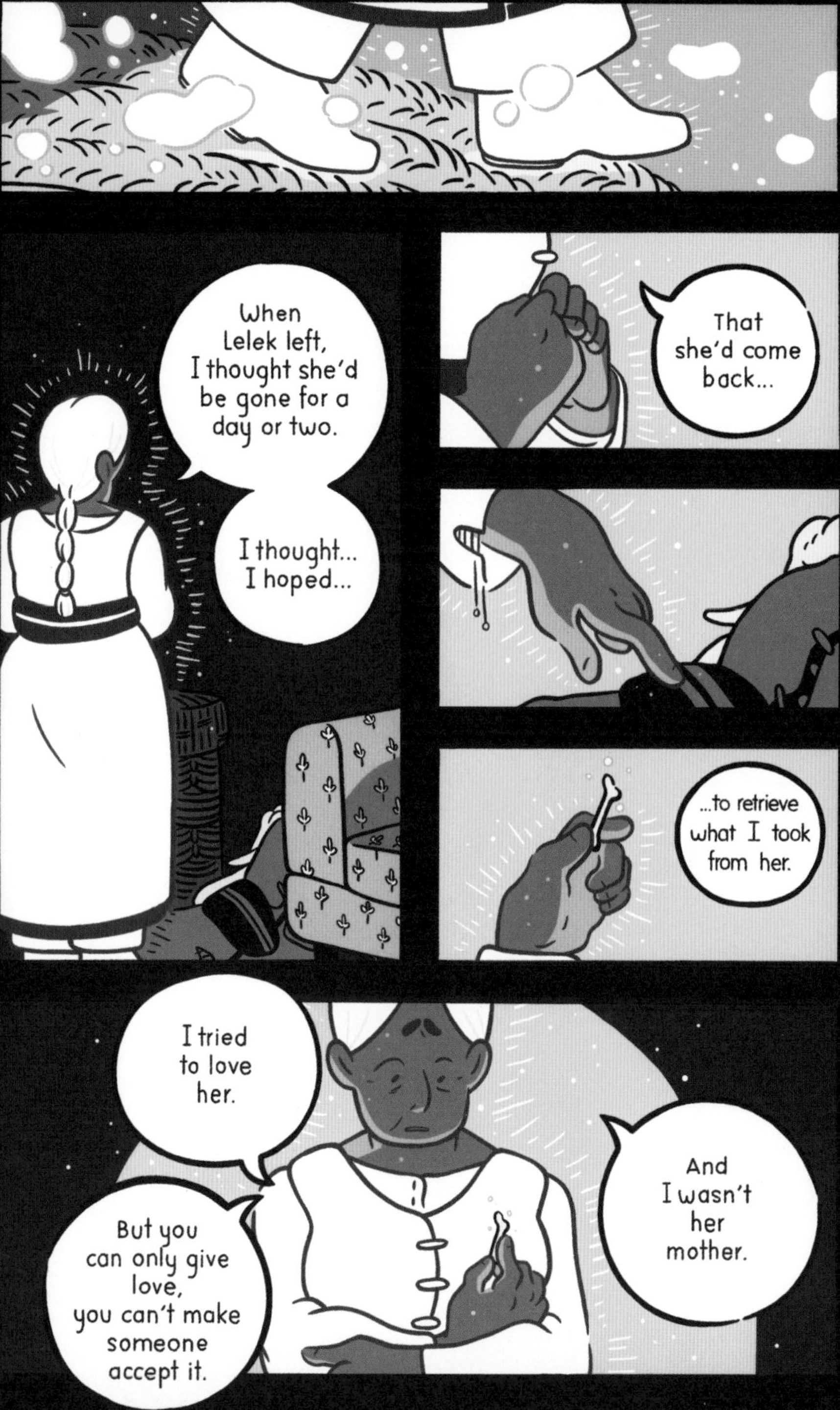
When Lelek left, I thought she'd be gone for a day or two.
I thought... I hoped...
That she'd come back...
...to retrieve what I took from her.
I tried to love her.
But you can only give love, you can't make someone accept it.
And I wasn't her mother.

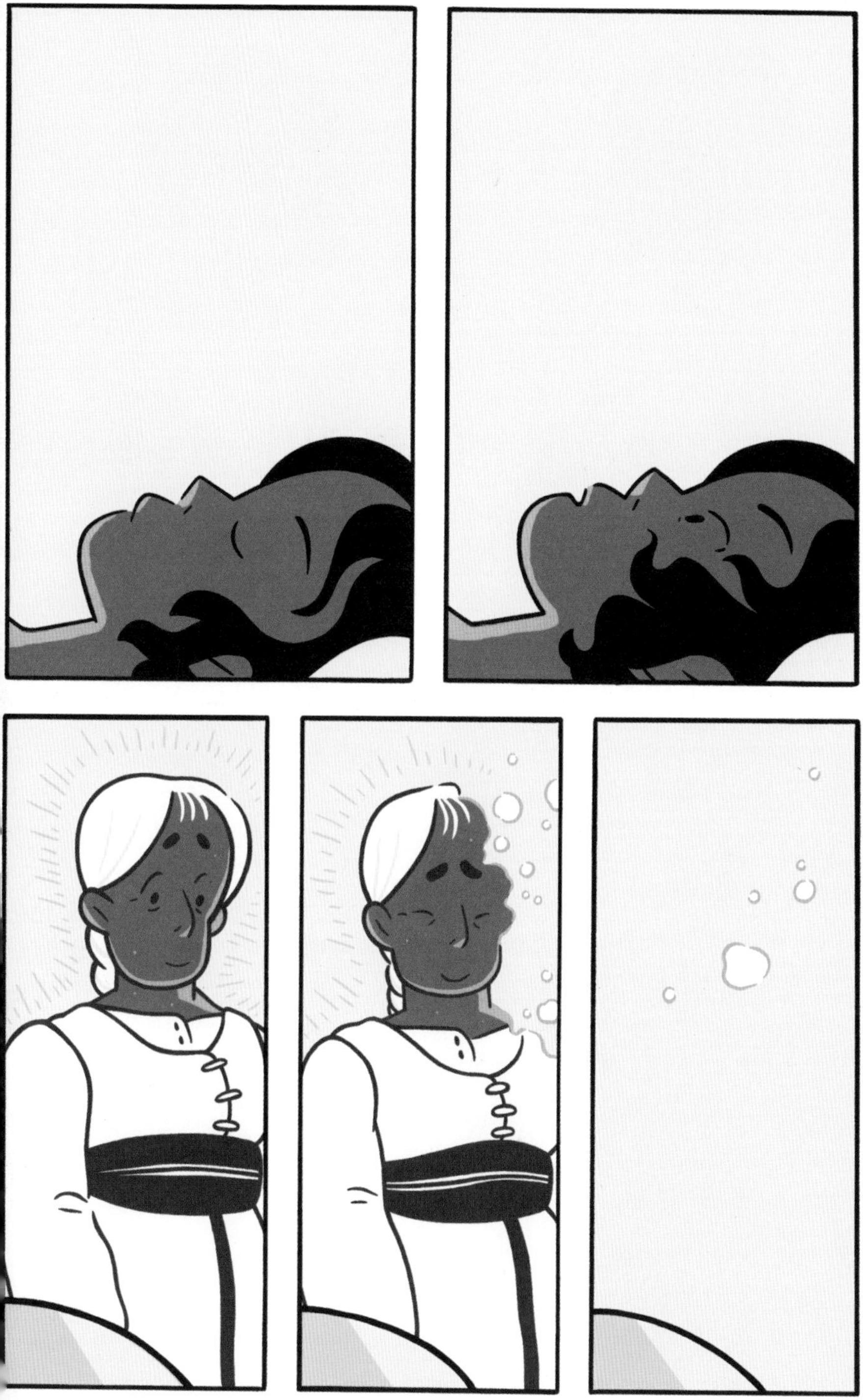

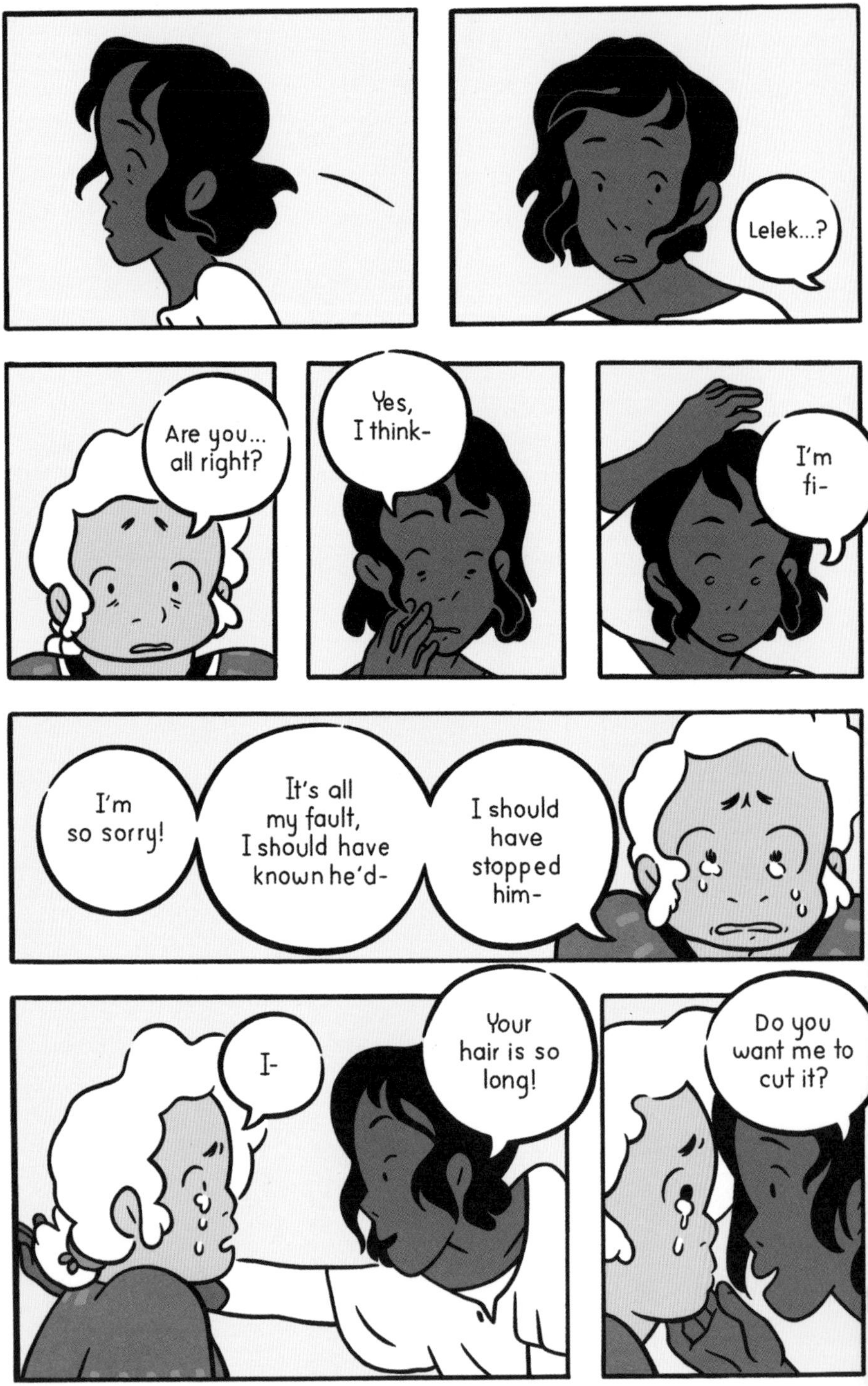

Lelek...?
Are you... all right?
Yes, I think-
I'm fi-
I'm so sorry!
It's all my fault, I should have known he'd-
I should have stopped him-
I-
Your hair is so long!
Do you want me to cut it?

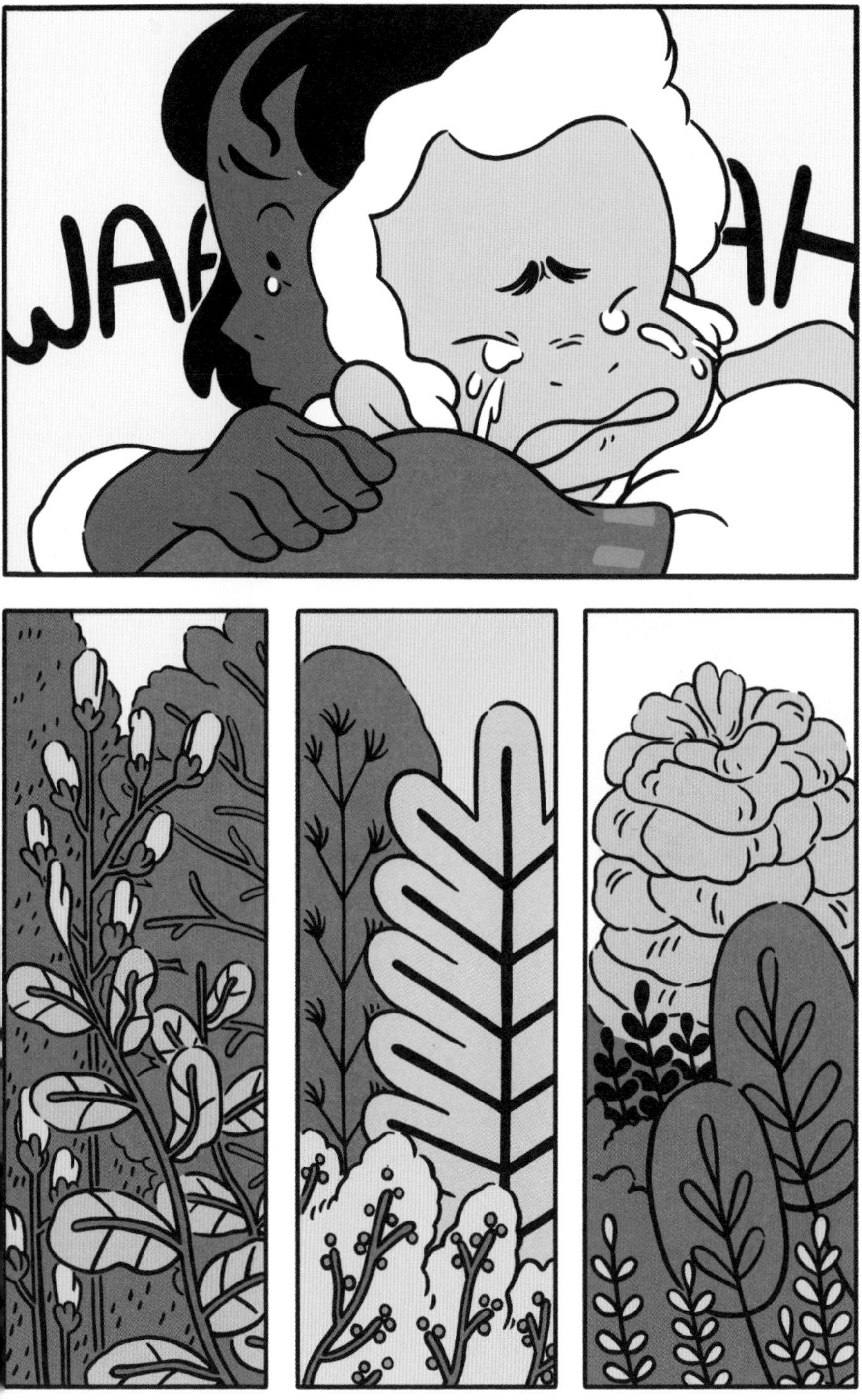

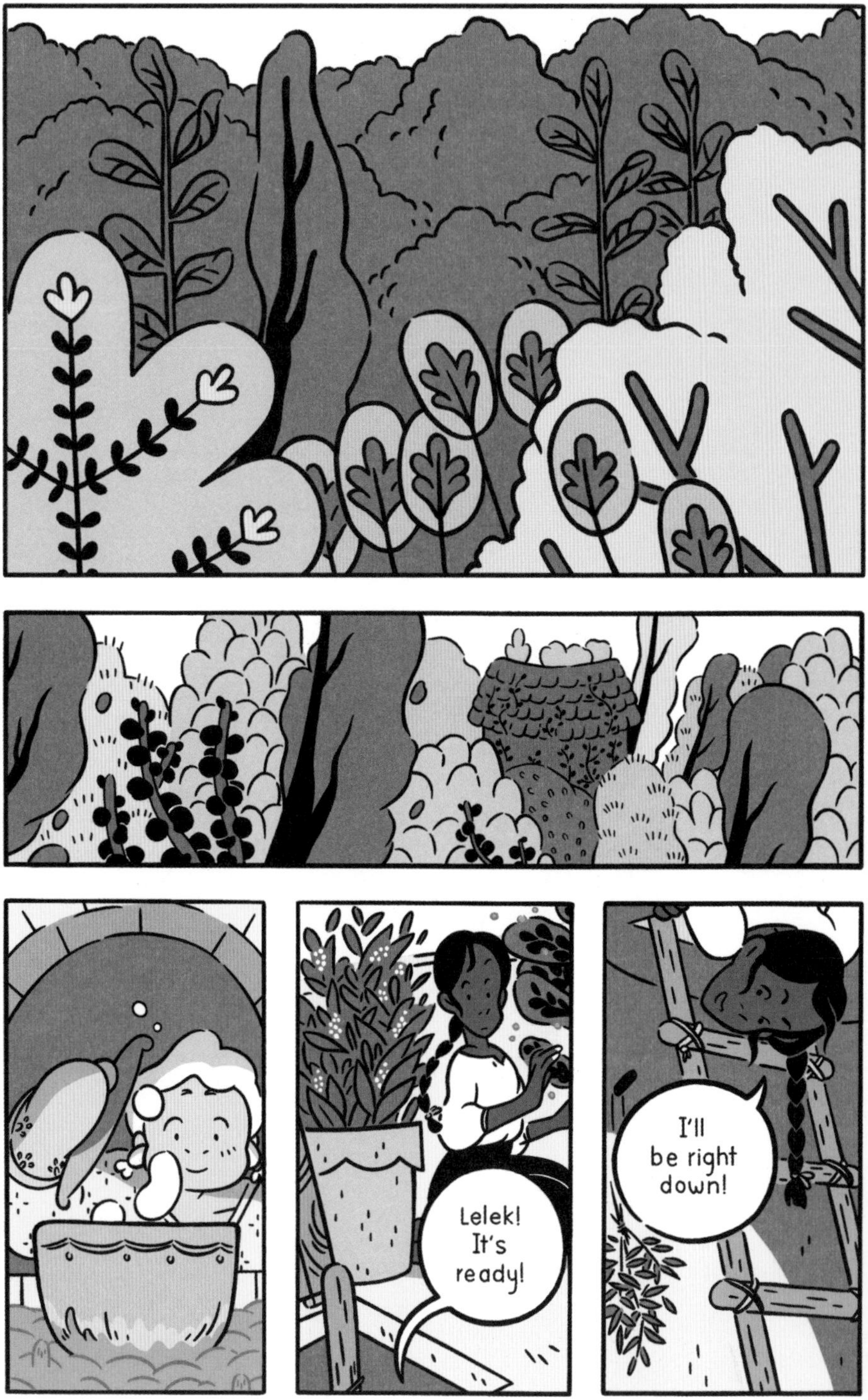
Lelek! It's ready!
I'll be right down!

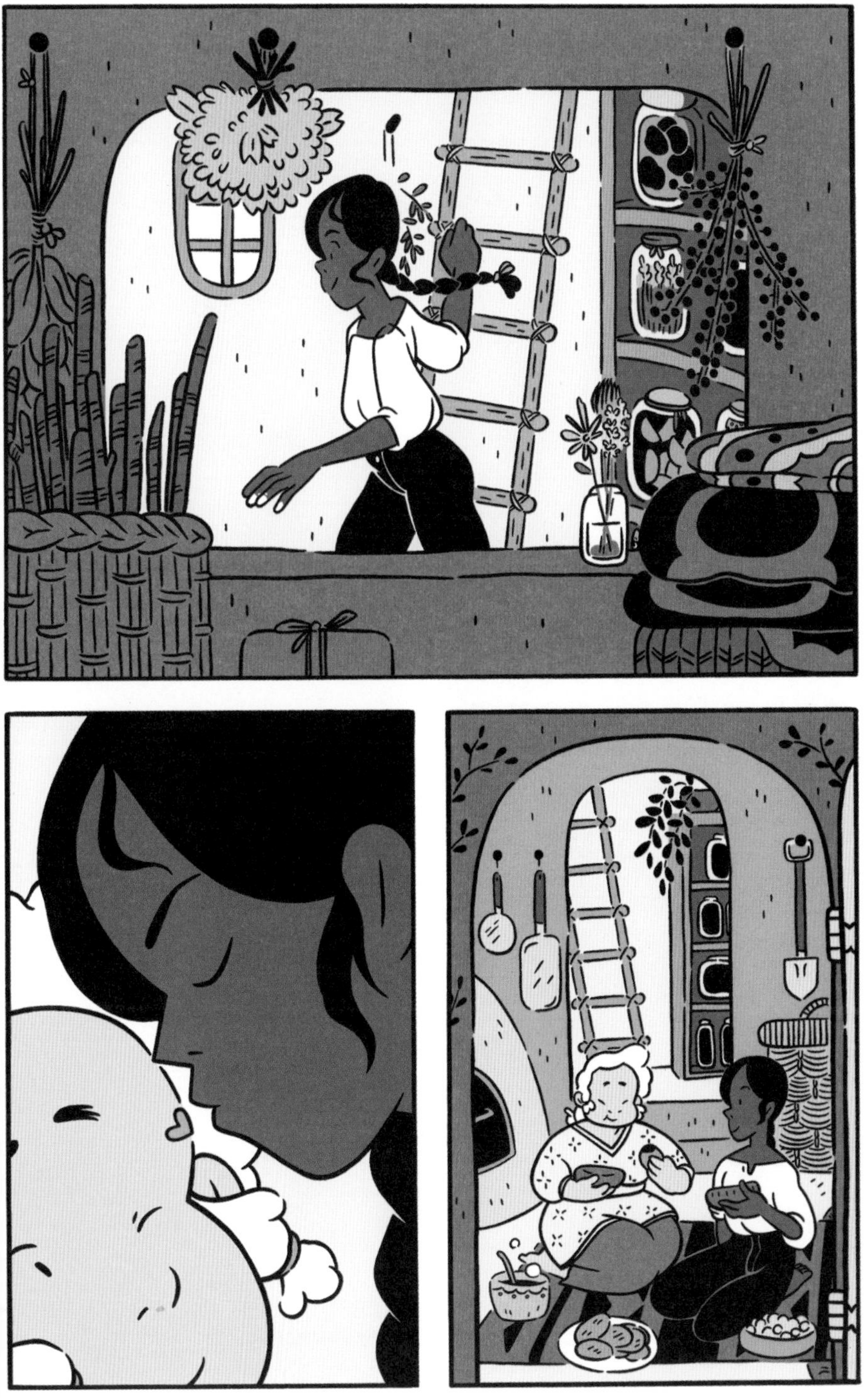

Epilogue

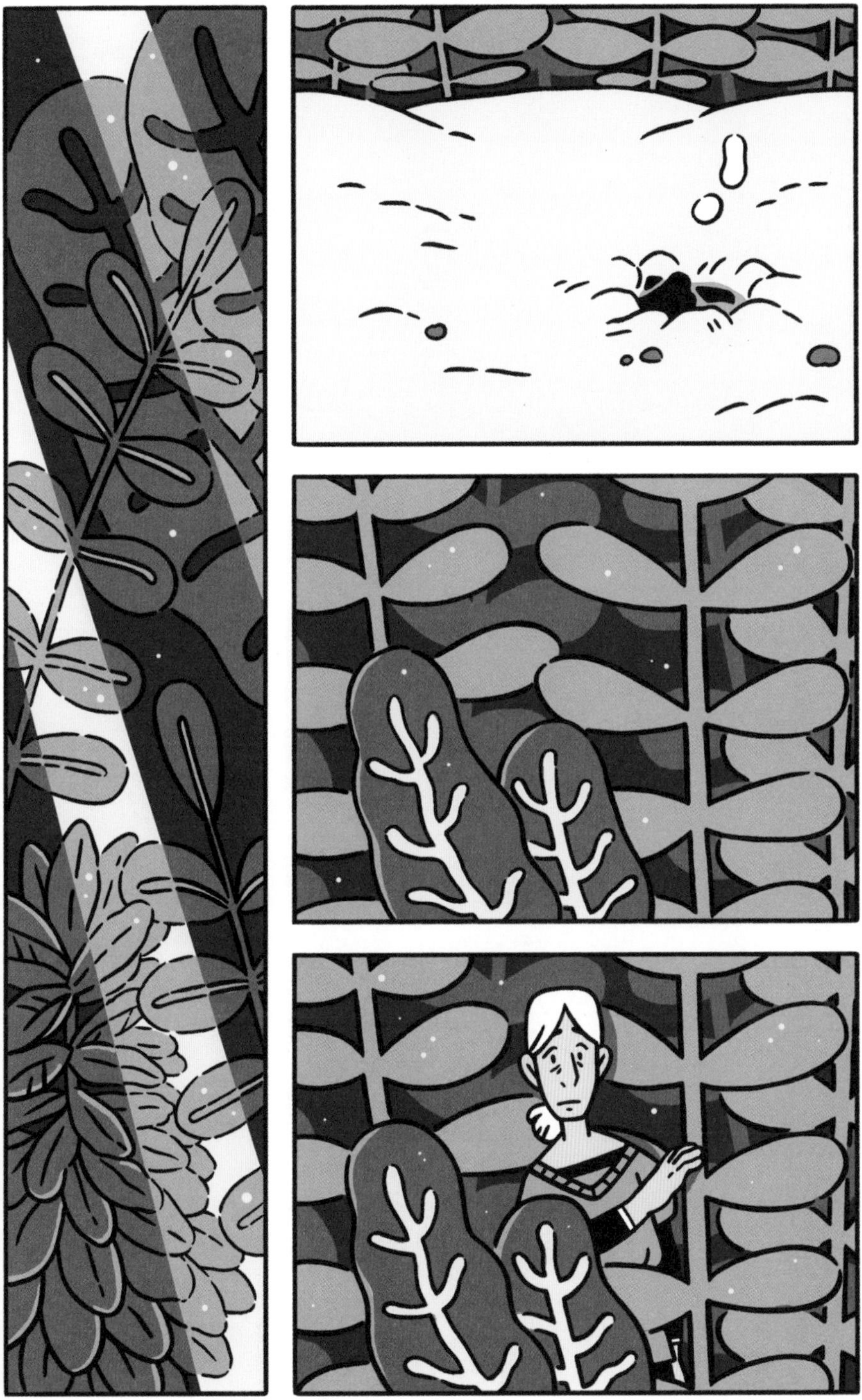

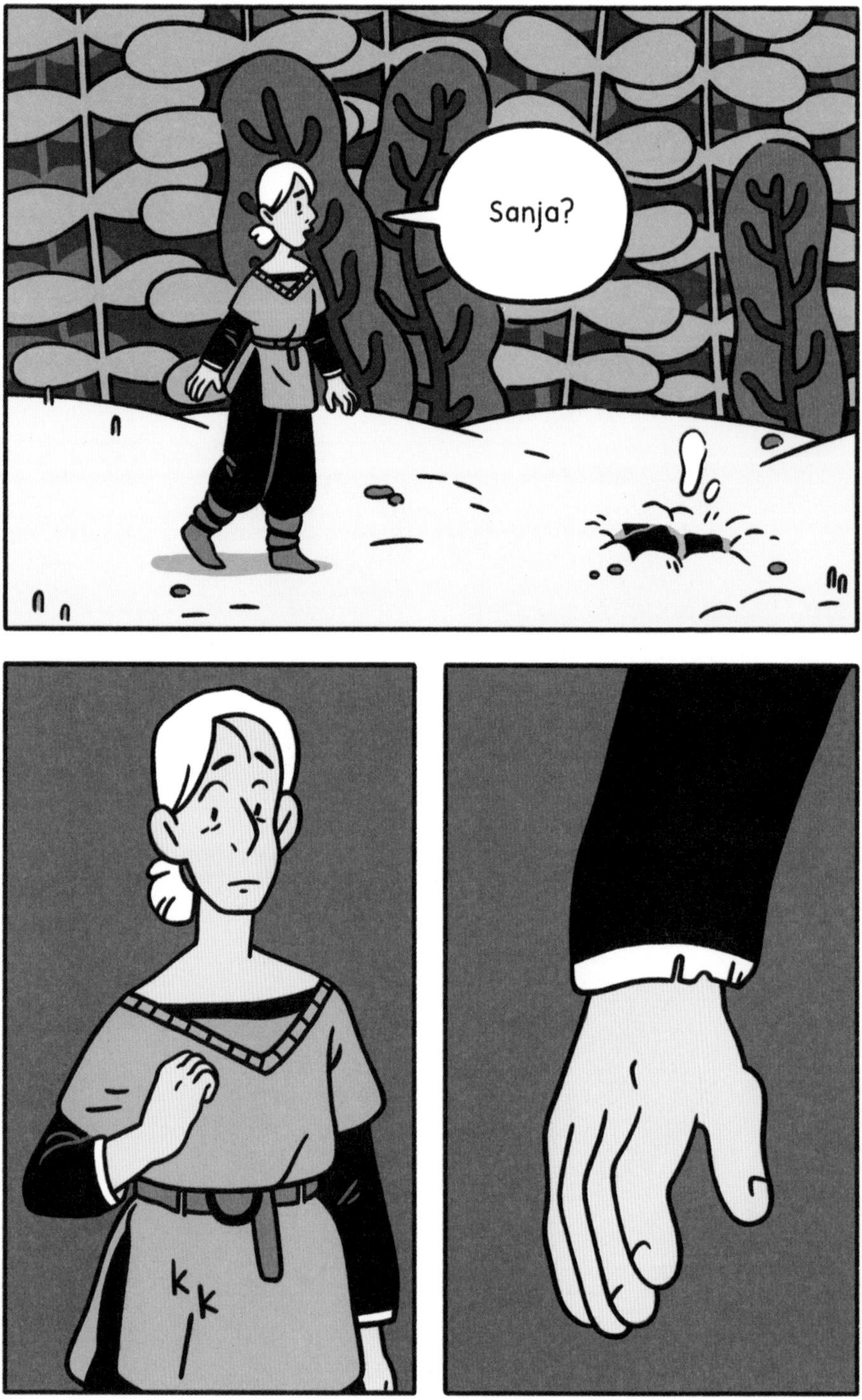
Sanja?
KK

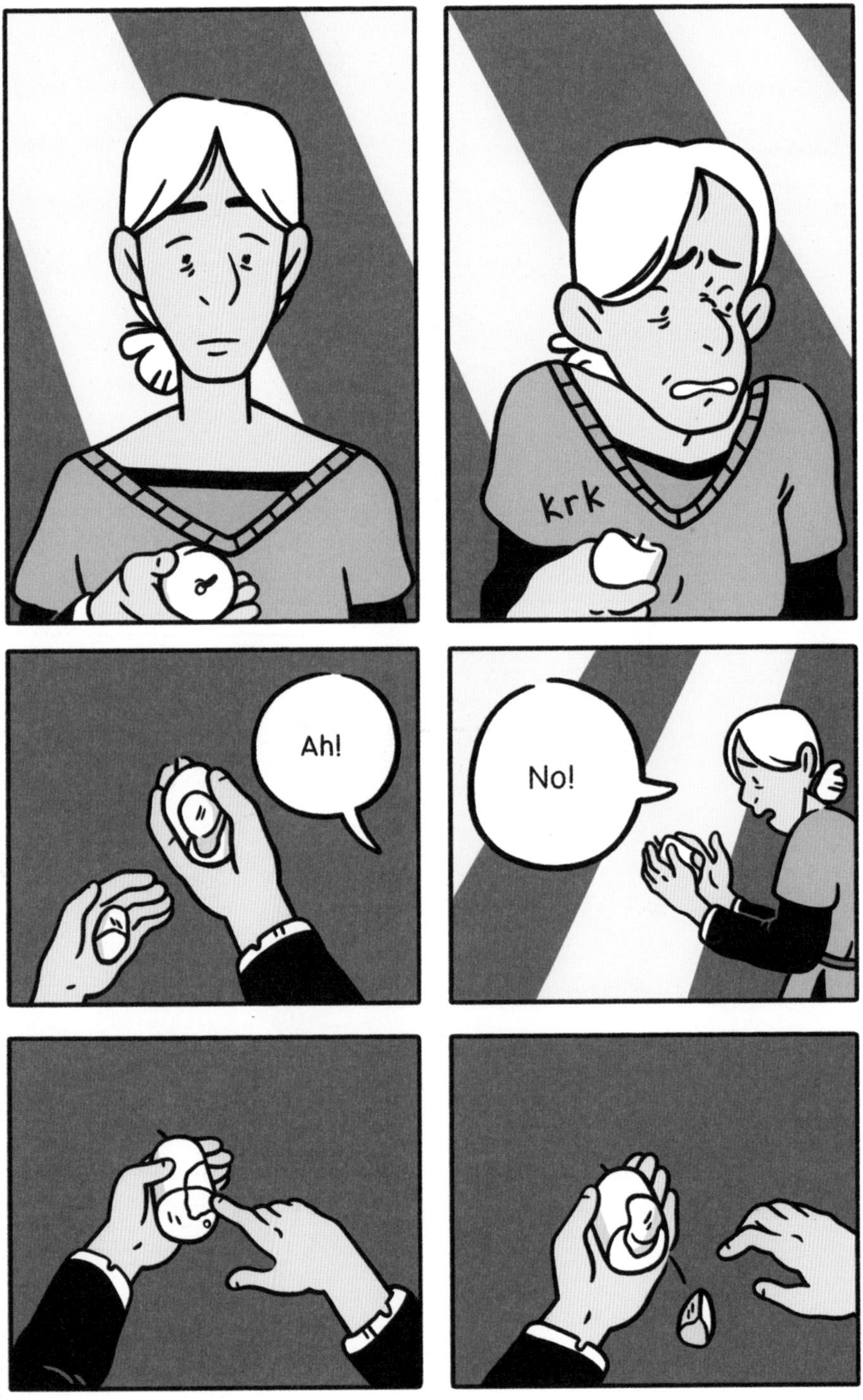
krk
Ah!
No!

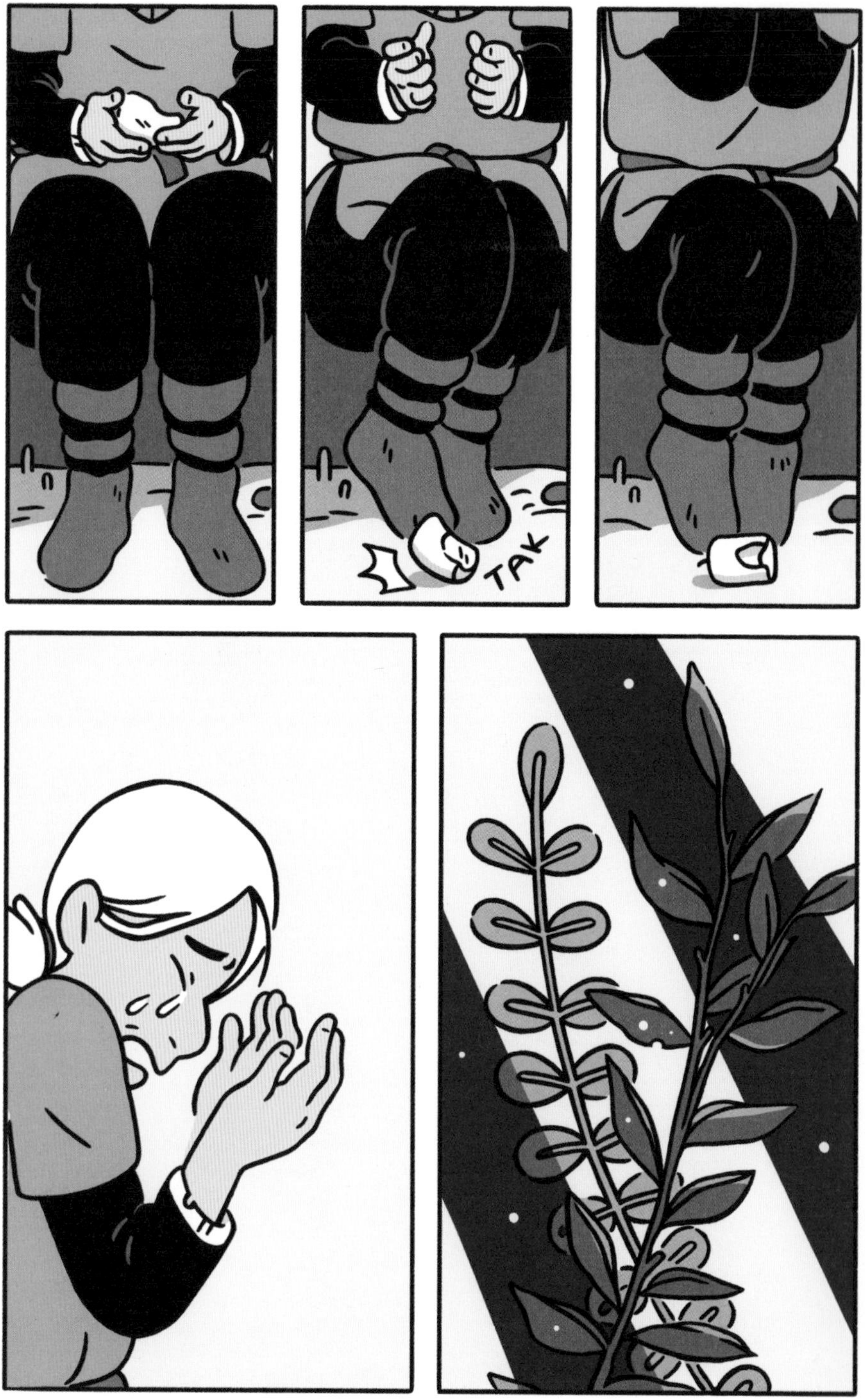
TAK

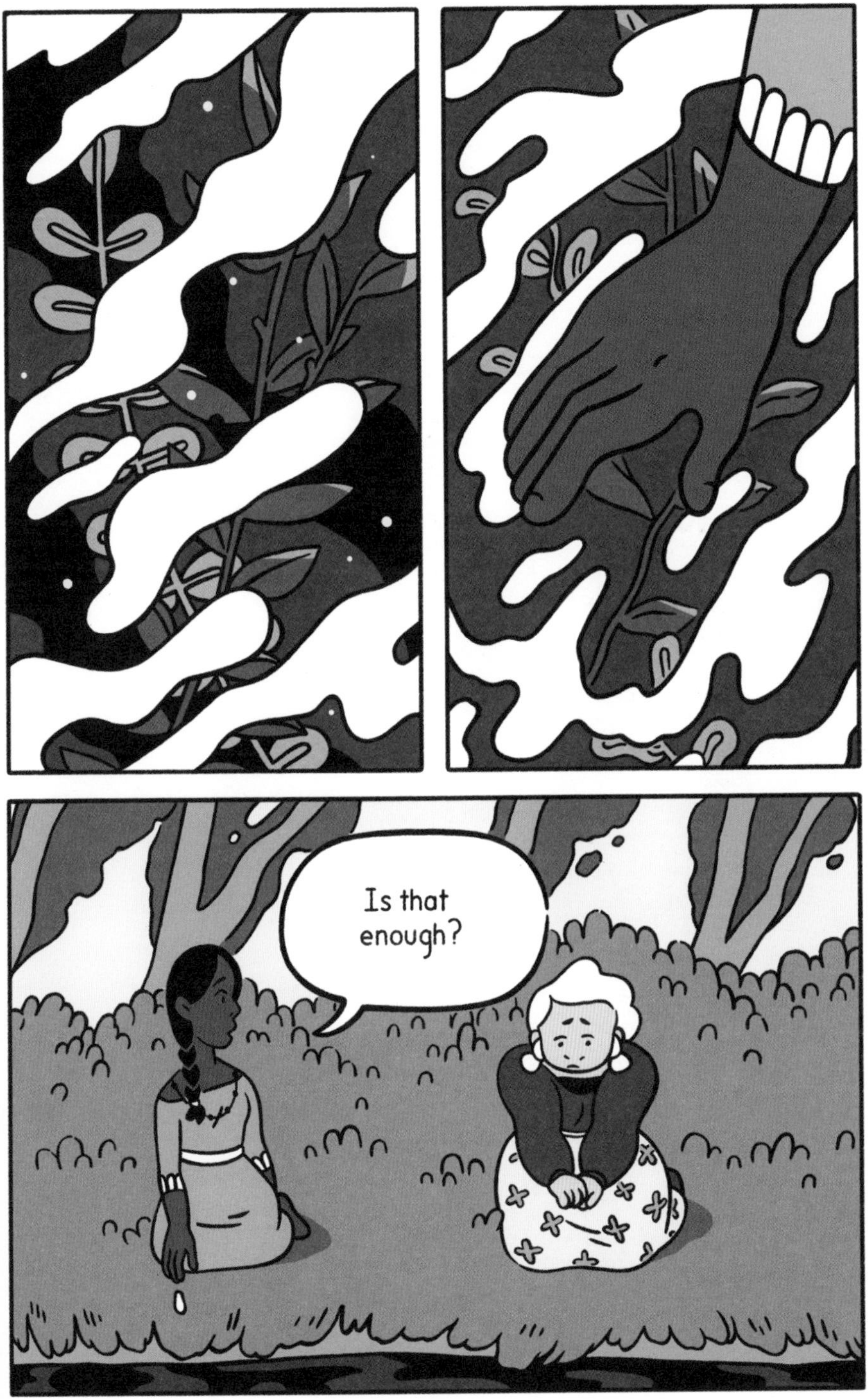
Is that enough?

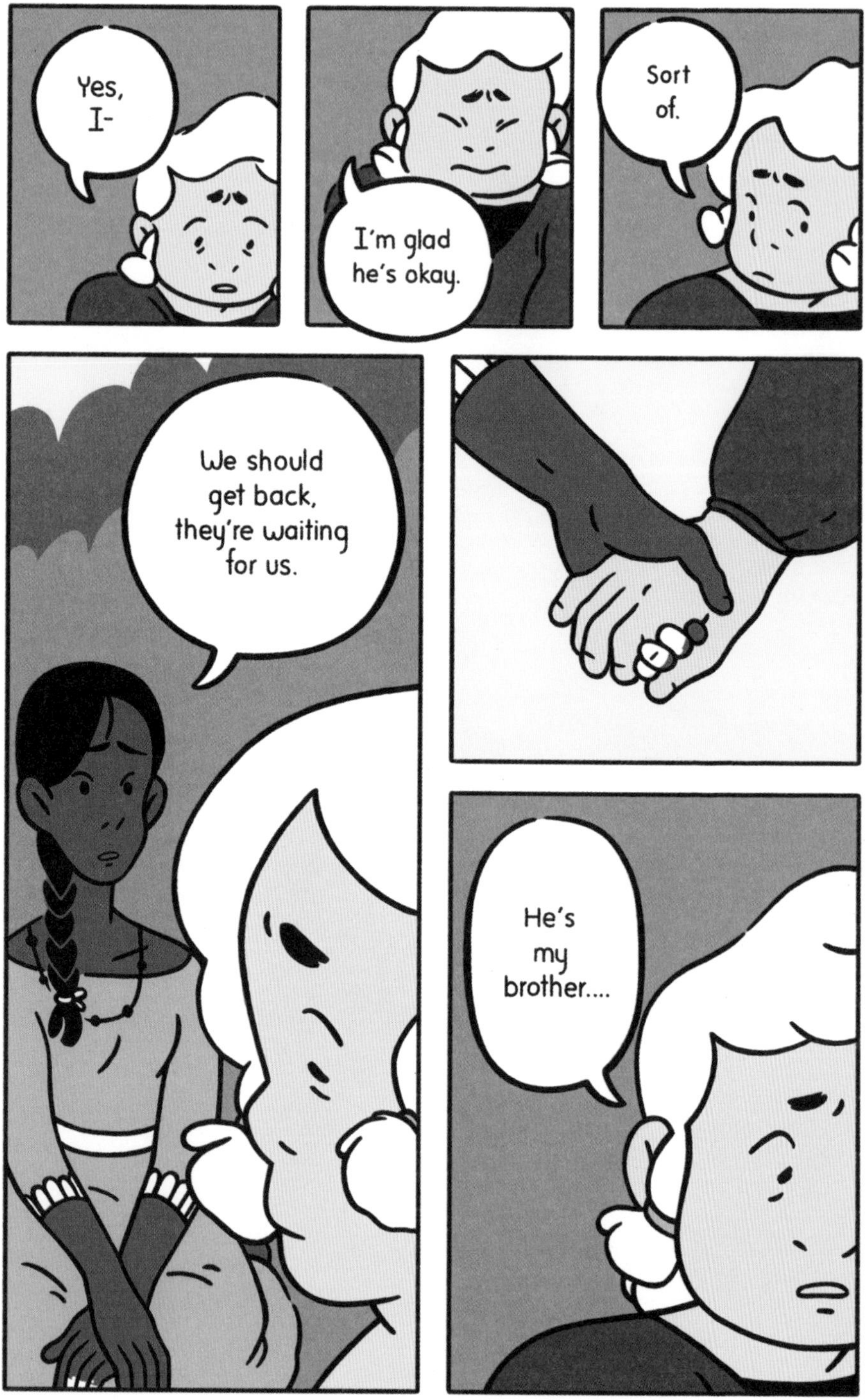
Yes,
I-
I'm glad
he's okay.
Sort
of.
We should
get back,
they're waiting
for us.
He's
my
brother....

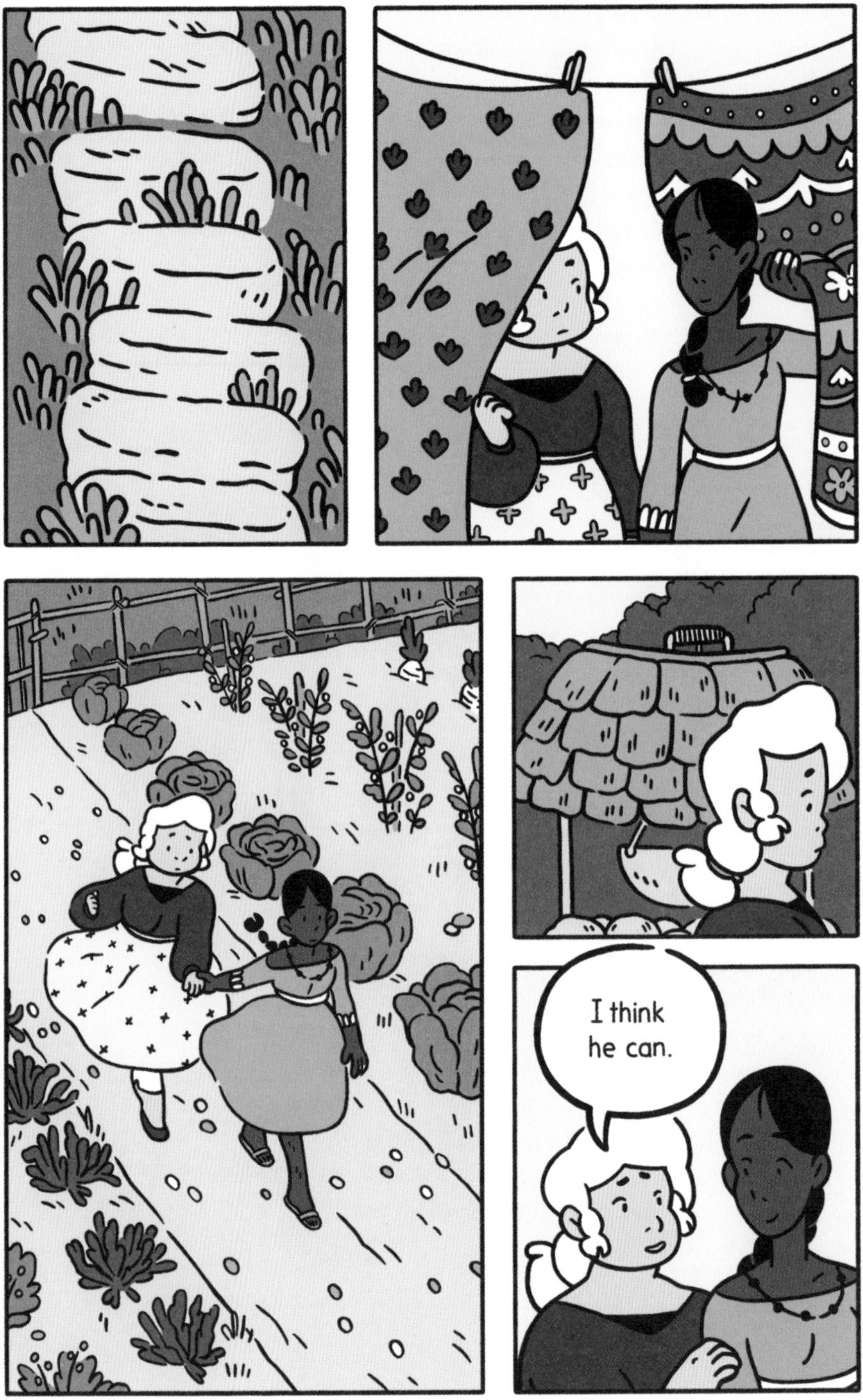
I think
he can.

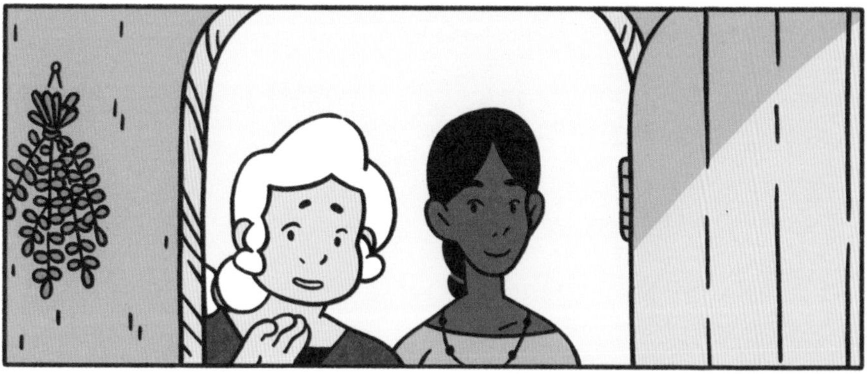

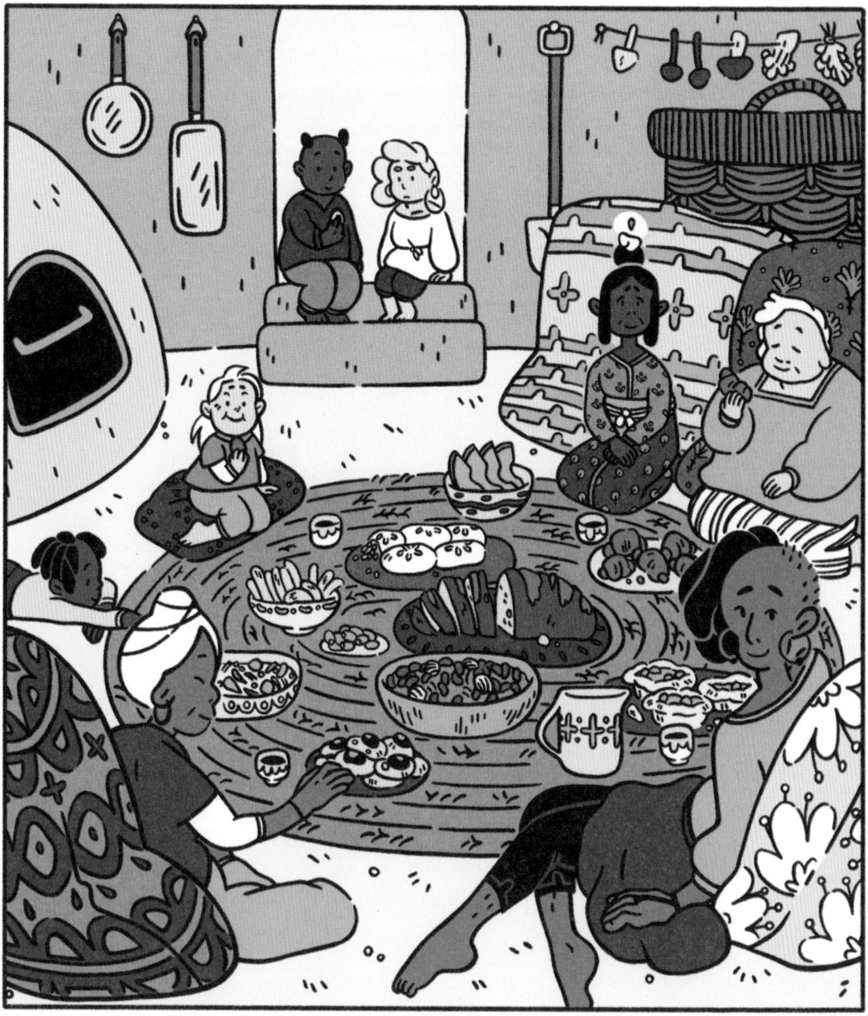

A note from the author:

From the start, *Witchlight* was an experiment in making exactly what I wanted to, and not worrying about what anyone thought it should be. I am incredibly grateful that so many people have embraced it.

A full half of *Witchlight* was made while listening to the podcast *Friends at the Table*, and I'm not sure how it could have gotten done otherwise. Their work has taught me so much about the joy and vulnerability at the core of all good storytelling. I am at heart a solitary and secretive creature, but their show makes me marvel at what can come out of true collaboration and trust.

Thank you to my parents for taking me to parks and museums and libraries, for teaching me how light works and the names of trees. Most of all, thank you for showing me how to tell stories for fun and taking the fear out of writing.

Thank you to Claire, for the good times. I hope we'll have more.

Above all others, thank you to Kevin Czap. When I first met them, I thought, "Who's this nerd?", one of many examples of my rude first impressions of the people who end up most dear to me. They were the first stranger to read my comics and say not just kind things, but insightful and true things about them. I am powered almost constantly by a brash and indestructible determination, but where that resolve stumbles, I keep going because I know Kevin believes I will.

RH GRAPHIC
THE DEBUT LIST

BUG BOYS
By Laura Knetzger

Bugs, friends, the world
around us—this book has
everything!
Come explore Bug Boys
for the fun, thoughtful
adventure about growing
up and being yourself.

Chapter Book

THE RUNAWAY PRINCESS
By Johan Troïanowski

The castle is quiet.
And dull.
And boring.
Escape on a quest for
excitement with our
runaway princess, Ro

Middle-Grade

ASTER AND THE ACCIDENTAL MAGIC
By Thom Pico & Karensac

Nothing fun ever
happens in the middle
of the country . . . except
maybe . . . magic?
That's just the beginning
of absolutely everything
going wrong for Aster.

Middle-Grade

WITCHLIGHT
By Jessi Zabarsky

Lelek doesn't have ar
friends or family in t
world. And then she
meets Sanja. Swords
magic, falling in love
these characters co
together in a journ
to heal the wounds
the past.

Young Adult

1999